MAPPING A SENSE OF HUMOR:
Narrative and Space in Terry Pratchett's Discworld Novels

By Daniel Lüthi

Mythopoeic Press 2023
Altadena, California, USA

Published by Mythopoeic Press, 2023

Copyright © 2023 by Daniel Lüthi

All rights reserved. No part of this publication may be reproduced, reprinted, transmitted, or distributed in any form or by any means, whether electronic or mechanical, now known or hereafter invented, without the written permission of the author, except in the case of brief quotations included in critical reviews and certain other noncommercial uses permitted by copyright law. Future publications of the work in its entirety must acknowledge its original publication here by Mythopoeic Press.

Mythopoeic Press is an imprint of the Mythopoeic Society. Orders may be placed through our website. For general inquiries, contact:
    press@mythsoc.org
    Editor, Mythopoeic Press
    P.O. Box 6707, Altadena, CA 91003, USA
    www.mythsoc.org/press.htm

ISBN: 978-1-887726-23-8
LCCN: 2022943087

ACKNOWLEDGMENTS
The author and publisher gratefully acknowledge the following for permission to include the images in this book:
- Discworld Emporium/Transworld Publishers. No title. *The Ankh-Morpork App*, 2013. Included with the permission of Discworld Emporium/Transworld Publishers.
- *Discworld*. Psygnosis, 1995. Included with the permission of Psygnosis/Sony.
- Kidby, Paul. Discworld Gods. *The Last Hero*, 2001. Included with the permission of Paul Kidby.
- Kidby, Paul. Lancre Map. *A Tourist Guide to Lancre*, 1998. Included with the permission of Paul Kidby.
- Kidby, Paul. Science of Discworld. *The Art of Discworld*, 2004. Included with the permission of Paul Kidby.
- Terraliptar. "Starting positions." Jan 20, 2005. https://boardgamegeek.com/image/64064/thud. Included with the permission of Terraliptar.

Cover art, *The Unreality of Time* by Francesca Baerald
Cover design by Megan Kornreich
Pre-press production by Leslie A. Donovan (Mythopoeic Press Editor), Paul Irwin, and Megan Kornreich
Index compiled by Janet Brennan Croft

Contents

Introduction i
Acknowledgments ix
List of Abbreviations x

Towards a Definition of Fantasy
A Note on Fictional Worlds 3
Chapter 1: Fantasy and Fictional Worlds 5
    Fantasy and Mimesis 11
    World-Making and Space in Fiction 15
    Postmodernism and Fantasy 20
Chapter 2: Fantasy and Humor 29
    Theories of Humor and Their Limitations 30
    Double Incongruity 32
    Parody and Postmodernism 37

Narrative and the Subversive Powers of Parody
A Note on Story Patterns in Fantasy Fiction and
    the Discworld Novels 47
Chapter 3: Beyond Parody 49
    Parody and Humor 50
    Parody and Theatre Fantasy 53
    Tolkienian Myth and Folklore on the Discworld 60
    Theatre Fantasy and Beyond 65
Chapter 4: The Threat of Clichés and Narrative Imperative 73
    The Subversion of Clichés 74
    The Dark Side of Clichés and the Dictatorship of Narrative . . . 82
    Happy Endings at All Costs 85
    Narrative Determinism 90
Chapter 5: Breaking the Spell of Narrative Imperative 95
    The Line of Duty 102
    The Problem with Heroes 104
    The Fiction of Morality 111

Chapter 6: Reflections on World-Making. 116
    The Fantasy of the Everyday 117
    Immersive Fantasy. 120
    The Science of Magic. 124
    Magic as a Creative Force. 127
    The Making of Reality. 131
    The Roundworld Project and Mental Narrativium 138

SPACE AND THE LAYERS OF NARRATIVE
A Note on Space in Fantasy Literature and
    the Development of the Discworld. 147
Chapter 7: You Can't Map a Sense of Humor 150
    Maps and Narrative. 151
    The Fear of Petrification 157
    Individuality and Maps 160
Chapter 8: Fairy Tales and Spatial Identity 171
    Too Much Geography. 172
    Land, Power, and Identity 177
    The Modernization of Fairy Tales 183
Chapter 9: The Urban Fantasy of Ankh-Morpork. 190
    Evading the Stage Set 191
    Urban Geography and Personal Experience 195
    Urban Dynamics on a Secondary World 200
Chapter 10: The Industrialization and
    Multimediality of the Discworld. 208
    The Victorianization of Ankh-Morpork. 209
    Technological Change on the Discworld 214
    The Discworld Franchise and Intermedial Narratives. 221
    Crossing Media and Narrative 223

A RECONSIDERATION OF FANTASY AND PRATCHETT
Outlook: Mapping and Storytelling in a Postmodern Era. 235
Afterword: Fantasy Beyond Escapism 241

Works Cited 247
Index 261

Introduction

Especially in its more inventive forms, fiction has received praise as a catalyst of alternate realms or speculative freedom and been branded as naïve make-believe and escapism. As both a representation and a violation of empirical reality, the worlds of fiction can be accessible and yet remain liminal spaces. Postmodern literature has increased the problems of this liminality by pretending to do away with it, erasing borders and limitations that were considered fixed and exposing the constructedness of not just these delineations but ultimately that of all meaning. Nevertheless, the traditions of literature have not so much been abolished as liberated from their confines to be used in often radically new ways. The postmodern has seen numerous expressions in art as genres have merged and hybrids constantly create new ideas of reflecting actuality. Fantasy is one of the more recent literary trends discussed in academic circles, a part of supernatural literature whose current popularity forms one of the core sources of postmodern imagination.

Specifically, the idea of creating not just literary scenarios but holistic secondary worlds that act as more than a simple spatial background of a story is the crucial feature of genre fantasy. The postmodern in such fiction derives from a curious interdependency: While fantasy authors take great care to make their secondary worlds believable and consistent, their cosmoses nonetheless underline their fictionality by featuring content that violates the rules of empirical reality. They thus present themselves in a constant flux or exchange, both representing and rethinking actuality. This problematic relationship finds further expression in the frequently derivative nature of fantasy fiction. An example of popular genre literature, fantasy tends to lean on proved patterns, first and foremost that of J. R. R. Tolkien's *The Lord of the Rings*. For all of fantasy's creative potential, numerous authors seem to prefer to repeat a given formula with little variation. Judging from the similarity of narrative plotting both in contemporary and classic fantasy, it would be all too easy to dismiss the genre as commercialized fiction, worth little critical attention.

However, it is exactly this conflicted nature of fantasy that provides the grounds for analytical reflection. Particularly since the late 20th century, fantasy, like postmodern fiction, does not exclude but tends to embrace the popular and formulaic—in order to then dismantle and reshape them in ironic and playful forms. When looking at fantasy and how it is often set within firm plotting patterns, at first glance, there seems to be little merit in comparing the genre to the postmodern, innovative manner of current critically and academically acclaimed literature. Yet, the reinterpretations of patterns of mythology and folklore reveal that the genre of fantasy itself is, at its core, the product of such playful disassembly and rearrangement, a development which did not begin with postmodernism. Prior to the coining of the term "fantasy" as a description of a literary genre, elements of it were present in literature and storytelling across all ages and cultures. Hence, this seemingly fixed genre and its roots in myths and folk tales are more than suitable to be considered in the light of postmodern fiction.

Nevertheless, while the genre itself has been undergoing constant renewal and reinterpretation particularly in the past few decades,[1] one element of fantasy has received little academic exposure so far, namely irony and, more directly, parody. Although irony is usually involved in reshaping elements of fantasy, and humor may form part of a narrative, authors who focus on full parodies of genre fantasy are comparatively rare, and their works appear to be rather predictable. Such parodies often merely act as distorting mirrors of "classic" fantasy,[2] and they offer no depth beneath superficial jokes and references as they

---

[1] Thanks to a myriad of subgenres and sub-subgenres ranging from grand reinterpretations like science fantasy to very specific niches such as young adult vampire college novel. Perhaps in slight conflict with my footnote just below, all of these works are "fantasy" insofar as they contain elements of the supernatural.

[2] What is considered classic fantasy has remained a topic of debate as much as the term "fantasy" itself. Critical consensus usually defines those works following the tradition of J. R. R. Tolkien's *LotR* as "classics" of the genre. Of course, there are numerous texts released prior to Tolkien's ground-breaking book that are also classics in fantasy literature, and they are given credit when relevant for my analysis. For the ease of identifying good examples, however, I count the works of authors such as Robert Jordan, Terry Brooks, Robin Hobb, and Tad Williams among books typical for genre fantasy in a Tolkienian formula.

reproduce their source-text as closely and ridiculously as possible. Titles such as *Bored of the Rings*, *Ronan the Barbarian* or *A Game of Groans* are instantly recognizable as spoofs of more famous originals. Since parody and pastiche form part of the postmodern in fiction, however, the question of its role in fantasy fiction arises, even when considering the various commercialized and superficial parodies in a—seemingly—commercial and superficial genre.

One author whose work could be considered part of this commercial parodist movement is Sir Terry Pratchett. It is easy to see why critics generally feel that he needs no introduction (see South, "Preface" x; Langford 3), when looking at the bestsellers' lists of fantasy fiction of the past decades—Pratchett being the second-most popular British fantasy author after J. K. Rowling.[3] All enthusiasm aside, the question of how he managed to attract and keep such a steady readership over the years remains. His work is typically classified as parody of fantasy, which normally only enjoys short-term success in the wake of the original parodied text. Yet by the time of Terry Pratchett's passing in 2015, there were 41 Discworld novels written over the course of more than 30 years, numerous play adaptations, video and board games, films, comics, with several companion volumes, maps, and other publications surrounding his secondary world.[4] Like *Harry Potter*, the Discworld has grown into a multimedia franchise.

A large part of this troubled relationship to the genre undoubtedly lies in the humor that characterizes Discworld novels. As in commercial parodies, nothing is exempt from Pratchett's jokes, ranging from William Shakespeare and philosophical considerations to film quotes and allusions to pulp detective novels—all of them combined in an absurd and seemingly whimsical fantasy context. In this regard, Pratchett's fiction is very much part of the postmodern, and most of its overt humor derives from the bridging of high and low, of kitsch and culture, although this combination is a delicate one to say the least: "One of the contradictions of postmodernism, I would argue, is that it does indeed 'close the gap' that Leslie Fiedler

---

[3] At the height of his popularity, Pratchett was the bestselling British author of fantasy in the 1990s and surpassed by J. K. Rowling's immensely successful *Harry Potter* series only in the early 2000s (James and Mendlesohn, *History* 167).

[4] Further special publications include cookbooks, daily planners and calendars, quiz books, and roleplaying game books. It would be exhaustive to try to include a comprehensive list, so a selection will have to do.

(1975) saw between high and low art forms, and it does so through the ironizing of both" (Hutcheon, *Poetics* 44). Still, here we have only one of many apparent contradictions inherent to postmodernism that Pratchett utilizes in his books. While fantasy constructs autonomous worlds as alternatives or reinterpretations of the actual world of empirical reality, another central topic of the genre (and indeed of postmodern literature in general) has received little to no attention, even though its importance for fantasy as for Pratchett's work must not be underestimated: Space. The conflict of making a secondary world which features impossible content and that is nonetheless supposed to be believable places fantasy—and consequently Pratchett's critique thereof—firmly within the postmodern reconsideration of space as construct and as an interpretation of reality.

Often treated as a concept secondary to narrative's focus on plot, space has been controversially addressed both in history and in literature. Specifically, it is part of a development that began with the artistic breakthroughs of the early 20th century,[5] and found its most liberating expression in the postmodern blurring of borders and constant reconsideration of space, as pointed out by eminent philosophers such as Michel Foucault:

> The nineteenth century found its essential mythological resources in the second principle of thermodynamics. The present epoch will perhaps be above all the epoch of space. We are in the epoch of simultaneity: we are in the epoch of juxtaposition, the epoch of the near and far, of the side-by-side, of the dispersed. We are at a moment, I believe, when our experience of the world is less that of a long life developing through time than that of a network that connects points and intersects with its own skein. (Foucault, "Other" 22)

Modernism both lamented and celebrated the dissipation of individual and communal life in an ever-more accelerating world and the shattering of beliefs in eternal progress and nationalist superiority during the First World War. Postmodernism marked an acceptance of this loss of fixed centers, demonstrated in fragmented and ludic

---

[5] Dadaism questioned the very center of meaning itself whereas Expressionism drew attention to new perspectives on space and time, reflecting not merely the repercussions of the First World War but also of new methods of transportation and other innovations in technology. While these artistic movements are not the main focus of my book, I still want to acknowledge that Pratchett's work channels their disruptive potential.

forms of art that constructed alternate spaces and referenced but did not become burdened by the past.

Like Michel Foucault, Fredric Jameson suggests that "it is at least empirically arguable that our daily life, our psychic experience, our cultural languages, are today dominated by categories of space rather than by categories of time, as in the preceding period of high modernism" (15). Fantasy, as a genre usually set in secondary worlds, is strongly conscious of its often-radical reinterpretation of space. Like postmodern literature *per se*, fantasy does not deny its historical sources—among them folklore, mythology, and romance—but reorganizes them in various manners, crossing paths with other genres[6] ranging from detective fiction to horror and space opera. Yet the making of a secondary world—a believable space despite its violations of physical and ontological laws—is of crucial importance. Pratchett's fiction is not excluded from this approach: Throughout his fiction, readers are constantly reminded of the spatiality of the Discworld—not simply its eponymous flat nature and the peculiarities implied by such a shape, but the very earthiness and tangibility of its extent. The secondary world we encounter may be impossible according to the laws of empirical reality, and be further undermined by constant humor, yet from this incongruous nature, the Discworld derives a hidden depth beyond mere jokes and references to popular culture.

Pratchett's work is thus a critical reflection of fantasy as well as of literature and culture in general, set at the core of the dynamics between fiction and empirical reality, between ideal make-believe and the facts of everyday life. He thereby addresses the dichotomy between art and life, between reality and representation, to an extent even between signifier and signified. Very much in postmodern fashion, he offers no ultimate resolution but reveals these conflicts to be continuous processes. Indeed, change is *the* crucial and recurring topic on the Discworld, shown both in a personified manner as characters progress over the course of his novels and in the technological innovations and sociological developments

---

[6] While I do not venture too deeply into genre theory itself, fantasy naturally draws influence not only from its immediate precursors in mythology, folklore, and preceding literature of the supernatural such as Gothic novels. Furthermore, it benefitted from parallel developments in supernatural fiction, for example science fiction or fantastic literature, and found further expression in later hybrid genres like Steampunk fiction.

that eventually begin transforming the Discworld itself. Thus, the Discworld is not simply a "mirror of worlds" restricted to mocking originals, but an endeavour that grew from its original parody into an increasingly intertextual and self-reflective phenomenon. As part of this development, Pratchett's work reconsiders not just space and storytelling but various topics from a wide range of influence with unusual and seemingly contradictory perspectives.

In the ensuing analysis, I generally aim to take the full scope of Pratchett's creation into account. However, in view of the abundance of Discworld content,[7] I also focus on topics specific to my purposes, and therefore certain volumes are given less emphasis than others. While storytelling (as one of the core features of the Discworld) is present in every novel to a certain degree, it is not *the* defining theme of all books. This is why individual novels clearly aimed at parodying particular aspects of culture (for example religion in *Pyramids* and *Small Gods* or Hollywood films and rock music in *Moving Pictures* and *Soul Music*, respectively) are given less attention than others that are more relevant for this study. To provide additional clarity, I refer to specific story arcs of the Discworld series as the "Rincewind books" (consisting of *The Colour of Magic*, *The Light Fantastic*, *Sourcery*, and *Eric*) the "Witches books" (consisting of *Wyrd Sisters*, *Witches Abroad*, and *Lords and Ladies*) the three "Tiffany Aching books"[8] *Wintersmith*, *I Shall Wear Midnight*, and *The Shepherd's Crown*, the "City Watch books" (consisting of *Guards! Guards!*, *Men At Arms*, *Jingo*, *Night Watch*, *Thud!*, and *Snuff*), and the "Moist von Lipwig books" (consisting of *Going Postal*, *Making Money*, and *Raising Steam*), as these form the most crucial texts of Pratchett's work for my intentions.[9] The titles of all novels quoted are written in full at first and thereafter abbreviated.

---

[7] As stated before, the main corpus of books comprises 41 novels alone—plus of course the corresponding companions, maps, as well as various other additions and extensions to the main texts. At the beginning of the creation of this book, there was still a plethora of Discworld content released on a regular basis. Looking back, I can safely say that trying to keep up with new primary and secondary reading material hitting the shelves at this pace poses a unique challenge to the writing (and editing) process.

[8] The Tiffany Aching arc consists of a total of five books.

[9] There are further novels in some arcs—while I also quote a few of them, their overall relevance for this study is secondary and they are thus not listed here.

Moreover, it is helpful to create a timeline of the books discussed — consisting of both the order in which they were released as well as what I call the "phase" they belong to. The first phase consists of Discworld novels that are mainly parodies of fantasy or other specific sources. During the series' mid-phase, beginning in the early 1990s, Pratchett redefines his secondary world as its own autonomous space and addresses more serious topics. Finally, by the mid-2000s, the Discworld enters its late phase, with an increased focus on world-completion as well as releases in additional media.

The classification of the series into three distinct phases is by no means definite and was conceived specifically for the purpose of this text. There are various novels that stand on the threshold of two phases, for example *Wyrd Sisters*, which is still largely parody but also features the beginnings of a critique of storytelling, or *Night Watch* with its intricate portrayal of Ankh-Morpork. Nevertheless, the following overview should provide a slightly more detailed chronology of the books:

Early phase: Parody
The Colour of Magic (CoM, 1983)
The Light Fantastic (LF, 1986)
Mort (M, 1987)
Sourcery (S, 1988)
Wyrd Sisters (WS, 1988)
Guards! Guards! (GG, 1989)
Eric (E, 1990)
Moving Pictures (MP, 1990)
Reaper Man (RM, 1991)

Mid-phase: Sophistication
Witches Abroad (WA, 1991)
Lords and Ladies (LL, 1992)
Small Gods (SG, 1992)
Men At Arms (MAA, 1993)
Soul Music (no abbreviation, 1994)
Hogfather (HG, 1996)
Jingo (J, 1997)
The Last Hero (LH, 2001)
Night Watch (NW, 2002)

Late phase: Saturation
Going Postal (GP, 2004)
Thud! (T!, 2005)
Wintersmith (W, 2006)
Making Money (MM, 2007)
I Shall Wear Midnight (ISWM, 2010)
Snuff (SN, 2011)
Raising Steam (RS, 2013)
The Shepherd's Crown (SC, 2015)

Acknowledgments

So many people were involved in the process of creating this book. Firstly, I would like to thank my two thesis supervisors, Prof. Dr. Ina Habermann and Prof. Dr. Philipp Schweighauser, for their support and advice throughout my research. The Doctoral Program of Literary Studies and the Department of English at the University of Basel provided an invaluable infrastructure for all my work. My gratitude also goes out to Leslie A. Donovan, Janet Brennan Croft, and the entire team of the Mythopoeic Press—your diligence and professionalism are all an author can wish for. I want to thank my parents René and Anita Lüthi, as well as my aunt Barbara Fey for nurturing my love of reading and my constant lack of shelf space. Big hugs to my proofreading elves Helena, Jasmin, Maria, and Jake. You made this book so much better than I ever could have. I am grateful for my closest circle of friends, the Disney Nights crew, and all the discussions, films, and times we spend together. A very special thank you and love to my partner in crime and so many other endeavors, Johanna Schüpbach. Thanks for always being there, for your patience, kindness, and wisdom. Finally, but certainly not lastly, an extended thank you to all the other friends who helped to turn this project into reality. See you all on the Disc.

List of Abbreviations

Works by Terry Pratchett

CoM	*The Colour of Magic*
E	*Eric*
GG	*Guards! Guards!*
GP	*Going Postal*
HG	*Hogfather*
ISWM	*I Shall Wear Midnight*
J	*Jingo*
LF	*The Light Fantastic*
LH	*The Last Hero*
LL	*Lords and Ladies*
M	*Mort*
MAA	*Men At Arms*
MM	*Making Money*
MP	*Moving Pictures*
NW	*Night Watch*
RM	*Reaper Man*
RS	*Raising Steam*
S	*Sourcery*
SC	*The Shepherd's Crown*
SG	*Small Gods*
SN	*Snuff*
T!	*Thud!*
W	*Wintersmith*
WA	*Witches Abroad*
WS	*Wyrd Sisters*

Other Works

BotR	*Bored of the Rings* by Henry N. Beard and Douglas C. Kennedy
H	*The Hobbit* by J. R. R. Tolkien
LotR	*The Lord of the Rings* by J. R. R. Tolkien
OFS	"On Fairy-stories" by J. R. R. Tolkien

Towards a Definition of Fantasy

A Note on Fictional Worlds

As a mass appeal phenomenon with undoubted presence in contemporary fiction and on bestselling lists, fantasy seems to be prevalent but hard to define upon closer inspection. In her critical examination *Rhetorics of Fantasy*, Farah Mendlesohn claims that "all literature builds worlds, but some genres are more honest about it than others" (59). At first glance, limiting this honesty to fantasy seems to neglect its wider implications: with the emergence of postmodernism in the arts, a focus on the constructedness—the very fictionality—of fiction and fictional worlds has become commonplace. Because the "intense self-reflexivity of postmodern literature thus leads to a constant interruption of narrative, an untiring reminder to the reader that he or she is reading a text, language, a fiction, and not viewing a world without mediation" (Best and Kellner 132), open displays of the fictionality of a text are a recurring feature of contemporary literature. Furthermore, endowing particular genres with more or less metafictional and self-reflexive traits is highly problematic when discussing literary criticism, especially since postmodern fiction also deliberately breaks the boundaries between genres and is, indeed, a highly ambivalent movement (Mortensen 179).

Yet fantasy, the genre that Mendlesohn singles out, is as ambiguous and mutable as postmodernism in literature. A term of equal dispute, fantasy in a wider sense "is Italo Calvino and Jorge Luis Borges; it is also Piers Anthony and Robert E. Howard" (Attebery, *Strategies* 1). It is not restricted to its delineations as genre; it exists in both the most elaborate forms of postmodern literature and in drugstore popular fiction. Core topics of postmodernist and fantasy fiction are in fact remarkably similar—they ask what does and what could define a "world":

> [P]ostmodernist writers (like Calvino and Pynchon) have been primarily occupied with ontological questions such as: what kind of world do we live in?

> [...] The question "what kind of world do we inhabit?" is akin to the question *"what if* the world we inhabited were like...?"*:* in both cases, the objective is to explore a world that cannot be understood according to our conventional notions of how reality functions. (Bolongaro 227–28)

Increased attention to world-making[10] is but one postmodern feature of the genre and its wider occurrences in fiction. However, "fantasy, by its very nature, challenges the dominant political and conceptual ideologies in a manner similar to that of postmodernism" (Casey 115). Far from being an ahistorical or otherworldly phenomenon, fantasy therefore both reflects and discusses subjects of empirical reality.

---

[10] Following Ansgar Nünning, I deliberately use the term "world-making" to underline not merely the literary act of creating a world but furthermore also the wider cultural area of alternative and speculative scenarios.

Chapter 1

Fantasy and Fictional Worlds

While fictional worlds can be traced back to the very beginnings of literature, they emerged as a theoretical concept via philosophy—most prominently in Gottfried Wilhelm Leibniz' thought experiment concerning possible worlds. Leibniz notoriously claimed that we live in the best of all possible worlds while there is "an infinity of possible worlds which [God] finds in his intellect; each possible world is a kind of blueprint for a possible act of divine creation" (Jolley 143). Twentieth-century philosophers such as David Lewis, Robert Stalnaker, and Saul Kripke expanded Leibniz' concept, using it to formulate hypothetical alternative worlds in formal semantics and modal logic. The proximity of these conceived worlds to fictional scenarios eventually resulted in their adaptation for literary research.

Literary critics like Lubomír Doležel, Marie-Laure Ryan, and Thomas Pavel picked up the theory of possible worlds from modal logic and combined its framework with fiction, overcoming the philosophical concept that "tends to lean more toward the abstract and the conceptual nature of imaginary worlds than practical particulars" (Wolf 19; see also Ronen 19). Compared to the rather hypothetical nature of philosophically possible worlds, fiction offered a more applied and detailed realm of speculation. Still, as a realm with an increased focus on inventiveness and a reliance on make-believe, storyworlds have also been a constant subject of critique.

Precisely because the alternative worlds encountered in literature do not primarily seek an ontological explanation in exact comparison to empirical reality but instead focus on content that favors creative input over logical thought, they show increased vulnerability to criticism and debate. Since it abandons a strictly rational and sequential argumentation for the benefit of freedom of fabrication,[11] a fictional world does not have the same basis as its philosophical counterpart from modal logic:

> What place in our semantics, then, should we reserve for fictional characters and fictional worlds? Is there something unintelligible about the concept of a unicorn that would cause Russell to exclude it from the realm of logic? Is a unicorn to be placed in the same category as a four-sided triangle? Would it not rather be preferable to say the concept can be logically conveyed—can be made intelligible in a meaningful way—without committing ourselves to its existence in the actual world? (Martin 86)

This argument touches on a problem which dates back to the very beginning of storytelling, namely the question of mimesis. Even though a fictional world can never be in strict accordance with our actual world, it nevertheless shares at least minimal connections with it. As Stephen Halliwell emphasizes, any fictional world derives its meaning from the relation between fiction and empirical reality:

> Artistic mimesis is conceived of as the representation of a world in relation to which the audience imaginatively occupies the position of an absorbed or engrossed witness. That is one reason why concepts of mimesis [...] inescapably raise questions about the relationship between the world *inside* and the world *outside* the mimetic work. (Halliwell, *Mimesis* 22)

The existence of fictional worlds is naturally based on ideas attained from the actual world; regardless of content, all fiction is processed through the mind of an audience which naturally exists in empirical reality and that compares the events and phenomena of fiction to real-world counterparts. Hence fiction is always a *construct* derived from a reflection, reinterpretation, and reinvention of empirical reality, a mimetic form and thought experiment for both authors and readers. The main problem arising from mimetic construction, however, is that the reflection can work in two ways: not only do real-world phenomena and situations influence or inspire fictional constructions (by providing hypothetical alternative outcomes or variations of actual scenarios, for instance) but fiction may also influence the perception of empirical reality.

Herein lies a conflict that has been a topic of long-standing philosophical controversy regarding mimesis. The Oxford English

---

[11] Which of course does not mean that logic is thrown away altogether. Fiction—and fantasy—is anything but irrational and simply making things up as you go along.

Dictionary translates the Old Greek word μίμησις as "imitation" (*OED Online*, "mimesis"), placing emphasis on the fact that the term is defined differently by Plato and Aristotle. As part of his troubled excursions on fiction, Plato famously derides mimesis[12] in *The Republic* (see Plato, Book III 387b–98b), proclaiming the banishment of all poetry from his concept of a future ideal state. His fears are inextricably linked with the *realm of ideas*. If reality is but a reflection of ideal forms, then accordingly any "art merely reproduces empirical reality and is illusory because it does not take us to the transcendental and perfect World of Ideas" (Alber et al., "Response" 378; see also Plato, *The Republic*, Book X 605b–c). Plato uses the metaphor of a mirror that only reflects and shows entities "so that they look like they *are*; however, they surely *are* not in truth" (Book X 596e). If we spend our time imitating actual scenarios, so Plato argues, we eventually start *preferring* mimesis to empirical reality and become lost in illusory daydreams instead of dealing with real situations.[13]

In comparison, the less purely idealistic and more practically minded philosophy of Aristotle defines the term differently in his *Poetics*. He claims that imitation is intrinsic to human nature:

> First, there is man's natural propensity, from childhood onwards, to engage in mimetic activity (and this distinguishes man from other creatures, that he is thoroughly mimetic and through mimesis takes his first steps in understanding). Second, there is the pleasure which all men take in mimetic objects. (Halliwell, *Poetics* 34)

For Aristotle, mimesis is not a deceptive illusion leading to pointless daydreams, but a crucial instrument in cognitive and social development—within moderation, of course. As confirmed by contemporary philosophy and anthropological research, imagination and mimicry indeed form a vital part not merely in the process of growing up and social interaction but in hominid evolution. Cognitive neuroscientist Merlin Donald outlines the importance of the genesis of a mimetic culture in pre-human communities through the development of a mental toolset:

---

[12] My focus in this book lies clearly on mimesis or the *representation* of a secondary world rather than on diegesis. While the Discworld is told diegetically by a narrating entity, my main goal is to uncover how the world is *shown* to readers—particularly in comparison with other secondary worlds.

[13] Or alternatively, we may deal with real situations in an irrational manner. In any case, Plato's argument remains firm in its denial of mimesis.

> Although the emergence of mimesis was primarily about the refinement and expansion of the skill-set of hominins as a species, by its nature it was also a potential channel for representing reality and communicating ideas. Once hominins were able to imagine actions and events, and re-enact what they imagined, groups of hominins would have had an elementary capacity for communication, improved imitation, and distributed cognitive events, such as sustaining toolmaking industries and maintaining fire. (Donald 192)

It would be a huge undertaking to trace the origins or full effects of storytelling and enactments for reasoning plus the entertainment derived from this evolutionary outset,[14] yet even on a general level, the human predisposition towards mimesis cannot be denied. Beginning with make-believe and childhood games that turn into what-if scenarios and considerations in adult life (see Gottschall 6–8), to imitate (and thereby reflect) reality is a natural and fundamental tool of our mental and social activity.[15]

However, this observation of mimesis as a mental tool does not entirely solve Plato's problem with mimesis. Especially in the more complex mimicry provided by fiction, the claim of literature being escapism is a recurring accusation: As "the human mind is capable of forming images currently not present" (Tolkien, "On Fairy-stories" 59), a myriad of creative images and ideas, for example, as in *LotR*, may seem to bear little relation to actuality, and the wondrous world and extraordinary situations of Middle-earth and other literary worlds may become preferable to the mundane and tiresome everyday life of empirical reality.

Yet keeping the aforementioned concept of the mental toolset in mind, Tolkien's arguments in his famous essay "On Fairy-stories" are remarkably close to Aristotle's idea of mimesis, whose approach to the concept is worth rendering further: "Unlike Plato, for whom mimesis is a mirror of something else and therefore potentially deceptive,

---

[14] One need only think of the thousands of films, books, TV series episodes, songs, podcasts, etc., released every year to get an idea of how central artistic mimesis is to our lives.

[15] While the importance of these two concepts in psychoanalysis cannot be denied, I refrain from adding Freudian or post-Freudian investigations to my book. Even though the role of imagination in the development of the human mind and society is discussed here and I move on to jokes and humor as equally crucial mental tools later, I believe that a psychoanalytical perspective would distract from rather than add to the main focus on the spatio-narratological evolution of the Discworld novels.

Aristotle defines mimesis as a craft with its *own internal laws and aims*" (Potolsky 33; my emphasis). Similarly, Tolkien is emphatic about the need for guidelines when creating a secondary world,[16] particularly regarding his notion of "literary belief":

> What really happens is that the story-maker proves a successful 'sub-creator'. He makes a secondary world which your mind can enter. Inside it, what he relates is 'true': it accords with *the laws of that world*. You therefore believe it, while you are, as it were, inside. The moment disbelief arises, the spell is broken; the magic, or rather art, has failed. You are then out in the Primary World again, looking at the little abortive secondary world from outside. (OFS 52; my emphasis)

For both Aristotle and Tolkien, it is crucial that we use our mental tools for a purpose and according to specific rules. Within the complexities of fiction, the act of mimesis is only successful if there "is an act of collusion between performer and audience" (Attebery, *Strategies* 51)—that is to say, only if the author manages to make a possible world which is not isolated from a cultural knowledge shared with readers and based in empirical reality.

Hence, be it for entertainment or for educational purposes, fiction builds on internal consistency as much as on the communal aspect of a shared mimetic culture. As readers, we certainly *know* that fictional characters are not real—but since they are based on concepts drawn from empirical reality and personal sensations, their emotions and motivations may *feel* real to us. While watching a tragedy on stage we may see moments where we then compare the staged events with similar events from our personal experience.[17] And in just the same way, the comparison of a possible world (or in the context of fantasy, a secondary world) to our real world may uphold the impression that what happens in a book *is real within a certain context*, provided the fictional world is portrayed in a believable manner.

---

[16] In Tolkien's terminology, our "Primary World"—empirical reality—provides the ideas and materials for the creation of secondary worlds. However, Ekman notes that the term "Primary World" is also "a literary construct whose setting imitates, on a general level if not in every detail, the actual world" (10). To avoid confusion between empirical reality and mimetic representation, I therefore follow this observation and stick to the terms "empirical reality," "actual reality," and "actual world" instead of "Primary World" to refer to our existing world.

[17] Naturally, this comparison of empirical reality to re-enactment need not be necessarily tragic, as the humor of comedy likewise derives from its relatability to factual situations and mishaps.

The importance of storytelling in human evolution, individual development, and daily life is clear. Here as for the ensuing analysis of Pratchett's approach to fiction and fantasy, my main priority is on the purpose and effects of stories. As the cultural dimensions of storytelling and narrative are essential for understanding Pratchett's work, it makes sense to investigate the idea of stories as a tool even further. That being said, I think it is also wise to know which road to take: "Inquiry into the nature of narrative can take two forms. The first, aiming at a description, asks: what does narrative *do* for human beings; the second, aiming at a definition, tries to capture the distinctive features of narrative" (Herman et al., *Encyclopedia* 345). Not just due to the fact that narrative also "resists straightforward and agreed-upon definitions and conceptualizations" (De Fina and Georgakopoulou 1), focusing on its functions and techniques to achieve immersion and believability rather than trying to pinpoint the exact notion of what a narrative or a story is yields the most relevant results in an analysis of the Discworld.

With the non-actuality of fictional worlds and the freedom, moreover the human instinct to invent narrative scenarios, there is consequently "an infinite size, number, and variety of possible worlds" (Doležel, *Heterocosmica* 15), both in philosophy and in literature. As laid out beforehand, one of the more general mistakes in literary research is to see the two approaches as identical, namely to think that the possible worlds of literature are subject to the same rules as those of philosophy. Wolf Schmid underlines the minor role of plain speculation in literature, since "the fictive should not be too closely linked to the concept of appearance, something tended towards by those theorists who explain fiction with an 'as-if-structure.' Fiction should rather be understood as the representation of a distinct, autonomous, inner-literary reality" (22). A reason for the comparatively dominant use of the term "world" in fiction is, therefore, the denotation of the autonomy of secondary worlds.

While Marie-Laure Ryan nearly always conforms to this terminology in her on-going research on narrative, she underlines that nomenclature such as "textual world" or "literary world" are but two of many possible metaphors for the spatiality of a text or a narrative:

> For immersion to take place, the text must offer an expanse to be immersed within, and this expanse, in a blatantly mixed metaphor, is not an ocean but a textual world. The recent emergence of other

analogies for the literary text, such as the text as game […], as network […], or as machinic [sic] assemblage […], should remind us that "the text as world" is only one possible conceptualization among many others […]. (*Artificial* 90)

Since fantasy literature in particular places strong emphasis on the term "world" to depict a literary space, it is the most fitting circumscription for my purposes. Not only does it include possible-worlds theory in fiction and Tolkien's reflections on secondary worlds in his essay, it also once more implies the importance of rules for any fictional literary world (Wolf 154), be it set in an entirely supernatural context or one with a more realistic background.

Fantasy and Mimesis

Regardless of the terms used to describe fictional scenarios—possible worlds, secondary worlds, network—the fact that the resulting texts have to mimic our actual reality (at least to a minimum), irrespective of their definition or genre, cannot be stressed enough: "Fiction, understood as mimesis in the Aristotelian sense, is an artistic construction of a possible *reality*" (Schmid 23; my emphasis). Having defined mimesis as the imitation of empirical reality, it would be easy to create a dichotomy between mimetic texts of so-called "realistic" fiction and fantasy as an example of non-mimetic texts. But even in extreme examples of postmodern fiction such as non- or anti-mimetic fiction, which indeed aim to counter "the mimetic bias" (Richardson 24), of narrative and consist of texts that actively try to sabotage accurate representation of reality by violating causality and continuity, there must always be a minimal given degree of mimesis involved—should a text display no representation of reality at all (i.e. no mimesis), reading or understanding the represented world and story will hardly be possible for readers.[18] Artistic mimesis is not dichotomous but a very nuanced affair.

In order to make the spectrum of mimesis clearer, it is helpful to include Brian Attebery's differentiation between high and low mimetic texts. Taking up this differentiation from Northrop Frye's

---

[18] Examples of texts with nearly no mimetic value are the Voynich manuscript and Luigi Serafini's *Codex Seraphinianus*, both of which are written in undecipherable fictional languages and feature absurd pictures that make little sense to readers (Wolf 30). Enjoyment can certainly be derived from books such as these, yet their mimesis of empirical reality is confusing to say the least.

Anatomy of Criticism, he stresses not only the importance of mimesis for fiction, but also that it must not be excluded from fantasy—nor *vice versa*: mimesis and fantasy

> can and do coexist within any given work; there are no purely mimetic or fantastic works of fiction. Mimesis without fantasy would be nothing but reporting one's perception of actual events. Fantasy without mimesis would be a purely artificial invention, without recognizable objects or actions. (*Strategies* 3)

Fantasy texts are not anti- or non-mimetic but what Attebery calls low-mimetic[19]—in fact, many of the more conservative fantasy worlds (despite their supernatural content) display more mimesis than postmodern texts that purposefully distort the boundaries between reality and fiction or the rules of linearity and causality in narratives.[20] For Tolkien, as for other fantasy authors, the representation of reality is of equal importance as invention: "Probably every writer making a secondary world, a fantasy, hopes that he is drawing on reality: hopes that the peculiar quality of this secondary world [...] [is] derived from Reality, or are [sic] flowing into it" (OFS 77). However, the tremendous variety and abundance of texts that contain supernatural elements are all products of different interpretations of reality; we need to keep in mind "the shifts in assumptions about reality which have taken place during the past 2500 years" (Hume 58; also Stableford, *Dictionary* xlii), and it would therefore not only be restrictive but indeed wrong to draw a final line between texts that are considered "fantasy" as part of a terminology and those that are not.

---

[19] Researchers of unnatural narratology like Brian Richardson differentiate between mimetic, non-mimetic, and anti-mimetic modes in literature. However, according to this terminology, "a non-mimetic text (such as a fairy tale) will follow non-realistic conventions" (Alber et al., "Really" 102)—a description which I—like Attebery—clearly identify also as valid for low-mimetic texts. I thus refrain from using "non-mimetic" throughout my analysis, as it is easily confusable with "anti-mimetic" (texts which willingly violate literary conventions in a postmodern manner).

[20] Richardson sees Salman Rushdie's books *Midnight's Children* and *The Satanic Verses* as anti-mimetic fiction (Richardson 31). Further examples of authors who deliberately counteract the mimetic spell of fiction are Franz Kafka, Gustav Meyrink, or, to name another clearly postmodern writer, Martin Amis, whose 1991 novel *Time's Arrow* depicts a world in which time is experienced as flowing backwards. In all these works, fiction is not just disrupted but at times actively sabotaged.

Fantasy is consequently not a genre that can be identified by a fixed set of parameters but may be traced in every fictional work which transcends the boundaries of reality defined as such by a certain era or culture. Far from being opposites, fantasy and realism are two sides of the same coin and both subject to reinterpretation and redefinition. As Edward James and Farah Mendlesohn point out,

> [f]antasy and not realism has been a normal mode for much of the history of Western fiction (and art). Arguably however, fantasy *as a genre* only emerges in response (and contemporaneous to) the emergence of mimesis (or realism) *as a genre*: only once there is a notion of intentional realism, so the argument goes, can there be a notion of intentional fantasy. Yet the ancient Greek and Roman novel, the medieval romance, and early modern verse and prose texts all commonly use what we consider to be the tropes of fantasy: magical transformations, strange monsters, sorcerers and dragons, and the existence of a supernatural world. (*History* 7)

Both supernatural and realistic texts existed before their definitions as genres or even as literary terms, subject to what was considered "real" at a certain time. Attebery's theory of fantasy underlines the relation of supernatural and non-supernatural content in literature. Instead of defining fantasy as one specific term, he opts for a threefold distinction, not only bridging the gap between non-fantasy and fantasy but also giving credit to the popular and subversive features of fantasy texts: "I can make an equally strong case for either claim. Fantasy is, indeed, both *formula* and *mode*: in one incarnation a mass-produced supplier of wish fulfillment, and in another a praise- and prize-worthy means of investigating the way we use fictions to construct reality itself" (*Strategies* 1, my emphasis). In this terminology, *mode* effectively consists of the building blocks or individual elements of supernatural content that may be used to greater or lesser extent in texts, whereas *formula* is a strict use of these elements in given narratological patterns. *Genre* is Attebery's third denominator, located "[b]etween the two, mixing elements of both in varying degrees according to historical and cultural factors" (Schallegger 32). In all three, the specific use or arrangement of supernatural elements creates a text with higher or lower mimetic content.

Although by no means a final explanation, this differentiation has proved to be the most fruitful and encompassing definition of fantasy, as fellow fantasy critics point out (Sandner, *Reader* 293; James and Mendlesohn, "Introduction" 1). It is an elegant compromise allowing a comparison of supernatural content in texts ranging from myths to works of high fantasy and postmodern metafiction. In addition, and perhaps even more importantly, Attebery expands his ideas of genre with George Lakoff's and Mark Johnson's concept of prototype theory (Lakoff and Johnson 69–72; Haberkorn, "Debugging" 172–73), applying the linguistic term "fuzzy sets" to a literary context. Any text with supernatural elements shares properties of a set of features encompassing a genre,[21] but none of the texts is fixed, nor is it the perfect example of the genre.

Not only does this modularity allow his three sub-definitions of fantasy to be overlapping (and at times congruent), it also provides fantasy with the potential to form part of any genre—a concept which itself must not be restricted to dichotomies such as realism/fantasy or other limiting labels:

> We often think of genres, like other categories, as territories on a map, with definitional limits marking off hard-boiled from classic detective, or fantasy from science fiction. [...] But another model proposed by logicians offers a more flexible means of categorization. Genres may be approached as "fuzzy sets," meaning that they are defined not by boundaries but by a center. (Attebery, *Strategies* 12)

Fantasy undoubtedly *is* a genre; however, it cannot be defined by isolating individual elements but rather by taking-into-account *any* array of supernatural elements, not all of which must be fulfilled in order for a text to be considered fantasy. Unsurprisingly, Tolkien's *LotR* stands "in the bullseye" for Attebery (14), of the fantasy fuzzy set,[22] incorporating the most elements considered part of the genre. Around this prototypical[23] fantasy novel, closer or further away in similarity, mode, genre, or formula are works that feature elements which violate the rules of empirical reality in different intensity.

While Attebery's open definition aims to include any text with even the least supernatural elements, it must again be underlined

---

[21] Naturally, various other literary genres such as horror or mystery novels overlap with fantasy by featuring supernatural content.

[22] In tune with my previous footnote, Farah Mendlesohn observes that "we can actually identify several fuzzy sets, linked together by what John Clute has termed *taproot* texts" (*Rhetorics* xvii). For the sake of my argument, however, I focus solely on the fuzzy set of fantasy.

[23] Even though *LotR*, although central, is not prototypical insofar as to incorporate *all* elements of the supernatural. In Attebery's terms, no text can thus claim to be one hundred percent fantasy by representing the entire scope of the genre.

that older texts "we might understand as fantasy" (James and Mendlesohn, *History* 7) or as fantastic were not subject to these terms at the time of their creation. Mythology, for example, is undoubtedly a precursor to modern fantasy (and one of its primary sources), yet its original function was neither plain entertainment nor an attempt to create a fictional world. Like mimesis, it was a mental tool to reflect on unknown or unexplainable phenomena of the actual world. Precisely because of these facts, its relation to fantasy cannot be denied:

> Fantasy has a long and noble heritage, beginning with the very first tales ever told around a campfire—of bowls over the sky with holes in them that let in the light of heaven, or of monsters named Grendel and heroes named Beowulf. We speak in metaphor when we don't have better poetry, and fantasy literature, over time, has evolved as a metaphor for human experience. (Thomas 60)

Again, the mimetic features of fantasy (and myth) are stressed: Attebery remains adamant about fantasy being "drawn in a comprehensible pattern" (*Strategies* 16), and thus close enough to empirical reality that readers may recognize at least some parallels to the actual world. Yet one of the more prominent problems of the genre is that fantasy as a modern phenomenon is usually set in a context which (regardless of mimetic value) tends to violate particularly spatial norms. Though derived from empirical reality, the secondary worlds of fantasy often feature few to no direct connections to any real-world places. Mythology, for all its inventiveness, explained actual phenomena (lightning or the change of seasons, for example) and provided stories not merely for otherworldly but also for existing places.[24] Fantasy, on the other hand, often has no real counterparts to its described spaces which could be visited or experienced, and must pay increased attention to the creation of non-actual spaces or—more problematically—that of entire alternative worlds.

World-Making and Space in Fiction

Having claimed that the secondary worlds of fantasy often appear to be holistic, one of the peculiarities in the making of a possible world in literature is that an author cannot possibly formulate everything and go

---

[24] Numerous examples of spaces in empirical reality act as inspiration for fictional treatment in myths and religion—among others Uluru in Australia and the mountain of Sinai in Israel. More than mere placeholders, they *are* the spaces told in stories.

into detail for every circumstance. As Doležel observes, fiction has the advantage (or disadvantage)[25] that it is "inevitably incomplete" (Wolf 19). No matter how detailed the possible world of a fictional creation becomes, it will never reach the actual detail of the spaces of empirical reality. The preference of the mimetic—or in the case of fiction, of the accurate representation of what is considered "real"—in favor of the invented is particularly apparent in theories of space. Even with the advent of the *spatial turn* and its focus on the importance of geopolitics, space, and place in culture and society, most research seem to be predominantly concerned with the representations of real spaces and less with those of purely (or partly) fictional spaces. As Soja explains,

> In what may be seen as one of the most important intellectual and political developments in the late twentieth century, scholars have begun to interpret space and the spatiality of human life with the same critical insight and emphasis that has traditionally been given to time and history on the one hand, and to social relations and society on the other. (qtd. in Döring and Thielmann 9)

In light of how mimesis is a natural part of human cognition, however, the spaces of literature are anything but removed from spaces of reality. Even so, Edward Soja's "possibilities machine" (81) of Thirdspace provides a foundation for their interconnectedness:

> For Soja, space must be understood as simultaneously real and imagined [...], for it always represents a link between physical, geographical spaces and mental, cultural constructions of space. [...] It is precisely in this bringing together of real and imagined places that his model of space could be picked up in literary studies[.] (Winkler et al. 254)

Since fantasy epitomizes the creation of imagined spaces that are based on mimesis and the reinvention of real-world space, the genre's cornerstones of imitation and imagination are given equal measure. There is, however, a caveat to the aforementioned incompleteness of fictional worlds: while both space and time are riddled with holes, the complexities of time are far easier to break down in fiction than those of spatial description.

---

[25] Literary critics debate the merits and challenges of the incompleteness of possible (or secondary) worlds. Doležel claims that incompleteness is a crucial feature of any fictional text (*Heterocosmica* 447), whereas Marie-Laure Ryan and David Herman propose *the principle of minimal departure*, according to which readers automatically "fill in the gaps" (Herman et al., *Encyclopedia* 51–53), when encountering such blank spaces in the text.

In simple terms, writing a text is a process of reduction: "Authors must take a set of complex actions that occupy the three dimensions of space and the fourth of time, and transform them into a linear sequence of words, so the mimetic process is selective" (Hume xi). Being linear[26] themselves, texts necessarily have to convey space in a linear, non-three-dimensional manner. Hence it is only logical that time is easier to portray and to analyze in fiction than space: Our perception of time as a one-directional and comparatively abstract process fits the successive linearity of writing and reading. Thus, a multi-dimensional and more complex construct such as space is harder to recreate fictionally (see Herman et al., *Encyclopedia* 551). Fiction is mainly concerned with time and its passing; without an adequate description of temporal circumstances, much fiction would be incomprehensible, its plots slow or an experiment at best.

Even in classic fantasy, with its tendency towards lengthy descriptions of surroundings, there needs to be a certain pace to keep the story going forward, although this is often the crux of the genre. As Wolf emphasizes,

> storytelling and world-building are different processes that can sometimes come into conflict. One of the cardinal rules often given to new writers has to do with narrative economy; they are told to pare down their prose and remove anything that does not actively advance the story. World-building, however, often results in data, exposition, and digressions that provide information about a world, slowing down narrative or even bringing it to a halt temporarily. (29)

According to Gérard Genette, time exemplifies the actions and events of a narrative while space provides the descriptions—the latter of which is secondary to the former: "Narration cannot exist without description, but this dependence does not stop it from always playing the first role. The description is naturally *ancilla narratienis* [the handmaiden of the narration], the slave always necessary, always submissive, never emancipated" (Genette, "Boundaries" 6). Despite Mikhail Bakhtin's chronotopical observation that in "literature and art itself, temporal and spatial determinations are inseparable from one another" (Bakhtin, *Dialogic* 243), time still enjoys a privileged role among the two—perhaps a bit less so in fantasy, yet events still need

---

[26] One could argue that hypertexts and other examples of non-linear writing do not follow this rule; however, what remains unchanged is the fact that the *reading* process of these texts still happens in a linear, word-for-word manner.

to happen regularly for adequate narrative progression.

This is not to say that texts of pure description are ruled out in fiction, but critics such as Genette place them in the speculative rather than in the literary realm (Genette, "Boundaries" 5). Therefore, "[l]iterature is basically an art of time" (Zoran 310), space emerging as the "stepchild" (Dennerlein 3–4), in the analysis or enjoyment of a story. While we can think and imagine spaces as well as we can imagine time, it seems to be a much more demanding—not to say secondary—task to portray them fictionally.

The main reason for this preference of time to space in fiction is, indeed, due to the problem that elongated spatial descriptions can break the (temporal) flow of a narrative. In the worst case, descriptions may become digressions or "descriptive pauses" (Genette, *Discourse* 99), in which little to no plot development occurs. One author who addresses this conflict both as a literary author and critic is Umberto Eco, particularly in his reflections on his first novel *The Name of the Rose*:

> I spent a full year, if I remember correctly, without writing a line [...]. Instead I read, did drawings and diagrams, invented a world. This world had to be as precise as possible, so that I could move around in it with total confidence. For *The Name of the Rose* I drew hundreds of labyrinths and plans of abbeys, basing mine on other drawings and on places I visited, because I needed everything to work well, I needed to know how long it would take two characters in conversation to go from one place to another. (*Literature* 314)

Thus, when reading the finished novel, we are presented with more than just a 14th-century crime fiction set in an abbey in the Apennines. Eco provides lengthy passages about monastic life and practices that often provide little to no insight concerning the murders, and seem to be the purely atmospheric digressions of a medieval scholar.[27] Yet like Eco's comments on the minute spatial descriptions in Alessandro Manzoni's *The Betrothed*,[28] so the author of *The Name of the Rose* himself "is designing a map; he is setting up a space [and] constructing his

---

[27] Interestingly, the book has many features of a fantasy novel: Besides intricate details about the daily routine of his literary world, Eco also provides a map of the abbey, translations of various Latin phrases, and a glossary.

[28] A novel whose author was notorious for interrupting his adventure novels mid-narrative (often when his heroes were in peril) in order to provide extensive information about specific aspects of his secondary world—mostly the political, economical, and sociological background of 17th-century Milan. Eco cites Manzoni's work as an example of description overshadowing events.

fictional world by borrowing aspects of the real one" (*Woods* 73). Herein lies the reason why space should not remain the stepchild of narratology: Wolf echoes Bakhtin and notes how "story and world usually work together, enriching each other" (Wolf 29)—space and time, descriptions and events are interlinked in every narrative and form two sides of a coin of "narrative comprehension" (Herman, *Logic* 211). Descriptions might detract from plot progression, but they add to the believability and autonomy of the fictional world.

The world-making techniques of fantasy authors are no different from those rendered above: A literary world is created as the spatial dimension of the narrative, which grounds it in an inner-literary reality and provides descriptions and information to enhance the main plot. The only crucial difference lies in the content: Staying within the theoretical framework given by Doležel, Ryan, and Alber, we see that fantasy depicts non-actualizable realms, possible literary spaces that could not exist in reality (Alber et al., "What Really" 104–05). Unlike the portrayal of France in Honoré de Balzac's work, for example, Tolkien's Middle-earth features elements that transcend our rules of physics and modern understanding—"the proportions between reality and invention are different" (Eco, *Woods* 78). As possible-worlds-in-fiction theory does not place particular focus on the impossibility of worlds, Jan Alber's investigations of unnatural narratives allow for a more precise view of these non-actualizable worlds. Although several interpretations[29] of unnatural narratives exist, fantasy as a genre is closest to Alber's idea thereof, which restricts the use of this term to texts about story worlds that contain physically, logically, or humanly impossible scenarios or events. That is to say, the represented scenarios or events have to be impossible according to the known laws governing the physical world, accepted principles of logic (such as the principle of non-contradiction), or standard human limitations of knowledge. In other words, the unnatural deviates from 'natural' cognitive parameters—real-world frames and scripts that are derived from our being in the world (Alber 449).

The appeal of transgression is one of the main motors of creative re-imagination. Doležel claims that "[w]hen it comes to

---

[29] Alber's co-writers and fellow researchers of unnatural narratives and narratology—Brian Richardson, Stefan Iversen, and Henrik Skov Nielsen, all propose slightly different approaches to the topic. For a good overview, see Alber and Heinze 3–4.

feats of imagination, nothing is more attractive than impossible worlds" (Doležel, *Postmodern* 35)—a technique that fantasy employs to oftentimes strong effect. Therefore, authors of unnatural fiction deliberately exceed the physical or logical limitations of our world in order to portray literary realms which, according to Alber and Doležel, challenge our familiar cognitive frames since "in order to reconstruct and interpret a fictional world, the reader has to *reorient his cognitive stance* to agree with the world's encyclopedia" (Doležel, *Heterocosmica* 181; my emphasis).

Yet while such cognitive reorientation is a crucial part in both postmodern texts and fantasy fiction, there is a vital difference: Postmodern texts often violate not just the rules of the actual world but furthermore the rules of their own fictional worlds, using techniques "such as linguistic play, new modes of narratological self-reflexivity, and referential frames within frames" (Woods 49), to emphasize the constructedness of fiction. Anti- or non-mimetic texts are examples thereof, but postmodern fiction generally features elements that underline the fact that what we are reading is a text, not a holistic world but the illusion thereof, if at all. This is problematic: While fantasy texts are also undoubtedly literary constructs with impossible content, they usually do not reveal their own fictionality in the same overt manner as postmodern literature. Inconsistencies and contradictions would destroy the Tolkienian belief needed to uphold the readers' immersion in the text and consistency of the secondary world—although the subversive potential of fantasy stems from the same sources as those of postmodernism. How the two terms share similarities despite their difference in approach to literature is another challenge.

Postmodernism and Fantasy

A term that defies being categorized or defined like fantasy, postmodernism[30] has become a substitute for a plethora of developments in mid-20th- to early 21st-century art. Reflecting on

---

[30] I mostly use the terms "postmodernism" and "postmodern" for my purposes, keeping in mind the distinction of "postmodernism" as an aesthetic movement and "postmodernity" as a political and socio-cultural phenomenon (McGuigan 3; Woods 10). Furthermore, despite various claims for the "end of postmodernism" since the turn of the millennium, I nonetheless regard this movement as a debatable but still valid and unfinished project.

Jorge Luis Borges' short story "On Exactitude in Science,"[31] Jim Casey remarks how "Brian Attebery describes fantasy as a 'fuzzy set,' and the same might be said of both modern and postmodern literatures. Fantasy, modernism and postmodernism are all disputed territories, and the boundaries of each vary from map to map" (113). Providing a similarly open and yet encompassing approach, Linda Hutcheon's interpretation of postmodernism establishes a link with fantasy in general and with Pratchett in particular. Having said this, perhaps the most enduring problem of postmodern literature is the fact that it "denies the idea of knowable origins" and "has acquired a semantic instability or shifting meaning that shadows and echoes its notes of indeterminacy and insecurity" (Woods 3). Yet in Hutcheon's view, this lack of precise distinction is not a defect but the greatest benefit and creative impetus of postmodernism, which at its core "is a contradictory phenomenon, one that uses and abuses, installs and then subverts, the very concept it challenges" (*Poetics* 3).

This resistance to definition or classification stems from similar sources as the rise of fantasy literature, namely the skeptical attitude of a society increasingly critical of the conservative climate after World War II:

> [The] openness and indeterminacy of Fantasy is the main reason why the young generation of the late 1960s, in their shared but individual rebellion against tradition and the economic dictates of capitalism, relied on Fantasy for their ultimately private search for universal, deeper meaning. (Schallegger 41–42)

As Best and Kellner underline, such individual rebellion was present throughout all the social strata:

> During the 1960s, a group of radical intellectuals and activists who became the first major postmodern theorists experienced what they believed to be a decisive break with modern society and culture. [...] At the same time, an oppositional counterculture emerged that called for a society which renounced the materialist ethos and success-oriented norms of capitalism. (4)

Fantasy was a part of the counterculture movement that embraced the "retrograde nostalgia" (Sandner, "Emergence" 34), message of *LotR*, in which the systematic destruction of Isengard and the scouring of the Shire seemed to mirror the loss of nature and innocence in an

---

[31] Characteristic for Borges, the story itself can be considered an early hybrid of postmodern and fantasy literature.

industrialized, post-Holocaust world. Both the rise of the fantasy genre and the emergence of postmodernism expressed a rebellion against the 19th-century belief in progress and prosperity that had prevailed until the repercussions of two global wars and which tried to continue in a purer form through capitalism thereafter. As an alternative to such disillusionment, fantasy provided the means of escape from post-war consumerist nihilism to the fictional, yet nonetheless seemingly better values taken from medieval romance, myths, and bucolic poetry. Yet despite the accusations of fantasy being escapist and reactionary,[32] the supernatural features of the genre successfully broke the conventions of so-called "realistic" representation in literature.

What Hutcheon and fellow theorists of postmodernism underline is consequently not just "the incredulity toward metanarratives" (Lyotard xxiv), such as the progressive message of post-War economic prosperity,[33] but furthermore a mistrust in conventions and definitions themselves. Similarly, even though fantasy offers the reader escape and replacement beliefs in secondary worlds, it also "suspends established truth and reality" and "directs attention not so much to the things in a world, as to the realization that the world has been constituted by mind" (Hull 35–36). It is here that postmodernism, in Hutcheon's sense, and fantasy overlap because in both cases the questioning of the real or of reality is often more important than what is represented as such.

Furthermore, this shared skepticism does not merely uncover the constructedness and cultural context of concepts and ideas but also that of binary oppositions, such as familiar/unfamiliar, fantasy/realism, fiction/empirical reality and time/space. Returning to the secondary role of space in fiction, the conflict between fictional time and fictional space points back to the challenge of world-making and confirms that in spite

---

[32] Following the monarchies and dictatorships that had plunged the globe into two catastrophic wars, the formation of the United Nations in 1945 heralded the (short-lived) promise of peaceful coexistence. Naturally, depicting major conflicts and reinstating kings in fantasy literature was a far cry both from the democratization and the spread of Communism in the world.

[33] The Marshall Plan, besides being an economic undertaking to rebuild a war-torn Europe, was also a new narrative promising a future to devastated nations and a rekindling of American exceptionalism in view of the looming Cold War (Pease 644). Other success narratives such as the German Wirtschaftswunder but also counter-narratives like the Soviet Union's fear of the "capitalization of Europe" were direct consequences of the reparations and support after the war.

of their seeming tendency to hinder each other, the description of a world and the progression of a story set in that world are interdependent:

> Recognizing that the experience of a *world* is different and distinct from that of merely a *narrative* is crucial to seeing how worlds function apart from the narratives set within them, even though the narratives have much to do with the worlds in which they occur, and are usually the means by which the worlds are experienced. (Wolf 11)

Particularly in light of postmodernist metafiction, the building blocks of a literary world can be revealed in this interplay. Going beyond Mendlesohn's statement that all literature is at its base constructing worlds, however, laying open the mechanisms of fictional world-making again mirrors the artificiality of *any* system or narrative:

> What [the postmodern] does say is that there are all kinds of orders and systems in our world—*and* that we create them all. [...] They do not exist "out there," fixed, given, universal, eternal; they are human constructs in history. [...] The point is not exactly that the world is meaningless [...], but that any meaning that exists is of our own creation. (Hutcheon, *Poetics* 43)

Underlining the aforementioned evolutionary importance of an increasingly mimetic culture, "narrative has been carried wherever human beings have gone" and forms an "essential strategy of human expression and thus a basic aspect of human life" (Altman 1). Postmodernism in Hutcheon's manner both celebrates and deconstructs this human affinity for storytelling as "a discursive world of socially defined meaning systems" ("Politics" 179–80), a world which offers the freedom of invention of further or alternative meanings but also eludes any attempt to define or grasp any of those meanings within any fixed or "final" systems.

Juxtaposing Aristotle's position on mimesis and Tolkien's statement regarding the creative potential of our minds, sub-creation indeed is a natural human activity, however one that spawns more conflict when the creation involves increased invention and less direct mimesis. While Tolkien stresses "the creation of a *believable* imaginary world" (Fimi 45; my emphasis), when writing fantasy, the postmodern blurring of the boundaries between fiction and reality reflects the unspeakable and the shattering of belief, namely "the crisis of storytelling, marked by the experience of the Second World War, and the way in which storytelling was then revived—in unprecedentedly self-conscious, metanarrative forms" (Meretoja 2). In the aftermath and shock that followed the First and the Second World Wars, the narrative cores of seemingly eternal truths, beliefs, and ideals were unmasked, giving rise to literature that explicitly addressed the "interchangeability of values and viewpoints" (Zima 23). Fantasy, however, took a radically different approach to this revelation than postmodern literature: rather than deliberately destroying the suspension of disbelief in fiction to showcase the constructedness of all meaning, authors of fantasy aimed at creating the illusion of holistic, alternate worlds which were strongly independent of empirical reality.

Having revealed the futility of searching for an ultimate meaning, postmodern literature could be inherently nihilistic and bleak, yet it thankfully also has a more light-hearted side: the freedom from any absolute meaning can also be celebrated with irony and humor. A vital part of this area of postmodern fiction is parody—a term that had a long history but now eclipsed any older definitions (Korkut 27–55). Hutcheon emphasizes the novelty of her interpretation of parody in the light of the 20th century, taking into account the ubiquity of parody in postmodern societies:

> What I mean by "parody" here is *not* the ridiculing imitation of the standard theories and definitions that are rooted in eighteenth-century theories of wit. The collective weight of parodic *practice* suggests a redefinition of <u>parody as repetition with a critical distance that allows ironic signalling of difference at the very heart of similarity</u>. ("Politics" 185; underlined emphasis mine)

The worlds of fantasy also act as repetitions or variations of empirical reality, engaged with the dynamics of similarity but also with the differences regarding their relations to our actual world. Indeed, fantasy, as other literary genres after World War II, became a mass phenomenon and subject to ever-stronger reinterpretation and reproduction. The success of genre and the increasing variety but also similarity of secondary worlds is intrinsically linked to the rise of popular literature, particularly in the second half of the 20th century.

Tolkien and the Mass Market

Radical as the changes at the beginning of the 20th century were, their infrastructure had its roots in 19th-century innovations: The Second Industrial Revolution had paved the way for mass production and provided the facilities for new uses of technology—with drastic consequences across the globe. Given the catastrophic events of World

War I, the shockwaves of high modernism and surrealism created new methods of storytelling, as authors attempted to break the unity of narrative and norms of literature. Likewise, the economic boom after World War II introduced consumption and demand at a level hitherto unseen. Due to increased literacy and leisure in Western societies, literature formed very much part of this movement. Indeed, the combined developments of "new technologies of industrial production to publishing, an expanding market driven by increased literacy and urbanisation, and the emergence of new commercial media [...] together decisively change[d] the conditions in which popular fiction [was] created" (Glover and McCracken 4).

Beginning with the cheap pulp magazines of the 1920s and 1930s and finding further exposure in comic books and paperback novels, fantasy was, like horror and detective fiction, at the forefront of entertainment literature. Fantasy texts had a long tradition, yet their mass appeal both for authors and readers stemmed from the increased demand for popular fiction. Next to its "twin" genre science fiction, by the early 20th century it had developed from Victorian fantastic texts into a growing field of alternate visions of worlds. Hence, it quickly found its way onto the mass market in both pulp magazines and ornate volumes alike. With the release of *LotR*, Tolkien's attention to detail brought fantasies set in extensive secondary worlds to the fore, turning fantasy into a staple of genre fiction: "Intermittent at first, it gained considerable impetus from Tolkien's *The Lord of the Rings* [...] to the point where much fantasy is now set in other worlds or in transformed versions of this one" (Manlove, *England* 4). Genre fantasy as we know it today was born from the mass-market appeal of Tolkien's use and creative reinterpretation of myth, folklore, and linguistics into a new whole.

Consequently, Tolkien's *magnum opus* was "embraced by the American counterculture of the 1960s, greatly expanding the readership of the genre" (Sandner, "Emergence" 33), and leading authors to write stories in the same vein, often hoping to repeat the commercial and critical success of *LotR*.[34] A problem soon arose from the repetition, since for

---

[34] It has become a commonplace phenomenon to proclaim newly successful fantasy authors "the next Tolkien" or to see their works surpassing *LotR* in terms of complexity or appeal. This unbridled acceptance of Tolkien as the prime fantasy author naturally assisted in the making of a multitude of secondary worlds that bear very close resemblance to Middle-earth or try to copy its linguistic and mythological depth—which may ultimately detract from narrative flow for purely decorative purposes, similar to Manzoni's digressions.

every good fantasy novel there were ten releases which were produced in a more haphazard manner. The consequences of commercialization in literature brought forth an ever-increasing stream of new fantasy novels that profited from the growing demand for the genre.[35] Still, none of them had the same erudite and intricate background as Middle-earth, which was deeply bedded in Tolkien's historical and linguistic research. Ironically, it was the freedom of storytelling beyond the rules of realistic representation that in the end restricted fantasy as a genre:

> The combination of novelty, semantic density, and freedom from many of the restraints of realism that characterises fantasy fictional worlds also furnishes them with unlimited storytelling possibilities. This, in turn, makes fantasy particularly suited to the processes of remediation and extension that have increasingly dominated commercial culture since the 1960s. (Herman et al., *Encyclopedia* 160)

No matter whether a fully-fledged fantasy world *à la* Tolkien or a cross-world portrayal of fantasy elements, the genre threatened to become an amalgam of clichés, similar to the rehashed sensationalist 19th-century Gothic novels[36] that had followed successful works such as Ann Radcliffe's *The Mysteries of Udolpho* or Matthew Gregory Lewis' wildly gory response *The Monk*.[37] The fantasy genre quickly earned a bad reputation, much in the vein of the pulp detective and horror fiction of the 1930s (Clute and Grant 612–15), the field of popular literature that it originated from but to which it certainly did not deserve being reduced to.

Nonetheless, the making of a secondary world became predominant—Tolkien had set the bar for creating a sophisticated

---

[35] As with Gothic fiction, the commercial success of fantasy literature heralded a plethora of authors whose prime aim was to make money or gain fame rather than to write a good story. This is not to say that such works are automatically bad examples of fantasy—but the monetary dimension of a popular genre should not be denied either.

[36] Gothic novels can be considered direct precursors to fantasy literature, as they employ various supernatural elements and are often set in highly artificial pasts that have been reconstructed from several epochs and cultural backgrounds. Some Gothic novels, for example, are located in an assembled past combining medieval imagery and feudal politics with highly romanticized plots that often draw direct influence from counter-enlightenment philosophy or the French Revolution.

[37] Although itself the inspiration for derivative blood-thirsty Gothic tales and a classic by today's standards, Lewis' novel was deemed an exaggerated caricature of Radcliffe's subdued form of Gothic fiction at the time of its release and provided a very fantastic alternative to her "supernatural explain'd" (Ellis 66–69, 83–84).

spatial expanse in supernatural fiction, and writers of the emerging genre followed his example. Descriptions of colorful backgrounds (such as the different cultures, languages, and vistas of a fantasy world) therefore took dominance over an original story, which in turn often followed a simplified formula *à la* "conflict-journey-resolve." Consequently, the narratives of many fantasy works, of the period and today, are laid out like beads on a string, one event following another: "Often, quests or other journeys function to structure the narrative as a series of encounters and conflicts that allow exploration of the fictional world as well as advancing the plot" (Herman et al., *Encyclopedia* 161).

Tolkien had set a new standard with the publication of *LotR*, simultaneously the starting point and arguably the ideal example of fantasy genre literature that spawned countless imitators in the decades to come. Attebery's summary of formulaic fantasy—"popular escapist literature that combines stock characters and devices" (*Strategies* 1), became the *mode d'emploi* of the genre. Quickly, the trend turned into a pattern, and began to transform genre fantasy into narratives that were often as predictable as they were consumable. Tolkien's world thus provided the building blocks for what John Clute and John Grant call "fantasyland":

> JRRT's influence on fantasy and sf has been not merely profound but also demeaning. It is his work which has given licence to the fairies, elves, orcs, cuddly dwarfs, loquacious plants, singing barmen, etc., who inhabit fantasyLAND, which itself constitutes a direct thinning of JRRT's constantly evolving secondary world. (955)

While there were always attempts to break the pattern,[38] it was much easier to reiterate the given structure, appealing to fans with recognizability.

When Pratchett published his first Discworld novel *The Colour of Magic* in 1983, it seemed that he had written what Diana Wynne Jones and other critics describe as the "Cook's Tour" (Wolf 158): An adventure across a secondary world, with characters travelling from point to point along an entertaining but, at its core, unoriginal narrative. While the humor that was the trademark of the Discworld

---

[38] Ironically, it was the same countercultural influences that had popularized the genre in the 1960s which also provided an antithesis to (stereo-)typical fantasy, finding expression in the works of authors like Ursula K. Le Guin or M. John Harrison. In a way, both the commercialization of the fantasy genre and its first critical reinterpretations occurred at roughly the same time.

was to reveal hidden depth as the series progressed, the emergence of humorous fantasy in the second half of the 20th century did not seem to offer a lot beyond mere mockery at first glance. Combining humor and fantasy in new and unusual ways would prove to be a tricky endeavor for Pratchett, to say the least.

CHAPTER 2

FANTASY AND HUMOR

Tolkien's impact on fantasy—whether regarded as positive or negative—is undeniable and has paved the way for a mass market for the genre. As James rightly states, Tolkien's work "looms over all the fantasy written in English—and in many other languages—since its publication; most subsequent writers of fantasy are either imitating him or else desperately trying to escape his influence" ("Tolkien" 62). Likewise, Pratchett remarks how "Tolkien has become a sort of mountain, appearing in all subsequent fantasy in the way that Mt. Fuji appears so often in Japanese prints," being present even when it is not in the picture (*Slip* 116). While Tolkien's imitators were (and to some extent still are) aiming to reproduce his formula as closely as possible, or at least attempting to depict their secondary worlds in a similarly erudite and serious manner, the main ways to avoid or criticize the Tolkienian formula within fantasy lie in either contrast or ironic exaggeration. In the former case, classic tropes are replaced with counterparts—the anti-hero[39] is a classic example, but one may also portray specific elements typical for the genre such as elves and dwarfs in uncharacteristic[40] manners.

The exaggeration of fantasy elements, on the other hand, is often linked to humor. Taking cues from Bakhtin's idea of the carnivalesque, typical elements are shown in a hyperbolical, even grotesque manner. For parodies of genre literature, this is the most straightforward method to escape the trappings of a stereotypical text, by inflating

---

[39] Michael Moorcock's "Eternal Champion" series protagonist Elric is a good example of an anti-hero, a weak and decidedly Byronic hero who relies on drugs and sorcery to survive the adventures he is involved in and who becomes increasingly weary and depressed by the oftentimes negative outcome of his endeavors.

[40] Untypical portrayals of elves and dwarfs are found in Andrzej Sapkowski's Witcher books, where the two races are subject to segregation and form parts of militant militia groups against human oppressors—a dynamic far removed from Tolkien's near-divine elves or dwarves living in isolation deep underground.

them to ridiculous levels. It does not suffice to label all parodist fantasy as merely humorous, however. Even though there is a multitude of parodies primarily aimed at very direct ridicule of a specific source text, the "critical edge" (Dentith 156), of parody as a general concept must not be forgotten—especially seen in the light of postmodern irony.

Theories of Humor and Their Limitations

While freedom of invention is one of the defining features of supernatural fiction, there have to be limits to this creativeness—first and foremost, through mimetic representation that provides common ground based on a shared cultural context. Not limited to the realms of fantasy, every secondary world must fulfill three axioms to a certain extent in order to evoke and hold the reader's attention, namely invention, completeness, and consistency:

> If a secondary world is to be believable and interesting, it will need to have a high degree of invention, completeness, and consistency. Of course, no secondary world can be as complete as the Primary World, inconsistencies are increasingly likely as a world grows, and no world can be the product of invention to the point that there is no longer any resemblance to the Primary World. Nevertheless, unless an effort is made in all of these directions, the resulting subcreation will fail to create the illusion of an independent world. (Wolf 33–34)

This delineation of secondary worlds is not just crucial for fantasy but for all elaborate fictional worlds, meaning that Wolf's three axioms apply to the literary worlds of Gustave Flaubert's *Madame Bovary* or James Joyce's *Ulysses* no less than to those of Jack Vance's *The Dying Earth* or Mervyn Peake's *Gormenghast*.[41] As mentioned before, an author must become a good "sub-creator" to achieve the effects of immersion and secondary belief. Since fantasy is often low mimetic, the believability of its secondary worlds has to be addressed more thoroughly to counter its impossible (or unbelievable) elements. Compared to fiction with higher amounts of mimesis, a fantasy world relies less on pre-established literary content and more on invention by making use of supernatural elements. Yet the "arresting strangeness" (OFS 60) of fantasy must be within appropriate measure in order to avoid breaking secondary belief—too much

---

[41] In all these works, we encounter artful descriptions of literary worlds—invention and mimesis may be employed in different manners, but completeness and especially consistency are of equal importance to Vance and Peake as they are to Joyce and Flaubert.

invention turns the world into a chaotic mishmash, and empirical reality cannot be avoided completely. In other words, invention and reinterpretation of elements in a supernatural context have to be approached in a serious manner.

Attempting to introduce humor into this delicate and often rigid framework is a challenge. Perhaps the most enduring and difficult problem of humor is the general tendency to equate it with ridicule or malice. The topic has certainly remained a controversial field of research in philosophy. Unsurprisingly, Plato does not condone humor or laughing, criticizing the laughter of the gods in *The Iliad* (*The Republic*, Book III 388e–89a) for being "an emotion that overrides self-control" and comedy in general as "a form of scorn" (Morreall, "Philosophy" 1). As with mimesis, Aristotle expresses a less strict view on laughter: He regards it as "part of the ugly, a form of defect or deformity which, however, is not harmful to anyone else" (qtd. in Gilhus 47), and thus acceptable within limits.

In later philosophy, three major theoretical approaches to researching humor emerged: superiority theory, relief theory, and incongruity theory. While superiority theory stems from Plato's and Aristotle's sentiments that humor effectively means feeling superior to others (Carroll, *Humour* 6; Bardon 463–64), and relief theory forms part of psychoanalysis explaining humor as a release of repressed feelings (Critchley 3), incongruity theory states that "an essential ingredient of comic amusement is the juxtaposition of incongruous or contrasting objects, events, categories, propositions, maxims, properties, and so on" (Carroll, *Aesthetics* 248). Incongruity theory is the leading approach in current humor research, even though it is not without its caveats and problems:

> Three major criticisms of the incongruity theory are that it is too broad to be very meaningful, it is insufficiently explanatory in that it does not distinguish between non-humorous incongruity and basic incongruity, and that revised versions still fail to explain why some things, rather than others, are funny. (Smuts 2.c.)

However, of these criticisms particularly the first two underline both the mental processing and reconsideration that characterize incongruous situations as well as the postmodern indeterminacy put forward by critics such as Linda Hutcheon. As it turns out, the cognitive playfulness typical of incongruity theory and the violation of mental patterns in low-mimetic literature such as fantasy are remarkably similar.

The prime reason why the incongruity approach to empirical reality comes close to the techniques of fantasy is because one of its core concepts is the production of an anomaly, meaning "that some thing or event we perceive or think about violates our normal mental patterns and normal expectations" (Morreall, *Comic* 11)—in the same manner as fantasy itself transgresses what is regarded as possible in the actual world or in a mimetic representation thereof. Combining these factors of humor, fantasy, and cognition, Gideon Haberkorn notes:

> The human brain is a device for making the world meaningful. […] Fantasy can foreground the tools we use to make meaning. Humour can help us notice and correct mistakes our mind makes in its meaning-making. The space opened up by the interplay between humour and fantasy is one in which readers can probe their mental patterns for mistakes and try out new ones. ("Debugging" 160)

What is underlined here is the invention of new content and the rearrangement of established tropes and phenomena—both humor and fantasy make us see our world differently by giving examples from possible worlds or hypothetical scenarios, even if we are aware that these scenarios are not empirically real (Gottschall 103–04).

Bearing in mind Donald's statement regarding the role of mimesis in human evolution, narrative is accordingly a crucial component not just for evolutionary purposes but also helps to gain an understanding of the pluralistic world we inhabit today:

> People incorporate stories into a wide array of practices, using narrative as a problem-solving strategy in many contexts. In this sense, narrative functions as a powerful and basic tool for thinking. (Herman, *Cognitive* 163)

Likewise, jokes (as with fairy tales or fiction in general) always contain at least a grain of narrative relevance, a relation to empirical reality and to factual scenarios. Disbelief is suspended for the duration of the story (be it a joke or a fantasy novel) because "knowing that those situations are not real, we can treat them playfully" (Morreall, *Comic* 53), and acknowledge their potential for subversion and challenge to our habitual mental patterns in either an amusing or a reflective manner. Nevertheless, combining two strands of incongruous narrative—that is to say, fantasy and humor—poses new problems.

Double Incongruity

Despite Tolkien's influence and the comparative seriousness of *LotR*, humor has a long tradition in fantasy. Looking back at Attebery's modular "fuzzy set" and its idea of individual supernatural elements, fantasy as a mode can undoubtedly be linked to more light-hearted topics. Examples of literary works that combine humoristic and fantastic elements begin as early as Aristophanes' *The Clouds* and Apuleius' *The Golden Ass* (Stableford, *Dictionary* xiii)—possibly even earlier.[42] Later satirists such as Jonathan Swift and François Rabelais show exaggerated worlds filled with supernatural elements that are both out of bounds and simultaneously mirth-inducingly absurd. In all these works (and worlds), "both the fantastic mode, to produce the impossibilities, and the mimetic, to reproduce the familiar" (Attebery, *Myth* 309), are made use of, a balance that strives towards reproduction while fantasy—and its parodies—form new literary genres.

Precisely because modern fantasy is usually set within the framework of supernatural elements already at its disposal, its more humorous exponents, in the same way as derivative fantasy, tend to "neglect" the creative recombination in favor of the repetitive: "Modern humorous fantasy has become an extensive sub-genre, in which imitation and bandwagon-jumping are rife" (Clute and Grant 487). In order to make fun of a literary genre, it appears, its constitutive elements must be isolated and exaggerated—in the case of fantasy, this concerns topics that are largely products of the imagination. The exaggeration of such elements by satirizing or parodying them effectively extends what is already supernatural with an overstated imitation (Butler, *Companion* 286), that may display even more impossibility and exaggeration[43] than the original.

While comic fantasy is hardly a stranger to English literature (Manlove, *Studies* 114–15), world-making and consequently the genre itself were treated more seriously with the advent of fantasy as a genre. In his theoretical reflections on how to make a secondary world, Tolkien sets a limit for the application of humor in fantasy

---

[42] Likely examples of political jokes might be found as far back as 2600 BCE Egypt or 3500 BCE Mesopotamia (Attardo 585).

[43] Marianne Wünsch's claims regarding qualitative and quantitative violations of reality might be helpful to underline this problem (25): As dwarfs and giants (quantitative violations of realistic representation or impossibilities in size) or magic (qualitative violations, meaning by allowing impossibilities such as teleportation or invisibility) are already supernatural elements typical for fantasy, a further exaggeration thereof in fantasy parodies stretches these violations to grotesque and possibly ridiculous ends. Wünsch's theory covers fantastic literature and is rooted in fairy tales but can be applied to fantasy texts in this regard.

as he defines it: "There is one proviso: if there is any satire present in the tale, one thing must not be made fun of, the magic itself. That must in that story be taken seriously, neither laughed at nor explained away" (OFS 33). Ignoring that, "the spell is broken; the magic, or rather art, has failed. You are then out in the Primary World again, looking at the little abortive Secondary World from the outside" (OFS 52). What Tolkien means by "magic" is the suspension of disbelief or immersion within a story achieved by attention to detail, as in Wolf's three axioms—even though a reader knows that the world presented is fictional, content with close resemblance to the actual world and skillful use of creativity and mimesis add to its believability. According to Tolkien, fantasy extends this initial moment of disbelief by its continuous yet *consistent* reliance on supernatural content in an otherwise recognizable and believable secondary world, expecting the reader to accept violations of real-world rules for a prolonged period and see them as "natural" in a secondary-world frame.

To achieve a high level of immersion, a fantasy author expects the reader to participate in the suspension of disbelief from the beginning to the end of a novel; otherwise, the enchantment of a secondary world will be broken. This is what is meant by successful "escapism" in the Tolkienian sense; we become absorbed in another world and momentarily accept it as a mimetic representation of an autonomous inner-fictional reality. We accept it as real despite its supernatural phenomena that violate our mental patterns and expectations based in empirical reality: "At such times, we do feel that we are in the text, that only the text exists for us. Our subjectivity has been temporarily dissolved. We are in the scene of fantasy the text creates, so that our reading experience is like dreaming. The outer world exists in another dimension" (McCracken 105). Here, we have one of the reasons why genre fantasy pays such close attention to detail. For readers to remain immersed in a secondary world, that world must contain strong consistency and internal logic, even if based on invented content that does not or could not exist in the actual world: "Thus when J. R. R. Tolkien states that [*LotR*] is an expansion of the historical record in an extant Middle-earth chronicle, the Red Book of Westmarch, his object is to increase the verisimilitude, not the verity of his work" (Manlove, *Studies* 2).

Like the supernatural elements that characterize the genre but work only in unison with elements representative of empirical reality, humor must be applied in moderate amounts, as too much of it would endanger the believability of the secondary world and portray it as ludicrous or inconsistent: A good example of the comparatively sober humor in *LotR* is the friendly rivalry between Legolas and Gimli which not only underlines their differing characters and worldviews but is also a good indicator of their eventual friendship. Even though Tolkien does not forbid humor[44] in fantasy, examples of humorous fantasy are fewer and often less elaborate—not to mention less attractive for authors. Brian Stableford notes that "'comic fantasy' led a slightly fugitive existence in the 1960s; the initial dominance of the nascent commercial genre by high fantasy did not immediately encourage experimentation" (Stableford, *Dictionary* 209). As pointed out at the end of the first chapter, the impact of Tolkien's popularity both as a literary and an academic author led to attempts at copying the pattern of *LotR*—not just to repeat his success but also to reproduce the erudition and subdued humor of his secondary world.

Many of these attempts at reproducing Tolkien's success resulted in what Attebery calls "formulaic fiction": Reflecting on his earlier observations in *Strategies of Fantasy* and comparing it to contemporary fantasy literature, Attebery laments "the interchangeability of a lot of what is called 'fantasy' on the supermarket book rack, much of it the unimpressive formula fiction that discerning fans call 'extruded fantasy product'" (*Myth* 1). Often, such stereotypical content can be summarized in Clute and Grant's idea of an entirely formulaic "fantasyland"—a word on which fantasy author and critic Diana Wynne Jones has written an extensive and tongue-in-cheek encyclopedia. Her book *The Tough Guide to Fantasyland*, composed as a tourist reference book, is both parody and criticism of genre fantasy, as it provides not merely entries on tropes which constitute much of formulaic fantasy but which also gives advice on what to do in order to achieve a typical narrative or quest:

> SAVING THE WORLD is something many Tours require you to do. You have to defeat the DARK LORD or WIZARDS who are trying to enslave everyone. It is about the same as a QUEST, except there is always a WAR, a personal CONFRONTATION, and a CATACLYSM before you succeed. Thousands of troops and DEMONS must be

---

[44] *H* is written in a rather humorous tone, owing to its intention as a children's book. *LotR* keeps some of the humor but enlarges the narrative by epic power plays and a mythological background, both being more serious matters for Tolkien.

>annihilated. The CITADEL or base of EVIL must be destroyed [...]. This usually triggers a semi-natural disaster. Sometimes large parts of the world you are saving go up in smoke. (167)

Filled with cross-references and dry remarks, Jones' account of the stereotypical elements of genre fantasy offers little direct critique of specific works but nonetheless lays bare the problems that may be caused by narratives too closely based on established source material—following the pattern of *LotR*, highly influential texts in this regard were Terry Goodkind's *Sword of Truth* novels and Robert Jordan's *The Wheel of Time* series among others. What Jones reveals in her *Guide* and equally in her fictional works[45] is how easy it is to imitate these patterns in genre fantasy, both in a serious and in an ironic manner.

The realization of the problem that narratives of a certain genre may be very similar to each other and follow particular patterns usually leads to two possibilities: An author either aligns their story with a given pattern (to a certain degree) or tries to break such patterns by actively avoiding its stereotypical components and plots.[46] A third possibility, however, is to address both of these dynamics in a postmodern manner, retelling famous stories from unusual points of view or to different ends. "Rather than inventing new materials, postmodernists quote what's already around and combine fragments" (Best and Kellner 133)—authors like Terry Pratchett and Diana Wynne Jones, but also Angela Carter or John Gardner, use this combination of methods to more or less ironic effect. While we should still be careful when applying the term "postmodern" to fantasy authors, it might well nonetheless be a "suitable vehicle for the postmodern imagination since contemporary fantasy may be thought of as the literary equivalent of deconstructionism" (Olsen 276)—the playful disassembly and rebuilding of fantasy in a different light. While never as comprehensive as Jones or as focused on a single source as Gardner

---

[45] A prolific author and equally as suspicious of stereotypical stories as Pratchett, Jones' books (prime examples being *Howl's Moving Castle* and *Dark Lord of Derkholm*) provide subtle but poignant jabs at the patterns of classic fantasy.

[46] China Miéville is probably one of the most radical contemporary fantasy authors who actively avoids any Tolkienian elements in his novels. Indeed, in his interviews and essays he criticizes Tolkien's fiction as reactionary and conservative, underlining the accusation that fantasy is often considered escapist and does not explicitly address problems that exist in empirical reality (James and Mendlesohn, *History* 110).

and Carter, Pratchett deals with the same problems of breaking the mold of stereotypical literature by subverting the status quo.

His decision to couple the genre with humor in the late 1970s and early 1980s was a reaction to a market oversaturated with derivative fantasy, but it also reflected a general tendency in Western society to criticize by disruption. As Linda Hutcheon remarked in 1988, "[p]erhaps the recent popularity of the theories of Mikhail Bakhtin owes much to the fact that they [...] offer a framework in which to deal with those parodic, ironic, paradoxical forms of postmodernist practice" (*Poetics* 54). It is exactly this subversive framework which was (and is) used by both postmodernist texts as well as fantasy authors (such as Pratchett) to address contemporary issues. After the success of the first Discworld novels, the intellectual climate of "the 1990s [was] an era when parody gained prominence in popular culture. [...] Terry Pratchett's Discworld novels, with their complex play on tropes from a range of genres including heroic fantasy, rose up the UK best-seller lists" (Webb, *Children* 65). Yet the combination of fantasy and humor[47] — two literary strands that both diverge from what is regarded as mimetic writing—remains conflict-laden when considering Tolkien's spell of escapism: it appears that with this combination, mimesis is attacked twice, not just once. And with the addition of postmodern play and fragmentation, any suspension of disbelief might have to be abandoned from the start. Since Pratchett's books on the surface seem to share many traits with parodies mocking *LotR* and other classics of genre fantasy, it would be easy to see them as works of the same strand of literature with little literary or academic merit.

Parody and Postmodernism

In 1969, the first parody of genre fantasy was published following the success of Tolkien's *LotR*. Appropriately titled *Bored of the Rings* and written by two Harvard students, the book retraces the plot of Tolkien's text in a "bawdy and psychedelic" (Chance 7) manner and channels the counterculture movement of the late 1960s. There is little original content to be found in this short novel: Beginning with the malapropisms of *LotR* character names[48] and a farcical foreword that misquotes Tolkien, the blueprint of the original text is clearly visible.

---

[47] Humor as parody, specifically.

[48] Examples thereof are often vulgar and simple: Frodo turns into Frito, Gandalf becomes Goodgulf, and, perhaps most crude, Bilbo is renamed Dildo.

Generally, parodies akin to *BotR* or contemporary examples such as *Barry Trotter* or *The Chronicles of Blarnia* lack invention; they rehash the plots and characters of their source text to achieve a maximum effect of recognition.[49] There is no sub-creation or attention to inner-literary reality: the worlds of Hogwash and Lower Middle Earth are riddled with inconsistencies, near-constant allusions to their source text and filled with white spots on their narrative maps. Within the context of such parodies, however, these inconsistencies are negligible because their goal is not to create a genuine secondary world but to make fun of an existing one, albeit in a near-parasitic manner.

These works just mentioned express one type of parody. Looking at subtler parodies outside these exuberant mockeries, the problem we are faced with is once more one of definition: clearly, the parody of Sherlock Holmes in Eco's postmodern reinterpretation as William of Baskerville in *The Name of the Rose* is a far cry from the blatant parodies of recent literary phenomena such as *Fifty Shames of Earl Grey* or the overt fantasy parodies mocking their originals. In literary research, there is a juxtaposition of two extremes regarding the definition of the term "parody," their representatives being Gérard Genette and Linda Hutcheon:

> Genette defines parody in a highly restrictive manner: a hypertext can be called a parody *only if* it playfully 'transforms' its hypotext. [...] The definition Hutcheon proposes instead is one that greatly widens the scope of parody [...] embracing all forms of intertextuality [and] not necessarily involv[ing] comic elements" (Korkut 18–19; see also Haberkorn, "Seriously" 138).

While Joyce's *Ulysses* thus falls into Genette's categorization, parodying one source (namely Homer's *The Odyssey*), his specification allows for no parody outside that of singular texts—if a text parodies several texts or a genre, it can only be pastiche according to his strict terminology.

Genette's definition becomes problematic when it is unclear whether a text transforms (parodies) or just imitates (pastiches) its source text: *BotR* seems to follow Genette's criteria for parody, being noticeably based on and transforming *LotR* into a mockery. Its tone, however, is not playful but rather acerbic, hence it would qualify as satirical caricature and thus not as a parody after all (Korkut 18). At the other end of the

---

[49] In the case of *BotR*, the parody of *LotR* even copies its map—the landscapes of Middle-earth and Lower Middle Earth are nearly identical (*BotR* vif), in shape.

spectrum, Hutcheon suggests a very wide range of parody, emphasizing the necessity of detecting layers of irony that may be hidden in the text:

> Parody is a bitextual synthesis [...], unlike more monotextual forms like pastiche that stress similarity rather than difference. In some ways, parody might be said to resemble metaphor. Both require that the decoder construct a second meaning through inferences about surface statements and supplement the foreground with acknowledgement and knowledge of a background text. (*Theory of Parody* 33–34)

The problem of Hutcheon's approach is her conclusion that humor (particularly incongruous humor) is not necessary for parody but rather the recognition of patterns—Rose summarizes Hutcheon's definition of the term as "repetition with difference [that] need not be comic" (282). In summary, *any* text that features allusions to other texts can be regarded as parody in her view, irrespective of its aims—the crucial element being the recognition of a second, potentially contrarian meaning in the text.

The plurality of a postmodern, ironic approach that I have laid out so far suggests that Hutcheon's open idea of parody is more adequate for my purposes when analyzing the Discworld novels—precisely because her definition supports but is not intrinsically dependent on humor. Pratchett's work displays both straightforward parody of stereotypical fantasy and survey of clichéd content beyond ridicule; it is, like Jones' *Guide to Fantasyland*, humorous *and* critical (Stableford, *Jaunting* 192). The troubles of combining genuine secondary-world fantasy with postmodern parody, however, remain: No matter what its extent or definition, parody often ignores the rules for fantasy set by Tolkien. Since it often "is fiction and metafiction at the same time" (Butler, *Companion* 286), parody breaks immersion and deliberately shows the artificiality of a secondary world by referencing texts outside the narrative. Although postmodernism and fantasy both illustrate the fictionality of any system (postmodernism more openly so), the parodist quality of postmodernist fiction can destroy the "magic" suspension of disbelief which is so crucial for the immersive value of fantasy texts. While fantasy is a construct as much as postmodern literature, it only achieves its goal of immersing readers by *hiding* its constructedness with the illusion of a consistent and independent secondary world rather than pointing out these mechanisms and destroying literary belief.

Besides such metafictional breaking of the suspension of disbelief, a problem of equal magnitude arises from the interplay between humor and fantasy: another of the core features of Tolkienian fantasy remains either unaddressed or is violated by parody, namely its idea of catastrophic transformation. Pratchett's Discworld is "an attempt to write comedy within the framework of the genre of fantasy, a genre whose structure is highly enabling of the comic novel, but distinctly unfriendly to formal comedy" (Clute 15). The difference between the two is that "a comic novel is ameliorative [...] [whereas] comedy is more worldly: it assumes that retention of a world once achieved is triumph enough" (Clute 16) and that a global alteration of the status quo is not necessary. Therefore, Pratchett breaks the pattern of genre fantasy in which a holistic transformation of the secondary world typically occurs as the story reaches its dramatic climax: "Full-fantasy narratives are stories of profound, all-transforming change. LOTR is such a narrative; and is subject, as noted, to the constant metamorphic meaning-drenched interplay between setting and tale which is essential to any definition of full fantasy" (Clute and Grant 341). Tolkien's eucatastrophe, the consolatory ending following cataclysmic events, is replicated in nearly every high fantasy novel that pits heroes against the impending doom of the secondary world and enables them to succeed against all odds (OFS 75–76). Yet stereotypical narrative patterns such as these are never fully enacted in Discworld novels, as they question the conservative features of the genre in a postmodern, comparatively open-ended manner. A possible explanation for this lack of closure is Pratchett's penchant for addressing not simply tropes and content of fantasy but using his "relentlessly intertextual" (Smith 135) novels to ridicule and reference across genres.

Especially in comparison to other works of fantasy whose style and narrative pattern prefer to follow "the deep structure of J. R. R. Tolkien" (Clute 16) and other classic texts of the genre, Pratchett's true sources appear to be found elsewhere: "Pratchett's work is very much in the tradition of British comedy, referencing both William Shakespeare and music hall, and acknowledging such comic forebears as Sellar and Yeatman, P. G. Wodehouse and the Carry-On films" (Butler, *Companion* 86). Even more so than the earlier fantasy parody *BotR*, Pratchett's first books were released at a time when the disillusionment of the 1960s' counterculture was turning towards the consumerism and brand awareness of the 1970s and early 1980s. Douglas Adams[50] mocks the clichés of science fiction in his *The Hitchhiker's Guide to the Galaxy* books by combining the genre with contemporary popular culture. Pratchett employs humor in the same manner to ridicule not simply the classic stories of fantasy but furthermore to provide tongue-in-cheek references to pop culture and reflections on the *conditio humana* in general. Indeed, the vast scope of the Discworld novels is one of the prime features that reveals them to be postmodern parody rather than being based on one source text or genre.

Judging from a direct comparison of *BotR* to Pratchett's first and second Discworld novels, *The Colour of Magic* and *The Light Fantastic*, the books appear to have a lot in common. Both authors use an ironic style that ridicules and subverts elements of classic fantasy and juxtaposes them with contemporary references, thereby exposing "the conventionality of their forms and their language" (Bakhtin, *Dialogic* 5) as in Adams' parody of stereotypical science fiction. Yet already in two descriptions of dawn breaking, a crucial difference between Pratchett's and *BotR*'s approach to fantasy parody becomes evident. Consider this sequence from *BotR*:

> In the eastern sky, Velveeta, beloved morning star of the elves and handmaid of the dawn, rose and greeted Noxzema, bringer of the flannel tongue, and clanging on her golden garbage pail, bade him make ready the winged rickshaw of Novocaine, herald of the day. Thence came rosy-eyeballed Ovaltine, she of the fluffy mouth, and lightly kissed the land east of the Seas. In other words, it was morning. (123)

Despite the deadpan final sentence, the immediate focus lies on ridiculing the purple prose of derivative fantasy by exaggeration and with references to Velveeta cheese, Noxzema skin cream as well as other well-known household products (at least for readers from the United States). Much of the humor derives from recognition rather than from absurdity.

---

[50] It is a lesser-known fact that Pratchett was also an author of humorous science fiction, writing two novels in this genre before focusing fully on the Discworld and fantasy. The first of these novels, *The Dark Side of the Sun*, was published in 1976, two years prior to the first BBC radio broadcasting of Douglas Adams' *The Hitchhiker's Guide to the Galaxy* (which was released before the subsequent 1979 novel). Whether the two authors knew of each other's work at that time and who might have influenced whom remains unclear, but the coincidence is certainly noteworthy.

Pratchett's second Discworld novel, on the other hand, opens with a deceptively simple statement: "The sun rose slowly, as if it wasn't sure it was worth all the effort" (*LF* 7). Instead of relying on established fantasy tropes and various irregularities that can be easily singled out, there is far more imagination at work here, with the second part of the sentence implying an almost cosmic cynicism that permeates the Discworld universe. While this idea is not explored any further afterwards, it nonetheless disrupts reader expectations without having to resort to crass overstatement. As is the case with so many of Pratchett's sentences, what seems to be a throwaway line at a first glance hides a deeply subversive element upon closer inspection.

Both of these excerpts are postmodern in Hutcheon's sense (breaking the typical patterns of genre fantasy), yet their method of achieving their effect is different: While *BotR* employs postmodern referentiality[51] and a list of numerous direct allusions to commercial products to break the cliché of mythical world-making and evoke comic reactions, Pratchett focuses more strongly on a singular incongruity[52] — one which is to the point and cuts a potentially romantic or mythical description of a sunrise short. This is not to say that Pratchett's parody does not include the pluralistic and self-referential features of postmodern literature. Yet, compared to *BotR*'s hasty parody with its quick succession of jokes and ridicule, Discworld novels are often more similar to what Plato would describe as mischievous humor.

Nevertheless, the problem of humor and fantasy still remains: If Tolkienian disbelief may be violated as postmodern fantasy breaks the stereotypical pattern of genre fantasy, a combination with the irony of postmodern approaches to texts provides a double collision of postmodern plurality, iconoclasm and humor with the conservative and meticulous background of fantasy. A question that inevitably arises from this conflict is whether Pratchett's fiction even *qualifies* as fantasy in terms of world-making or if his Discworld novels are but crude and loosely connected collections of well-known fantasy. Yet despite the ridicule — particularly in the context of Pratchett's continuing "typical humorous style and verbal wit" (Schnitker and Freiburg 175) in the Discworld novels — the deeper implications of parody must be stressed:

---

[51] Apart from the product names and its inspiration from clichéd fantasy, the lengthy description of the sunrise in *BotR* is also strangely similar to the poetic descriptions of dawn in the works of Homer and Virgil.

[52] Namely that of the sun being sentient and having a rather bad day.

> One of the typical ways in which parody works is to seize on particular aspects of a manner or a style and exaggerate it to ludicrous effect. There is an evident critical function in this, as the act of parody must first involve identifying a characteristic stylistic habit or mannerism and then making it comically visible. (Dentith 32)

While the sunrise from *BotR* cited just before displays the preposterous aspects of parody, it does not serve any deeper function besides evoking laughter. For Pratchett, however, the active disturbance of mental patterns both exemplifies and undermines the genre and tropes that he parodies.

Pratchett therefore fulfills and at the same time violates Wolf's principles of world-making *as well as* Tolkien's idea of sub-creation by utilizing the familiar and showing it in a new, paradoxical perspective. The humorous style might seem to detract from the believability of his fictional world, but it is precisely this technique that Pratchett continuously uses to address both the comical and serious topics of fantasy literature, secondary worlds, and storytelling in general. Such a technique rests in an uneasy balance: If postmodern fantasy "comprises one of the fuzziest of all sets" (Casey 113), then the question is perhaps less whether Pratchett's fiction can or cannot be considered fantasy but rather how many different genres and influences play a role in the making and elaboration of his secondary world and whether he is able to uphold his unique take on fantasy throughout his entire work.

Narrative and the Subversive Powers of Parody

A Note on Story Patterns in Fantasy Fiction and the Discworld Novels

Despite countless accusations of secret conservatism and cliché, fantasy is a genre that never eschews innovation. It is easy to create new elements in a work, yet they usually still remain within an established array of plots and characters typical for the genre. Attebery's "fuzzy set" of fantasy exposes the vast possibilities of connections, combinations, and variations of these tropes; however, if we read several classic fantasy novels back to back, their basic structure is arguably the same:

> Most fantasy novels have many similarities to fairy tales. [...] However, just as fairy tales are not a homogeneous genre category, featuring magical tales as well as animal and trickster tales and so on, so fantasy is a generic heading for a variety of different types of narratives, some taking place in a fairy-tale realm, some depicting travel between different worlds, some bringing magic into the everyday. (Nikolajeva 139–40)

Regardless of the pattern used, *recognizing* these patterns opens up a path to mockery. Parody forms an intrinsic part of fantasy's relation between tradition and innovation, but its focus lies primarily on exaggeration and not on subversion. In cases such as *BotR*, the pattern is revealed but remains unbroken; Frito goes on a journey similar to Frodo's and still follows Propp's schematic fairy tale formula. On the surface, Pratchett appears to copy the formula as well: In novels like *Witches Abroad* and *Guards! Guards!*, the plots of classic fairy tales and fantasy novels are re-enacted in a very literal manner, the only difference being that his main characters appear to be not the protagonists but little more than ciphers in a larger story.

Yet even though Pratchett's protagonists such as the witch Granny Weatherwax or the city guard Samuel Vimes conform to their roles as secondary characters, they add their own twist to them. As marginal figures, they traditionally stand on the threshold of classic narratives, and thus see them differently than the characters at their center. They express a strong mistrust in the idealistic promises and happy endings that these stories entail—stories that may occur in different forms, but largely follow the same or at least a similar pattern. Indeed, Pratchett draws his own conclusions regarding stereotypical stories: "This is called the theory of narrative causality and it means that a story, once started, *takes a shape*. It picks up all the vibrations of all the other workings of that story that have ever been. This is why history keeps on repeating all the time" (*WA* 8). If done often enough, repetition leads to habituation. When applied in a determinative manner, the basic structure of stereotypical plots and characterization allows for little to no deviation from the narrative sequence of events. Pratchett showcases how stories can ultimately take priority over characters to such an extent that their personal choice—indeed, their personality— is subjugated to the dictates of a given story pattern that is re-enacted in a Discworld novel. While part of this re-enactment, Pratchett's marginal (and, it should be mentioned, often also marginalized) protagonists challenge narrative causality and refuse to accept the preset and often simplified outcome of a story.

Linked to this mistrust is the harsh reality of their everyday life—as characters that do not possess entitlement or vast riches like the protagonists of classic fantasy at the end of their respective stories, they must work to live. Their unsentimental and down-to-earth nature reflects Pratchett's credo of writing fantasy that *works*—providing not merely a simplistic stage for the main story but including the supporting factors of a secondary world beyond the plot. All of these factors add to the completion, believability, and consistency of Pratchett's secondary world—his world, though a parody, still functions according to Tolkien's rules (despite the incongruity at work on the Discworld) and Wolf's ideas regarding world-making. For all its mockery of the clichés of fantasy fiction, it nonetheless acknowledges their necessity and—herein lies the crux of the Discworld novels—points out the shortcomings of much of derivative genre fantasy and simplified storytelling. The Discworld is beset with constant reminders of an inner-fictional reality as well as with indicators of the pitfalls of the idealistic, artificial endings of stereotypical fantasy stories.

Chapter 3

Beyond Parody

The evolution of humor and parody of the Discworld follows the development of the series over the decades. After the fast-paced jokes of the earlier novels which almost followed a list of fantasy clichés to make fun of, many of the mid-to-late Discworld books reflect the refinement of Pratchett's world into a fully-fledged secondary world. While his earliest books therefore still "raided the closets of fantasy, almost at random" (James and Mendlesohn, *History* 179) and provide only little of the characteristic wit and depth that the series was to become famous for, they set the stage for later parodist critiques covering, amongst other topics, "genre-play, socio-political satire, [...] economics, mythology, geography, and folklore" (Alton and Spruiell 4). Even though there may be traces of these subjects in *CoM* and *LF*, they are, for the most part, parodies of Tolkienian and other fantasy—not as commercial and blatant as *BotR* and fellow direct parodies, but likewise nowhere near the sophistication or satire[53] of later Discworld novels.

Pratchett's indebtedness to myth, and especially to folklore, also reflects the refinements in his books written and published beginning in the 1990s. Going beyond mere mockery of the stereotypes of fantasy, these books explore its sources in order to criticize both the genre and its history through subversion and irony. If we think back to the conflicted overlapping of fantasy and incongruity theory, then the Discworld constantly renews the subversive qualities of mythology, folklore, and popular culture in a postmodern manner, revealing the problem of merely copying them without denying their importance for fantasy. Such parody, in Hutcheon's understanding, reveals Pratchett as "more than a writer of good jokes" (Clute 16) and the Discworld as anything but a mere humorous background for them.

---

[53] As the mid-period Discworld novels reveal in particular, Pratchett's books also "handle darker themes with greater maturity" (Westfahl 974).

Despite the problematic relationship laid out in the last chapter, fantasy remains remarkably resilient yet at the same time open to parody. Precisely because the supernatural elements in fiction can be traced back to antiquity (Clute and Grant 432–35), fantasy as a mode has undergone parody and mockery throughout its existence;[54] individual elements were cherished by one generation and ridiculed by the next. But parody reached a new height after fantasy as a genre was formed—without detracting from its continued success and adaptability: "It is as if emphasizing the ludicrous aspects of the genre, rather than denigrating or diminishing the mode, actually augments it. Less robust cultural phenomena would be exterminated by such mockery; fantasy, on the contrary, thrives upon it" (Roberts 28). When Tolkien paved the way for fantasy as a genre, its modular elements were cast in a more recognizable pattern—a formula that was easier to mock and parody than individual traits, exemplified by works repeating the pattern such as *BotR*. Pratchett took this more humorous outlook on fantasy as his starting point for criticism of genre fantasy of the 1960s and 1970s: Humor, in spite of its danger for disbelief, was a method of emphasizing stagnation and stereotypical features in various derivative fantasy novels which followed the success of Tolkien's *LotR*.

Parody and Humor

The most striking feature when first reading a Discworld novel is undoubtedly the humor.[55] Here, we encounter amusing characters, clearly based on the established tropes of fantasy, among them "eccentric wizards, down-to-Earth witches, obstinate trolls, fire-breathing dragons, talking dogs, and personified Death" (Pratchett et al., *Science* 9). Their adventures are set on a flat world which "is supported by four elephants who are standing on the back of a giant turtle swimming endlessly through space," a postmodern reimagining of Hindu mythology (Schnitker and Freiburg 175). All

---

[54] Some of the earliest examples of fantasy mockery are Aristophanes' comedies *Peace*, portraying the Greek pantheon in humorous fashion, and the city of Cloudcuckooland in *The Birds* that parodied both Athenian politics and visions of Utopic metropolises.

[55] Among the many ill-fated attempts to define a subgenre for Pratchett's take on fantasy, "funny fantasy" or "funtasy" are perhaps the most prominent examples. While they did foreground his humor, they largely left out the more serious and satirical aspects of his fantasy, placing him close to parody as simple mockery instead.

of this is presented to readers in a light-hearted and playful manner, emphasizing the jokes and ironic takes on classic fantasy. As the author of the Discworld novels "is a master of the double laugh—the first laugh is at the joke, the second one, a few seconds later, is at the *other* joke which is revealed as the first one sinks in" (Pratchett and Briggs, *Companion* 267–68), it would be easy to conclude that Pratchett's books are multi-layered but, ultimately, still simple parodies of genre fantasy. Having seen the direct adoption of *LotR*'s plotting, characters, and tropes in *BotR*, a superficial comparison of Discworld novels with distinctive works of fantasy would indeed display a similar levity of content, and specifically the first two novels are indeed comparable to the farce of commercial parodies.

This said, the first crucial difference between the Discworld novels and *BotR*-style parody lies in the former's increased scope—they encompass not just the genre's sources and success but also extended cultural contexts. Rather than a limited parody of one source text, down to a mockery of its title, Pratchett mocks more than just *LotR* or any other fantasy classic in particular. Having experienced the rise of modern fantasy as a reader in his youth, he decided to address its exploitation and commercialization (Stableford, *Jaunting* 183) once he became a fantasy author himself. In an interview, Pratchett stated how one of the reasons for the conception of the Discworld lay in a conscious move against the many failed attempts to create a work as ground-breaking and influential as *LotR*:

> Discworld started as an antidote to bad fantasy, because there was a big explosion of fantasy in the late 70s, an awful lot of it was highly derivative, and people weren't bringing new things to it. The first couple of books quite deliberately pastiched bits of other writers and things—*good* writers, because it's the good ones most people can spot. (Pratchett, "Discworld & Beyond" 4)

As *BotR* was a reaction to the rising popularity of Tolkien's *magnum opus* in 1960s' counterculture, so was Pratchett's creation of Discworld in the 1980s a stage for humorous reflections on the genre and its exponential growth after the success of its most archetypical text. Pratchett's parody incorporates not just Tolkienian genre fantasy but far more of the fuzzy set of fantasy—authors who were published both before and outside of the immediate influence of *LotR*. Hence "there is incidental mockery of the *Conan* stories [...] and of Anne McCaffrey's 'Dragonworld' books" (Manlove, *England* 136) in the first

Discworld novel as Pratchett parodies his contemporaries, but also popular fantasy writers of the 1930s' pulp magazines such as Robert E. Howard, H. P. Lovecraft, and Fritz Leiber.

If we take a closer look at the first Discworld novel *CoM*, Pratchett's parody still remains largely limited to these authors and thus within the framework of fantasy in that book. Picking up *BotR*'s mockery of names, the novel starts with a dialogue between two heroes named Bravd and Weasel—a clear reference to Fritz Leiber's pulp fantasy heroes Fafhrd and the Gray Mouser (Butler, *Companion* 220–21). Apart from such rather passing resemblances, other characters and situations are modeled even more closely on literary forerunners.[56] During the journey across the Discworld in *CoM*, we encounter Hrun the Barbarian, one of the overt extended parodies in the first novel:

> There was a figure there, sidling along stealthily with its back against one wall. Rincewind saw the gleam of gold and bronze.
> There was no mistaking that shape. He'd seen it many times. The wide chest, the neck like a tree trunk, the surprisingly small head under its wild thatch of black hair looking like a tomato on a coffin... (119)

The resemblance to Robert E. Howard's Conan the Barbarian, "a man [with] broad shoulders and sun browned skin" as well as a "square cut black mane" (Howard 27), is undeniable. But Pratchett's humor is still close to *BotR*, and his description of Hrun, even though succinct, makes the Barbarian appear equally ridiculous as threatening. And tellingly, the parody mainly covers the physical features of the original, remaining superficial and foregoing any attempts at addressing underlying problems such as macho culture, sexism or racism.

Howard's Conan was meant to be a critique of decadent civilizations, a mirror image of barbarism coupled with fatalism (Clute and Grant 481), yet Hrun exaggerates the outward appearance but loses most of the characterization of the original. As Rincewind, one of the protagonists of the first Discworld novel, remarks, Hrun "could speak words of more than two syllables, if given time and maybe a hint or two" (*CoM* 119). Pratchett thereby mocks both the original Conan and the cliché of a "not terribly bright, muscle-bound, over-sexed adolescent fantasy hero" (James and Mendlesohn, *History*

---

[56] Haberkorn provides a detailed overview of the works parodied in *CoM*, using the term "echo people" to underline the proximity of the copies to the originals of characters ("Seriously"140–42).

36), with a version that even surpasses the simplified Conan of later stories and the Arnold Schwarzenegger movie portrayals. Here we have straightforward parody bordering on Bakhtinian grotesque, imitating the original character in a caricature (Korkut 18) of crass overstatement. Hrun is a one-dimensional character with little originality, much like *BotR*'s Frito, who is a nearly one-to-one parody of *LotR*'s Frodo. This lack of depth is emphasized by the fact that we do not encounter Hrun again in consequent novels, a circumstance which occurs rather rarely in Pratchett's later fiction.[57]

CoM presents itself as a referential cosmos filled with a panorama of jokes and quick-paced plotting. Other early Discworld novels featuring the inept wizard Rincewind as the protagonist are equally sweeping in scope, making fun of particular texts, countless tropes, and stereotypes from across literature and culture in general without the satirical depth of later books. And although intertextuality beyond fantasy occurs, the first Discworld books are mainly focused on parodying its classic texts and topics. Pratchett breaks the bonds of single-text-parodies (such as *BotR*) and his tone is different, yet he nonetheless employs similar methods to the parody of Tolkien's text—the hero is a coward, the evil witch turns out to be good, and "the whole flat world becomes a stage" (Rayment 47) for exaggerations and ridicule.

Parody and Theatre Fantasy

The first Discworld novels are therefore representative of the aforementioned fantasyland, a term strongly related to what James and Mendlesohn describe as *theatre fantasy*. In this definition, "the fantasy world provides a theatre stage on which stories can be played out" (James and Mendlesohn, *History* 105)—theatre fantasy is thus fantasy, which makes strong use of familiar tropes and narrative patterns that Tolkien cemented in *LotR*. Often, the most theatrical aspect of the term lies in the representation and use of a secondary world as little more than the space which is at stake and must be

---

[57] In his stead, there is a more refined (and recurring) parody of Conan in other Discworld books—Cohen the Barbarian. Rather than merely an exaggeration like Hrun, Cohen is a tragi-comic satire of the original: An 87-year-old barbaric hero who is still fighting foes and simultaneously battling the ailments of his advanced age. He, as many other characters of the later Discworld, shows far more depth and complexity than the ones we encounter during the first excursions.

saved. Closely related to the conflict-journey-resolution pattern of quest fantasy, the important but nonetheless inferior role of world-making is typical for theatre fantasy:

> Nonspecific landscape is unrolled like a carpet in front of the character. This landscape even embraces the contrived design of Romantic landscape painting. [...] The entrant into the portal-quest fantasy is precisely this kind of tourist [...] positioned gazing at a vista [...]. But in the absence of real depth, history, religion, and politics must receive a similar treatment. (Mendlesohn, *Rhetorics* 13)

It is not surprising, then, that the second major character of the first Discworld book besides the protagonist Rincewind is, indeed, a tourist named Twoflower. While not necessarily as blatant as in fantasy parodies, the secondary world of such a theatre fantasy work is treated as background, as a picturesque view to be enjoyed or traversed, and, at least in the first novel, not threatened by destruction. In Pratchett's context, the two main characters and their quest are ironically focused exactly on this depiction of space as something "to merely *look* at" (*CoM* 45). Paraphrasing Genette, time is more crucial in these narratives than space, although viewing the secondary world is important as part of the touristic journey. Hence, the world Rincewind and Twoflower are travelling through must exist; yet it is largely there to provide a stage and opportunities to be in awe of its vistas.

In this regard, theatre fantasy or stereotypical quest fantasy bear close resemblance to Jones' as well as Clute and Grant's ideas of fantasyland and form a summarized space filled with elements that can be easily exploited by parodies. While authors taking direct inspiration from works like *LotR* or *Harry Potter* often make worlds that are clearly based on their sources, the secondary worlds of parody are not genuine creations, but rather hasty copies of other secondary worlds: *BotR* and fellow commercial parodies appear to mock the fantasy genre in general, yet their focus usually lies on one source text/series and author—good examples being J. R. R. Tolkien, J. K. Rowling, C. S. Lewis, and their literary worlds.

The shared key trait of theatre fantasy texts (expressed more strongly in parodies) is the fact that their secondary worlds are seen as fixed[58] background material:

---

[58] "Fixed" in a twofold manner: For one, they are based on a precursor secondary world (often Tolkien's Middle-earth), and secondly, they are mere background to the story that is told.

> Fantasyland's relationship to the secondary world parallels the relationship of genre fantasy to full fantasy. [...] Fantasyland, it follows, is a secondary world which is fixed in place; it is inherently *immobile*; it is backdrop, not actor; and it is still the case that Fantasyland is a natural home for unambitious tales. (Clute and Grant 341)

Even more so than fantasy directly inspired by preceding fantasy, the "stage" of *BotR* and other parodies offers a simplistic background for the jokes that their authors want to make, and it is easy to regard the early Discworld novels as standing in this tradition. While the Discworld has to be saved from destruction in the second novel, this event does not result in a dramatic change for the world itself[59]—unlike *LotR*, where the end of the Third Age ushers in the age of humans and transforms the whole of Middle-earth (*RK* VI.5.1272, 1420). Similarly, literary tropes such as salvation or change are rarely taken seriously in parodies, whose worlds and characters, as mentioned, are merely replicas of source texts.

Yet despite their parodist qualities and lack of Tolkienian eucatastrophe and resolution, *BotR* and the first Discworld novels still follow the narrative *pattern* of high or heroic fantasy (and theatre fantasy): A quest has to be fulfilled through travelling the secondary world and mastering strange encounters. By making one of the two main characters of *CoM* a tourist, Pratchett ironically achieves a very humorous yet close adherence to the pattern, as his motivation to explore the Discworld subverts but also perfectly mirrors that of a stereotypical fantasy protagonist:

> Characteristically the quest fantasy protagonist goes from a mundane life, in which the fantastic, if she is aware of it, is very distant and unknown (or at least unavailable to the protagonist) to direct contact with the fantastic through which she transitions, exploring the world until she or those around her are knowledgeable enough to negotiate with the world via the personal manipulation of the fantastic realm. (Mendlesohn, *Rhetorics* 2)

The "quest" of *CoM* is indeed a variant of the quests that heroes encounter in fantasy, however with a parodist twist: The inept wizard Rincewind must guide the tourist Twoflower across the Disc and show him the wonders of the world—the typical genre fantasy pattern of the journey chronotope (Bakhtin, *Dialogic* 243; Smith 136) remains untouched, although the goal is anything but heroic. Rincewind is the

---

[59] We witness the birth of eight new Discworlds in outer space at the end of *LF*, but they are never seen again nor referred to in consequent novels.

opposite of a hero and prefers to run away from dangers; combined with Twoflower's naiveté and desire to see the sights of the world, the comedic but also the creative[60] value of the first Discworld novel is therefore very high. As Colin Manlove deduces almost sarcastically, "we move further and further out on the Disc and to wilder and more novel imaginative flights, until there can be only one conclusion, to fall off the Edge" (Manlove, *England* 136). Considering the plot, however, the first novel is little more than an array of unfortunate situations and coincidences that make fun of the clichés of fantasy—very much like the hasty rehashing of Tolkien in *BotR*.

In spite of its hastiness, one of the side effects of this touristic journey across a secondary world is a feeling of mutuality between readers and protagonist: Twoflower is an incongruous yet relatable character for a fantasy novel—he is a sightseer, not a hero—and has "the ways of the [Disc]world explained to him for the sake of the readers" (Butler, *Companion* 387), who themselves are new to the sights of Pratchett's secondary world. It is for this reason that Pratchett alludes to the parodist dimensions of tourism on a fantasy world within the presentation of his newly created realm. Some passages of *CoM* unsurprisingly remind us of a tourist brochure:

> The discworld offers sights far more impressive than those found in universes built by Creators with less imagination and more mechanical aptitude.
>
> Although the disc's sun is but an orbiting moonlet, its prominences hardly bigger than croquet hoops, this slight drawback must be set against the tremendous sight of Great A'Tuin the Turtle, upon Whose ancient and meteor-riddled shell the disc ultimately rests. Sometimes, in His slow journey across the shores of Infinity, He moves His country-sized head to snap at a passing comet. (*CoM* 95)

Yet even though sublime descriptions imbue Pratchett's world with a sense of wonder beyond the simplistic depictions of landscapes or blatant parody in *BotR*, their immersive value is repeatedly broken by jokes, puns, and parodies which also interrupt the narrative and suspension of disbelief.

The alternation between descriptive and parodist moments are a sort of *leitmotif* of *CoM*: The actual journey across the Discworld

---

[60] As with much of fantasy, invention was at the fore of the creation of the Discworld—completeness and consistency followed as more novels were published.

is a selection of vistas and encounters that introduce us to various parts of Pratchett's secondary world, spanning from its premier city Ankh-Morpork to the very edge of the world. Taken as a whole, the realization that the first novel "is really four novellas, set over a period of months, and without a strong overall story line beyond Twoflower's trip" (Butler, *Companion* 86) underscores the status of the early Discworld as a colorful stage which is ultimately subordinate to humor and as disjoint as the plot.

Rincewind and Twoflower thus disappear and reappear at given places, and the different parts of the book seem like a series of images showing the best sights of the Discworld rather than a consistent story—the theatricality, indeed the background nature of the secondary world for the sake of humor is continuously underlined. Pratchett states that he deliberately wrote his first Discworld novel as a photo-album tourist journey through a world of pastiche and caricature that he had created for the purpose of mocking fantasy clichés:

> Discworld started out as a genuine tourist trap. I wanted to journey through a familiar fantasy universe where the people didn't stay in character, where barbarian heroes could be old men, wizards could run away and Death could hold a conversation. A tourist seemed like a good idea, especially if he believes in heroes and wizards and can't quite seem to take on board the facts that the ones he meets aren't like the ones in the books. (Pratchett and Kidby [43])

The tourist Twoflower thus functions as a sort of alter ego for the reader (or, thinking further, perhaps even acting as a reader-parody), who is being led through the world and whose expectations of genre fantasy are about to be taken apart (Haberkorn, "Debugging" 176). While he is, in fact, an inhabitant of the Discworld, Twoflower has not seen a lot of it since he is "sitting at a desk all day, just adding up columns of figures" (*CoM* 38)—his day-to-day life consists of a mundane profession, the Discworld equivalent of an accountant, which allows the readers to identify with him.

The irony of Twoflower's position is the fact that like many protagonists of classic fantasy, he still leaves his home to follow a call to adventure (even if only to be a bystander),[61] ergo fulfilling a

---

[61] Twoflower desires to see the Discworld and experience adventures, but it is Rincewind who (involuntarily) takes him on these adventures. In his recruitment by Ankh-Morpork's de facto ruler Vetinari, Rincewind is also reminiscent of *LotR*'s Sam, who is added to Frodo's journey by Gandalf after being caught eavesdropping on their conversation.

stereotypical plot device: "Narratively speaking, having the main character come from a marginal region also naturalizes expository passages, since the main character is learning about the world along with the audience" (Wolf 158). If we keep this and the tourist role of Twoflower in mind, *CoM* is once more strongly evocative of the narrative pattern of quest fantasy, where "a character leaves her familiar surroundings and passes through a portal into an unknown place" (Mendlesohn, *Rhetorics* 1). Naturally, these patterns are turned upside down and exaggerated to ridiculous dimensions, yet their core message remains largely the same. Adding to this impression, is the fact that the second Discworld novel, *LF* (a direct continuation[62] of *CoM*), features even stronger adherence to the pattern. Taken together, *CoM* and *LF* are, in fact, one story told over the course of two novels linked by their focus on the "quest" aspect of fantasy. Whereas *CoM* is essentially a "directionless story [...] intended in part as a parody of the journey of Tolkien's Frodo with the wizard Gandalf across Middle-earth" (Manlove, *England* 136), *LF* is less interruptive and much more plot-driven—a plot that is eventually revealed as the second half of a traditional quest-fantasy narrative. *CoM* covers Rincewind and Twoflower's journey from the middle to the edge of the Discworld, but Pratchett's second novel tells of their return homewards. In addition, it features a goal with more depth than the disconnected narrative of *CoM* and puts the two novels even more firmly into the tradition of quest or theatre fantasy. Already in the first Discworld novel, we learned how the bumbling wizard Rincewind once read one of the eight spells of the mystical "Octavo" tome, ending up with the spell stuck in his head that disables him from learning any further magic (*CoM* 60–61).

During his travels with Twoflower, Rincewind feels the spell welling up in his mind from time to time, seemingly but a nuisance. Only at the end of their journey in *CoM*, as they fall off the edge of the disc, does the spell reveal itself as being of major importance to the plot. Setting the stage for the second novel, the personification of Death is summoned at the beginning of *LF* and prophesies "that

---

[62] The serialism of fantasy novels is another stereotype of fantasy that Pratchett abandoned in later Discworld novels. While characters recur and several novels feature the same protagonists, their stories do not necessarily have to be read in order—each book is a self-enclosed story that may allude to preceding events but does not require knowledge thereof.

the world will be destroyed unless [the wizards] speak the eight great spells of the Octavo" (Butler, *Companion* 236) in unison. Hence, the second Discworld novel turns out to be the return-home-part of a quest fantasy and Rincewind its hero, reluctant and cowardly as he may be. As in a classic fantasy novel, the world itself is now at stake and must be saved from destruction—the eighth spell inside Rincewind's head acts as the prime plot device, a copy of Tolkien's One Ring in *LotR*. Like the ring, the spell must be returned to where it originally came from—here, the spellbook holding the other seven spells—and a heroic deed has to be accomplished to turn back the forces of evil that have arisen during the journey back from the edge of the disc. It is not surprising, then, that the finale of the second novel reads rather more like classic fantasy than straightforward parody.

We ironically arrive at the conclusion of many quest fantasies (mocked but nonetheless repeated by many parodies), namely the realization "that a quest is a process, in which [...] the real reward is moral growth" (Mendlesohn, *Rhetorics* 4). It seems redundant to apply any of this moral to Pratchett's fragmented and joke-riddled journey, as to any other parody, yet on the final pages of *LF*, Rincewind considers re-enrolling at Unseen University (the Discworld's premier school for wizards), seeing himself "getting to grips with magic and graduating really well" (*LF* 280). The second Discworld novel thus qualifies as a quest fantasy in the tradition of Tolkien, combining both an external and an internal quest (Clute and Grant 796), or a journey to an end that leaves the protagonist/s with increased knowledge about themselves whilst also having learned more about the world. Yet the stage ultimately remains unchanged, as do the characters: although the Discworld has escaped near-destruction, it does not undergo a transformation as Tolkien's Middle-earth does in the epilogue of *LotR*. Likewise, Rincewind does not graduate[63] despite his claim—his journeys in later Discworld novels always present him as a cowardly wizard still unable to cast even the simplest spell.

In the long run, the character Rincewind is inextricably bound to the parody of quest fantasy we encounter in the first Discworld novels; while a near-absolute antithesis to a classic fantasy hero (see

---

[63] Although he eventually receives obsolete and honorary professorships, thus giving him a more "fixed" position at Unseen University. Nevertheless, he becomes entangled in further adventures as his character is revisited in *The Science of Discworld* books and later novels.

Butler, *Companion* 185), he is still "continually forced to try and save the world, while running from trouble to something worse" (Schnitker and Freiburg 176). He is automatically drawn to adventures wherever he goes, a recurring and predictable narrative pattern in his series of novels. Taking this and his mostly unchanged character into account, the early Discworld stories focusing on Rincewind are therefore limited in their potential:

> There is little character development possible—[Rincewind] is a slapstick figure who does little more than get into danger and run away, or avoid getting into danger by running away. By now he seems to have explored most of Discworld, each location being a parody of a real world culture, and there seems little more to do with the role. (Butler, *Companion* 318)

Limiting the Discworld to books featuring Rincewind would have left it a mere stage, an arrangement of set pieces for parody, bad puns, and a few wise jokes in between. In order to widen the scope and storytelling possibilities of his emerging secondary world, Pratchett began to introduce characters who at first appeared to be parodies (just like Rincewind), yet displayed qualities that were far beyond the stereotypical heroism of quest fantasy or Rincewind's complete reversal thereof. Slowly, the Discworld novels following *CoM* and *LF* began to peek over the horizon of parodying the genre and contemporary culture. Simultaneously, Pratchett refocused on specific parts of genre fantasy in addition to given texts.

A large part of the world-making aspect of secondary worlds has its roots in mythology, and Tolkien's reliance on myths to make his Middle-earth more believable is not the only example. Providing an elaborate, macrocosmic background to a secondary world had become a key feature of successful fantasy. Parodists have not refrained from using this trait to ridiculous ends. For Pratchett, however, mythology— and even more so, folklore—became important stepping-stones for his move beyond such superficial parody.

TOLKIENIAN MYTH AND FOLKLORE ON THE DISCWORLD

In their *Encyclopedia of Fantasy*, Clute and Grant speak of "taproot texts" (921) that act as prime sources for much of today's genre fantasy. Tolkien summarizes the roots of fantasy as "Faërie" in his essay, wisely refraining from defining it with precise parameters and thus allowing myths and fairy tales, oral and written storytelling to form part of it (OFS 32). Some of the originality of the Discworld stems from these sources: Hutcheon's idea of acting from within a system to criticize it in combination with incongruity theory is demonstrated in Pratchett's humorous treatment of fairy stories and mythology, even though their roles in his secondary world have different purposes. Before moving on to a more in-depth analysis of Discworld texts, it is therefore important to illustrate how Pratchett sees the use of myths and fairy tales in fantasy fiction.

Tolkien's consideration of myth-making as a sub-creative power (OFS 42) underlines the importance of mythology in cultural development and the explanation of cosmological phenomena, as do the numerous fictional pantheons and stories of origin in contemporary fantasy. Attebery likewise stresses "that fantasy cannot be understood in isolation; rather, the story of its emergence as a modern genre is best told as a counterpoint to the history of myth" (*Myth* 22). What both authors underline thereby is the fact that mythology is more than merely a historical document of former world-views[64] but, tying in with Donald's remarks about mimetic culture, a tool for thinking:

> Many feel that mythology was how people before Christianity and the scientific and technological revolutions explained the things that they did not understand. Mythology, however, is more subtle and complex than that. Mythology is somewhat like poetry in that it creates metaphors: a fiery chariot, for example, represents the Sun and its passage through the sky. Mythology is, therefore, a narrative method people developed to discuss things that they did not understand and could not explain. (Westfahl 548)

As a result, mythology is not simply a device for meaning-construction because "we abhor explanatory vacuums" (Gottschall 121). It serves as a means and springboard for inquisitive thought and—underlining Tolkien's idea of humanity as sub-creator—for creativity. In sum, Tolkien's analysis of myth pertains to "the power of language and the way it affects not only our perception of the world but also our imagination" (Fimi 44). Abandoning the religious roots of myth in favor of a secular treatment, fantasy as one of the modern usages of myth is exempt from its former claim to truthfulness: "Unlike myth, fantasy speaks with no authority. It pretends to be a mere game"

---

[64] Clute and Grant too claim that "a myth may be almost anything once believed and subsequently proved false" but that it is nonetheless an idea that remains in the "national consciousness" (675).

(Attebery, *Myth* 21) and hence offers more possibilities to engage freely with imagery and imagination.

In Pratchett's fiction, mythology appears to be addressed in a thoroughly humorous manner, beginning with the exaggerated cosmological image of the world-turtle. He takes his initial inspiration from Hindu mythology and turns it into an extended, if ironic, making of the Discworld, especially in later books:

> Upon [the turtle's] back stand Berilia, Tubul, Great T'Phon and Jerakeen, the four giant elephants on whose shoulders the disc of the world rests. A tiny sun and moon spin around them on a complicated orbit to induce seasons, although probably nowhere else in the multiverse is it sometimes necessary for an elephant to cock its leg to allow the sun to go past. (Pratchett and Briggs, *Turtle Recall* 41)

Even though Pratchett does not shy away from providing context grounded in (fictional) reality by mentioning how seasons come to pass on the Discworld, the overall impression remains tongue-in-cheek and (given the cosmic scale) comparatively impersonal. Here, fantasy's freedom to create and reimagine elements of mythology goes hand in hand with the fragmented and playful manner in which postmodern literature rearranges existing concepts and historical motifs.

In addition to the cosmology of the Discworld, Pratchett addresses another typical element of mythology often reused in fantasy, namely a pantheon of deities which at times bear a close resemblance to those of various historic mythological backgrounds (Pratchett and Briggs, *Turtle Recall* 106–08). A reflection of Pratchett's aim to parody a wide range of fantasy tropes in his novels, the Discworld pantheon is thoroughly mixed and collaged, a decidedly postmodern and manifold affair. It is, therefore rather unlike Tolkien's duality-inspired pantheon of *The Silmarillion*—there is no Satanic antagonist as Melkor/Morgoth on the Discworld, whose gods are portrayed as a "quarrelsome and bourgeois" (Butler, *Companion* 313) medley with no prime creator[65] or destructor. Like the Discworld itself, its deities are portrayed in a humorous manner often bordering on ridiculousness. Nevertheless, and true to postmodernist fiction, they have an ironical but also a metafictional dimension: Pratchett's first novel plainly

---

[65] In *Eric*, a Discworld novel parodying Goethe's *Faust*, we encounter the creator of the Discworld, but his role remains marginal and is not addressed again in other novels.

presents the Discworld as a playground for the gods—perhaps not incidentally, its flatness imbues it with a resemblance to a board game. And indeed, there is a replica of the secondary world laid out in front of the deities at the beginning of the book: "The gaming board was a carefully-carved map of the Discworld, overprinted with squares. A number of beautifully modelled playing pieces were now occupying some of the squares" (*CoM* 96). Pratchett revisits this idea throughout his career—perhaps most vividly in the illustrated Discworld novel *The Last Hero* (see fig. 1). Pratchett may appear to use mythology in the same ridiculous manner as *BotR*'s whimsical portrayal of deities, yet the board game metaphor holds more than meets the eye—not to mention that it underlines the staged and theatrical nature of the Discworld. The true core of Pratchett's creation must, therefore, lie in another central source of fantasy—namely folk tales.

Fig. 1: Discworld Gods by Paul Kidby. A group of Discworld deities gathered around their "game board." Note the dice in the hand of Blind Io in the middle. See *LH*, pp. 82–83. (Used with permission of Paul Kidby.)

Folklore, another important source for fantasy literature, is a no less vital part of the spectrum of Tolkien's Faërie. Like mythological motifs, it provides the building blocks for stories that have been told and retold throughout history, forming part of the elements that account for the supernatural in literature: "The traditional narratives of folklore, refracted through the literary developments of earlier centuries and into the literary and popular forms of a more technological age, have retained a relevance which demonstrates their power and endurance as a cultural artifact" (Tiffin 1). Their cultural importance often relies on the morals[66] or message that they convey; consequently, folkloristic tales are mirrors of their time and yet universal in their appeal.

Written fairy tales, as well as the oral heritage of folklore (Clute and Grant 359; S. Jones 2–6) are, therefore—like mythology—characteristically typical for parody precisely because of their recognizability and century-old traditional retellings, offering Pratchett a repository of tropes for the Discworld novels:

> Fairy tales, the extensive body of stories embodying folk-wisdom and wonder handed down from generation to generation, pervade the Discworld series. Because of their status as common-stock stories that many readers will remember at least the bones of from childhood, they are particularly important as the source of jokes (because they can be easily and recognisably parodied), as recognisable motifs and allusions and as sources for darker ironies. (Butler, *Companion* 138)

The remembering of the "bones" of stories is a point worth deeper analysis, as it emphasizes what Tolkien terms "the cauldron of story" (OFS 39–40) and uncovers narrative patterns that reappear in the oral and written traditions of fairy tales and folklore—one of the central topics of Discworld novels following *CoM* and *LF*. Looking at Pratchett's whole oeuvre, folkloristic content forms a large part of the Discworld, "based on a blend of British folklore, benign satire of modern Wicca, and a reinterpretation of the Triple Goddess myth" (Butler, *Companion* 417), themes which are of particular importance to his novels featuring witches.

Upon closer investigation, it becomes clear that Pratchett feels more indebted to folklore and fairy tales than to mythology—only one of his novels, *Small Gods*, has mythology in a religious sense as its central topic, whereas more than ten Discworld novels cite and parody folklore as their main source.[67] The reason for such emphasis lies in Pratchett's preference for earthly matters. In another one of his essays, he states that:

---

[66] Even though these morals might be dubious or troubling. Pratchett was keenly aware of the problematic and sometimes even disturbing implications of fairy tales, as demonstrated in novels such as *WA* (see Chapter 4, pp. 85–94, in the present study) and the Tiffany Aching books.

[67] Most prominently in the Witches series of books, but folklore also plays an important role in the one series that I largely (and sadly) leave untouched in this volume—the Discworld novels featuring Death. Pratchett's version of this entity is both fascinated and astounded by humans, and consequently Death attempts to grasp human nature and its love for storytelling, which includes a large array of folkloristic content.

Brewer's Dictionary of Phrase and Fable was a major discovery. I still have the second-hand copy I bought in a local bookshop for ten-and-sixpence; I may have been the only twelve year old to read through it, end to end, for the dark pleasure of realising that the world is a fascinating and complicated place. [...] I tended towards folklore rather than mythology, because gods seemed rather dull and stupid and in any case mythology just seemed to be the folklore of the winners. (Pratchett, "Worlds" 161)

Instead of creating a secondary world with a vast and detailed mythology akin to Tolkien's extensive portrayal of several historical and pre-historical ages of Middle-earth and Arda (not to mention his successors), Pratchett's interests lie elsewhere: "In tune with the deeply secular cast of Pratchett's mind, in so far as it expresses itself clearly through Discworld, the maintainers of the decency of the Discworld are secular creatures; their solutions to problems are pragmatic, realistic, sagaciously resigned to an unreligious, untransformable world" (Clute 26). As with mythology, Pratchett's approach to folklore is postmodern and does not refrain from combining classic motifs with elements of popular culture to poke fun at their recognizability and stereotypicality in fantasy literature.

However, this leads back to the problem of whether the Discworld novels—as parodies of fantasy in general—can be considered more than mockeries of the genre at all. If the Discworld is truly just a stage populated with clichés from folklore and mythology, a mere game board for the gods to play with, there seems to be neither individuality of character nor any escape from genre-related humor. Pratchett's creation would be an ultimately stale and superficial world (as parodies akin to *BotR*), literally and figuratively flat, a realm where Tolkienian suspension of disbelief is impossible.

THEATRE FANTASY AND BEYOND

With the fourth Discworld novel, *Mort*, Pratchett began to veer away from the popular parody of fantasy as a genre—Clute and Grant provocatively call it "the first Discworld novel with a successfully integrated plot" (784), an innovation which is mainly due to a more subdued and not as anarchic perspective on the secondary world. While Pratchett employed wild pacing and incessant joking in *CoM* and *LF*, and even though the fourth book's "primary targets of humour [are] still fantasy, science fiction and story-telling rather than the much wider pastiche, parody, satirising and lampooning of society" (Butler, "Theories" 69–70) found in later Discworld novels, this book extends the confines of fantasy-ridicule with philosophical considerations. "YOU DON'T SEE PEOPLE AT THEIR BEST IN THIS JOB" (*M* 27), the character of Death tells his apprentice early on, reflecting the less farcical and slightly somber tone of the novel. The Discworld's version of the Grim Reaper had been introduced in *CoM* as a rather cruel trickster who actively attempts to murder Rincewind, but he is a far more complex and sympathetic entity in this and subsequent stories. What *M* begins to exhibit is that as the secondary world is revisited, Pratchett does not limit himself to parodying fantasy but starts to include material from a far wider field of literature and culture.

An even better example of this increased scope and complexity is the sixth Discworld novel *Wyrd Sisters*, which references and ridicules numerous Shakespearean plays. As in the first novels, a plot—in this case, *Macbeth*—is replicated with even more accuracy than the quest-fantasy narratives of *CoM* and *LF* and provides, first and foremost, the (nearly literal) stage for the book: "*Wyrd Sisters* is a parody of *Macbeth* told from the perspective of the witches [...] and the most palimpsestic of the Discworld novels. [...] Though *Wyrd Sisters* features parodic moments derived from multiple intertexts, from *Hamlet* to the first *Superman* movie, its basic structure is firmly based on the Scottish play" (Smith 135). Indeed, what was still fast-paced parody in the first two Discworld novels, with thinly veiled humorous copies of originals such as the aforementioned "things from the chaotic Dungeon Dimensions" (*LF* 14) evidently based on H. P. Lovecraft's Cthulhu mythos, began to slowly turn into a finer assessment of the elements and texts parodied. What is more, the Discworld eventually started to undergo its first changes—the "books acquired a sense of purpose, which lifted them up above the 'theatre fantasy' tradition of which they are part" (James and Mendlesohn, *History* 179). The stage, untransformable and superficial as it seemed, began to show subtle modifications in further novels.

Comparing Pratchett's earliest books from the 1980s with the final Discworld novels from the 2010s, they are clearly not set in the same (secondary) world. By the publication of the 24th Discworld novel in 1999, Pratchett reflected on the necessity of change if his creation was to not become stale or a rehashing of the stories told before: The Discworld "ha[d] to evolve to keep going. If I'd written 25 versions of *The Light Fantastic* by now, I'd be ready to slit my wrists" (Pratchett, "Discworld

& Beyond" 75). While the humor was still very much present, it too had been refined. As part of such development, the scope and focus of the parody had indeed shifted—or more precisely, been expanded:

> Parody is intrinsic to the Discworld books, at the more complex end of a literary spectrum that extends from simple light entertainment featuring continual cheap gags to literature involving an intricate pastiche of genres and human issues. [...] The first Discworld novel, COM, was almost entirely a simple parody of genre fantasy, but the baffling and wonderful thing about the Discworld novels is that they did not remain simply fantasy, parody, or anything else. (Butler, *Companion* 286)

Following the rather quest-oriented structure of the first novels (emulating *LotR*), narratives set on the Discworld soon began to be much more character-driven than the comparatively simple early Rincewind stories with their fragmented, if unbroken, journey narratives.[68] Staying true to its roots in parody, the protagonists of further books were still exactly opposite to what is traditionally considered a fantasy hero: witches, con-men, and alcoholic guards. And yet, like the jokes and puns that seemed to be only perfunctory, they displayed increased depth as new Discworld novels were published in the 1990s and 2000s.

Nevertheless, the essence of the Discworld—mockery of numerous topics from culture, history, and other fields, self-ironic passages that address the constructedness of the world—remained intact. While Pratchett undoubtedly "plunders popular culture" (Mason 55) and literary history for inspiration, thereby eclipsing the simple parodies such as *BotR* by later releases, his parody is nonetheless set on a secondary world of fantasy; albeit one that makes fun of everything including itself. Again, this self-mockery can be problematic: Authors of humorous fantasy such as Piers Anthony or Robert Rankin use humor to give color to certain characters or absurd situations, but the satire or irony rarely extends to the internal consistency of their secondary worlds.

Terry Pratchett, on the other hand, constantly transgresses these boundaries, be it via meta-commentaries, footnotes, or characters

---

[68] The penultimate *Discworld Companion* lists up Rincewind's numerous adventures across the whole Discworld—compared to other protagonists, his journeys are vastly longer and cover wider expanses of Pratchett's secondary world (Pratchett and Briggs, *Turtle Recall* 315).

breaking the fourth wall.[69] In doing so, he reveals the very fictionality of his world, seemingly destroying the Tolkienian "spell" of suspension of disbelief, which is necessary for the reader's immersion in a believable secondary world. Because of this openness about its fictionality, "we never quite forget that the Discworld is a game, an experiment. There is, at times, a sense of vulnerability about the *mise en scène* of the Discworld books, a sense that the entire edifice could be dissolved with the flick of the Owner's wand, that Discworld was created for its Owner to do something with" (Clute 25). More apparent than other literature, the Discworld thus stands in a fragile balance between possibility and impossibility, between reality and fiction. The metaphor of the secondary world being a game board or "a playground" (Stableford, *Jaunting* 183), is one of the crucial postmodern features of Pratchett's fiction. Throughout the Discworld novels, we never really leave the stage that has been set[70]—James' and Mendlesohn's idea of theatre fantasy applies to the whole series, but what is acted out on the stage of each book explicitly addresses the fictitiousness of all these enactments in yet another twist of constant indeterminacy.

It is thus no surprise that theatricality is defining for the Discworld: "Theatres, theatrical performances, and theatrical performers are the very stuff of Pratchett's Discworld novels" (Rayment 46). Much as postmodernists "deployed language to turn in on itself with a new energy" (Best and Kellner 132), Pratchett uses metafictional irony to expose the stage sets of fantasy, including his own. What he achieves thereby is a curious hybrid. His Discworld novels

> are critiques of the genre but they also play fair: they work as fantasy novels [...].
> In addition, the novels are structured so that the entire world is both a parody of a fantasy world and an engaging world in its own right; each novel reads as a parody of the fantasy genre as a whole. (Butler, *Companion* 287)

---

[69] In the fourth *The Science of Discworld* book, the very nature and impossibility of the Discworld are debated by Discworld characters themselves, leading one character to the exclamation that the turtle carrying their world may be "an unlikely turtle, but nevertheless the turtle in front of us, or rather below us" (Pratchett et al., *Judgement* 209).

[70] The three only instances of characters leaving the Disc occur in *CoM* (marginally so when Rincewind and Twoflower nearly fall off the edge of the disc), *E* (depicting a journey to the beginning of time to experience the creation of the Disc), and, most extensively, in *LH*, where an expedition to the Discworld's moon and back to the Disc is carried out.

Pratchett consequently operates inside the very system he disassembles, a Bakhtinian circle "of the collapse or reversal of hierarchies" (Butler, "Theories" 84) being staged in each novel.

The Discworld series thereby both utilizes and challenges the norms of fantasy, an example of Hutcheon's idea of postmodernism as parody that does not restrict itself to merely ridiculing its targets: "Parody is a particularly double-edged form of humour. It is not a matter of simply satirizing a target: in fact, the most successful parody is hardly satire at all, for to parody a form or an institution effectively one has to understand it to the point of affection" (Sawyer, "Librarian" 114). While *BotR* is a carbon copy of *LotR* with brand-names and satirical real-world references mocking the original text, Pratchett's Discworld novels aim at a deeper parody, namely that of the fantasy genre as a whole, its full historical background and the inspirations from the real world that it is based on. Going hand in hand with this refinement, the protagonists of later Discworld books (most prominently Granny Weatherwax and Samuel Vimes) are not simply anti-heroes but characters whose inner—and outer—conflicts are even more complex.

Acting beyond parody of fantasy towards an analysis of genre and reader expectations, "the Discworld series is peppered with unlikely heroes and challenges to the notion of hero" (Smith 185). The true implications of this playing with the notion of heroism became apparent as Pratchett abandoned the direct antithesis of heroes still present in the Rincewind novels:

> Terry Pratchett says that as the series developed, so he himself acquired a deeper interest in the art of plot-making. Witches Abroad [the twelfth Discworld novel] is transitional in that regard also. Like the first novels, it sets its main characters on a journey, and during that journey, they encounter a number of fictional universes, ranging from Tolkien's Lord of the Rings, through several fairy tales, such as Sleeping Beauty and Little Red Riding Hood, and moving on to 60s television series and The Wizard of Oz. But whereas Rincewind, the central character of the early novels, was little more than a cipher, and the episodes of his journey no more than beads upon a string, in Witches Abroad the protagonists change through their experience, and the different scenarios each make their own contribution to the development of the tale. (titles not italicized in the original; Mason 58)

Repeating Mendlesohn's comment that moral growth is crucial to quest-fantasy narratives, this process became more complex in later Discworld novels. Rather than continuing to litter his invention with parodies of derivative or classic fantasy works, Pratchett began to work on the Discworld with increased focus on a self-contained and independent secondary world.

Like the protagonists of *LotR* during their travels across Middle-earth, Discworld characters began to change and grow during their journeys through the parodies of quest fantasies (Downes 56–60). Since most Discworld novels feature recurring characters, the increase in complexity was eventually mirrored in the books themselves—references to previous adventures and the previous history of characters appeared more frequently. Eventually, Pratchett could no longer "ignore what ha[d] gone before" *(LL 5)*, since his creation demanded greater attention to detail the further he removed it from mere parody.

For Pratchett, this meant rethinking the biggest weakness of his works—not so much the parody as the self-parody threatening the internal consistency and suspension of disbelief—and turning it into one of the Discworld's greatest strengths, namely by using said challenges to more serious ends without abandoning their funnier side. Like Jonathan Swift and Oscar Wilde (Butler et al. viii; Brown 263), Pratchett began to employ humor not simply to evoke laughter but to address contemporary issues by ridiculing them with a sharp edge:

> Humour is much more than laughing at the ugly, whether it be at ugly people or ugly situations—at what Bakhtin labels the grotesque, the physically excessive body. It is a chance to describe and to some extent criticise the real world. In his fantastical comic space Pratchett can, good-humouredly, offer such criticism. [...] It seems likely, as Socrates argued, that a writer like Pratchett knows how to write a tragedy, but for now we should appreciate the liberation through laughter he offers us. (Butler, "Theories" 87–88)

Over the years, the Discworld books lost most of the explicit pastiche seen in the first novels and stopped merely making fun of stereotypical plots and protagonists. Using humor in an engaging manner, Pratchett's on-going stories eventually arranged the Discworld within an autonomous system of rules. However, he also continued to expose this "rule set" of fantasy and allowed readers to peek behind the curtain of secondary belief through humorous or metafictional elements.

This is where the Discworld differs from all contemporary fantasy parodies that stand in the tradition of *BotR*, such as *The Chronicles of Blarnia* or *Barry Trotter*. His parody can therefore not be properly categorized within Genette's structure: while "true" parodies in Genette's sense mimic one text and may pay homage to its characters and plot or on the other hand exploit them for fun and possibly profit—the introduction of *BotR* even explicitly states that this "book is predominantly concerned with making money" (5)—Pratchett's texts quickly evolved from their parody guise after the first Discworld novels had been released. As Butler observes, however, while the "level of parody has decreased steadily since the beginning of the series, [...] existing parodistic elements have been carried forward" (Butler, *Companion* 286)—foremost the parody of classic fantasy tropes and references to popular culture. Abandoning the humor[71] altogether would have been as drastic a move for the continuance of the Discworld series as overdoing the parody.

After the success of the first few Discworld novels, Pratchett could certainly have remained in his niche (which had been labeled "funny fantasy" by various critics), writing parody after parody and mocking all the clichés of fantasy fiction.[72] "Suffering under the triple damnation of writing popular, humorous fantasy" (Butler et al. viii), he was in danger of being typecast as an author who merely ridiculed and copied what other authors had achieved creatively. Looking back at the parody typical of the first two Discworld novels, they indeed offer a fast-paced persiflage of fantasy, using elements from classic fantasy novels, mythology, and folklore to achieve a maximum number of jokes per page. *CoM* is especially, as we have learned, little more than a patchwork of stories linked by the main characters stumbling from one absurd situation into the next.

However, it is evident that Pratchett's humor is not without foundation. Revealing a darker side to stereotypical content and patterns in fiction, his later novels outmatch the mere parody and retelling of classic stories and enter what could be called "the realm of the serio-comical" (Bakhtin, "Characteristics" 129), a mirror of both fantasy and of our actual world.

---

[71] A few of his later novels (first and foremost *Night Watch*) have nevertheless been described as "supernatural thrillers" rather than as humorous fantasy—whilst jokes still abound in these books, they unmistakably deal with more serious matters.

[72] Looking at the abundance of fantasy fiction in the 1990s and the turn of the last millennium, Pratchett certainly would have had enough material to work with. One might, for instance, claim that his adolescent witch Tiffany Aching was directly inspired by the *Harry Potter* series, but reading the books it becomes clear that she is a fully fleshed-out protagonist and far from any parody or mere copy of J. K. Rowling's characters.

> [I]f the Discworld has gone from strength to strength (rather than petering out as many theatre fantasies do) it is not because they are funny (although they are) or because the characters have become so interesting, but because Pratchett has used the storylines and characters to poke and prod at the "givens" of our own world, of the stories we tell about it, and of the fantasy worlds many of his colleagues write. (James and Mendlesohn, *History* 181)

Being firmly grounded in empirical reality, the Discworld offers fresh and critical insights into topics that exceed yet never exit their literary stage. "The world Pratchett has created is, like our world, broken and morally complex" (Foster 198), and its problems cannot be resolved with magic or any other supernatural element as in typical wish-fulfillment escapist fantasy written by Tolkien's imitators. While the Rincewind novels mainly covered quest fantasy and closely followed its narrative pattern, the further iterations and variations of the Discworld began to address the more serious meanings of fantasy and accusations of escapism, not only parodying clichés but moreover investigating their sources and powers.

Chapter 4

The Threat of Clichés and Narrative Imperative

ONE OF THE DECISIVE FEATURES of classic fantasy is that eucatastrophe applies to the main characters as much as to their secondary world. As we follow the narrative of a fantasy novel, both world and protagonist are subject to conjoined dramatic events. Compared to literature considered more mimetic and representative of empirical reality, fantasy often exaggerates the consequences and development of a character within a larger context — Bilbo and Frodo undergo ordeals that make them cross an entire world, unlike, for example, Madame Bovary or Stephen Daedalus.[73]

Nonetheless, the Discworld also offers a space for this trait of fantasy, and Pratchett makes strong use of main characters who display a noticeable sophistication over the course of their novels:

> The Discworld is a series, and many of the characters are used in several different books. [...] As with other such serial productions, stories may continue from one volume to the next. Although each of the books in the Discworld series does bring some kind of resolution to its own particular plot, there are overarching storylines that continue from one to the next, and which may, indeed, never come to a conclusion. (Mason 56)

However, instead of putting personal development secondary to the quest-fantasy stereotype of saving the world (a pattern which we still encounter in *CoM* and *LF*), the later Discworld novels put character first and narrative expectations second. In each individual volume, Pratchett challenges the stereotypes of characters and, more importantly, narrative. If the Discworld grew into a complex world reflecting fantasy and storytelling with each new novel, it seems to be a logical step that its recurring characters likewise developed morally complex personalities that do not fit the simplistic patterns found in derivative quest fantasies and particularly in their parodies.

---

[73] Although in Daedalus' case, his one-day journey through Dublin is still based on the epic travels of Ulysses in Homer's *Odyssey*.

What is more, "marginalized narrative groups have greater representation in postmodern fantasy" (Casey 118)—a feature clearly found in Pratchett's unusual choice of protagonists of later novels: the two witches Esmerelda Weatherwax and Tiffany Aching, as well as city guardsman Samuel Vimes. Their relation to storytelling, and being part of a story themselves, is one of the central unresolved conflicts at the dynamic core of the Discworld, all the more so since their marginality (particularly from the perspective of classic fantasy) means that they would either not play a major role in genre-typical novels or be cast as villains.

THE SUBVERSION OF CLICHÉS

Given fantasy's roots in fairy tales and mythology—both of which often feature simplified distinctions of morality and justice—one recurring stereotype of genre which must not be left unconsidered is the problematic dichotomy of good versus evil. It should be noted that the fantasy genre uses the terms "good" and "evil" in a literary context and, more specifically, as they are classified in fantasy and fairy stories, that is to say, in an oftentimes binary manner.[74] For the sake of narrative ease, the two concepts are frequently opposed, allowing for a clear if rather unrefined juxtaposition and a potential outset for easier characterization. Indeed, the deeper problematics of this either-or mentality are not always taken into account in fantasy fiction—which is not to say that they are entirely absent from the genre but nonetheless have the advantage of providing a recognizable template: "The phrase good and evil describes a *dynamic opposition* which drives much fantasy, SUPERNATURAL FICTION and horror; the Good and the Evil themselves are seldom examined" (Clute and Grant 422). Authors of novels set in fantasyland rely on predominantly binary moral models, reducing the complexities of empirical reality— and thus morality—to create a more clear and unambiguous message regarding the agenda of characters.

Looking at Tolkien's ideas of good and evil, whilst they are not a direct allegory of Christian motifs but certainly inspired by them (Manlove, *England* 72), they nonetheless allow for some depth and

---

[74] Which do not have to be absolutes but often *can* be: Particularly in contemporary fantasy strongly influenced by Tolkien, characters (and their surroundings) are often assigned to be either good or bad, with no finer shades in between. See also the next three footnotes.

reflection on the nature of evil. As Burns notes, "the greatest evil in Tolkien's view is 'possessiveness', a sin which includes simple materialism as well as domination, enslavement, and arbitrary control; and these, of course, are qualities which may be as manifest in those who inherit power as in those who acquire it by force, stealth, or deception" (Burns 50). The One Ring, as both symbol and object of ultimate power, leads to the corruption of Boromir and reveals its duplicitous nature to Frodo, a conflict that finds its purest expression in the character of Gollum. Torn between desire for the Ring and loyalty to his new master Frodo, "Gollum [comes] very close to repentance" (Nagy 246), but in the end succumbs to the allure of power.[75]

That said, Tolkien's book nonetheless often follows dichotomous patterns based on mythological and folkloristic motifs. Throughout, characters mostly conform to either end of the good-evil spectrum: Hence Aragorn is the classic figure of the lost and rightful king and Sauron his satanic "mirror image" (James and Mendlesohn, *History* 49), a fitting "*parody* [and in this respect, as pointed out just before, a subversion] of good" (see Clute and Grant 746).[76] In later fantasy novels inspired by *LotR*, the Christian undertones might be less obvious or even completely absent, yet their echoes are still visible in clear oppositions of good and evil as exemplified in Guy Gavriel Kay's *Fionavar* trilogy or Stephen R. Donaldson's *Chronicles of Thomas Covenant* series (Senior 190, 199; Habermann and Kuhn 271).

The earliest Discworld books, being parodies of quest fantasies, leave these borders mostly untouched. Evil is parodied, but not in order to criticize its oversimplified role as a direct opposite to an equally unreflected representation of "good." Pratchett rather exaggerates individual elements: While "it is not in [Pratchett's] nature to create any character who is nothing but evil" (Mendlesohn, "Faith" 244–45), antagonists such as the bureaucratic wizard Trymon vie for control and power with "a mind that was as bleak and pitiless and logical as the slopes of Hell" (*LF* 111) — a character whose malign

---

[75] A power that for him means immortality: Apart from needing the ring as a physical object (his "precious"), Gollum is not interested in the political implications of the Ring but hopes to attain what Tolkien calls "the oldest and deepest desire, the Great Escape: the Escape from Death" (OFS 74).

[76] What is more, specific races of Middle-earth are portrayed as good (exemplified by the angelic elves of Rivendell who act as saviors and wise advisors) whereas a race such as the Uruk-hai is seen as predominantly evil.

tendencies turn into an exaggerated version of evil once he becomes possessed by otherworldly demonic forces. Further evidence and a direct inspiration from H. P. Lovecraft's Cthulhu mythos, the malevolent and chaotic deities of the Dungeon Dimensions that feature prominently in the first Discworld novels pose an equally pure evil and otherworldly threat as Tolkien's Sauron and the absolute evils of other fantasy works.[77] Only in later Discworld novels did this exaggerated portrayal of evil give way to a more humane and diversified idea of morality, reacting against the simplistic black-or-white moral distinctions of fantasy novels of the 1960s and 1970s.

More importantly, Pratchett's refinement of 'right or wrong' behaviour reveals how one of the cores of modern fantasy—folklore—may provide source texts with definitions like "good" and "evil" that need not be challenged but merely reproduced:

> [A]n awareness of narrative runs through all Pratchett's work, seen most explicitly as a recurring and somewhat satirical sense of the nature and importance of fairy tale. Reacting against the Disneyfication and general cuteness of fairy tale in the twentieth and twenty-first centuries, his awareness of narrative is folkloric, returning to a more earthy and brutal pattern which denies idealism in favor of a certain bloodiness. (Tiffin 162)

His books also reflect the need for these constructs and at the same time show "that such systems are indeed attractive, perhaps even necessary; but this does not make them any less illusory" (Hutcheon, *Poetics* 6). Therefore, instead of providing a radical rewriting akin to Angela Carter's feminist subversion of fairy stories in *The Bloody Chamber*, Pratchett sets the stage for a fantasy parody with all of its motifs seemingly intact: Unheroic heroes, overstated or ridiculous villains, absurd plots filled with numerous allusions to popular culture. His radical departure from this outset lies within the re-enacting of specific stories and laying bare the illogical or unreflected matters hidden in such stories through closer attention to details and by thematizing questions normally unposed. Pratchett also "looks at a convention from a different perspective" (Haberkorn, "Seriously" 145); but he utilizes and undermines the stereotypical elements of

---

[77] An excellent example being the "Dark Lord" (Clute and Grant 524) Shai'tan of Robert Jordan's *The Wheel of Time* series. Like the hero Rand al'Thor, who signifies a severely conflicted but ultimately absolute good, his adversary Shai'tan is a nearly direct evil counterpart.

his source in a less crass manner than Carter, criticizing the genre of fantasy and its adoption of often simplified ideas such as good and evil from within its confines.

With this insight, we arrive at one of the defining characteristics of the Discworld: although the Discworld itself is a secondary world filled with magic and narratives that are undoubtedly fantasy or a parody thereof, all of these well-known tropes are examined with a sharper and more critical sense of humor in the novels following *CoM* and *LF*. Echoing not just Bakhtin but furthermore Viktor Shklovsky's concept of defamiliarization, Pratchett clearly states his views on how he sees fantasy (as exemplified in his books) by recounting an anecdote of one of his travels in Australia:

> I looked down towards the horizon and there was Orion. It was the first constellation I ever learned to identify, when I was about eight or nine. I know Orion off by heart. But I was seeing Orion upside down. [...] The other constellations weren't unfamiliar. They were just ones I hadn't seen before ... [...] But Orion was *un*familiar—something old and commonplace presented in a new way so that you're almost seeing it for the first time. That's what fantasy should be. (Pratchett and Briggs, *Turtle Recall* 421)

Although turned on its head, Orion—or fantasy on the Discworld, respectively—is still recognizable from its original pattern or shape. Such defamiliarization, like incongruity and irony, is another determining factor of Pratchett's books. By referencing sources ranging from mythology and folklore to Shakespeare, popular culture, and Hollywood films, the Discworld highlights unusual sides of events and phenomena as a parodist counterpart of our actual world and becomes a mirror of popular culture as well as various other aspects of empirical reality.

Yet ironically, Tolkien criticizes such close proximity of fantasy to empirical reality, as in his opinion it does not create new images or ideas but prefers to focus on mere subversion of existing phenomena (in a literal mirroring, by turning something on its head or showing a reversed image of it). Chestertonian fantasy, as he defines this process of defamiliarization by mirroring, lacks the intricacies of literary invention and reinterpretation, Tolkien claims:

> *Mooreeffoc* is a fantastic word, but it could be seen written up in every town in this land. It is Coffee-room, viewed from the inside through a glass door, as it was seen by Dickens on a dark London day; and it was used by Chesterton to denote the queerness of

things that have become trite, when they are seen suddenly from a new angle. That kind of "fantasy" most people would allow to be wholesome enough; and it can never lack for material. But it has, I think, only a limited power; for the reason that recovery of freshness of vision is its only virtue. (OFS 68)

True fantasy in the Tolkienian sense uses imagination to create a secondary world that is not principally based upon defamiliarization of the familiar but employs a creative retelling or combination of several ideas—case in point being his *LotR*.

Pratchett's Discworld, on the other hand, makes extensive use of Chestertonian fantasy with its penchant for open allusion to content that is familiar not merely to fantasy readers but to readers in general: One novel introduces rock'n'roll music to the Discworld, for example, while another parodies Hollywood's film industry. As a parody of fantasy but also a satire of empirical reality, such Discworld novels in particular exaggerate and subvert aspects of the actual world as much as the stereotypical content of classic fantasy novels.[78] Still, as pointed out in the preceding chapter, Pratchett's take on parodying fantasy goes beyond the merely laughter-inducing parody of works such as *BotR* or *Barry Trotter*, and the same can be said of its representation of empirical reality. While subversion and exaggeration are key to the Discworld as they are to fantasy parody per se, Pratchett aims for goals that exceed mere defamiliarization of individual tropes—his entire world undergoes such a process.

Ironically, the vast scope of the unfamiliar ultimately becomes part of the familiarity that exists on the Discworld, where incongruous content and reversals form and constantly reshape Pratchett's creation. Pratchett extends the process of defamiliarization so far that it is, in fact, accepted as part of everyday life on the Discworld. Through the combination of a humorous perspective on the unheroic facets of a secondary world with the aforementioned reversals of classic tropes of fantasy, the familiar and the unfamiliar enter a coexistence on his secondary world.

The content of Pratchett's works is much closer to the familiarities of daily routine than in other fantasy novels, whose focus usually favors

---

[78] These being *Soul Music* and *Moving Pictures*. They, more so than any other of the Discworld novels following *CoM* and *LF*, feature extensive parodies of their core topics by referencing an overabundance of songs or films.

grand schemes and pays less attention to smaller, personal stories. Mason offers a fitting summary of this unique feature of the Discworld:

> The Disc came to be a world in which fantasy and the most mundane reality existed side by side, in which ordinary people, living ordinary lives, might expect to bump into a werewolf, or a dwarf, in which magicians and witches might be found having a drink in a pub, and in which metaphors and other figures of speech could take on the solid reality of a brick. (Mason 55)

By expanding the subversive qualities of the Discworld while still making use of the recognizable clichés of fantasy and placing emphasis on the daily life on a secondary world, Pratchett creates an almost Kafkaesque intermingling of the ordinary and the supernatural, a realm "where gods had a habit of going round to atheists' houses and smashing their windows" (*CoM* 103). What he, in fact, achieves is a refamiliarization process similar to Scarinzi's idea of literariness (270–75): For all the constant jokes and meta-commentaries aimed at clichéd fantasy content, the people of the Discworld intrinsically accept them as part of their life and world. In other words, the Discworld and its inhabitants continue working[79] despite all the absurdity.

Such a combination of mundane reality with the stock tropes of a fantasy world yields a fresh approach to the oftentimes highly elusive genre. Neither abandoning nor simply parodying Tolkien's pattern, Pratchett instead addresses the pitfalls and unresolved dilemmas of genre fantasy in each Discworld novel. Be this by reflections on those characters traditionally branded as "good" or "evil" or by asking questions that normally remain unasked in fantasy fiction,[80] his critical enquiries are nearly always relatable to readers and far from the simple mockery of his first releases:

> On the one hand, in many ways [Pratchett] debunks fantasy and its conventions—and he certainly doesn't subscribe to mediaevalist nostalgia for a world of lost faith in quite the backward looking, conservative way that, *mutatis mutandis*, one might see Tolkien and Coleridge doing. But he does often do something akin to

---

[79] With their ordinary, everyday lives, Discworld protagonists once more bear a close resemblance to the homely and unheroic hobbits in Tolkien's work—and like Bilbo and Frodo, Pratchett's characters experience involuntary calls to adventure.

[80] Indeed, Pratchett's approach to fantasy can be seen as childlike: Critics point out that a major part of what makes his mid-period novels so entertaining and astute stems from his habit of asking "some of the awkward questions avoided by the original authors" (James and Mendlesohn, *History* 179).

> what Angela Carter has done with fairy stories: revisit them, not to undermine them in a spirit of rational scepticism, but to reveal them in a different light. (Brown 292)

Pratchett neither dismisses nor copies, but actively reutilizes the conservative features of fantasy fiction, showing familiar elements in unfamiliar ways. This is perhaps why Pratchett proceeded rather methodologically when inspecting different clichés of fantasy fiction in *CoM* and *LF*: He revisited the most important tropes of fantasy with his duo of Rincewind and Twoflower, using a cowardly hero and a tourist to portray them from a new and unusual perspective—creative yet comparatively simplistic characters for an entertaining if unoriginal tale.

It is precisely such close adherence to typical fantasy quest structures in these two novels that reveals their overuse in the genre and provides the groundwork for Pratchett's more critical endeavors. While still indulging in the lighter side of the tropes he made fun of, Pratchett simultaneously began to uncover the narrative mechanisms which are at work behind stories in books such as *WS* or *GG*. With every story that has been heard over generations, there consequently comes a certain expectation—and if the story structure is repeated often enough, readers anticipate specific outcomes and events to follow one another. The vital role of mental patterns and narrative for the human mind is among Pratchett's most important topics in his books:

> A theory that arose in my mind as a result of my reading, and later my writing, was that of narrative causality—the idea that there are "story shapes" into which human history, both large scale and at the personal level, attempts to fit. At least, a novelist would put it that way; it's probably more sensible to say that we ourselves for some reason have the story shapes in our mind, and attempt to fit the facts of history into them, like Cinderella's slipper [...] And we like things in our stories that fit. We may have begun as *homo sapiens* but we have become *homo narrans*—story-making man. (Pratchett, "Worlds" 166)

Pratchett's idea of narrative and storytelling in human life lies in the same vein as what Jonathan Gottschall describes as *"Homo fictus* (fiction man), the great ape with the storytelling mind" (Gottschall xiv) and echoes the idea of "narrative [...] as a powerful and basic tool for thinking" (Herman et al., *Narrative Theory* 163). As events happen and experience shapes our lives, we tend to reflect and interpret them as a pattern that forms a narrative in a logical sequence of causality.

Since these storytelling patterns occur naturally in our minds (Donald 185), events are being processed in a manner that we can make sense of easily, specifically in the form of a causal chain.[81] Whenever a new situation arises and we recount events to others or remember them later, our minds attempt to form the sequence of experienced events into a pattern resembling a story for easier memorization and retelling. This "narrative fallacy addresses our limited ability to look at sequences of fact without weaving an explanation into them, or, equivalently, forcing a logical link, an *arrow of relationship*, upon them" (Taleb 63–64). Especially in a written culture and literary context, this tendency to narrate events establishes patterns of storytelling that are often repeated for ease of recognition—and may turn into stereotypes or genre blueprints. Indeed, due to its formality, genre fiction is particularly prone[82] to the recurring use of certain topics or the successful narrative patterns of specific works, fantasy being no exception. Pratchett calls such "unquestioning echo of better work gone before" EFP—Extruded Fantasy Product, using the same description as that of fantasy critic Brian Attebery (Pratchett, *Slip* 84; Attebery, *Myth* 1). By EFP, both authors mean fantasy that does not have to be an obvious copy of preceding texts but usually displays little original content, setting its characters within a clear-cut and recognizable framework of binary good and evil and well-known story patterns.

Critical of this unreflective recycling of storytelling and simplistic morality, Pratchett imbues his protagonists with an awareness of the power of stories[83] that challenge the manner in which their counterparts

---

[81] It must be stressed that these events need not be connected on their own but we can *interpret* and order them as such; that is to say, the causality of several linked events arises from our impression as much as it may from the events themselves. While I do not want to fall into Humean skepticism with this argument, the human tendency to create and recognize patterns in unrelated events is, as Donald and Gottschall underline, undeniable.

[82] Even in the case of fantasy authors who actively avoid Tolkien's inheritance such as China Miéville, their work is often still categorized within a specific framework: *Perdido Street Station*, a truly genre-defying novel, has seen labels ranging from urban fantasy to plain science fiction, and Pratchett's fiction, as pointed out before, has seen similar variety of attempts at a "definition."

[83] Which is not to say that they have a meta-awareness of their own fictionality—Pratchett's fiction remains classic fantasy insofar as it does not venture into the postmodern breaking up the barriers between character and reader or character and author. The characters certainly know about the features of their secondary world—that it relies on narrative and storytelling to a strong degree, and that stories can come true on the Discworld—but their knowledge does not feign to expand to an empirical reality outside of their fictionality.

in other fantasy books accept their roles. First and foremost among these unresolved conflicts is what Pratchett terms *narrative imperative*.[84] More than the mere realization of the story patterns that organize thought and fiction, the narrative imperative reveals the power that these patterns hold both for mind and for life. Starting with *GG* and particularly *WA*, Discworld novels begin to show the frightening implications of narrative expectations: readers' assumptions about how stories proceed and should normally end might, in fact, lace a sort of pre-established corset[85] around fiction: "[A]s a story works its way through it acquires the power of inevitability; it spawns more stories which structure the narratives people are capable of conceiving" (Butler, *Companion* 265). Interestingly, this form of habituation is remarkably close to the concept of refamiliarization: Once the new or unfamiliar has been accepted (and reformed into a familiar and recurring pattern), its repetition can ultimately rob it, not just of its unfamiliarity, but also of its originality. In the long run, such narratives may nullify any alternative or variation.

The Dark Side of Clichés and the Dictatorship of Narrative

A metafictional approach to storytelling had been discernable from the postmodern bricolage of genre fantasy in the first Discworld novels, yet its narratological reflections became evident only as the sophistication of Pratchett's discussion about "the interplay of belief and Story" found its expression in later books (Clute and Grant 784). In particular, the initially simple "world as a stage/game board" metaphor and the image of a flat world taken from Hindu mythology were extended with increased philosophical attention after their first humorous portrayals. It is, therefore, crucial to see how the investigations into the narrative and humor of the Discworld novels complement each other.

The protagonists we encounter in Pratchett's books evoke a humorous or at least incongruous reaction to begin with, since they

---

[84] It should be noted that the term *narrative imperative* is applied in various fields of research, among them medicine, marketing, and politics. Naturally, my attention lies on the literary and fictional implications of the term, although intersections with the aforementioned areas may occur at given parts of this book.

[85] These may be both genres or larger narrative patterns that are repeated in stories across the literary spectrum. While extensive research continues in this area of literary and cultural theory, Joseph Campbell's monomyth is perhaps the most enduring idea, one which has found expression in narratives from Homer's *The Odyssey* to George Lucas' *Star Wars* films.

are not normally the "heroes" of the stories they are drawn into. In many other novels, they would only feature on the margins of the narrative and provide comic relief or hinder the hero's progress. By shifting the perspective to these margins and showing stories of classic fantasy from their point of view, Pratchett indeed creates a funny and self-reflective environment. Echoing Hutcheon's postmodern idea of parody by giving a voice to "those who are marginalized by a dominant ideology" (*Poetics* 35), in Pratchett's context, secondary characters experience their own narrative within a classic framework of a typical fantasy narrative—the dominant narrative of classic Tolkienian fantasy, so to speak.

Story is thus not simply vital for fantasy: In a strict way, it *defines* fantasy, beginning with formulas such as "Once upon a time"[86] and further signified in the framework of high fantasy being set in different storyworlds complete with additional stories implied in maps and glossaries. What is more, characters may possess at least some knowledge that they are in a story or that their everyday life follows certain patterns—a concept whose importance is essential within a Discworld context and Pratchett's idea of narrative imperative:

> Part of the definition of fantasy is that its protagonists tend to know that they are in a Story of some sort, even if at first they do not know which one; at moments of RECOGNITION they find out just which Story it is that has, in some sense, *dictated* them. (Clute and Grant 901)

In Tolkien's literary oeuvre, the characters, therefore sometimes express how their current situation is comparable to a story;[87] *H* and *LotR* are books *based* on the adventures of the protagonists and written down by them—Bilbo and Frodo, respectively—in the (fictional) *Red Book of Westmarch*. The characters turn their journeys into a story by

---

[86] A formula that ensures that the story following this mantra is set in another time and in another place—both of which can remain unexplained as to their precise where- and when-abouts. While genre fantasy has replaced the time- and placeless marvel of fairy tales with vastly detailed secondary worlds, it still evokes the same displacement in time and space in readers.

[87] Very memorably so at the end of *LotR* when Sam and Frodo are standing at the foot of Mount Doom after the One Ring has been destroyed and Sam exclaims: "What a tale we have been in, Mr. Frodo, haven't we?' [...] 'I wish I could hear it told! Do you think they'll say: *Now comes the story of Nine-fingered Frodo and the Ring of Doom*? And then everyone will hush, like we did, when in Rivendell they told us the tale of Beren One-hand and the Great Jewel. I wish I could hear it! And I wonder how it will go on after our part" (*RK* VI.4.1244–45; see also McMurry 223–25).

recounting their life as a tale, one might say. Fantasy in the vein of Tolkien often relies on such storytelling frames to put the personal journeys of its protagonists into a larger context—the fate of the individual influences that of the whole world, which in turn exerts influence on the development of the character.

In Pratchett's case, however, such proximity to stories and the role of a character within a bigger story becomes problematic. Being skeptical of the trappings and dangers of stereotypical storytelling that fantasy authors use, he began to devise ways to cover them from another perspective in his novels. His protagonists are therefore not simple parodies of stock fantasy characters—they must ultimately fight against the confines of story and narrative imperative that would either force them back into voiceless marginality or silence their subversive powers by putting them center-stage and thus annulling their outsider's perspective.

Terry Pratchett's criticism and subversion of storytelling naturally extends to characters. His protagonists are not the shining heroes or "chosen ones"[88] who eventually learn about their destiny and must hence inevitably prevail—tropes which are employed frequently in classic genre fantasy and which "reliably pull in [...] steady readership" (Attebery, *Myth* 98). It is easy to regard the main characters of the mid-to-late-period Discworld novels as mere parodies on a superficial level, yet once more, this would result in overlooking the development that has gone into their refinement and their overall role in Pratchett's secondary world.

Not being heroes in a classical sense, Pratchett's protagonists are prone to be overlooked or seen as caricatures from the viewpoint of genre fantasy: "From COM onwards, the Discworld series has been ambivalent about who the heroes are. It is not Hrun the Barbarian or the naïve explorer Twoflower, who features as the central protagonist, but rather Rincewind, who seems anything but a hero" (Butler, *Companion* 185). But Rincewind, like Tolkien's hobbits, still qualifies as a hero

---

[88] One seeming exception to this deviation from stereotypical heroism—although again merely on the surface—is Pratchett's non-Discworld novel *Only You Can Save Mankind*. Ironically, the book title is that of an arcade video game, thereby ruining the promise of the main character being "the one," as there are countless chosen ones who can all choose to play the game. In the end, the protagonist Johnny has to help the *enemies* in the game to prove himself a true hero, subverting the role of hero as defender into hero as savior.

chosen by narrative imperative despite his cowardice and reluctance: While he is a failed wizard, his mind nonetheless harbors one of the vital spells that will save the Discworld from destruction—while the opposite of a hero (not an anti-hero but rather a coward who runs away), he is trapped within the narrative patterns of heroic fantasy and at the end of *LF*, he acts accordingly and defeats the otherworldly threat.

Yet the main characters of later novels—the witch Esmerelda Weatherwax and city guard Samuel Vimes—are traditionally (read: in classic fantasy novels) considered either background characters or villains, not heroes.[89] What is more, they display a comparable awareness of larger stories happening outside their daily lives as Tolkien's hobbits and a similar reluctance to going on adventures[90] linked to those stories. Like Bilbo or Frodo and much more so than Robert Jordan's Rand al'Thor, Christopher Paolini's Eragon and so many other fantasy protagonists with humble beginnings, they aim to remain marginal and not to become a larger part of an overarching narrative. Yet in each Discworld novel they are put into "classic stories" of fantasy and must cope with situations beyond their normally liminal role.

Happy Endings at All Costs

For all its emphasis on creativity over mimesis and telling stories filled with supernatural content, classic genre fantasy nonetheless follows established values. Its villains and heroes usually adhere to a clear-cut schema between good and evil, black and white. This dichotomy is one of the most enduring features of fantasy fiction—as pointed out before, partly due to the influence of the recurring narrative patterns of fairy tales (Fimi 56–57)—and has given rise to the stigmatization of the genre as being simplistic: As Attebery underlines, a "character in a fairy tale *is* what he *does*" (*Strategies* 71–72), a method also used by numerous fantasy authors to establish clear definitions of roles such as hero and villain in measurements of absolute differentiation. Thus

---

[89] Witches and particularly city guards do not often have important roles in classic fantasy—unlike Rincewind, whose profession as a wizard is closer to what is considered a crucial character. While Gandalf and Saruman represent "good" and "evil" wizards in *LotR*, nobody would argue that they are background characters.

[90] As Bilbo Baggins famously disclaims in *The Hobbit*: "We are plain quiet folk and have no use for adventures. Nasty disturbing uncomfortable things!" (7). It is only through Gandalf's perseverance that the hobbit eventually does join the expedition to the Lonely Mountain—one could claim that the wizard therefore acts as the *narrative imperative* for Bilbo.

characters that *do* wicked deeds automatically *are* or *look* wicked, and vice versa; Tolkien's Uruk-hai or the scheming Gríma Wormtongue are good examples because their inner workings must correspond to their hideous outward features. Taking morphic determinism to its extreme, "form shapes function" (Mendlesohn, "Faith" 240), in fairy tales as it does in fantasy. Such characters of stereotypical fantasy offer little depth and complexity, their destiny and personality are preset by narrative causality, regardless of whether they are heroes,[91] villains, or secondary characters.

In his books, Pratchett is highly critical of this acceptance of narrative conventions, seeing them as a simplification of facts and complexity. His twelfth Discworld novel, *WA*, best exemplifies his skeptical attitude towards such unquestioning adherence to traditional story patterns. Narrative expectations are challenged from the outset: As in his first novels, we experience a shift in perspective. Taking inspiration from Shakespeare's *Macbeth*, Pratchett's protagonists are a trio of witches—a literary trope associated with treachery and dark magic in Shakespeare's play, in classic fairy tales, and in much of genre fantasy. Their adventure is set in an at times very pastiched fantasyland (in the vein of *BotR*), featuring numerous parodies of classic fairy tales, and the goal of their journey—to stop a prince from marrying a princess—appears to be in tune with their stereotypical role of villains. However, seen from the witches' perspective, what they aim for is not to harm people but to change a constructed story and allow individual choice. Pratchett emphasizes that knowing storylines is the witches' prime power, perhaps part of their magic. As we learn in *WA*, "[a]ll [Discworld] witches are very conscious of stories. They can *feel* stories, in the same way that a bather in a little pool can feel the unexpected

---

[91] However, it would be to the detriment of Tolkien to conclude that his characters strictly adhere to this simplistic model. Hence even though ultimately "Frodo performs the role of hero, [...] he fits into that role only approximately; in some ways, he barely fills the outline, in others he is too solid to be contained within it" (Attebery, *Strategies* 72). In other words, he does not conform to his role as hero from the beginning of *LotR* in the same manner as Aragorn, the figure of the lost king (Armstrong 23). Frodo feels unhappy about leaving the comfort of his home and embarking on an adventure (*FR* I.3.85)—yet towards the end of his journey, he accepts his role as Ringbearer and thus also the troubles of heroism: "I can manage it." [...] "I must." (*RK* VI.3.1222). Tolkien's hobbits therefore may not be archetypical heroes, but in the long run they become subject to the demands of storytelling and acquiesce to their destined role.

trout" (*WA* 102). On the Discworld, the parodist retelling of classic stories from literature had been commonplace since the first novel, yet the story-awareness did not feature so prominently until *WA*.[92] Indeed, with their magical ability to sense stories, the witches are capable of detecting the enactment of metatexts within the Discworld to a degree.

The power of stories is apparent already in the first major Witches novel *WS*. At its base a humorous retelling of *Macbeth*, the book shows a more serious side of parody when the witches see the Discworld version of the play and realize for the first time how the *tale* of the crooked old witch can change their *reality*:

> That's us down there, [Granny Weatherwax] thought. Everyone knows who we really are, but the things down there are what they'll remember—three gibbering old baggages in pointy hats. All we've ever done, all we've ever been, won't exist anymore. (*WS* 214)

Pratchett is using parody to hold up a mirror and go beyond mere quick-fire jokes at the expense of the fantasy genre. What we see here, as in *M*, are the first steps towards a Discworld that is both more complex and mature. At the end of *WS*, the witches manage to derail the performance and thus avoid being misremembered, but this is only the beginning of "the metafictive nature that will become a hallmark of the Witches series" (Smith 135).

To prove this "power of story" even more so in *WA* than in the preceding Witches novel, Pratchett moves on from the stage and effectively creates a fairy tale realm within his fantasy world: There, the witches not only find themselves deprived of their actual role in people's lives on the Discworld—wise old women with medical knowledge and advice—but they are now *assigned* new roles as villains in a context constructed from classic fairy tales.[93] They suddenly become subject to a refamiliarization with a negative reinterpretation of their lives; their society begins to recast them as wicked witches because on the Discworld—as in empirical reality—"we can deny the facts of life: we can redescribe them and, in doing so, come to think

---

[92] Of course, *GG* (which was released two years before *WA*) also has storytelling and belief among its central topics, but it is still placed within a larger plot involving other elements. The message is the same in both books, but the consequences of narrative causality are more far-reaching in the Witches book.

[93] As his Witches series of Discworld novels reveals, Pratchett clearly favors the idea of witches as healers and advisors to their darker and malevolent portrayal in Grimm's fairy tales and the stereotypes deriving from this image.

about the world differently, and cause others to do so as well" (South, "Destiny" 33). Here, the role of narrative in cognition is revealed as deeply ambivalent: It can help us understand the world in an orderly manner but might also make us accept it in prepatterned ways and habits, positions which can be very hard to break and reconsider.

In the worst case, narrative thus does not remain a mental tool but becomes an instrument for the abuse of power: The penultimate *Discworld Companion* provides a succinct summary of the implications of narrative causality and imperative. While written for the context of the Discworld, the description stresses that realizing about these forces must not remain limited to Pratchett's creation:

> Finally, there is narrative causality, the power of stories. This is perhaps the strongest force of all and, again, *weaker echoes of it are found in this world*. Not for nothing do we say: History repeats. History does have patterns, clichés of time. People find themselves again and again in situations where they are playing roles as surely as if a script had been thrust into their hands [...]. And there are bigger patterns: the rise of empires, the spread of civilizations...
> (Pratchett and Briggs, *Turtle Recall* 119; my emphasis)

Pratchett thereby establishes a direct link between our actual world and the Discworld. In empirical reality, as on Pratchett's secondary world, people are often faced with the choice between behaving according to a role or being regarded as outsiders—fates that Pratchett's main characters have to deal with constantly.

The full implications of narrative causality in *WA* are brought to the fore when the witches arrive in the magical kingdom of Genua,[94] a fairy tale country within the Discworld. From the start, the artificiality of this part of Pratchett's secondary world becomes plain, as does its resemblance to Disneyland. The streets are swept clean, citizens are unanimously happy, everything seems tranquil and peaceful[95]—an unreal counterpart to the gritty Discworld metropolis of Ankh-Morpork bustling with life or the earthbound daily routine of the more rural areas of the Discworld. The city palace of Genua bears a crystalline majesty, every tower seemingly "designed to hold a captive princess" (*WA* 148).

Soon, the witches learn about the truth behind this facade: Lilith, the sister of head witch Granny Weatherwax, has established a strict

---

[94] Not to be confused with the real-world city of Genua in Liguria, Italy.

[95] Besides Disneyland, Genua also eerily resembles the Lordship of Duloc in Pixar's animated film *Shrek* (2001)—both the movie, as well as Duloc, are a parody that was obviously inspired by Disney films and theme parks.

rule upon the whole land and taken on the role of a fairy godmother whose benevolence is based on narrative conventions: The beauty and happiness of Genua and its inhabitants are run by a fairy tale dictatorship where everything must happen as it does in stories. Lilith's ideas of the old patterns of tales have shaped her rule over the land and are to be followed to their bitter end at all costs:

> Lil[ith] appears to believe that happiness can be achieved by conforming to the rules of the imaginary world of fairy tales. In the city over which she rules, she has decreed that cooks must be fat and jolly, that toy-makers should whistle, sing, and tell children stories. Those who do not follow the prescriptions are hauled off to the castle dungeons, and tortured until they promise to reform. Her pursuit of happy endings is postulated upon a reign of terror. (Mason 60)

Citizens of Genua must behave in given ways and proclaim to be happy because this is what all the stories spell in the end. In this Discworld novel, narratives "seem to behave like ideologies— the oppressed daughter has to marry the prince, the sister of an evil sister has to be good, and so on" (Butler, *Companion* 421). The relation of Genua to the tales of progress and national superiority spun by despots of empirical reality is evident, yet Pratchett takes the narratives of dictatorships into a wholly storified direction on this part of his secondary world: For every single inhabitant of Genua, a life-path that overrides individual preference has been laid out— which is also why the marriage that the witches aim to prevent has to happen according to the logic of the classic fairy story, no matter whether the bride and groom truly love each other or not.

Perhaps the most frightening fact about Genua is that both its political power and the power of story, as well as Lilith's concept of good and evil, are all drawn from the paradigms of fairy stories. True to indoctrined rules and regulations of dictatorships, this ideal is more important than the actual (inner-fictional) real, regardless of its roots in fairy tales. While the country itself most likely existed prior to Lilith's rise to power, her dystopia hidden underneath a quasi-utopia governed by narrative imperative goes beyond any normally conceivable reality:

> Lilith's Genua is a perfect example of what Jean Baudrillard labels the 'hyper-real' or a 'third-order simulation'. [...] Baudrillard views Disneyland as a perfect example of [...] 'hyperreality', and we can say the same thing about Genua, a place where 'the model precedes the real', the model here being the fairytale stereotypes which Lilith uses to structure the real world [...] (Smith 144)

Like Disneyland, Genua is "[m]ore real than the real" (Baudrillard 81), its obedience to the narrative structure of fairy tales has been turned into a scripted reality that allows for no intrusion of actual reality— hence the biggest offense in the kingdom are literally "crimes against narrative expectation" (WA 75). Lilith overrides the lives of her citizens with conformity and the dictum of story, even though her "stories all rely on artifice"[96] (Mason 60), that ignores individuality and enforces conformity to narrative conventions. Since the "shared cultural knowledge offered by fairy tales" is part of everyday life on the Discworld (Tiffin 163; WA 113), and particularly in the context of Genua, its inhabitants find it natural to believe in them and thus eventually accept and submit to their power and simplified versions of truths.

NARRATIVE DETERMINISM

WA and other novels in the Witches series constantly remind us of the determinative potential of stories: If a story has become popular by repetition and/or formula, other possible outcomes or variations of its narrative pattern are rarely taken into account due to the dominance and popularity of the formulaic retelling. On the Discworld, such influence is reciprocal, and narratives display animistic features. Not only can stories take on a specific "shape" when told repeatedly throughout generations, but in Pratchett's fiction they can also actively influence lives if given enough power by repetition through retelling:

> People think that stories are shaped by people. In fact, it's the other way round. [...] Stories, great flapping ribbons of shaped space-time, have been blowing and uncoiling around the universe since the beginning of time. And they have evolved. The weakest have died and the strongest have survived and they have grown fat on the retelling ... stories, twisting and blowing through the darkness. (WA 8)

Narratives are one of the defining forces of the Discworld—the right story at the right time can attain "inevitability [and] spawns more stories which structure the narratives people are capable of conceiving" (Butler, *Companion* 265), and, in a larger context such as Genua, may influence the personal life narratives of individuals. While "for Tolkien story is like a portal onto a different land, in Pratchett's writing story intervenes in people's lives and imposes itself on them, regardless of

---

[96] Certainly, *all* stories are artifice (that is to say, constructs); yet Lilith's dictated stories are even more artificial and staged since they have been reduced to repetitive patterns that must be followed in an unquestioning and almost pathological manner.

their preferences, their intentions, their plans" (McMurry 227). Since characters like Lilith put stories to wrong ends, the belief that they have to progress and end in a given way can be so powerful that it leads people to believe that they are someone else than their true identity.

The belief in stories on the Discworld may be a mere assignment of a different role within a certain narrative (such as the inhabitants of Genua have undergone to create the perfect fairy tale country with perfect inhabitants), yet Pratchett takes the potential of this story power in a world filled with supernatural forces one step further. If literary belief is a creative technique that can shape secondary worlds like Middle-earth, then on a self-referential, story-centered secondary world such as the Discworld "[w]hat is believed in strongly enough is real" (Pratchett and Briggs, *Turtle Recall* 119). In Pratchett's creation, this belief is consequently not limited to thought but extends to what, in fact, exists on the Discworld—we are faced with a physical consensus reality[97] that relies on stories as one of its guiding principles. In other words, belief in stories and story patterns on the Discworld can create, shape, and modify objects as well as—more frighteningly—subjects.

Perhaps the most horrifying example of this link between a power that shapes reality and the belief in stories is a wolf encountered by the witches during their journey in *WA*. At first glance, the creature appears to be the Discworld's equivalent of the famous wolf from the classic fairy story "Little Red Riding Hood" who threatens the lives of the eponymous heroine and her grandmother in the woods. On the Discworld, however, the depiction of an animal *unwillingly* behaving like a human bears an unnatural edge:

> A normal wolf wouldn't enter a cottage, even if it could open the door. Wolves didn't come near humans at all, except if there were a lot of them and it was the end of a very hard winter. And they didn't do that because they were big and bad and wicked, but because they were wolves.
> This wolf was trying to be human.
> There was probably no cure. (*WA* 129)

A story variation that could easily be portrayed in a ridiculous manner (for instance, a talking wolf displaying the same ineptitude

---

[97] Remaining at basic terms, I follow Kathryn Hume's description of *consensus reality* as the agreement "that food, oxygen, and liquid are necessary for human life; that bodies fall; that stones are solid and hard; that humans die" but also that "the impulse to depart from consensus reality is present for as long as we have had literature" (Hume xi, 30).

as Rincewind's lack in wizardry) instead becomes a harrowing subversion of fairy tales (Mason 59, 63). Pratchett provides his parody of the classic story with an unexpected twist by featuring a wolf, which is not simply an animal that behaves like a human, but moreover an animal that has been *forced* into behaving like a human by narrative imperative. Thus, it spends its life in a miserable state as neither one nor the other,[98] providing a poignant critique of "the sentimental tendency to anthropomorphize animals in many fantasy and fairy-tale contexts" (Tiffin 168). The wolf has been shaped into a human-like behavior mold because the inhabitants of the forest have heard of and *believe* in the story of "Little Red Riding Hood"—namely that the wolf must walk upright, speak, and so on.

As Kevin Paul Smith stresses, Pratchett puts a marginal character center-stage: "*Witches Abroad*'s version of 'Little Red Riding Hood' brings out the hidden voices of the tale. [...] The wolf here is no sexual predator, but a real predator warped through human interference" (142)—meaning that the wolf has begun exhibiting human behavior because he was forced to do so by the shaping powers of literary belief. Narrative imperative is at its core narrative determinism, yet rarely as absolute as in this example—*LotR* characters do not have "full control over their destiny, but they do have the use of free will, and can choose"[99] (McMurry 227), and Pratchett's protagonists generally also have the choice to remain marginal. However, in the kingdom of Genua, a place where literary belief is employed like a magic spell, such freedom of choice is negated by the power of story.

Remaining within the narratological context that epitomizes Pratchett's fiction, the most extreme form of narrative imperative ultimately denies personality. If mimesis and hypothetical scenarios are crucial components of human cognition, they consequently also form important parts of identity in a continuous and constantly

---

[98] Even though it should be in accordance with Lilith's simplified idea(l) of a fairy-tale wolf. While she does not waste any deeper reflection on the topic, Pratchett clearly shows throughout his novels how the real constantly stands in an uneasy balance with the ideal.

[99] Again, Frodo's and Bilbo's reluctance to go on an adventure is typical for such choice, as is Frodo's decision to proclaim himself Master of the One Ring at the end of *LotR*. Naturally, the characters in a novel have no true "real" choice—being fictional constructs created and directed by an author—yet on the Discworld, the concept of narrative imperative having a direct influence on characters far exceeds the destined paths of the hobbits.

revised narratological process: "*Narrative identity* is a person's internalized and evolving life story, integrating the reconstructed past and imagined future to provide life with some degree of [...] purpose" (McAdams and McLean 233), and even though fictional characters do not possess such autonomy, the stories they are part of certainly impinge on their personalities. The decisive influence of the narrative imperative on the Discworld is that it can enforce a specific preset of personal narrative bound to a larger metanarrative[100]— as with Genua, where each inhabitant must perform a certain role according to a perfect fairy tale kingdom.

On its surface, the idea of staging fairy tales to repeat their stories with actors is ridiculous, providing much of the humor and postmodern parody in the novel; digging deeper, however, the dehumanizing[101] and enforcing factors of such involuntary re-enactment are underlined. Rather than being funny, it robs people of their individuality and free will instead:

> The analysis of the classical fairytales used in *Witches Abroad* [...] shows that the values taught by these fairytales are directed at making their audience view the world in a certain way. Sleeping Beauty is rewarded for her passivity, Red Riding Hood is punished for her disobedience [...]. Granny Weatherwax does not hold with this function and disapproves of the way that stories predetermine people and make them less than human, and her deconstruction of the stories in each case acts as an intertextual revision which, by giving the narrative point of view to someone typically excluded from the fairytale, exposes and subverts the underlying premises of fairytales which we usually ignore. (Smith 152–53)

As with the Disneyland-inspired nature of the land of Genua, the ideal of a personality overrides the real personality—Lilith has an exact idea of how people ought to behave and imposes her vision on the populace. As a consequence, there is no escape from narrative imperative, also since "what people *call* each other has a very real effect on their lives" both on the Discworld and in our actual world (Webb, *Fantasy* 30). Taking up the aforementioned example regarding the role of Pratchett's witches in the novel, a person called a wicked witch

---

[100] A personal narrative is usually bound to a personal construction of a future (e.g., the aim to become an expert in a specific field of work or the wish to start a family). While these potential futures are necessary for life planning and may take inspiration from fiction as well, they become problematic when they interfere with the future of others to such a degree as to limit their own personal options.

[101] Or humanizing, in the wolf's case.

will eventually be treated as such—namely shunned or even killed in the worst-case narrative scenario.[102] In a cruel twist of Pratchett's penchant for featuring seemingly clichéd characters, it thus appears that the theatre stage of the Discworld should be prone to pogroms and literal witch hunts. There is, however, one way to fight narrative imperative—namely from within.

---

[102] As a witch remarks in *I Shall Wear Midnight*, "it's very easy to push an old lady down to the ground and take one of the doors off the barn and put it on top of her like a sandwich and pile stones on it until she can't breathe any more. And that makes all the badness go away. Except that it doesn't. Because there are other things going on, and other old ladies" (165). The bitterness of history—and a story—repeating all the time is evident.

CHAPTER 5

BREAKING THE SPELL OF NARRATIVE IMPERATIVE

ON THE DISCWORLD, REALITY IS CONSTITUTED by narrative imperative: "In Pratchett's world everything has a story in it [and] everything is part of a story" (McMurry 226), and what is believed to be true strongly enough is true. The narrative imperative should, therefore, be ubiquitous. Taking up the metaphor of the Discworld as stage again, not just the inhabitants of Genua but every individual on Pratchett's secondary world ought to live in more or less strict accordance to a fixed script, their every move and word dictated by the conventions of fantasy, fairy tales, and the numerous narrative patterns that form part of Pratchett's parody. Yet throughout his novels, there is one common method to fight the inevitability of narrative imperative—namely "the use of story to undermine the power of story" (Butler, *Companion* 266), that is to say by accepting the powers of narrative causality and then in turn utilizing said powers to undermine this causality. Since witches have a natural talent for perceiving story patterns, they can play a certain role inside these patterns to their advantage.

It is here that we come back to James' and Mendlesohn's idea of *theatre stage fantasy*, because another part of what makes the Discworld eminently postmodern is the fact that its protagonists[103] deliberately emulate stereotypical roles from specific stories and narrative patterns. Often, we see main characters perform as if they were on a stage: For instance, when Granny Weatherwax enters a card-playing competition in *WA*, at first she "strode as she usually strode. Though as soon as she passed through [a doorway] she was

---

[103] Theatricality is seen to a lesser degree in Rincewind—even though he wears a hat with the letters "Wizzard" written on it, he rarely attempts to be what he is not but would like to be (namely a powerful wizard). Instead, he often merely evokes laughter by being a coward and running away, particularly in his first appearances. Pratchett's later protagonists Vimes and Granny exhibit this deliberate acting out of a specific role (that of a witch or a city guard) to a much larger extent.

suddenly a bent old woman, hobbling along, and a sight to touch all but the wickedest heart" (WA 100–01). By acting like an inexperienced old lady she outwits card-sharks, disarming the competition by cleverly employing the narrative conventions of Beginner's Luck and "working this story to her advantage" (Smith 137):[104] Because "when an obvious innocent sits down with three experienced card sharpers and says 'How do you play this game, then?', someone is about to be shaken down until their teeth fall out" (WA 102). Following Hutcheon's observations regarding postmodern parody and its tendency to exploit artifice, Pratchett underlines the popularity of this narrative pattern and allows Granny to use it to her benefit by having her recognize its stereotypicality and exploit its power—a recurring motif in WA and the Witches series of Discworld novels in general.

However, it would be going too far to endow Pratchett's characters with an awareness that truly challenges the borders of the fictional. While postmodern literature is known for breaking down the barriers between fiction and reality, Discworld characters never go so far as to address readers directly or recognize an authorial force that guides them. Nonetheless, the Discworld's main strength—as that of postmodern literature—lies in showing the similarities between the narrative patterns of fiction and those of empirical reality:

> At its deepest level—unannounced by any direct authorial interjection—on the Discworld conditions are such that Heraclitus' axiom that "character is destiny" is upheld, and character is a fictional device. To some extent, this is trivial: the witches, wizards, and other creatures that figure in the Discworld series are written constructions, and obey the rules of plotting as we might expect them to. Part of the pleasure in reading Pratchett is derived from the way in which the reader is able to recognise the subterranean plots that the major characters are subject to, and the ways in which they breathe new life into old stories through subtle alterations in tone. (Mason 56)

Beyond this mockery and revelation of narrative patterns, however, lies a still deeper incentive within the theatricality of the Discworld. In a subtle homage to the famed Shakespeare quote that "[a]ll the world's a stage / And all the men and women merely players" (*As You Like It*

---

[104] Of course, in the end we learn that Granny is an excellent card player, but in order to win inconspicuously, she took on the role of a beginner to trick the other players and win back their brooms, which Nanny Ogg lost in an earlier game (WA 98–99, 111).

2.7.140–41) and masquerade and crossdressing, "Pratchett is actually proposing a radical social ontology for his characters. For, on Discworld, [...] acting is not something secondary, reduced to that which takes place in the theater, but rather is universalized into *the primary condition of being*" (Rayment 48–49). Acting indeed is the only manner with which one may challenge the powers of narrative imperative—by first choosing to conform to a certain role and then actively undermining narrative causality and the passivity[105] of these roles from within.

At its best, such masquerade is not a dictate but rather a personal choice for the main characters—a choice which reflects, reconsiders, and indeed constructs their identity. Consequently, acting in a certain way means *being* a certain character following a certain story, at least superficially so. We "recognize ourselves in the stories we tell about ourselves" (Ricœur 214)—and recognizing the patterns of these stories allows Pratchett's protagonists to conform to a specific role by personal choice before one is forced upon them. Herein lies the cruciality of knowing narrative conventions and how stories tend to proceed in established patterns: Pratchett uses postmodern metafictionality not to break the boundaries between author and character, as for example in Paul Auster's *City of Glass*.[106] Instead, Discworld main character Granny Weatherwax is aware of the fairy story of the old, wicked witch and decided to become a witch of her own accord before people could even begin to call her a crone[107] (Butler, *Companion* 406), thereby establishing her own role and idea of a witch within the narrative imperative. The fact that she chose "to be a witch whatever they say" (*Lords and Ladies* 12) at a young age does not change her role *per se*. What is crucial is that *she herself* consciously decided to be a witch, thereby gaining freedom to shape her reputation and self before others could do so: She is as strict and stern as stereotypical witches, but also

---

[105] The heroes of commercial parodies also act as subversion of stereotypes yet rarely achieve prominence as characters with real motivations or personal goals—there is no depth to them beyond their acting in a certain way, following a stereotypical plot, all in order to amuse readers.

[106] In which the protagonist famously visits a representation of his author.

[107] An appellation that she strongly resents because it not only highlights the darker features of a witch according to classic fairy tales but also falls into the either/or category that Lilith is so fond of. What is more, by her active choice to be an outsider, she avoids becoming an outcast instead. Thus, she lives alone (because she wants to) but is still important to her community rather than being shunned and hated.

helpful and not truly wicked. It is a freedom in a chosen role—one, however, that in turn comes with a cost.

The witches, as Jennifer Jill Fellows rightly observes, "are the moral compasses of their respective communities" (204), not because they are or consider themselves better than other people but because they are "regularly called upon to make the most awful and precise of judgments, when the choices are never clear" (Sayer 141). In other words, as deliberate outsiders at the margins of their society, they have the obligation of making the decisions that nobody else more central to the community will make.[108] Marginal but still part of society as they are, they provide a different perspective on the world and the story patterns it is subject to, and even though they potentially have tremendous power[109] to subvert or restore its order (as it also happens in the eucatastrophe that occurs at the end of *LotR* and other secondary worlds), they prefer to provide subtle corrections instead.

Pratchett's witches are aware of the necessity of trying to make sense of the world by ordering it, yet they also know of the futility of every attempt at making any such ordering final: "*Witches Abroad* is postmodern in the sense suggested by Linda Hutcheon, as a form of art that 'questions centralized, totalised, heirarchized [sic], closed systems: questions, but does not destroy [...] It acknowledges the human urge to make order, while pointing out that the orders we create are just that: human constructs'" (Smith 161). Their knowledge in marginality also holds the key to free will, to seeing grand narratives from the outside or, more fittingly, from their boundaries. For others, being affected by the determinist powers of narrative imperative more strongly, there seemingly "is no choice about ends, only about means" (Vacek 285)—yet the witches realize that even preset endings can be challenged. Throughout the entire Witches series of Discworld novels, Granny Weatherwax remains "suspicious of stories" (Mason 53), and their innate potential to dictate given outcomes. Her skepticism, however, harbors a fear of wielding narrative power herself.

The main problem for Granny is that even though she has firmly established her role as a witch, the narrative imperative might

---

[108] Being midwives and the equivalent of doctors, many of the witches' decisions involve matters of life and death.

[109] *WS* has the witches project the entire country of Lancre fifteen years into the future using a powerful spell. In later books and in general, such feats are exceedingly rare on the Discworld.

ultimately still exercise control over her. As we are reminded again and again, "Granny has everything it takes to be the perfect wicked witch, but chose long ago to reject a scripted life" (Butler, *Companion* 408). She performs her role as a witch according to her own personal interpretation, yet the intrinsic features of her personality are similar to stereotypical portrayals, among them "a quick temper, a competitive, selfish and ambitious nature, a sharp tongue, an unshakeable conviction of her own moral probity, and some considerable mental and occult powers" (Pratchett and Briggs, *Turtle Recall* 402–03). This overlapping of stereotype and personal choice leads to a constant struggle over who she is and who she could become if she embraced her full potential as a classic fairy tale witch.

Pratchett underlines that the greatest danger of becoming a stereotypical witch after all, apart from being branded as such, lies in abusing one's power, exemplified by clichéd evil laughter as a sign of madness and loss of control:

> "Cackling," to a witch, didn't just mean nasty laughter. It meant your mind drifting away from its anchor. It meant you losing your grip...It meant you thinking that the fact you knew more than anyone else in your village made you better than them. It meant thinking that right and wrong were negotiable. (*Wintersmith* 29)

Granny's sister Lilith appears to be the opposite of a cackling witch on the outskirts of town—indeed, she wants to be seen as a benevolent fairy godmother—but this is a mere mask. While feigning to be "good," she uses the power of narrative causality to the same ends as a self-superior, "evil" witch would. Granny likewise is not the opposite of Lilith but closer to her than she might like. As her sister, she too would have the possibility to utilize narrative imperative like a weapon since witches are naturally aware of its implications—it is a power prevented only by a firm moral intuition and not giving in to feelings of superiority.

The eventual confrontation of Lilith with Granny at the end of *WA* leads to a veritable clash of mindsets. Even when pushed into this role by Lilith, Granny rejects her role as the evil witch from fairy tales and continues to act out a life that defies her destined part in traditional folklore. Simultaneously, she must always keep her powers over narrative imperative in check:

> Granny Weatherwax is able to disrupt Lilith's tales for precisely the same reason that Lilith can manipulate them—she recognizes the

> power inherent in them. This means that, while exerting her abilities to combat Lilith, she must fight continually against *becoming* Lilith by interfering with people "for their own good." (Tiffin 165)

Pratchett's critique of the unreflected use of the terms "good" and "evil" as absolute measurements is shown perfectly in this broken duality expressed in Granny Weatherwax and Lilith. For all her traits typical of a wicked witch, Granny's "practical history puts her on the 'good' side of the ledger, in the same way as a cold shower and brisk run are good" (Pratchett and Briggs, *Turtle Recall* 403). Indeed, it is her down-to-earth nature and preference for the real instead of the ideal that makes her prevail and underlines another cornerstone of the Discworld novels, namely the sense of tangible reality inherent in Pratchett's secondary world. Lilith, on the other hand, pretends to be an ideal to such a determined degree that in her hands, it turns into its opposite. As a twisted mirror image of what is considered "good" in fairy tales, she does not actively aim to be evil, but her unwillingness to see the individuality of people in her grander scheme of stories makes her immoral—not merely due to her belief in the power of stories but coming from her abuse thereof to create the perfect fairy tale.

We arrive at the paradoxical conclusion that, while telling a story in *WA* (and in all the other Discworld novels), Pratchett remains deeply suspicious of the implications of his sources (fantasy and its sources in folklore and myths) as well as their often simple, preset, stereotypical patterns and happy endings—as we learn, happy endings mean "that life stops here. Stories *want* to end. They don't care what happens next…" (*WA* 267). Endings, one could be led to think, are a sort of narrative death.[110] Pratchett agrees with Tolkien's claims in OFS and shows that fantasy without critical reflection and a connection to actual reality is but escapism, much like Twoflower's expectations as a tourist in a fantasy realm in *CoM* and *LF*.

Still, Pratchett does not abandon the happy ending entirely. Having revealed the factitiousness of any ending, there is an ending for *WA* all the same, thus favoring the traditional penchant of fantasy

---

[110] The ending of a novel with no sequel leaves open the question of whether characters continue leading their lives or whether a happy ending renders the rest of their fictional lives either uninteresting or obsolete. Pratchett addressed this conundrum particularly in his narrative-heavy Witches novels with their critical glance at clichéd phrases such as "… and they lived happily ever after."

for holistic closure over postmodern openness and lack of an ending. Despite this, adding a further twist, it is an ending that is neither happy nor entirely final:

> The ending of *Witches Abroad* may seem satisfying, even happy, if the reader identifies superficially with its heroines. But it is an open ending [and] Pratchett [...] reaffirms a number of well-embedded cultural values, typified in binary pairs such as superficial and deep, authentic and factitious, real and illusory, while simultaneously leaving open the possibility that they might not, when pushed, account for the complexities with which he hopes to imbue his fictional universe. (Mason 65)

While Pratchett's perspective is not fully postmodern, endings are an ambiguous motif in any Discworld novel—he is aware of their artificiality, yet nevertheless aims to offer a momentary conclusion for the narrative arc of each book. His main criticism regarding such narrative closure is that while life is ongoing, be it on the Discworld or in empirical reality, it does not have a true ending. Imposing an artificial "end" or a goal on continuing personal narratives would restrict individuals or protagonists in their potential and freedom and cut their narrative identities short.[111]

The marginality of his witches, their role as outsiders to society, is therefore pivotal to identity and integrity, since "one of the things a witch did was stand right on the edge, where the decisions had to be made" (*LL* 33) and where endings are but the next threshold to be crossed. Interestingly, Pratchett's work also constantly follows Yuri Lotman's observation that fiction functions only when characters cross thresholds[112] and break boundaries by finding an *edge*—in other words, a marginal place—from which new ideas and narrative situations derive. What is more, his witches do not simply travel to

---

[111] Again, I should emphasize the fact that fictional lives always remain fictional and do not continue in the same manner as lives in empirical reality. Additional text such as fan fiction or encyclopedias can extend fictionality far beyond the pages of a novel, but a fictional narrative identity is, as all fiction, a finite and descriptive affair.

[112] Ekman highlights a crucial but also very underrated aspect of fantasy: "Borders and boundaries unite rather than divide [and] expand the world by joining different realities together" (126). Fantasy has been heavily influenced by folklore in this regard. Crossing from the known (one's home) into the unknown (for example the old forest outside of town) is one of *the* core elements of fairy stories and has found expression in thousands of fantasy novels. Secondary worlds are held together by the seams of thresholds, one could argue.

these transgressional places but actively fight to remain there by their choice of a marginal, outsider personality.

However, freedom in marginality is never a given but must constantly be defended against the narrative imperative at all costs, and Pratchett's protagonists are, in a way, in a constant transit:

> As story tellers we like to be at the centre of the narrative [...], although frequently the margins are both more realistic and more comfortable places to be. Granny Weatherwax is one of the rare people who fiercely preserves her marginality (while also insisting on her importance of course—she is a witch!), she is always and ever the interferer in other people's stories. (Butler, *Companion* 266)

Granny is, therefore, neither heroine nor villain but a character continuously fluctuating between the two extremes.[113] She epitomizes Pratchett's ambiguous relationship with narrative and his conflicted dependence on stories—as exemplified in the postmodern, open-ended, and yet traditional, holistic nature of the Discworld novels.

> Discworld, although technically a world run on fairy tale rules, derives much of its power and success from the fact that they are consistently challenged and subverted, most directly by the witch Granny Weatherwax, who cynically uses them or defies them as she sees fit. [...] But she herself is part of a larger story, and they follow rules, too. In a sense, she's always trying to saw off the branch she's sitting on. (Pratchett et al., *Globe* 79)

Even beyond fairy tales, marginality is necessary to escape the dictating power of narrative imperative, and the struggle to remain an outsider is not restricted to Granny Weatherwax. Pratchett's preference for marginal characters is expressed in all of his protagonists—even Rincewind, as a failed wizard, is an outsider. But in light of Granny's adamant refusal to be neither heroine nor villain, the protagonist of another series of novels can reveal additional insight into the development of the Discworld's take on narrative from the early parodies to the social criticism and satire of later books. I am, of course, talking of Samuel Vimes.

THE LINE OF DUTY

The narrative imperative is a frightening concept for Pratchett's marginal protagonists: it ensures that stories proceed in given patterns, that certain characters must succeed because they are

---

[113] Underlining that these concepts too, like good and evil or mimesis and invention, are the ends of spectrums and should not be considered binary absolutes.

defined as the heroes and that others must fail because they are the designated villains. However, this dictum is constantly broken in the Discworld novels, be it by casting a not-so-wicked witch as the main character or by having no clear villain to identify.[114] Pratchett uncovers such patterns and tropes of fantasy novels by interrupting them with constant metafictional and genre-unspecific commentaries:

> This is an element that has been present in Pratchett's novels from the first: little asides, footnotes, small riffs, all destroyed the smooth impermeability of the characteristic mass market fantasy [...] [that] depends on the willingness of the audience to suspend judgment, depends absolutely on the main character's willingness to accept everything the mage figure tells him/her about the world. (Butler, *Companion* 265)

Even more so than in the stories focusing on Granny Weatherwax, this maxim applies to the series of City Watch novels. On the surface, they are a combination of urban fantasy[115] and detective novel and have a main character who is both detective and city guard within a fantasy metropolis: Samuel Vimes, commander of the Ankh-Morpork City Watch. As we follow his investigations and patrols through Ankh-Morpork in the novels beginning with *GG*, we learn about the dynamics of the city—but also about its citizens. Moving from a fairy tale-like scenario to an urban environment, the implications of the narrative imperative adopt a greater dimension in Ankh-Morpork because, with more people that may believe in a story, narrative belief also gains more power. Instead of forcing stories on individuals to control their behavior, here, the spark of one idea can lead to a vastly bigger story, and the social implications of these movements allow for an even more variable approach to storytelling and the question of putting secondary characters center-stage in a far more complex space.

---

[114] Or, perhaps even more drastically, by making villainous characters both realistic and relatable. More often than not, they are driven by urges that are anything but otherworldly: Inquisitor Vorbis is driven by religious fervor, Jonathan Teatime by brutal ambition—Pratchett flatly refuses to paint his antagonists as mere caricatures.

[115] Not to be confused with the *genre* called urban fantasy which is predominantly set in modern metropolises and offers a more contemporary background to the supernatural. I describe Pratchett's City Watch series as "urban" because the novels are often taking place entirely within the city walls of Ankh-Morpork, which is however still more of a clichéd mock-medieval fantasy city than an urban sprawl—at least in the earliest Watch books.

The Problem with Heroes

As noted, Pratchett's protagonists normally do not choose to be, or are not forced into the role of a hero—their *choice* is a different one but nevertheless one that unexplicitly confirms their status of major importance to the stories they become part of. Consequently, his main characters are not categorized as such neither in the Discworld companions nor in the novels, "hero" being a term that Pratchett is skeptical about, to say the least: "[...] I dislike heroes. You can't trust the buggers. They always let you down" (Pratchett, *Slip* 104). The reason for such dislike stems from Pratchett's knowledge of derivative fantasy of the 1960s and 1970s and their simplified portrayal of heroes. When the Discworld stages the clichés encountered in these books, being a hero means adhering to narrative expectations of such precursors since characters in this role are naturally at the center of attention—fates that Pratchett's non-heroes constantly try to evade. Marginality is therefore also sought by Samuel Vimes, protagonist of the City Watch series of the Discworld novels. A character equally as inspired by fantasy as by hard-boiled detective stories, Vimes knows his city and its goings-on. Echoing Ed McBain, Raymond Chandler, and film noir (*GG* 10; James, "City Watch" 197–98), Pratchett's merging of detective fiction and fantasy is one of the defining features of the City Watch novels and underlines Mason's observation that on the Discworld, the everyday life of everyday people in a fantasy world is of central importance—be it in rural parts or in an urban environment.

The reader thus follows Vimes' everyday duty of keeping law and order in a melting pot of humans, dwarfs, trolls, and other species. His relationship to the city is "loving but critical, and as the series extends, he adds to a world-weary resignation, an increasing cynicism" (Mendlesohn, *Rhetorics* 91). For a fantasy character that we consider the protagonist, he exhibits an uncharacteristically unheroic and practical-minded, even embittered attitude towards his secondary world. Like Granny Weatherwax, he does not hold to the lofty ideal that the heroes of fantasy worlds aspire to but must constantly face the harsh daily life of the people outside the main narrative—a defining characteristic that he retains even as he develops in different adventures:

> Vimes is the lens through which we see Ankh-Morpork. His attitude to the poverty he sees and the culture of entitlement which undermines protest is [...] essential and it is easy to miss the point that he *does not* have to be this way. Compare this to any other fantasy

> author who springs to mind. Social mobility almost always includes a change in moral understanding in which the hero/ine is co-opted to paternalism and suppressions. [...] Vimes retains his original critique in which hard work and honesty lead not to success in life but to an existence as everyone's victim. (Mendlesohn, "Faith" 251)

Due to this harsh outlook, Vimes constantly keeps himself marginal. While he indeed rises both in social status and in fame over the course of several books, his identity continues to derive from this unchangedly critical view of the city, its inhabitants, and most importantly himself. As Leverett underlines, "Vimes acts not for the physical rewards of the trope, but for his own integrity" (168). Indeed, his very sense of morality is dependent on his marginality—like Granny Weatherwax, taking on an authorial role as a guard whose decisions are beyond any doubt would result in the loss of this realist perspective. In Ankh-Morpork, a simple everyday life (as compared to the grandiose heroics of classic fantasy) is key to keeping one's senses sharp and moral code intact.

Yet throughout the City Watch novels, the peace of daily routine is constantly threatened by civil unrest or plots to overthrow the government. The inherent ambiguity of many Discworld novels is underscored by the combination of two classic narratives in *GG*: While the progress of Vimes' investigations largely follows the patterns of detective stories, the main plot he investigates is driven by another story straight out of fantasy, namely the return of the lost king and true ruler. The fantasy aspect of the Discworld remains dominant, and therefore a secret group summons a dragon solely for the purpose of it being defeated by a rightful hero (who is but a strawman hero that they recruit and then can enthrone). Using the narrative imperative for a political upheaval, the conspirators re-enact an entire plot of clichéd fantasy, knowing that if enough bravado and drama are added to staged events, people *will* believe them and this belief will spread as truth among the populace. As a citizen of Ankh-Morpork puts it, when "a stranger comes into the city under the thrall of the dragon and challenges it with a glittery sword, [...] there's only one outcome. [...] It's probably destiny" (*GG* 205). It is no wonder, then, that the false "hero" must slay the dragon that terrorizes the city because narrative imperative demands so—but the story does not end there, since the dragon returns after the crowning of the king and wreaks more havoc.

Again, Pratchett peeks beyond the endings of "classic" fantasy stories and points out that a so-called (ideal) happy ending is either premature or illusory—the cynical endings of many detective stories act as a (real) counterweight to fantasy make-believe. Adding a further ironic twist, Pratchett lets characters who are normally of no major importance to a story be heroes in spite of their sarcasm or resistance to this stereotype. While many detectives of film noir must ultimately accept their defeat, Vimes and his fellow watchmen emerge successful and manage to defeat the dragon for good. Yet in this success, similar to Granny's powers, lies the danger of becoming used to being center-stage and thus losing one's marginality, moral code, and integrity.

Vimes stands on the fragile balance of denying heroism in favor of marginality and rising to the need for a hero and thereby garnering attention. In order to make a larger-scale difference, he must step out of his marginal role, yet only in crucial moments (mostly to keep the peace in the city) in order not to put himself under the influence of increased narrative imperative by longer center-stage exposure. On the Discworld, the role of the hero consequently must not be accepted for an extended period of time, as it is too close to an illusory ideal that will ultimately overshadow the real. A preference for the "real" in a low-mimetic context, here in a secondary world of fantasy, may seem highly incongruous and ironic, but it also triggers a necessary shift in perspective.

The dedication at the beginning of *GG* is a perfect example of this conscious shift and shows that the narrative "ideal" of the hero brutally neglects and marginalizes less central characters affected by such story patterns:

> They may be called the Palace Guard, the City Guard, or the Patrol. Whatever the name, their purpose in any work of heroic fantasy is identical: it is, round about Chapter Three (or ten minutes into the film) to rush into the room, attack the hero one at a time, and be slaughtered. No one ever asks them if they want to. This book is dedicated to those fine men. (*GG* 7)

Once more, it is a Hutcheonesque "desire to tell the story of those who, in fantasies or films, are given no lines at all, and no voices of their own" (James, "City Watch" 199), showing the importance of the postmodern for the Discworld novels. Yet Pratchett goes further than just giving a voice to outsiders: his characters, while being at the center of their story, still have to fight narrative conventions that threaten them from every side. In a classic fantasy story, being identified by what their normal roles are—witches or guards, in this context—they would very quickly be pushed to the margins of interest again. On the other hand, if they were to embrace any extended heroism thrust upon them, they would quickly outgrow their original roles and abandon their marginality for the lime-light.

To add to this skepticism regarding heroes, there *is* a classic heroic figure in the City Watch novels. Watch member Carrot Ironfoundersson has all the stereotypical features of a hero: He is exceptionally tall, muscular, benign, and believes in doing good for its own purpose.[116] He appears to be of royal descent, yet like Sam Vimes and Granny Weatherwax, he actively and successfully tries to escape the role that narrative imperative has in store for him (being king) despite having obvious signs of rulership:

> He has a crown-shaped birthmark at the top of his left arm. Coupled with his sword, his charisma, his natural leadership, and his deep and almost embarrassing love of Ankh-Morpork, this rather suggests that he is the long-lost rightful heir to the throne of the city. It is a subject that he avoids, to the point—it has been hinted—of destroying any written evidence to the fact. (Pratchett and Briggs, *Turtle Recall* 73)

Carrot defies his destined role by taking on another one in this "theatre of the real," namely that of a watchman.[117] He is happy with his occupation as a guardsman of the Ankh-Morpork City Watch, and never is it even suggested that he desires to claim his right to the throne. This is far from the crowning of a false king in *GG* or, to pick a classic example from genre fantasy, Aragorn's eventual inheritance of the throne of Gondor at the end of *LotR*. While it may take him a long and arduous journey to get there, narrative convention demands that the rightful king must be crowned at the (happy) ending of a story.[118]

As pointed out before, Pratchett is critical of such closure to narrative patterns—the ending of *LotR* is by no means an example of bad fantasy, but it spawned numerous further fantasy novels ending with a return of the "true" king or just ruler. As Stephen Potts asserts,

---

[116] These characteristics and the manner in which he is usually illustrated in the Discworld comics and companions make him strongly reminiscent of "classic" Disney heroes. Indeed, his unshaken belief that all people are good at heart has ironically earned him respect even in the sarcastic, cutthroat metropolis of Ankh-Morpork.

[117] Taking this factor into account, he is basically a fantasy version of comic-book-alter-ego Clark Kent. Carrot's secret identity is also his life, however—he never shows himself as Superman or in his case as king.

[118] It is no surprise that Aragorn's crowning in *LotR* follows a classic fairy tale pattern. Even more so than in the book, the multiple endings of *The Return of the King* (2003), Peter Jackson's third film of his *LotR* adaptation, are essentially an overtly kitschy and extended happy ending as in a prolonged fairy tale.

Tolkien too actively tried to avoid the simplistic heroism that abounds in the portrayal of heroes in fantasy inspired by *LotR* and which Pratchett parodies with Carrot:

> In *The Hobbit*, Tolkien intentionally avoids a hero in the romance mode, since he found most classic heroes subject to a vice he called by the Anglo-Saxon word *ofermod*, defined as "overmastering pride" (Clark 49). Bilbo, on the other hand, is anything but overly proud. Although middle-aged for a hobbit, he comes across as a child in many respects: obsessed with food and comfort, leery of participating in adventures—in short, a little guy content to remain wrapped up in his own little world. (Potts 222)

Nevertheless, both Bilbo and Frodo, as pointed out before, eventually accept their role in the grander scheme of Middle-earth and the War of the Ring—they do not express pride in this role but they ultimately cannot escape the narrative imperative (insofar as it applies to *LotR* as a specific story pattern). As with Tolkien's complex but in the end still largely binary approach to the good/evil dichotomy, the simplification of heroes in the fantasy of the 1960s and 1970s was a direct consequence of the adoption of his blueprint for the genre.

Pratchett's City Watch novels offer a contrast to these fantasy books and reveal the dichotomy at work beneath the surface, expressed in the two "heroes" we are faced with. Vimes "is the Everyman, with whose degradations and triumphs we almost invariably sympathise" (James, "City Watch" 194), while Carrot is the archetype of heroes encountered in classic fantasy—although he aims to be an everyman[119] as well. Over the course of the novels, both Vimes and Carrot develop and rise in society; yet it is Vimes who—while not being crowned like Aragorn—becomes part of the aristocracy of Ankh-Morpork at the end of the second Watch novel, *Men At Arms*. Here we have another subversive move by Pratchett, because through "a combination of merit, circumstance, and the Patrician Vetinari's Machiavellian patronage, [Vimes] rises to become His Grace, the Duke of Ankh, Commander Sir Samuel Vimes" (Butler, *Companion* 399).[120]

---

[119] A much more positive-minded everyman than the cynic Vimes, though.

[120] Another major factor that should not be left unmentioned is his wife, Lady Sybil Ramkin. As "the richest woman in Ankh-Morpork" (Pratchett and Briggs, *Turtle Recall* 390), and a part of the city's aristocracy, she introduced Vimes to high society after they got married in *MAA*. While he despises the upper class (apart from Lady Sybil herself, who is remarkably down-to-earth and kind) since they are far removed from any of the harsh realities that he is dealing with on a daily basis, it nonetheless played a role in his becoming a member of nobility himself.

A background character from classic fantasy novels is moved from the margins toward center-stage, which means that his struggle to still remain obscure—and morally intact—grows harder in later novels. Nonetheless, Vimes is keen on maintaining the constant doubt between appearance and sense of self like Granny Weatherwax:

> Sam Vimes shaved himself. It was his daily act of defiance, a confirmation that he was ... well, plain Sam Vimes.
> Admittedly he shaved himself in a mansion, and while he did so his butler read out bits from the *Times*, but they were just ... circumstances. It was still Sam Vimes looking back at him from the mirror. The day he saw the Duke of Ankh in there would be a bad day. 'Duke' was just a job description, that's all. (*Thud!* 11–12)

As he becomes more involved in Discworld politics, Vimes' individuality—his "real"—is under threat of becoming too central (Neely 233), and thus being subsumed by an abstract political or aristocratic "ideal." Vimes, like Carrot, affirms his sense of self by denying the role that has been given to him—that of a Duke—and aims to remain in his chosen role of watchman. Nevertheless, "he oscillates between his own gaze of himself in his room dressing up in nobbish clothes and his gaze of himself playing an ordinary policeman on the streets" (Rayment 50)—the view of his image in the mirror acts as a literal reflection of the role he is currently expected to play and a reminder of the difference between his appearance and his identity.[121]

Vimes and Granny are both suspicious of appearances even as they form part of who they are. For them, what people *do* is decidedly more important than whom they appear to be. Despite all the theatricality that the Discworld encourages, dressing or pretending to belong to a specific role or group does not automatically complete one's personality—without individual action, there is no individuality, just a mask, an unreflected narrative or an image like Lilith's Genua, one that has no basis in reality:

> In the end Lily loses to [Granny] because she cannot tell the difference between 'what's really real and what isn't', between her own image and her-*self*. Fascinated by stories and mirrors she lives in the world of what Lacan has called the Imaginary—the world a child lives in before it recognises that it is an individual separate and distinct from its mother. (Sayer 149)

---

[121] Vimes and Granny never forget that the role they play also *is* their identity—hence, they are very careful about changing their appearance and behaving in a radically different manner to their original roles as witch and watchman.

Instead of enacting an ideal in front of the mirror and then using this storified self-image to perform a role in the Discworld's reality, Vimes and Granny accept their reflection as what it is—a mere reflection and not what they are. But they also know it is a reminder of what they appear like and might become if unchecked.

As the end of WA reveals, mistaking the reflection for the real means losing oneself and not knowing who you are in the long run.[122] Trapped in an otherworldly realm filled with countless mirrors, Granny is tasked with finding a way back to the Discworld. She instinctively realizes that she needs no mirror to know who she is:

> Esme turned, and a billion figures turned with her.
> 'When can I get out?'
> WHEN YOU FIND THE ONE THAT'S REAL.
> 'Is this a trick question?'
> No.
> Granny looked down at herself.
> 'This one,' she said. (WA 281)

Unlike her sister Lilith, who is facing the same challenge earlier and ends up running "on through the endless reflections" (WA 278), Granny remains *grounded* in reality and finds a way out of the illusions by looking at *herself*, not her mirror image.

Accepting the image for the real ultimately means losing touch with reality and moral behavior: The witch would start cackling, and the guard would embrace his hard-earned aristocracy—the uniting factor being that each would regard themselves as something ideal and abandon their true identity. "Vetinari [...], Vimes, Granny Weatherwax—all are aware that, as far as power is concerned, appearances do not just matter but *must be maintained at all costs*" (Rayment 59). Carrot, for all his heroic features and signs of entitlement, also refrains from such *ofermod* arrogance. He, like Vimes and Granny, has a moral code and personal integrity that must constantly be defended against outside forces as well as the "characters' own *darkness within*" (Rana 7), be it alcoholism, righteousness, or claims to power. For Pratchett's characters, to give in to entitlement, as it happens so often in classic fantasy, would mean becoming entangled in the meshes

---

[122] Another famous example from fantasy fiction is the mirror of Erised in *Harry Potter and the Sorcerer's Stone*. Rather than showing one's reflection, this object instead shows the innermost desire of anyone who stands in front of it—and depending on the intensity of this desire, the viewer may prefer vision to reality.

of narrative imperative and losing the possibility of expressing doubt about stereotypical story patterns. There is thus a constant altercation between real and ideal, between inner self and appearance.

THE FICTION OF MORALITY

All of this self-realization of Discworld characters in the face of narrative imperative culminates in their knowledge of clichés and the patterns of stories. The Discworld's protagonists must be aware of their pre-determined role in classic storytelling to evade its implications. Yet even more importantly, this realization of a role does not simply allow characters such as Sam Vimes and Granny Weatherwax to escape the dictates of their stereotypes and retain a sense of self in a secondary world determined by narrative conventions. It is also a sensible way to live and not to aim for a happy ending or power but rather to maintain a healthy sense of critical doubt in one's world—even if this world is a fantasy world filled with impossible phenomena and incongruous situations.

The fight against narrative stereotypes effectively means destroying prejudice and false assumptions, beliefs that hold hidden dangers and may lead to single-sided conclusions. Specifically, Pratchett underlines how doubt is the crucial instrument in dispelling any "absolute" claims to truth or how life should be led—assumptions that his headstrong protagonists are not far away from: "The ability to commit evil in the belief that one is just doing one's job, or, worse, that one is doing it for the good of the community or for one's god [...] reconnects with Pratchett's continual assertion that our only salvation lies in a clear and truthful sense of our own identity" (Mendlesohn, "Faith" 245). By realizing their position on the margins of narrative conventions, Vimes and Granny can see beyond the superficiality of stories about perfect heroes and happy endings, and reveal the darker motifs and untold stories that lie behind them. At the same time, as we have learned, their capability "to insert the sharp axe edge of refusal into the tale" (Butler, *Companion* 265), ensures that they are both under the constant danger of becoming too central and themselves falling prey to the patterns of stereotypical stories or using their power beyond moral constraints.[123]

What Pratchett makes clear is that in his incongruous fiction, the dichotomy of good/evil so typical of fantasy is neither applicable

---

[123] Even though they constantly violate story constraints.

nor acceptable. Nevertheless, he remains aware of the necessity of a differentiation between good and evil as ends of a spectrum that allows for moral improvement—as Granny claims in another novel, "[t]here's no greys, only white that's got [sic] grubby" (*Carpe Jugulum* 210). Clearly reflecting Pratchett's critical but ultimately benign view of humanity, his main characters show kindness and live morally without ever falling into the stereotypical portrayal of "good" characters in classic fantasy. Their innate sense of justice is relatable for readers, yet their thoughts and deeds are far from being beyond any doubt:

> Pratchett is too ruthlessly honest to allow us to take the connection too far. We are not even allowed to assume that we have identified the good guys. […] That we assume we know which side we are on is entirely due to a set of cultural expectations which have become embedded in the action adventure genres: reverting back to the 'us' and 'them' divide. It is the unquestioned *belief* that we do what we do because we are good, and you do it because you are evil: identity (and all too often skin colour or scales), rather than motive or result is the distinction. Pratchett makes good use of this moral trap and provides all the evidence we need to question our assumptions. (Mendlesohn, "Faith" 242–43, my emphasis)

Pratchett unmasks the false simplicity that storytelling may create. This is why his characters seem to be *so* at odds with their world again and again: The Discworld being a secondary world mirroring countless other worlds and motifs, it would be easy for its inhabitants (and readers) to simply become refamiliarized with dichotomies and accept them without reflection—they are surrounded by stories, and recounted stories are easier to digest than a "real" inner-fictional life.

On the other hand, postmodern philosophy and literature have revealed that *any* belief is a construct, and Vimes and Granny are "self-aware enough to recognize that these beliefs themselves are fictions, and thus can be bent as needed" (Fellows 224). They thus refrain from accepting the absolute measurements often encountered in classic fantasy and allow for a more open and pluralistic idea of fiction as well as good and evil on the Discworld—while at the same time fiercely defending their own positions.

The prevalent down-to-earth nature of the Discworld thus applies to the portrayal of evil in Pratchett's fantasy as well. Reflecting his progress from the earlier to later Discworld novels, Pratchett largely abandoned the idea of a larger, supernatural evil for more human evils by the late 1990s and early 2000s. Evil forces on the Discworld are not symbolic and all-powerful as in *LotR* or *LF*, but deeply human and personal.[124] Lilith is no Sauron but a flawed individual who tries to force her own version of what she thinks is "good" onto others. Tied to this very relatable concept is Hannah Arendt's idea that for evil to succeed, remaining neutral is all which is needed—behavior which we also find on the Discworld. Rather than using a binary model of good and evil like much of classic genre fantasy, Pratchett instead opts for a far more realistic and unsettling alternative. Clearly, the moral core of Discworld characters is dependent on passive acceptance or active choice:

> The nature of evil is central to any construction of morality. Here Pratchett is firmly with the likes of Bonhoeffer in his belief that evil is more about the complicity of the ordinary human being than the result of madness or the desire to inflict pain. [...] Pratchett understands the nature of evil and it is not in his nature to create any character who is nothing but evil. (Mendlesohn, "Faith" 244–45)

After the first Discworld novels, which still featured an almost entirely supernatural evil—most prominently the Dungeon Dimensions, akin to Tolkien's dark forces or other "absolute" villains—the obstacles that hinder the main characters took on a more relatable form.

Instead of putting the whole world at stake as in quest fantasy novels, Pratchett's protagonists are confronted less frequently with evil but rather the aforementioned reluctance to do good or preference to remain neutral. Lord Havelock Vetinari, de facto ruler and tyrant of Ankh-Morpork, sums up this "passive evil":

> 'Down there,' he said, 'are people who will follow any dragon, worship any god, ignore any iniquity. All out of a kind of humdrum, everyday badness. Not the really high, creative loathesomeness of the great sinners, but a sort of mass-produced darkness of the soul. Sin, you might say, without a trace of originality. They accept evil not because they say *yes*, but because they don't say *no*.' (GG 392)

Vetinari, too, acknowledges the dangers of blindly following a

---

[124] At a first glance, one notable exception seems to be the so-called "Summoning Dark" in *T!*—a sentient demonic power which begins to possess Vimes over the course of the novel. Regardless, Vimes does not destroy this entity but instead drives it away. By the later Watch novel *SN*, the Summoning Dark has in fact become a sort of "companion" for Vimes (170), acting both as a reminder of his own darker side and as a supernatural helper. While otherworldly, this force is thus not stereotypically evil but—like so much else on the Discworld—far more complex than it appears.

doctrine without hesitance or doubt, yet also emphasizes that people are often not really evil but merely passive instead. Such an approach to the nature of evil is rather unusual for fantasy fiction of the 1980s and 1990s—particularly in novels considered to be a parody of the genre—and shows the sting beneath Pratchett's evident humor.

In the end, Pratchett's characters refuse to conform to Mendlesohn's observation that in fantasy, "function follows form." Characters who appear evil are evil—this is the cliché. Pratchett undermines it by making his characters appear one way and yet having them not comply to their role in classic fantasy narratives. As we have seen, they act to survive in the face of the overpowering narrative imperative, but on related terms, they also embrace this struggle. For them, it is an active choice of a certain role, one which reminds them of whom they could become if they do not remain on guard. All of Pratchett's protagonists are deeply moral in this respect:

> So [...] Rincewind the wizard is neither brave nor honourable in the terms of conventional fantasy, but he has a clear view of the way the world works, and the extent to which he is willing to be complicit in the actions that most people take to get along in it, [and] his much trumpeted cowardice [...] is a consequence of his ethical code. Similarly, Granny Weatherwax's rigidity masks compassion, while Vimes, for all that he burns with indignation, understands compromise and mercy. In all three cases, their moral weight rests on their identity and sense of self. (Mendlesohn, "Faith" 240)

In classic fantasy, cowards, witches, and city guards are neither the center of attention nor predominantly "good" characters—in any stereotypical story, their perspective would be either bad or unimportant. Pratchett's characters escape this clichéd storytelling by an unusual amount of down-to-earthness and a personal idea of morality beyond the will to do good for the narrative's sake of a happy ending.

The power of narrative imperative is linked to the reduction of complexity. If stories are a method of easing understanding of the intricacies of empirical reality and retaining information necessitates the fictionalization and thus simplification of actual experience, then this method holds a hidden danger. As the real is turned into fictional recounting of empirical facts and situations, it is only one step away from elaborating these fictionalities into an abstract goal or impression. The narrative imperative simplifies and nullifies the real, replacing it with an ideal that may gain more relevance than the real itself. Linked to this simplification is the reduction of individuals to a 'means to an end' as exemplified by Lilith's fairy tale kingdom. Paraphrasing Immanuel Kant, Granny Weatherwax places the categorical imperative above the narrative imperative: "You shouldn't turn the world into stories. You shouldn't treat people like they was *characters*, like they was [sic] *things*" (WA 270).[125] Life on the Discworld is always in danger of falling victim to narrative (or philosophical) trappings, and although Granny is an immensely powerful character herself, she remains opposed to any position or measure that abuses their privilege. Likewise, Vimes is a fierce idealist in his occupation as a watchman, yet he does not let himself be defined by it in an abstract, entitled way.

Paying such unusual attention to the potential lives of fictional characters instead of their narrative function within the larger story does not remain limited to the plot of Pratchett novels—as it turns out, the ambiguity between real and ideal is rooted in his secondary world itself, both on a macro- and a microcosmic level. Although the Discworld might appear to be a simple stage that provides the environment for his characters to play chosen roles, here, too, the difference between appearance and actual inner-fictional reality reveals Pratchett's secondary world as much more than merely background.

---

[125] Granny's exclamation about turning people into characters remains one of the few instances where an (arguably) truly metafictional moment occurs in the Discworld novels, one which is however never followed to a wider extent as in the fiction of authors like Italo Calvino or Paul Auster. Doing so would break the spell of a believable secondary world.

Chapter 6
Reflections on World-Making

MUCH OF GENRE FANTASY AIMS to present us with a secondary world which, while clearly influenced by empirical reality, nonetheless exhibits a specific otherworldliness, providing readers with an unfamiliar and supernatural space. Pratchett's world both follows and rejects this technique: his secondary world is undoubtedly vastly different from our actual world—the Discworld is flat and exists only thanks to the abundant powers of magic and narrative causality—yet at the same time it is a realm that refrains from emphasizing these supernatural features so much as to overshadow the daily chores of the main characters in the novels. Doing so would focus on the world as a representative stage to merely awe readers and would leave out the common factors of everyday life that are so characteristic of the Discworld.

On the other hand, fantasy often focuses on *presenting* a story set on a secondary world—story being the dominant force, the secondary world often acts merely as an elaborate background. Pratchett is equally critical of this approach to fantasy, emphasizing the importance that (as with individuality) the portrayal of a secondary world must not be neglected in favor of a story. Indeed, just like space and time are joined in the chronotope, story and world are intertwined and not opposites (McCabe 268). As exemplified in the preceding chapters, any fiction placing emphasis on an artificial, ideal story following narrative imperative is one-sided because it neglects inner-fictional reality: "The only weapon of power, its only strategy against this defection, is to reinject the real and the referential everywhere, to persuade us of the reality of the social, of the gravity of the economy and the finalities of production" (Baudrillard 23). On the Discworld, the generally skeptical attitude of characters reminds us of this neglected "real," even if it is literary, and in extension stresses that a secondary world must also function according to "real" rules.

For instance, it may feature allusions to the mechanisms that nurture and keep a society running even if they do not form part of the main narrative. Nevertheless, these dictums are never so strict as to detract from Pratchett's sources—unlike China Miéville's fantasy, which criticizes stereotypical fantasy by replacing its overt features with socialist ideas, the Discworld remains open about its indebtedness to Tolkien and fellow authors of classic fantasy.

The Fantasy of the Everyday

The aforementioned reinjection of the real is inextricably linked to the interdependency of defamiliarization and refamiliarization. Featuring content typical for a genre is not only convenient but of course also necessary when writing in said genre—for Pratchett, both to acknowledge one's sources and to find a method of turning them to new ends: "The reason clichés become clichés is that they are the hammers and screwdrivers in the toolbox of communication" (*GG* 176)—and by extension, of innovation. Pratchett is far from simply ridiculing or pointing out the fallacies of stereotypical content in literature—he is neither commercial parodist nor cultural pessimist[126] in this regard. What he does instead is underline the uses as much as the fallacies that lie in this toolbox of the human mind, reflecting his ideas regarding "human" nature.[127]

> [T]hese are basically literary devices Pratchett uses to produce quintessentially humanist tales: not humanist in the modern sense of a scientific and universal secular religion—Pratchett's idiom is unmistakably local, that is, English (not even 'British')—but in the best classical, pre-modern tradition (and this is a link with Tolkien) of the human, sceptical and tolerant. [...] As such, Pratchett's

---

[126] The "Grimdark" subgenre of fantasy can be considered a dark parody of fantasy clichés. Arguably the most popular (and undoubtedly famous) example are George R. R. Martin's *Song of Ice and Fire* books: Classic fantasy tropes such as the knight in shining armor are revealed as fatally flawed concepts (a good example being Jaime Lannister), and the general mood of the books is deeply misanthropic. Pratchett's novels, in contrast, still feature hope for all their cynicism.

[127] Since "humanism" has seen numerous interpretations in philosophy, I continue to refer to this matter as the aforementioned "moral code" of Discworld protagonists and characters. For one, it underlines what Pratchett deemed most important in his books, namely protecting one's morality and sense of self even in the face of overwhelming odds. Secondly, with all the various fantasy races populating his secondary world, "humanism" would be a strange term to apply to dwarfs, trolls, and other species—"moral code" is much more encompassing and thus appropriate.

> stories partake of a postmodern emphasis on the local, plural and contingent; they refresh rather than dessicate the contemporary soul. (Curry 137)

While his breaking of boundaries is indeed postmodern, Pratchett never loses himself in debates about fictionality and world-making to such an extent that they might interfere with the pragmatic nature of his characters or the progressing of his stories—despite his criticism, narrative and its powers on his world remain the focus. The Discworld consequently accepts the multitudinousness of contemporary culture, but Pratchett's main attention rests on the subtle irony and self-awareness of postmodern literature rather than on its iconoclastic dimensions.

Therefore, his use of incongruous humor is not applied as the ultimate tool to deconstruct meaning, but rather for emphasis of clichéd storytelling—that is, to point out the constructedness of any meaning in the same manner as its necessity. The tropes and clichés established by Tolkien and reused by later fantasy authors are ridiculed throughout all the Discworld novels, yet on the level of world-making, Pratchett does not resort to parody in the same manner as *BotR*'s gleeful mocking of Middle-earth. The internal consistency of the Discworld as a world in itself is undoubtedly one of its major and long-term appeals, and its only superficially humorous or incongruous display of everyday life on a fantasy world reveals a hidden depth beneath the jokes and absurdities:

> [T]his *is* a fantasy world, with all the unusual suspects: wizards, witches, gods and heroes. The twist is that it is taken seriously; not taken seriously as a fantasy, but taken seriously as a world.
> In this I owe a debt to G. K. Chesterton, who pointed out on many occasions that the fantastic, when looked at properly, is much less interesting (and a lot less fantastic) than the everyday. (Pratchett and Kidby [1])

The everyday life of fantasy people was a central topic of the Discworld from its beginnings, yet it became even more important as the series progressed—and was responsible for its success and credibility despite the continuous parody.

It is perhaps the most enduring and robust aspect of Pratchett's fiction that he turned the genre on its head in more than one way—not just in making fun of it, but in filling it with a healthy dose of reality and a focus on individual lives rather than the epic proportions of a secondary world:

> The comedy itself depended in part on puns, gags, and—often very obvious—jokes, but its mainspring was in the absurdities opened up by placing characters and tropes drawn from the fantasy genre in the context of a world that otherwise followed the rules of ordinary life, as conceived by English readers of the late twentieth century. (Mason 55)

Discworld humor, for all its parodist potential and abundance, is nonetheless part of a secondary world that can be taken seriously even as it makes fun of itself. Stories of classic fantasy are parodied, yet their problematic features—favoring the ideal over the real, putting individual lives into a greater, impersonal context of quests that have to be fulfilled—always shine through. The constant struggle between ideal and real applies to the world-making of the Discworld as much as to its storytelling. Opting for neither one nor the other, Pratchett's creation rests in an uneasy balance between (inner-fictional) reality and physical impossibility: As underlined in several novels, "the Discworld exists right on the edge of reality" (*WA* 8; Clute and Grant 783). More precisely perhaps, it seems to stand on the edge of reality and fantasy; on the one hand, it is an impossible world that does not follow the rules of physics and the probability of a representation of empirical reality; on the other hand, as pointed out before, too much impossibility or narrative freedom would make it irrational and impractical to read. The interdependency of the narrative imperative therefore acts as a kind of framework, which remains in play even as it is broken. It is imperative that story is followed: The characters need to fulfill certain narrative conventions (even while they may express doubts about them or break them in favor of others) in order to guarantee reader enjoyment—the pattern may be broken but must be replaced with another one.

Therefore, even though the Discworld novels also provide stories that surpass the life of individuals and put them into grander (narrative) schemes, in the end, their personal perspective and attitude remain the prime focus. In addition, it should again be emphasized regarding Pratchett's protagonists that what we read about them is but *part* of their ongoing narrative lives, of which we are given the illusion that they continue beyond the novels. The fictionality of the Discworld (as with that of any other fictional creation) must not be denied, yet it is implied that neither its spatial expanses nor the lives of its characters end when we close one of the books. Once again, the "as if" portrayal of fictional worlds is replaced by the mimesis of an automonous, self-contained, inner-literary reality.

Nevertheless, a large part of Pratchett's skepticism towards stories lies in the aforementioned fact that endings always seem artificial. In several Discworld novels, the story continues beyond a happy ending has been forced upon the world—and therefore, the dragon returns despite having been defeated, the mighty barbarian has grown old, and the witches see the cracks beneath the surface of the staged fairy tale ending. For Pratchett as for his characters, "there's more to life than narrative" (*Sourcery* 207), and an imposed sense of closure at the end of a story.

However, this is not to say that the Discworld novels completely abandon endings altogether. To do so would mean to deny the fantasy core of the books: As closure is an integral part of classic fantasy, the Discworld novels both ridicule and yet feature endings of their own. John Clute notes that "salvation provides the understory for all of Pratchett's work" (30), a crucial component of fantasy à la Tolkien, yet the apparent lack of global eucatastrophe in each novel offers a much more personal perspective compared to the large-scale salvations we encounter in classic fantasy. The light-hearted and ironic commentary in the novels on how stories should end and what is implied thereby once more puts the Discworld novels close to postmodern irony. All the same, Pratchett *knows* that endings, though as artificial and constructed as any meaning, are nonetheless necessary. The mimesis of empirical reality both challenges and reaffirms the human predisposition for understanding life through narrative frameworks. Derived from such observations, the Discworld is likewise not a realm which is visible only in the novels, but a world that seemingly extends beyond the parts of it that we read about.

IMMERSIVE FANTASY

Particularly in fantasy, with its strong emphasis on world-making, providing the impression that the spatial expanses of a world continues outside of the narrative provided in the text is essential. Pratchett presented the Discworld as a series of both connected and segmented spaces in *CoM*, yet these connections became ever more intricate as further books set in the same world were released. The increasing complexity operating behind the novels puts the Discworld close to one fantasy sub-categorization[128] by Farah Mendlesohn that deals with world-making in particular: immersive fantasy. In this definition, the secondary world aims for a completeness and continuity that ventures far beyond the immediate story: "In the *immersive fantasy*, the point of world-building is to create something that can be existed in. If one turns the corner of the street, one will not run off the page of the author's speculation because the coherence of the world is such that out of sight of the author *it forms itself*" (Mendlesohn, *Rhetorics* 71; my emphasis). In Mendlesohn's framework, Tolkien's Middle-earth is a prime example of fantasy that gives readers the illusion of being a holistic and continuous secondary world, and the influence of its claim to completeness concerning the languages, mythology, and historical background of a fictional realm cannot be underestimated for the development of the genre.

But where many fantasy authors failed to reproduce the academic thoroughness and knowledge of Tolkien,[129] Pratchett follows his example insofar as he focuses on a smaller, more personal scale. The quest-fantasy structure of the early Discworld novels, in which "the reader learns about the alien world along with the main character(s)" is replaced by characters that "are at home in the strange world […] and the reader has to work out how it works from the clues that are given" (Ekman 7).

Mendlesohn's obversations regarding immersive fantasy point back to the problem of narrative imperative: As the grand story of saving a secondary world is central for the plot of a stereotypical fantasy, the smaller problems and everyday lives of individuals are far less important. On a world-making scale, this effectively means that the focus of a novel abandons the perspective of the personal for a larger, more impersonal view—in the worst case, as we have seen most evidently in *WA*, the pursuit of a greater ideal can replace the individuality of the real. Critical of this perspective-shift from personal (real) to impersonal (ideal), Pratchett's fiction constantly

---

[128] In her book, Mendlesohn features this theorem among four sub-categories of fantasy, yet also emphasizes that "[t]his book is not intended to create rules. Its categories are not intended to fix anything in stone. This book is merely a portal into fantasy, a tour around the skeletons and exoskeletons" (*Rhetorics* vii).

[129] Tolkien is also unique in fantasy since he has received an unparalleled academic and critical attention over the years. Looking at the sheer abundance of material that exists about his life and work, no other fantasy writer comes close.

places reminders of the background of a secondary world: Just like the smaller stories that continue outside of and parallel to the main narrative, so the readers should realize that while it may not be explicitly addressed, characters nonetheless have to eat, sleep, and undertake numerous other actions outside of what is of importance to the plot. Jasper Fforde, himself an author who combines postmodern parody and fantasy in his *Thursday Next* novels, highlights this largely uncovered problem:

> All the boring day-to-day mundanities that we conduct in the real world get in the way of narrative flow and are thus generally avoided [in fiction]. The car didn't need refuelling, there were never any wrong numbers, there was always enough hot water, and vacuum-cleaner bags came in only two sizes—upright and pull-along.
> [...]
> There was a peculiar lack of cinemas, wallpaper, toilets, colours, books, animals, underwear, smells, haircuts and, strangely enough, minor illnesses. If someone was ill in a book it was either terminal and dramatically unpleasant or a mild head cold—there wasn't much in between. (Fforde 1–2)

To Fforde's meaning as well as to Pratchett's, narrative imperative ensures that stories follow certain patterns and focus on specific details, leaving out any other personal additions or variations that distract from the main plot. This is done mainly to achieve narrative flow and thus create enjoyment for readers, but if such secondary features are neglected entirely, the result will be a plain story whose secondary world is neither believable nor very immersive. Case in point are the rashly-produced fantasy parodies we discussed before, but also Pratchett's first Discworld novel with its disjoint narratives attempting to form a whole.

Taking up Pratchett's idea of everyday life on the Discworld, however, non-crucial information about the secondary world is constantly underlined and brought to light in later books, breaking up the greater narrative chain with smaller instances of necessities such as Vimes patrolling the streets or Granny tending to her garden. The immersive value of the Discworld derives from such breaks; they point toward a more in-depth world than the often superficial and "staged" secondary worlds in derivative genre fantasy or parodies. At the beginning, Pratchett's novels, making fun of fantasy fiction, still used and largely accommodated its cliches; in the first three

Discworld novels, it is therefore little surprise that the world itself is threatened and that Rincewind—even though anti-hero—must save the Discworld repeatedly. The increased detail and more in-depth immersion of the later novels mirrors the change in focus: It is not the Discworld itself which is at stake anymore; the perspective shifts onto smaller, more personal narratives.

Instead of needing a hero against all odds, the plots of later Discworld novels are resolved by cunning and thinking outside of narrative stereotypes rather than by heroics (reluctant as they may be) or magic. This narratological refinement went hand in hand with the increasing complexity of the secondary world. Clute states that "[...] it was only after half a dozen Discworld novels that Pratchett became inclined to create stories that develop in one place—this growing disinclination being another sign, incidentally, of the decreasing prominence of the Discworld as a geomorphic conceit" (23). In reducing the scale of his novels—not excluding the fate of the Discworld per se, but giving more credit to personal conflicts— Pratchett moved even further away from the clichés of quest fantasy and its emphasis on travelling the whole (secondary) world following points of narrative interest, as if retracing them on a map. Pratchett's approach to providing an immersive experience for his secondary world, however, is as ambiguous as his general idea and treatment of fantasy. While authors like Mendlesohn and Tolkien are adamant about the immersion remaining intact, i.e., not breaking it by irony or metafictional content in a text, the Discworld deliberately puts such conflicts and violations of secondary belief center-stage.

What is more, Pratchett redoubles his increased attention to the daily routine of characters in a supernatural realm. The absurdity of focusing on the everyday life of individuals who are normally non-central in a genre of literature that can be highly dependent on stereotypical "heroes" and plotlines is always apparent and never hidden from the reader. This idea is then taken one step further: The absurdity of combining a classic fantasy framework with postmodern fragmentedness and marginality is itself referenced and explained repeatedly throughout the novels. Like the outsider nature and unheroic mannerisms of Discworld protagonists, the trappings of breaking disbelief and immersion are addressed directly instead of being hidden or remaining in the background. This puts the Discworld on the aforementioned edge of reality—yet another marginal position—and provides further explanatory material for the absurd yet consistent nature of Pratchett's secondary world. Indeed, the delicate positioning of the Discworld between possibility and impossibility sets the stage for another vital component of fantasy fiction explored in a unique manner by Pratchett: Magic.

The Science of Magic

Magic is one of the central concepts of fantasy fiction, and while nearly all of its authors employ this plot device in various ways, "there is a remarkable consensus among fantasy writers […]: magic, when present, can do almost anything, but obeys certain rules" (Clute and Grant 615). The believability of a secondary world often depends on such rules, since inconsistencies or a laughable portrayal of magic would destroy the reader's suspension of disbelief. Therefore, judging from such a premise, the humorous and self-ironic Discworld novels appear to be a poor example of a sensible depiction of magic. If we go back to the beginning of *LF*, Pratchett shows a first clash of magic and humor in an absurd description of a fresh dawn on the Discworld:

> Another Disc day dawned, but very gradually, and this is why.
> When light encounters a strong magical field it loses all sense of urgency. It slows right down. And on the Discworld the magic was embarrassingly strong, which meant that the soft yellow light of dawn flowed over the sleeping landscape like the caress of a gentle lover or, as some would have it, like golden syrup. (*LF* 7)

Pratchett appeals to his readers to suspend disbelief by applying their empirical knowledge to a secondary world—in this case, by accepting that the speed of light is influenced by magic. Nevertheless, the workings of Discworld magic are explained in detail not to prove its believability or probability, but rather used to create a fantastic image—in other words, to produce the Tolkienian spell of immersion. And even though he repeatedly breaks this spell with irony in all of his books, Pratchett's depiction of magic likewise becomes increasingly complex without losing its humor.

In many fantasy novels, magic is—first and foremost—the affair of wizards and witches, whereas its importance to the Discworld as a world (beyond its use as a plot device) turned out to be crucial as the series progressed. Pratchett expanded his initial idea of magic possessing scientific properties to a standing magical field[130] in later

---

[130] Obviously inspired by magnetic and gravitational fields of real-world science.

novels—which both ensures the Discworld's existence within the fictional reality of Pratchett's secondary world and expands on the method of scientific metaphors being used to explain magic. Asked what would happen if this magical field collapsed, the wizard Ponder Stibbons[131] speculates that the Discworld's "seas will run dry. The sun will burn out and crash. The elephants and the turtle may cease to exist altogether. [...] You see, magic isn't just coloured lights and balls. Magic holds the world together" (*LH* 21). Discworld magic thus works on an atomic level, ensuring the existence of such an improbable (and yet speculatively possible) realm.

Although Stibbon's declaration is strongly absurd and remains within the fictional framework of Pratchett's creation, it is likewise strongly similar to established theories about secondary worlds. According to Wolf, "[t]he deepest level [of world-making] is the *ontological* realm itself, which determines the parameters of a world's existence, that is, the materiality and laws of physics, space, time, and so forth that constitute the world" (36). On the Discworld, we thus encounter a microcosmic level of attention to detail compared to the macrocosmic, far-reaching mythological background of Tolkien's *LotR*. Magic, for Pratchett, may also be a consequence or an echo of divine creation, yet his focus clearly rests on the role of magic on a tinier level.

It is here that Pratchett's indebtedness to science fiction comes to the fore—and I think it is helpful to remind ourselves that he also wrote several novels set in fantasy's twin genre.[132] It should therefore not come as a surprise to encounter the first flat world in his pre-Discworld science fiction novel *Strata*,[133] and the later adaptation of this concept into fantasy retained at least some roots in the other genre. Accordingly, several of the opening paragraphs of the earliest Discworld novels are both fantasy and science fiction, as in this (re-)introduction to Great A'Tuin in *LF*:

---

[131] Much more so than other faculty members, Stibbons is the equivalent of a scientist on the Discworld: Even though a wizard at Unseen University, he specializes in the use of magic on an experimental and atomic level.

[132] This differentiation between fantasy and science fiction began to dissolve as subgenres and crossovers between the two main genres became more prominent in the 1980s, but it persists as a rudimentary juxtaposition to this day.

[133] A novel in which a disc-shaped world is engineered by an alien race rather than created by divine entities (James and Mendlesohn, *History* 179).

> Great A'Tuin the star turtle, shell frosted with frozen methane, pitted with meteor craters, and scoured with asteroidal dust. Great A'Tuin, with eyes like ancient seas and a brain the size of a continent through which thoughts moved like glittering glaciers. Great A'Tuin of the great slow sad flippers and star-polished carapace, labouring through the galactic night under the weight of the Disc. (*LF* 8)

The turtle is described as floating through space—judging from a science fiction perspective, Great A'Tuin is a starship, with the inhabitants of the Discworld and the four elephants as its crew. More relevant than this, however, is the fact that Pratchett did not stop using elements of science fiction to enhance the believability of his fantasy world as the series progressed. Although hybrid descriptions like the one quoted above are less prevalent in later books, which focus more strongly on the Discworld than on its journey through space, some origins of Pratchett's creation in science fiction remain. Evidently, the most important element of science fiction on the Discworld is its penchant of addressing fantasy concepts in a scientific manner.

Science fiction is a literary genre that pays strong attention to detail and which follows "closely on the heels of science" (Wolf 97). Many of its authors spend great amounts of time explaining the technological developments of their secondary worlds—the "big three" authors of science fiction, Isaac Asimov, Robert A. Heinlein, and Arthur C. Clarke, were writers keen on scientific accuracy or at the very least on internal consistency within their novels.[134] In a similar manner, Pratchett's Discworld novels display an unusual attention to details going beyond the normally grand scope of fantasy: its authors hardly ever decided to explain the physical properties of magic on their secondary worlds. Likewise, Tolkien's core goal lay in the development and refinement of a full mythological, linguistic, and cultural history for his secondary world, a hobby clearly inspired by his academic research. Pratchett, on the other hand, focuses on the creative aspects of world-making, on a secondary world creating and constantly reinventing itself through stories and an almost scientifically inspired system of magic.[135]

---

[134] Which is also why they are known as exemplary authors of "hard science fiction"—a part of the genre that pays close attention to creating believable, if not feasible scenarios of the future.

[135] Remaining in the field of science fiction, Arthur C. Clarke's famed dictum that "any sufficiently advanced technology is indistinguishable from magic" (Prucher 22) comes to mind.

Magic as a Creative Force

Science fiction attempts to answer questions regarding the nature of its literary worlds with speculations about possible scientific developments and discoveries in times to come. Pratchett proceeds in a similar manner, although with fantasy as his main target, he prefers to explore the possibilities and implications of its perhaps most vital component: "Magic glues the Discworld together—magic generated by the turning of the world itself, magic wound like silk out of the underlying structure of existence to suture the wounds of reality" (*WS* 6). Pratchett's explanations for its existence go deeper than a simple creation myth and look at the structure of the Discworld both on the cosmological (Great A'Tuin) and the microcosmic level. On the larger scale of world-making, Pratchett uses parody of fantasy and science (fiction)[136] clichés to comic effect, however not as his primary goal. Thus, even though the Discworld may exist "because the gods enjoy a joke as much as anyone" (*S* 13), there is a deeper reason behind it. By analyzing magic in a scientific manner, Pratchett strips away the mystery so prevalent in most works of fantasy that refrain from explaining the existence of magic. He destroys none of its functionality nor its role within a secondary world. Magic, as we encounter it in fantasy, is an irrational concept and impossible in empirical reality; yet in the context of Pratchett's writing, it is a system that makes sense within its parameters of a fictional world. By reflecting the pragmatism of its inhabitants, the inner workings of the Discworld are addressed with the same prosaic approach.

Even in his cosmogony, Pratchett relies on logic and dry humor rather than on supernatural explanations. The absurdity of this logic deliberately makes use of irony and paradoxes to achieve a sort of justification that asks for suspension of disbelief in a tongue-in-cheek manner. But at its heart, it once more reflects Pratchett's literary endeavors to uncover narrative patterns:

> There is a sensible way to make a world. It should be flat, so that no one falls off accidentally unless they get too near the edge, in which case it's their own fault. [...] It should have a sun, to provide light. This sun should be small and not too hot, to save

---

[136] Rana observes that "Pratchett isn't so much imitating science fiction as science itself"—particularly in his *Science of Discworld* books, but certainly also in the novels involving the wizards of Unseen University (6).

energy, and it should revolve around the disc to separate day from night. The world should be populated by people, since there is no point in making it if no one is going to live there. (Pratchett et al., *Judgement* 1)

The mindset of Discworld logic invites readers not to abandon common sense but to reconsider literary belief even as it is constantly broken by irony—it challenges them to see the Discworld as a place where magic and rational thought can coexist and belief can create as much as uncreate. In other words, it wants us to question established patterns of thought and see them from a new, unusual perspective without ignoring their importance as tools for cognition and understanding. Regarding the latter, Pratchett's scientific view of magic does not forget to emphasize the creative powers that underlie the making of a secondary world.

On the Discworld, secondary belief is a primary belief that requires no "elvish craft" (OFS 16), to create something new. The concept of literary belief, however rudimentary, has existed on the Discworld since its beginnings. Therefore, in a manner similar to the conspirators in the later novel *GG*, Twoflower can create a dragon by mere belief in the first book (see *CoM* 185–86). In his fiction, Pratchett links one of the major tropes of fantasy (magic) to Tolkien's analysis of secondary belief to achieve his own interpretation of the powers of narrative and storytelling: "Because of the magical field in which the Discworld is bathed, belief systems are very important and powerful, so that anything which is believed in strongly enough does exist" (Butler, *Companion* 122). As stated earlier, belief is such a universal force on the Discworld that it can call things into existence that have been imagined with enough vigor. Providing a critical reflection of this interplay between real and ideal, between imagination and actual existence, Pratchett explores the concept in numerous instances in later books. While his novels always remain within the fantasy context of its original parodies,[137] the influence of science fiction cannot be denied.

On the Discworld itself, the rules of magic can be measured with an almost mathematical precision, the absurdity of which is subject to the reader's willingness to accept or deny. At its most basic level,

---

[137] Except for the Moist von Lipwig series and the final Discworld novels, but these books and their change in tone are covered in more detail in the last three chapters of this book.

magic consists of thaums,[138] the definition of which demonstrates how Pratchett uses humor to accentuate the role of incongruity and refamiliarization for his world-making:

> Thaum: The basic and traditional unit of magical strength. It has been universally established as the amount of magic needed to create one small white pigeon or three normal-sized billiard balls (a smaller measure for purposes of calculation is the milli-thaum). A thaumometer is used to measure the density of a magical field. (Pratchett and Briggs, *Turtle Recall* 350)

Not only does Pratchett allude to physics of empirical reality, he also establishes a link to his earlier concept of a "standing magical field." The irony of this idea—measuring magic by the energy required to perform certain tricks—finds its match in the actual use of magic on the Discworld. Because the Discworld literally "runs on magic" (Pratchett et al., *Science* 9), it poses dangers to the uninitiated and thus paradoxically lowers the urge to put it to use: "Magic has pretty much the same status as nuclear power: under control it is useful, perhaps even essential, but too much reliance on it comes with a disproportionally high price, and only a lonny [sic] would use it to catch fish..." (Pratchett and Kidby [1]). The inhabitants of the Discworld are so accustomed to magic that to them, it is nothing particularly miraculous anymore.

Like gravitational forces in empirical reality, magic may appear awe-inspiring at first, but in the end, it mainly fulfills its one central function, which is keeping the world together. "Pratchett [...] often explores the world of magic in the most down-to-earth way" (Brown 275), and while magic is essential to the Discworld, lighting a match is far quicker and easier—and most importantly, less dangerous—than casting a fireball. Citizens of the Discworld take magic for granted, since it is what created their world in the first place, yet there is no overindulgence in fantastical devices due to the dangers inherent in overuse. Like everything else on this secondary world, the marvels of magic have their purpose, but not more than that. The core of the Discworld mentality toward magic lies not in the wonders of the world but in the behavior and generally practical attitude of its inhabitants.

---

[138] A term undoubtedly inspired by the Greek θαῦμα ("thaûma", transl. "miracle") and the word "thaumaturgy" which occurs as a concept or school of magic in fantasy fiction.

Nonetheless, a large part of the internal consistency of Pratchett's world remains subject to the magic which permeates everything, ranging from the turtle carrying the world down to its smallest grain of sand. As a consequence of the Discworld being saturated with magic, a rule that arises from this abundance is that any abuse of it could have catastrophic consequences—the previous analogy to nuclear power is on point. Pratchett underlines the implications of this comparison by equating the misuse of magic with nuclear war. A violation of the magic-usage rules resulted in the Mage Wars, a cataclysmic event that left parts of the Discworld contaminated. Akin to radioactive waste or the impact of an atomic bomb, the use of strong magic affected the "places on the disc which, during the wars, had suffered a direct hit by a spell. The magic faded away—slowly, over the millennia, releasing as it decayed myriads of sub-astral particles that severely distorted the reality around it" (*CoM* 151).[139] I think it is highly likely that this idea has a biographical inspiration. Prior to his occupation as a full-time writer, Pratchett was press officer of the Central Electricity Generating Board in Britain, a position that included coverage of four nuclear power stations. The link of idealist fantasy to empirical reality is obvious: The disillusionment with atomic power being not just a clean but also a safe way to provide energy is used as a metaphor to point out the failings of magic as a catch-all *deus ex machina*.

What Pratchett does is combine the pragmatic mindset that characterizes the Discworld with a set of internal rules. This grounds his world, despite all the jokes and absurdities, in a frame that is consistent and offers an internal logic. Butler states that Discworld magic has a "sense of it needing to have a cost" and that it is thus "not to be entered into lightly" (*Companion* 301), a concept we are more likely to encounter in science fiction and not in the comparatively free inventiveness of fantasy. This limitation of magic in a world powered by magic seems to be yet another paradox of the Discworld—however, when analyzed on a broader scale, it reveals Pratchett's ongoing experimentation with literary belief and reader expectations; of both the potential and pitfalls of narratives as mirrors and distortions of empirical reality.

---

[139] China Miéville uses a similar analogy to nuclear power and atomic bombs in his novels *Perdido Street Station* and *Iron Council*, where so-called Torque bombardments resulted in long-term mutations and disfigurements that are strongly reminiscent of the effects of increased radiation in contaminated areas in empirical reality (Miéville 279–81).

The Making of Reality

If we follow Pratchett's scientific excursions further, we arrive at extended explanations on the nature of his secondary world and its proximity to narrative and storytelling. Magic is crucial for the Discworld, but mainly the result of its location at the edge of reality. Pratchett extends the absurd scientific linking of gravity and magic to emphasize the forces at work on his secondary world:

> The Discworld creates an extremely deep well in Reality in much the same way as an incontinent black hole creates a huge gravity well in the notorious rubber sheet of the universe.
> The resulting tension seems to have created a permanent flux which, for want of a better word, we can call magic. (Pratchett and Briggs, *Turtle Recall* 118)

The continued coupling of fantasy concepts with the science of empirical reality is amusing—the four *The Science of Discworld* books being the best example—but as with Pratchett's treatment of clichés, this is not the main intent. Pseudo-scientific as the reasonings may be, they add to the internal consistency of the Discworld on a literary level. Even more importantly, they link narrative causality with this scientific treatment of magic, showing that "the basic laws of physics [...] can be examined and interrogated in fiction" as much as in science (Sawyer, "Narrativium" 160).

In the same way that the power of thaums allows the creation of certain objects and magic tricks, given enough thaums, they influence narrative concepts as well. "Things that might *nearly* exist in a 'real' world [...] have no difficulty at all in existing in quite a natural state in the Discworld universe; so here there will be dragons, unicorns, sea serpents and so on" (Pratchett and Briggs, *Turtle Recall* 118). What is literary belief in empirical reality turns into literal belief on the Discworld. The premise is simple and once more reflects Pratchett's version of a consensus reality: If enough people believe in something, it exists. Or, to put it in other words, "while events cannot change belief and expectations, belief and expectation *can* change events" (Moody 154). Calling to mind my previous observations regarding the treatment of belief in novels such as *WA* and *GG*, this underlines the narrative causality described in the fourth chapter—expressed most evidently in the enforcement of stereotypical storylike behavior in Genua but already present in earlier novels. Therefore, the witches can change the course of the main story in *WS*, although it is "a very obvious riff on *Macbeth*" (Butler, *Companion* 264), and appears to follow its plotting like other early parodies of

Pratchett. They refuse to be cast as the villains (the three witches as they appear in Shakespeare's play) by convincing themselves and everyone else that they *are* not the villains in this story. At the end of *WS*, the citizens involved realize that wicked witches "are just stories to frighten people" (*WA* 304)—yet as the extended use of narrative imperative in *WA* implies, these stories can influence existence on a far wider scale and even shape the inner-fictional reality of the Discworld.

The internal logic of this system powers the consensus reality on a creative level: Since it is located at the edge of reality, close to impossibility, the Discworld can create its own reality or possibilities by belief. The more people believe in something, the more real it is. On the Discworld, Death is consequently "the Ultimate Reality" (Pratchett and Briggs, *Turtle Recall* 98), because everyone believes in his existence.[140] In a few of his novels, Pratchett goes so far as to create entities that feed upon holes in reality—ideas, metaphors, and even mere thoughts can come into existence simply because they slipped through a breach in reality and nourished themselves on the belief of people.[141] *Hogfather*, perhaps the Discworld novel most focused on literary belief and creation, has "creatures just popping into existence because someone's thought about them" (*HG* 216)—possibly the Discworld equivalent of Doležel's idea of "a language that would give us direct access to reality" (*Postmodern* 30), turning speech acts into actuals. As is implied in more than one instance, "reality is in constant flux" (Moody 165), on the Discworld, and alternative outcomes or objectifications of abstracts are sometimes a mere thought away. Nevertheless, as with narrative, Pratchett rarely allows his characters to wield this tremendous power: True magic, on the Discworld, is not about solving problems by waving a hand and casting them away but rather about *believing* in prevailing against all odds and acting correspondingly. Naturally, this belief is often powered by a magic going much deeper than the magic portrayed in other fantasy, but it ties in with narrative expectations and individuality.

---

[140] For the simple reason that death is an inevitable part of life and hence Death—as a personification of an idea on the Discworld—must exist. While usually in his archetypical (not to say stereotypical) form as a hooded skeleton with a scythe, it is implied that the appearance of Death too is shaped by the belief of the people who encounter him.

[141] The prime examples of this feeding on reality being *Moving Pictures* and *Soul Music*, both of which feature fictional constructs (music and films) that become more real the more often they are performed or played and consequently evoke more belief by their audiences. See also the "movie logic" of *MP* below.

Returning to Pratchett's main characters, Granny Weatherwax is instinctively aware of the powers of narrative and how it ensures that people *believe* she is a witch—a witch, however, whose role and characteristics she carefully chose herself. Likewise, the cynical mind of Vimes knows that history is repeating itself all the time, reiterating the same stories, and he aims to remain marginal in order not to get caught up too tightly in the weavings of narrative imperative (hence his reluctance to accept, if not denial of his role as Duke of Ankh-Morpork in later books, which he did not choose himself). For both main characters, the knowledge that what is believed in strongly enough exists is intrinsically linked to the roles they play and the characters people believe they are.

Once again, the importance of stories and the powers of narrative are highlighted and linked to the very existence of Pratchett's secondary world: "The Discworld is a place where stories happen" (Pratchett and Briggs, *Companion* 7), both on a grand and small scale. The powers of fiction and storytelling on the Discworld are made up from equal parts of belief[142] and the certainty that on the Discworld things happen because the narrative imperative ensures that stories get told even as others are broken. Yet looking at this determinist certainty in even more detail reveals another, deeper layer of the complexity that makes up the Discworld and sheds further light on the dynamic interplay between fiction and reality. Written stories consist of text that is created by the author in empirical reality, and Pratchett represents this act of creation on the Discworld through the fictional element of narrativium.

Coming back to Pratchett's reimagining of nuclear power as magic on the Discworld, further parallels can be drawn between the science of empirical reality and his secondary world. Apart from the practical usage and limitations of magic, equal to the initial optimism and later caveats concerning nuclear power,[143] Pratchett's paradoxically scientific

---

[142] Both for readers, whose enjoyment of reading and immersion into the secondary world derives from suspension of disbelief, and for the inhabitants of the Discworld, who believe in their world as much as they believe in gods or other abstract or magical concepts.

[143] An example of the change in attitude regarding nuclear power is Dwight D. Eisenhower's 1953 "Atoms for Peace" speech that addressed the fear of atomic weaponry and warfare in the Cold War as well as the hope to utilize their power in another, more peaceful manner. By the mid-to-late 1960s, this cautious optimism was already less prevalent and soon fell on further criticism with nuclear accidents in Chernobyl and on Three Mile Island—the latter of which occurred shortly before Pratchett took up his position as a press officer of the British Electricity Board.

approach to a non-scientific concept such as fantasy also includes allusions to the basic chemical elements of his secondary world—far from the "mundane, non-magical elements" (Sawyer, "Narrativium" 170), of empirical reality. Discworld magic, as we have seen, does not simply exist on a large scale to shape unfolding stories, but also extends to an (to remain in Wolf's world-making terminology) ontological level that binds the powers of storytelling to magic and literary belief:

> What runs Discworld is deeper than mere magic and more powerful than pallid science. It is *narrative imperative*, the power of story. It plays a role similar to that substance known as phlogiston, once believed to be that principle or substance within inflammable things that enabled them to burn. In the Discworld universe, then, there is narrativium. It is part of the spin of every atom, the drift of every cloud. It is what causes them to be what they are and continue to exist and take part in the ongoing story of the world. (Pratchett et al., *Science* 10)

The Discworld is not merely a place where stories happen—in this view, it is literally made from stories on a material level. Magic and narrative complement each other, and while the analogies used to explain their relation are highly incongruous—they are a fictional-scientific explanation for a fictional world, after all—they nonetheless add to the consistency and completeness of Pratchett's secondary world within a fictional framework.

Thus language itself is magic on the Discworld. It can cross the threshold between what is *said* and what *exists*—speech acts provide not merely direct access to an inner-fictional reality but, in fact, allow the modification of this reality through words. While most novels focus more on the shaping power of stories rather than literal creation by speech, Pratchett does not forget to repeat the problematic relationship between ideal and real here as well: if on the Discworld, things can exist simply because enough people believe in them, then the powers that control this belief—first and foremost narrative imperative—can enforce existence. In the most extreme case, specific situations and phenomena "should happen because people want it to (magic) or because the power of story (narrativium) demands it" (Pratchett et al., *Judgement* 1). While this extended idea of a consensus reality that may manipulate existence itself is mostly explored humorously in novels such as *HG*, Pratchett's postmodern treatment of magic and literary creation brings the general dangers of fictional constructions to the fore again.

Given enough credibility and belief, the powers of language can override and reshape reality—both fictionally and in empirical reality. Particularly with the rise of mass and social media, the number of stories we tell, retell, and reshape has grown almost exponentially:

> Postmodern societies are characterised by an abundance of stories that surround their subjects and that are to be found in all forms of the mass media. The fairy godmothers of our society are the ones that convert the chaos of events into stories, people in positions of power who use the formula of stories to make the public think about events in 'mythical' ways[.] (Smith 153)

The human mind, as discussed in Chapter 4, seeks patterns, and part of the reality we create for ourselves derives from the stories around us, big or small. While Discworld speech-acts have, on their own, the potential for a simple *creatio ex verbo*, their true shaping strength is unlocked by telling stories, that is to say, through longer strings of events or words. Lilith's idealized fairy tale kingdom of Genua rests on an overarching set of master narratives—those of fairy stories—the power of which is backed by narrative imperative and narrativium.

The births of specific creatures by the mere act of naming them in *HG* are therefore secondary creations to the causal chain of situations told in a larger framework. Coming back to narrativium, this element[144] is the direct cause of narrative imperative and thus the anchor for the stories that unfold on Pratchett's secondary world. It imbues all instances and uses of narrative on the Discworld with a power that is hard to resist and even harder to escape from:

> On Discworld, abstractions show up as *things*, so there is even a thing—narrativium—that ensures that everybody obeys the narrative imperative. [...] Even if a character tries to behave contrary to the story in which they find themselves, narrativium makes sure that the end result is consistent with the story anyway. (Pratchett et al., *Science* 267–68)

Narrativium acts as the prime source of creative power of the Discworld. Naturally, Pratchett is the creator of his secondary world, yet narrativium acts as his inner-fictional explanation of why the Discworld has been filled with echoes and repetitions of classic stories,

---

[144] Strictly speaking, narrativium is only one of several fictional elements that occur on the Discworld (Pratchett et al., *Science* 67–69, 374), and ensure its existence, the details of which would potentially cover a whole sub-chapter of its own. Yet it is safe to say that narrativium is the element with the most prominence in Pratchett's novels and companions.

and herein lies the crux of the novels. Again, it is only the skepticism of the protagonists regarding these recurring story patterns that saves their individuality from being completely ruled by narrative imperative in a determinist manner. It also reinforces one of the rules of immersive fantasy: Even though their secondary world is their home, protagonists have to understand the workings of this world to a certain degree in order to succeed; they "see knowledge as argued out of the world, by breaking it open" (Mendlesohn, *Rhetorics* 65). Therefore, Granny Weatherwax's and Sam Vimes' repeated efforts to derail preset stories (Clute and Grant 784) are virtually an application of their increasing knowledge of the Discworld and its reliance on narrative. Their cynicism and mistrust towards stories hide a rational way of understanding their secondary world.

The Discworld novel *Moving Pictures* is perhaps the strongest proponent of such empowerment through knowledge. In this novel (as in *HG*), things are called into existence through belief, albeit to a far greater extent: *MP* sees the introduction[145] of film to the Discworld, another concept that soon takes up the powers given by narrativium. It applies the narrative imperative not just to the movies that are made on Pratchett's secondary world, but in the end, transgresses to the Discworld's inner-literary reality, finding its cinematic climax in "[a] giant woman carrying a screaming ape up a tall building" (*MP* 300). However, as the main character of this book has learned, "by the Hollywood logic of Story brought into operation through his belief, he can win by behaving not prudently but in wildly heroic, filmic style" (Clute and Grant 784). The narrative imperative, it turns out, also works *vice versa*, and one can use it to one's own advantage—an idea that is constantly present in the mindsets of Granny Weatherwax and Samuel Vimes when they actively change well-known story patterns.

The possibility of influencing a narrative by belief lends power to those who are aware of it. In Pratchett's novels, the characters who think outside the box and use or evade the clichés of storytelling are the true "heroes," rather than the heroes traditionally shaped by stories to be heroes. In this regard, Pratchett's works are approaching postmodern narratives insofar as they focus on metafictional play.

---

[145] To be precise, it is the re-introduction of film to the Discworld, as the narrative powers of movies are literally unearthed akin to discovering an Egyptian tomb at the beginning of the novel.

While they never display an awareness of their own fictionality,[146] Pratchett gives his characters the unique opportunity to divert their story from the usual patterns, provided that they recognize them: "The inhabitants of Discworld are themselves fully aware of the narrative conventions of the adventure film: it is almost as if they have seen Errol Flynn, or any of the numerous screen reincarnations of Robin Hood" (James, "City Watch" 199). For the protagonists of Pratchett's novels, we have seen, this awareness is not merely a useful skill but a means for survival. By spotting the narrative threads that normally dictate their lives, they can go so far as destroying "narrative by destroying linearity"[147] (Butler, *Companion* 265), of a given narrative and thus giving way to another, more beneficial strand of story. While the confines of stories cannot be truly escaped on the Discworld, they can certainly be modified and used to one's advantage.

Pratchett's idea of the narrative imperative always implies that not only knowledge but stories themselves are power—an observation equally valid for empirical reality and a postmodern society. For his first science book written with Stewart and Cohen, Pratchett took inspiration from a scientific story—the fictional element of phlogiston—to create his own fictional element called narrativium. Both this concept and its summary in *The Science of Discworld* bear more than a passing resemblance to the role of narratives in science:

> 'Narrative' is what is left when belief in the possibility of knowledge is eroded. The frequently heard phrase 'the narratives of science', popular in the new field of science studies, carries the implication that scientific discourse does not reflect but covertly constructs reality, does not discover truths but fabricates them according to the rules of its own game in a process disturbingly comparable to the overt working of narrative fiction. (Herman et al., *Encyclopedia* 344)

---

[146] As touched upon in the previous chapter, the self-awareness of Discworld characters remains within their secondary world—they understand the narratological features of their world but do not identify an author/narrator who controls them.

[147] Which, it could be claimed, happens every time a traditional or stereotypical story pattern is broken by characters behaving differently than they should—a feat achieved by Discworld characters repeatedly thanks to their knowledge about these patterns or stories.

Using Niels Bohr's metaphor of an atom as a solar system, the scientists Ian Stewart and Jack Cohen point out the inaccuracy[148] of this model but at the same time acknowledge that the "search for understanding leads us to construct stories that map out limited parts of the future" (Pratchett et al., *Globe* 248). As new methods of understanding are created and new claims replace obsolete theories, the narratives of science change. In a similar and very literal manner, Pratchett uses stories to ground his Discworld in a pseudo-scientific explanation of its existence that undergoes changes as the novels progress.

Even though the Discworld is said to teeter on the edge between reality and impossibility, narrativium enables this secondary world to exist. Each Discworld book reflects "Pratchett's interest [...] in the power of narrative expectation" (Butler, *Companion* 264), and offers the opportunity to address topics like narratology and clichés in a humorous yet insightful way, to expose narrative fallacies—and as expressed in the Science of Discworld books, often by adopting a scientific approach.

Like the references from popular culture and other sources, the scientific excursions and footnotes in the Discworld novels and companions show the proximity of Pratchett's secondary world to empirical reality and other texts. Compared to *LotR* and fellow classic fantasy, whose roots in mythology and fairy tales are often subdued or have been changed dramatically, the intertextuality and references of the Discworld are decidedly more direct. Having said this, Pratchett reveals yet another layer of the importance of narrative both for his secondary world and for our empirical reality in his *Science of Discworld*—indeed, the quartet of books analyzes Pratchett's creation on a meta-level that goes far beyond ironic footnotes in the novels.

THE ROUNDWORLD PROJECT AND MENTAL NARRATIVIUM

Looking back at the power of literary belief that allows protagonists to create dragons or influence the proceedings of a story, creative acts like these are powered by the strong magical field that engulfs the Discworld. Bound to the rules that characterize Pratchett's secondary

---

[148] Or what they provocatively call "lies-to-children" (Pratchett et al., *Science* 43–44)—metaphors and concepts we *know* are wrong, but which help children understand the world until they learn more complex correlations. The provocative element of their claim lies in the idea that these lies are not exclusively for children but apply to adults as well (for instance, when a newly proven scientific theory replaces outdated models of the world).

world, an overabundance of magic is dangerous and, while it can be used for scientific experiments, "the results are likely to be unpredictable, i.e. predictably fatal" (Pratchett and Briggs, *Turtle Recall* 243). Having used the metaphor of residual magic as the Discworld's equivalent of background radiation, Pratchett revisits this topic for even further elaboration in the *Science of Discworld* books. At the beginning of the first of these books, the wizards of Unseen University split a thaum to harness its energy—creating the Discworld's first (and thankfully only) "nuclear" reactor akin to the Chicago Stagg Field Experiment of 1942 (Pratchett et al., *Science* 22). Yet as the experiment gets out of control by producing too much random magic, "the Wizards of Discworld attempt a number of thought-experiments by building themselves a round world in order to figure out such important questions as why people don't fall off" (James and Mendlesohn, *History* 182).

The analogy of magic and nuclear energy from *CoM* is picked up in a less violent manner here. In the *Science of Discworld* books, Pratchett largely refrains from telling a story about the dangers of nuclear power. His interest lies in the narrative potential that has been unleashed by the splitting of the thaum: with the sheer amount of magic available, the wizards are able "to create [...] an area where the rules of magic don't apply" (Pratchett et al., *Science* 48). What happens with the appearance of this so-called "Roundworld" on the Discworld is the creation of a secondary world within a secondary world (Wolf 233), opening a new literary space to be explored with Pratchett's usual humor, but also with extensive scientific reflection (see fig. 2).

The appearance of Roundworld within the Discworld is a truly metafictional and much more openly postmodern discourse on Pratchett's work. After having been created, this fictional representation of our own empirical reality[149] is regarded with much marvel in the secondary world of Discworld. Even though Roundworld is created through magic, it is still radically different from the Discworld beyond mere shape:

> If legend, myth and one extremely unreliable eye-witness account can be believed, the Discworld was created some time after the rest of the universe, using *traditional craftsmanship* rather than the impersonal modern method (which involves taking nothing whatsoever and splitting it in half). (Pratchett and Briggs, *Mapp* [24]; my emphasis)

---

[149] It is *not* a direct mirror of our empirical reality—the Roundworld develops in vastly different directions and even features split timelines as well as the possibility to visit it backwards and forwards in time, again evoking possible-worlds theory.

Fig. 2: Science of Discworld by Paul Kidby. The creation of Roundworld. Kidby's inspiration for this picture was undoubtedly Joseph Wright's famous 1768 painting, *An Experiment on a Bird in the Air Pump*—effectively placing the wizards in the position of scientists. See Pratchett and Kidby [52–53]). (Used with permission of Paul Kidby.)

As a far more accurate representation of empirical reality than the Discworld, Roundworld naturally has more features from our actual world than Pratchett's flat creation. Perhaps the most crucial difference between this fictional representation of our world and the Discworld— apart from one of them being spherical and the other being flat—is that on Roundworld, there is no narrativium. For the wizards of Unseen University, this means that the Roundworld should technically not exist at all, since "you can't make a world out of bits and pieces" and "you certainly need narrativium, otherwise the life you get is a lot of opening chapters" (Pratchett et al., *Science* 374).[150] Life simply "has a tendency to exist" on the Discworld, thanks to narrative causality (Pratchett and Briggs, *Turtle Recall* 118–19). To the wizards' amazement, however, the Roundworld continues to thrive and develop a narrative over several books despite its apparent lack of narrativium.

What they miss is the realization that while narrativium does not exist as a chemical element on the Roundworld or in empirical reality, it is still *believed* in—even though it does not exist as a real entity, it

---

[150] On their world, the theory of evolution is, as all other theories, a story powered by magic and made true by literary belief and the narrative imperative (the third *Science of Discworld* book, *Darwin's Watch*, addresses this topic in depth).

nonetheless finds expression in actuality as an abstract concept. Of course, we are all proof that life can well develop without narrative in actual reality, but "Pratchett's Discworld series is always pointing out that humans do not live in the real world, but an imaginary one of their own creation" (Smith 161). The human sphere is "addicted to story" and to "spinning fantasies" (Gottschall xiv, 11), be it in daydreams, fiction, everyday life, or science. Doing so, we create our own narrativium, namely one that exists in our minds:

> Discworld narrativium is a substance. It takes care of narrative imperatives, and ensures they are obeyed. On Roundworld, our world, humans act as if narrativium exists here, too. We expect it not to rain tomorrow *because* the village fair is on, and it would be unfair (in both senses) if rain spoiled the occasion. (Pratchett et al., *Globe* 24)

Pratchett's continuing examination of narratology and fictionality on his secondary world is nothing less than an exploration of how stories shape and influence our actual world. The Discworld novels (and the Discworld science books) unravel what Nassim Nicholas Taleb calls narrative fallacy.[151]

According to Taleb, "[w]e like stories, we like to summarize, and we like to simplify, i.e., to reduce the dimension of matters" (Taleb 63) in order to process information more easily and make it readily available. Specifically, as Rescher explains:

> Fictions, unlike real things, have finite descriptive depth. [...] And so while fact is often *stranger* than fiction, it is always more *complex*. And the reason for this is straightforward. Fictions are creatures of thought, and the capacity for complexity management that we finite creatures possess is limited. [...] The cognitive depth of fiction is always finite because fiction—unlike reality—is the finite product of a finite mind. (36, 259–60)

It is in our nature to think in stories since they form a normal part of growing up (Gottschall 22–23), and later adult life—be it fairy tales told by relatives, the ongoing story of a television series or the narratives we read in books. Going back to my claims regarding narrative identity

---

[151] Aptly titled *The Black Swan*, Taleb's book about the prediction of events and luck theory places strong emphasis on the human tendency to form habits: If we have never seen a black swan before, we may well conclude that there *are* only white swans—a theory that becomes obsolete as soon as we encounter a black-feathered specimen. In other words, we believe the narrative imperative about the white swans unless proven otherwise.

from the previous chapters, we constantly organize and retell details about our lives as if they were a story—certainly not a fixed story with a forced happy end as Lilith attempts in *WA*, but rather a fluid set of narratives that change according to how our life develops.

Nevertheless, the methods of storytelling and sense-making are, as some critics claim, identical: "The most fundamental mental operations that we perform to extract a story out of a text are the same ones that we execute to interpret the behavior of our fellow humans and to make decisions in our own lives" (Ryan, "Parallel Universes" 647). No matter their identity or similarity, however, narrative cognition certainly extends both to fiction and empirical reality, and as Pratchett exemplifies, the two are anything but mutually exclusive—even on an absurd secondary world where magic and science coexist.

For the Discworld characters as for readers based in empirical reality, there is a constant conflict between real and ideal, between what we think our lives should be and what they in fact are. While both are a natural part of existence, neither of the two should dominate the other: Thinking in patterns or stories forms an intrinsic part of our minds, but we (hopefully) never stop adapting our narrative identity to new situations and developments as they arise. Incongruities disrupt those patterns, be they humorous or simply incompatible with what we are currently thinking. Doubt and critical thought both derive from such disturbances, and it is the merit of postmodernism that it draws increased attention to the numerous fallacies that await in increased indulgence in the ideal.

Pratchett's secondary world seemingly acts as a playground for postmodern parody of classic fantasy and its stereotypical elements. However, it embraces the deconstructive and reassembling features that characterize postmodern art and, furthermore, its controversial and (to a lesser extent) iconoclastic powers. The Discworld is a world rife with conflict and paradoxes; instead of ridiculing the misconceptions of stereotypical genre fantasy, it presents an increasingly complex secondary world that simultaneously destroys and reconstructs its own plausibility and internal consistency.

> [I]f the Discworld has gone from strength to strength (rather than petering out as many theatre fantasies do) it is not because they are funny (although they are) or because the characters have become so interesting, but because Pratchett has used the storylines and characters to poke and prod at the "givens" of our own world, of the stories we tell about it, and of the fantasy worlds many of his colleagues write. (James and Mendlesohn, *History* 181)

Likewise, the main characters that we encounter in the books are both parodies of what is considered a "classic hero" in contemporary fantasy literature and elaborate protagonists in their own regard. Their success—in some cases, their very survival—depends on their capability to interpret and adapt to a world ruled by narrative expectations. The conscious choice of a specific role within this narrative framework leads to a freedom that remains fictional but nonetheless acts as a reflection on the nature and the powers of storytelling. The process of self-realization is pivotal to the development and the upkeeping of a moral code for Discworld protagonists, a constant rejection of entitlement or claims to superiority.

While free will naturally remains an illusion for characters confined to books, this topic poses one of the recurring questions in Pratchett's fiction. Unsurprisingly, it is the Discworld's personification of death, an entity who sees life narratives from their beginning to their end, who reflects on the implications of determinism and free will—ironically whilst being part of a narrative himself:

> HAS IT EVER STRUCK YOU THAT THE CONCEPT OF A WRITTEN NARRATIVE IS SOMEWHAT STRANGE? said Death.
> [...]
> IT IS A MADE-UP STORY. VERY STRANGE. ALL ONE NEEDS TO DO IS TURN TO THE LAST PAGE AND THE ANSWER IS THERE. WHAT, THEREFORE, IS THE POINT OF DELIBERATEDLY [sic] NOT KNOWING? (*T!* 387–88)

Story patterns naturally occur on the Discworld and influence all aspects of existence from a micro- to a macrocosmic level. However, precisely since narrative imperative forms the core of this secondary world from the ground up, there is a general awareness of such clichéd story elements among the Discworld populace. Particularly for Pratchett's protagonists, this knowledge is bound to a choice to mistrust any promises of an unattainable ideal and to go their own way against all (narrative) odds instead—to find alternatives to established narrative patterns, specific roles, and preset endings. Each Discworld novel, in this regard, is an exercise in not becoming complacent.

As further novels were released following the success of the first books, Pratchett's postmodern playfulness with storytelling and narratives eventually reached the point where keeping track of all the sub-narratives and character development became hard to follow, both for him and his readers. Although reluctant to give his secondary world more contours with glossaries and maps, he eventually realized that the Discworld had become too big (Pratchett and Briggs, *Companion* 8–9) to remain a vague creation. Reading allows only a certain extent of information retention—our brains are not capable of having a whole secondary world constantly visualized—and thus, maps were one of the next logical steps in the development of the Discworld.

The Discworld had revealed itself as a fantasy world with unusual detail regarding its own inception and the mechanisms at work behind the stories. The initial parodies of classic fantasy novels had turned into a fully-developed secondary world that did not primarily rely on jokes anymore. Among the topics addressed in the later novels were serious matters—be they racism, war, or religion. Not stopping at fantasy clichés, the "mirror of worlds" also reflected the darker sides of the human condition. Furthermore, beginning in the 1990s, Pratchett gradually adopted fictional counterparts to technological developments such as computers, e-mail, and Internet into his creation. More than mere cosmetics, these innovations would not simply add more layers and threads to the "metaphysical backcloth" (Stableford, *Dictionary* 330) of the Discworld but change it on a fundamental level. As the 20th century came to its end, Pratchett's creation embraced new emerging media and trends and ultimately left parts of its roots in fantasy behind.

Space and the Layers of Narrative

A Note on Space in Fantasy Literature and the Development of the Discworld

FANTASY NATURALLY CONFRONTS READERS with an implied world beyond the text, as does all literature. Indeed, it has become one of the crucial and most recognizable features of the genre that, when opening a fantasy novel, we are treated to a visual representation of the world inhabited by the characters—most commonly in the form of a map. Due to this conscious move to depict the spatial expanses of a secondary world in cartographic dimensions rather than describing them in all detail and thus potentially interrupting the narrative flow, maps are a sensible alternative in order to provide a more encompassing overview without detracting from the main story:

> In narratological terms, space is not to be conceived as a backdrop for the characters and their actions, but it is continuously created within the text (Dennerlein, 2009, p. 93, passim). In contrast, the maps produce spatial expanses which appear to be 'already there', without gaps, before the story unfolds, suggesting a material reality which serves like an anchor for the story's flights of fancy. (Habermann and Kuhn 264)

Therefore, regarding the textual descriptions and the pictorial depictions of space as entirely different methods of storytelling would be as unwise as continuing to see time and space in fiction as narratological opposites. The two sides of spatial representation influence each other—naturally, the map must be compatible with the text and vice versa if inconsistencies are to be avoided. This reciprocal influence between visual and textual narration and description of space is driven by a similar dynamic as laid out in the first part of my analysis: The question of being an individual person versus forming part of a larger community.

One of the prime examiners of this mutual influence, Foucault addresses the powers inherent in spatiality, namely its role for both individuals and their society: "Space is fundamental in any form of communal life; space is fundamental in any exercise of power" (Foucault, "Knowledge" 252). Regardless of whether we read it in a text, experience it personally, or see it as an abstract map, space always implies connection and authority—an authority that demands a certain conformity:

> However, while we are pushed in the direction of forming communities, a conflict arises with our desire for individuality. In some ways, a community functions more smoothly when its members share certain values and ideals; a relatively homogenous community is more likely to reach consensus about what it is trying to accomplish and methods for achieving those goals. This creates a certain pressure to conform and an incentive for avoiding too much individuality among a group's members. (Neely 230)

The problematics of individuality in the light of narrative imperative on the Discworld have been covered in detail in the first part of the analysis. However conforming or rebellious it may be, coupled with the need to form part of a community, the conflict extends to yet another level. Undoubtedly, the power dynamics between keeping one's identity and sense of self intact and conforming to the rules of a larger group and the ideals they might embrace pose also a constant balancing act in Pratchett's fiction.

As the Discworld grew in detail and density, this uneasy equilibrium became harder to maintain—which eventually detracted from the sharp satire of the mid-period novels. While Pratchett's world never fully lost its impetus and core issues, particularly the last releases before his passing[152] bear less impact and reflection on the various topics from empirical reality, even though the Discworld itself was to undergo vast and drastic changes.

That said, for the second part of the analysis, we cannot forego to take into account the expanses and evolution of the Discworld beyond its novels and also its extended texts. Over the decades, it grew from a set of novels into what we could call a franchise: Not only are there movies and illustrated guides; in addition, Discworld video games

---

[152] I believe that the more large-scale changes on the Discworld towards the end of Pratchett's life are bound to his Alzheimer's disease, but I also want to stress that this is a very delicate subject and moreover a partly personal opinion. Even though some critics and readers have noted that the final novels show less strong plotting and characterization, the topics addressed in these books undoubtedly reflect the general direction that the Discworld was taking. I return to these observations in more detail in Chapter 9.

and various further content have been released since the early 1990s. This again ties in with Doležel's notion of a possible world that can be refined but never completed, and of course with storytelling per se:

> More and more, storytelling has become the art of world-building, as artists create compelling environments that cannot be fully explored or exhausted within a single work or even a single medium. The world is bigger than the film, bigger even than the franchise—since fan speculations and elaborations also expand the world in a variety of directions. (Jenkins, qtd. in Wolf 10)

Therefore, as a final note, the intermedial development of Pratchett's world—focusing mainly on the Discworld video games—forms a sort of addendum to my survey of the Discworld, giving a speculative overview of its differing methods of narration. Since providing a fully-developed theoretical overview of media theory would go beyond the scope and main goal of this study, as would a thorough coverage of the intermediality of Pratchett's work, I hope that the selective nature in Chapter 10 offers some ideas for a detailed media study in future Discworld criticism.

CHAPTER 7

You Can't Map a Sense of Humor

ALTHOUGH PORTRAYING FICTIONAL REALMS, maps of secondary worlds can be regarded as representative of a reality insofar as they use the same methods of mapping as cartography in the real world: "As such, the map which seeks to ground 'secondary belief', the reader's belief in the fantasy world as real, is valuable thanks to the practices which surround 'real' mapping" (Hills 228). Both maps of actuality and of literary worlds provide readers with a representative overview and, more importantly, a sense of the reality of the mapped spaces. Yet, the flipside of this similarity in the mapping of fictional and real places provides evidence for the fact that all maps are *representations* of a reality. The believability of fictional spaces undergoes a similar claim to authenticity as that of real spaces when either are mapped out, but we need to remain aware how any attempt at mapping is and remains a construct.

While certainly not limited to the genre, fantasy is literature that makes strong use of maps to account for a believable, consistent world and to add to the suspension of disbelief. Such consolidation yields further rules to be accounted for:

> The more complete a world is, the harder it is to remain consistent, since additional material has to be fit into existing material in such a way that everything makes sense. Completeness also demands more invention, as more of the world is revealed. The more invention a world contains, the more difficult it is to keep everything in that world consistent, since every Primary World default that is changed affects other aspects of the world, and those changes in turn can cause more changes. Likewise, consistency will limit what kind of invention is possible as a world grows. Therefore, all three properties must be considered simultaneously as the world takes shape and develops. (Wolf 34)

As his secondary world grew, mapping became part of Pratchett's parody, resulting in the mockery of the overabundance and strong reliance on these maps in stereotypical fantasy. Pratchett was aware of the trappings of clichés regarding maps of fantasy worlds, satirizing "the pretensions of fantasy to realism" (Butler, "Theories" 86) by deliberately not including maps in his first novels—a choice which was to change with the release of separate maps after the persistent success of his books. Nevertheless, the role of maps on the Discworld is never as crucial as in the fantasy parodied by Pratchett. It is certainly helpful for readers to have a map as the series progresses, yet the trajectories of characters across the world are as much personal experience as a journey that can be traced and plotted.

Maps and Narrative

Maps are more than simply a means of orientation. Likewise, space "is social morphology: it is to lived experience what form itself is to the living organism, and just as intimately bound up with function and structure" (Lefebvre 94). In other words, space, like maps—or narrative, for that matter—can be a tool, and thus forms part of human cognition. Moreover, reflecting Pratchett's ideas regarding storytelling, maps are part of mimesis and speculation just as much as stories—indeed, in fantasy fiction they are often illustrated stories that act as mental projections. As Lotman describes, "The semiotics of space has an exceptionally important, perhaps even overriding significance in a culture's world-picture. And this world-picture is linked to the specifics of actual space. For a culture to get to grips with life, it must create a fundamental image of the world, a spatial model of the universe" (150). Pratchett sees this technique at work both in written and in oral tales about the state of the world—storytelling is employed to explain the spaces and phenomena of empirical reality in the same manner as those of fiction:

> Putting 'Hy Brasil' on the map is a step in the right direction, but if you can't manage that, then 'Here Be Dragons' is better than nothing. Better dragons than the void.
> Right at the bottom, at the tip of the root, is the fear of the dark and the cold, but once you've given darkness a name you have a measure of control. Or at least you think you have, which is nearly as important. (Pratchett, *Slip* 99)

As mapping becomes more accurate—be it in fiction or in empirical reality—the white patches begin to disappear, and the speculation and storytelling about the unvisited spaces are replaced with facts from exploration and discovery. In the long run, the mythical, speculative approach to mapping gives way to a logical and more fact-based cartography—a development that also finds expression on the pragmatic Discworld.

Even mapping and orientation are grounded in everyday experience on Pratchett's secondary world. In the preface to their first version of a Discworld map, Pratchett and his co-designer Stephen Briggs venture that if "the first question an intelligent species formulates for the universe at large is 'Why are we here?' the next one must be 'Where is here, exactly?'" (*Mapp* [5]). The move from mythical to logical thinking reflects the constant reminder of the real on the Discworld: Instead of providing background material for the causes and origins of the world or of one's species, as well as speculation about unknown places and unexplainable phenomena, the world itself—in its inner-fictional reality—is explored. The approach might be mythical at first—the Discworld is based on a mythological image, after all— but eventually, it gives way to a perspective guided by rational rather than inventive thought. What is more, the individual becomes more center-stage than the larger picture of a whole world. Looking back at the first part of the analysis, the third question an intelligent species could ask is, therefore, "Who am I?"—and part of the answer can be found in a combination of the two questions mentioned above. Not just one's purpose but also one's position in a world, be it secondary or an empirical reality, is crucial to forming one's identity. The "Where is here?" is explored much more strongly by Pratchett in combination with characters learning more about themselves in his novels.

It is one of the defining features of fantasy that it aims to provide answers to questions outside of the main narrative: Tolkien is known for having written down large parts of the prehistory of his fictional universe long before he began writing *LotR*, and numerous drawings and sketches of the spaces of Middle-earth and Arda exist as well (*Shaping* 76, 219–34). The secondary worlds modelled after the pattern of Middle-earth display an equal, if not bigger, claim to completion. Yet, for all their elaboration and extensive mapping, it would be redundant, not to say fruitless, for any author to attempt a full cartography of any secondary world.[153] What can be said, however, is

---

[153] Arguably the most famous attempt to create a map identical with the territory is shown in Borges' short story "On Exactitude in Science." The resulting map of a 1:1 scale brings about the death of cartography, as any map that has the same size as the land it depicts ultimately cannot be used and shows the absurdity of exact mapping.

that the narrative enmeshment of a secondary world becomes denser as more content is produced—which is not restricted to mapping but applies to any additional material released. "As more information is added," Wolf shows, "the narrative material of a world grows more complex than that of a set of braids, and becomes what we might call a *narrative fabric*" (201). Looking at the secondary worlds presented in *Harry Potter* or *Game of Thrones*, to name but two famous recent examples, it is easy to follow their development from comparatively simple to increasingly complex narrative strands.

One of the main effects of such narrative enmeshment is a growth in believability, as a stronger "narrative fabric greatly increases a world's illusion of completeness, as well as the audience's engagement with the world" (Wolf 201, 33–48). Due to its long-term success, the Discworld also naturally became subject to such densification. Critics, as well as readers, have noted the multi-layered plots and overall substructural growth in later Discworld novels (Stableford, *Dictionary* 329; James and Mendlesohn, *History* 179–82), a densification of the narrative fabric that undoubtedly reflects Pratchett's distancing from his mere parody in the first novels. What is more, the increasing complexity of the Discworld is in accordance with Mendlesohn's arguments concerning immersive fantasy. The scientific excursions into the mechanics of the Discworld, as well as the overall sophistication in plotting and characterization, add significance and believability to the secondary world; in short, they help "to deepen the immersion and build the world" (Mendlesohn, *Rhetorics* 63).

Precisely because Wolf's narrative fabric becomes ever denser as the mesh of interconnected stories grows in complexity and relatedness, so any attempt to create a holistic map of the Discworld, Middle-earth, or any other fantasy realm would be as exhaustive as it would be ultimately futile.[154] As a secondary world is represented in different iterations, every new text set in the same space adds changes to this space. Specifically, in the context of fantasy, the travel metaphor is key both to world-making and narrative development over the course of one or several texts.

---

[154] One is reminded of George Perec's famous attempt at recording every single moment happening at a certain point in time in a French apartment building in his 1978 novel *La Vie mode d'emploi*, an ultimately failed experiment to describe a literary world down to the last detail.

The first Discworld novels are—as pointed out before—mainly linear quest fantasies. The journey of Rincewind and Twoflower in *CoM* and *LF* is literally a creative act, as a new world is constructed around them and presented as they travel—a stage for their adventures, again emphasizing the crux and problematics of theatre fantasy. While the creative process of writing is central, it nonetheless remains superficial: the secondary world is little more than the ground that characters walk on or play their roles upon. The comparative lack of detail is not due to bad quality but rather because of the aforementioned narrative economy—since a whole world is traversed from center to edge, describing everything in painstaking detail would exceed the attention span of any reader, let alone the energy of the author. That said, the technique is still similar to Tolkien's method of depicting Middle-earth: exemplary for fantasy literature, both are travel narratives. Be it with Bilbo, Frodo, or in our case Rincewind and Twoflower, the ideal way to introduce readers to a fantasy world is by letting characters travel its expanses. The tourist journey that happens in *CoM* mocks the trope of fantasy characters undergoing a long and arduous journey, but it still largely serves the same purpose as other voyages. Diana Wynne Jones underlines this cliché: "JOURNEY is of course your Tour. No discovery or action can take place in Fantasyland without a good deal of travelling about. This is in the Rules" (D. Jones 104). Looking at maps of secondary worlds of fantasy less complete than Middle-earth, they are often drawn to represent the journey of the hero: The trajectory on the map provided follows the narrative—space may become subordinated to the plot or time of the novel, and a map may thus be little more than a thread of narrative points of interest.

The other side of this subordination of space for the sake of narrative representation is the importance of the secondary world as a whole—even in theatre fantasy. The hero may be the central character of a story and the description of space limited to their journey, yet the goal of this journey is predominantly a variation of the stereotypical world-saving that provides the climax of the narrative. A lot of clichéd fantasy, for all its heroism and spatial linearity, ultimately focuses on a mythical, macrocosmic view, instead of remaining within a personal perspective and an individual experience of space. We first see Middle-earth through the eyes of hobbits and not through the idealized view of a narrator. Their lack of heroism is personal, something that we can relate to—beyond the clichéd orphan-turned-hero or lost-king trope encountered so often in stereotypical fantasy. Yet, as pointed out in the first part of the analysis, in the end, Bilbo and Frodo fall victim to narrative imperative and their larger role in a grander scheme—the fate of Middle-earth rests on their shoulders, and personal problems bear little weight. The journey of these characters is often fixed to a world-encompassing destiny, both in Tolkien's book and in those of his successors, and the power dynamics of space exert their influence through the protagonist's responsibility for the destiny of an entire secondary world.

The problem arising from the far-sweeping nature of the first Discworld novels is identical: Rincewind is a constant subject to narrative imperative. He is secondary to the plot and to a macrocosmic perspective of space, a character turned protagonist *nolens volens* and driven out of his comfort zone at Unseen University to be sent across the secondary world. Unlike later protagonists, he lives in a certain place but does not derive a strong personal sense of self from it—yet as a failed student, he is nonetheless a member of the university and tries to fit into this society as well as he can. His roots in Ankh-Morpork become part of his melancholic nostalgia once he must leave the great city, exemplified by his constant reminiscence and drive to return home. That there is great comedic potential in this role cannot be doubted, but Rincewind remains a rather two-dimensional character for all his clunky charm. His personality, in a nutshell, is survival—a skill that he admittedly is extremely good at—and the hope of eventually returning home.[155] This comparatively simplistic personality is backed by further evidence: Unlike any other Discworld protagonist, his fictional biography practically begins with his first appearance in a novel, and rarely[156] do we learn about his past beyond his enrollment at Unseen University. Rincewind's life before the first novel is doubtful at the very least, adding to his rootlessness and predominant use as plot device rather than as a genuine character. Nevertheless, these deficits in characterization make him the perfect character to be chased across the whole of the Discworld and back—

---

[155] This naturally links him to Tolkien's hobbits, whose longing for comfort and reluctance to leave their home is of similar recurring urgency and a source for amusement.

[156] The problematic status of Rincewind's family history is briefly mentioned by him in *The Last Continent*, albeit in a drunken state: "Never had a *relative* before, come to that. Never ever" (373).

the white spots on the early Discworld of *CoM* and *LF* are mirrored by the comparative lack of background information about Rincewind. He does not try to understand his surroundings but rather hopes to traverse them unscathed. While not yet thematized as explicitly as in *WA*, narrative imperative ensures that he continues his journey and is drawn to further adventures.

Rincewind is a main character with limited use for Pratchett beyond repetition of the journey metaphor. Reflecting these limits, while the basic structure of the world had been set out in the first Discworld novels, the finer meshes of its intricacies followed in numerous novels published after the initial success of the 1980s. As the series kept its bestselling status well into the 1990s, and further books were only a matter of time, Pratchett realized the need for a fixed reference—not just for himself but, more importantly, for his readers.

For all the freedom that humor and parody provided, the Discworld nonetheless would soon rest in a firm and largely consistent structure. In the introduction to the first *Discworld Companion*, the downside of this need is underlined by Pratchett:

> The golden age of reckless invention has passed.
> [...] It was a surprise because I've always been against too much chronicling. I've never felt that the author's job was to say what happened after the hero rode into the sunset, or to follow the fortunes of characters once they have strutted their way across the little stage.
>   But the Discworld is too big. [...] And sometimes even I forget who was who, and where things are. Readers don't like that sort of thing. They write me letters. (Pratchett and Briggs 8)

It seems a bit strange to learn that Pratchett was rather reluctant about showing his characters' destinies after their adventures on the Discworld—a statement that stands in sharp contrast to his equal resistance against providing a "questionable happy ending" (Smith 139) to ongoing narrative lives. As it turns out, however, Pratchett's reluctance stems from another concern regarding the limitation of fiction, namely the fear of Tolkienian completeness that plagued other fantasy series.

Pratchett was less worried about there being a map of the Discworld than by "the 'map first, then chronicle the saga' school of fantasy writing" (Pratchett and Briggs, *Mapp* [1]). As we have seen, he began the first book *sans* detailed map before sending characters on their jaunt. Coming back to Wolf and his concept of narrative enmeshment, it is clear that the more novels Pratchett wrote, the more complex and intricate the narrative (and later, its cartographic representations) became. However, one major problem arising from fixing a world in order to achieve consistency and avoid contradiction is the fact that providing a world with a solid ground of consistent reality may also limit its creative potential by having to resort to material which is already there instead of having full freedom of invention. Precise description can thus hinder the development of further tales. Increased depth, equally important for fleshing out characters to showcase their personal journey, can be restrictive to their world. Pratchett addresses this problem just as he does the trappings of narrative imperative—with incongruous, ironic, and yet serious parodies of mapping in fantasy.

The Fear of Petrification

True to Pratchett's approach to his sources, maps are a stereotypical feature of genre fantasy as much as the plot devices he addresses in his parody. Therefore, it is hardly surprising that his attitude towards mapping is ironic at best.[157] The beginning of the fifth Discworld novel even claims sardonically: "This book has no map. If this bothers you, feel free to go and draw one of your own" (S 5). In later books, however, mapping became an intrinsic feature of Pratchett's secondary world as inconsistencies could otherwise not be avoided. Matthew Hills argues that "Pratchett's use of invented geography and space both underpins the effect of his humour, and provides a sense of trust and continuity for his fans" (218)—to which I would like to add the fact that such a humorous underpinning also extends his irony and incongruity to the cartography of the Discworld. Whilst mapping became as important for the Discworld as for any other fantasy world, its penchant for criticizing the genre from within did not stop at this aspect of fantasy.

Still, the mapping of the Discworld displays similar care and consistency as the portrayal of magic—it is treated in an absurd yet pragmatic manner. Pratchett and illustrator Stephen Briggs paid attention to create an accurate first cartographical picture of the Discworld in 1995, especially since they were not the only ones attempting to map the world:

---

[157] It is perhaps telling that Twoflower brings no map to his touristic journey across the Discworld but rather a dictionary in order to understand people. He aims to have a personal guide—in the end, Rincewind—and does not rely on cartographic orientation. A more exact manner of knowing where to go would have limited Pratchett's excursive creativity in the first Discworld novels.

> People send me maps of [the Discworld] all the time, which usually look pretty much like the sketches I have doodled over the years. [...] Readers are perceptive. They notice little details. If a journey that takes someone three days in one book takes someone else two hours in another, harsh things get written. Irony is employed. (Pratchett and Briggs, *Mapp* [1])

The need for a map underlines Wolf's demand for consistency within secondary worlds: The more complete a fictional world becomes, the more attention to detail must be paid—and since there are several stories covering different areas and eras[158] on the Discworld, being consistent has become very important for Pratchett's invention. Nonetheless, consistency has a strong disadvantage: In setting certain facts in stone, "the rules remain unchanged" (Ekman 127) and cannot be modified without giving rise to further inconsistencies.[159] The secondary world becomes subordinate to certain fixed points, and the initial freedom of storytelling gives way to precise narratives.

Perhaps the greatest fear, not of Pratchett but of his readers, was that a definite portrayal of Discworld cartography could render the world stale: "After an earlier map, *The Streets of Ankh-Morpork*, was published, people asked me if this fossilization of the imagination will prevent future stories" (Pratchett and Briggs, *Mapp* [2]). For the most part, this fear has proved to be wrong. In fact, I think it is safe to assume that without mapping, the Discworld would not have enjoyed such long-term popularity with readers of all ages. Yet remaining true to his initial skepticism concerning maps, Pratchett does not rely on the cartography of his Discworld to such an extent that it gets in the way of reading. Rather, one should regard the ensuing abundance of Discworld maps as part of the narrative process: They did not immediately fossilize but added to the storytelling powers of Pratchett's secondary world—looking back at the implications of narrative imperative in Chapters 4 and 5, the stereotypical stories that have been told and retold countless times provide not merely narrative paths but also the incentive to break away from them: "Stories etch grooves deep enough for people to follow in the same way that water follows certain paths down a mountainside. And every time fresh actors tread

---

[158] Though never as exhaustive as other fantasy authors, Pratchett alludes to a prehistory of the Discworld in several books—most prominently *E* and *SG*.

[159] As Ekman claims further, the exception to this rule is when a border is crossed—but even though such crossings occur on the Discworld, they rarely lead to a different rule set in later novels.

the path of the story, the groove runs deeper" (*WA* 8). It is apparent that Pratchett's protagonists step out of these narrative pathways to find new tracks, and in so doing they also create further paths that have not yet been travelled. Ironically, both narrative patterns and cartographical mapping allow characters to go off the beaten paths in the first place as they let them know about the paths which already exist. While traditional for modern fantasy, a map thus remains an abstract generalization and not "every damn place shown on it" (D. Jones 120) must be necessarily visited as if on a linear journey.

Furthermore, the fear of petrification of the Discworld was also mostly unnecessary because while some parts of Pratchett's secondary world eventually became *spatially* fixed (through cartographical and textual means), they could still be expanded *temporally* with more stories that happened in said spaces at other times. This observation goes hand in hand with Wolf's idea of narrative fabric: The density of stories can be increased not just by expansion into other spaces but by a more intricate densification of the space that is already there. The white spots on the first narrative forays into the Discworld were explored and filled in in more detail in later novels, each book adding another layer of information to the secondary world, like the songs, poems, genealogies, and timelines that accompanied the main narrative of *LotR*. As with everything on the Discworld, this was a constructive process, which drew attention to its own constructedness while simultaneously employing these very methods to make a secondary world more detailed.

As Habermann and Kuhn point out, "successful world-making in a modern vein is crucially based on the treatment of setting [...] — both visual, as already emphasized with regards to maps, and textual, in the composition of the narrative itself" (264). While Pratchett originally parodied this typical feature of fantasy fiction in *CoM* by employing elements from travel guides and tourist brochures to ridicule his setting, the crucial bond between making a secondary world believable, both through text and image, has become evident in later novels and their corresponding maps. Like space and time, the visual[160] and the textual should not be regarded as limiting each

---

[160] While there are two main illustrators responsible for the visual portrayal of the Discworld — Jack Kirby and Paul Kidby — their work has been unanimously accepted by readers and Pratchett alike as canon. And while never intended as a definite visualization of the Discworld, their illustrations nonetheless act as an important extension and addition to the texts.

other's potential—on the contrary, they complement and eventually begin *completing* each other. "If a certain vagueness is called for by the genre, then this indistinctness—running counter to the map's purported realist trickery—becomes more and more difficult to sustain as narrative geography is established through the iteration of a series of novels. The 'unmappable' Discworld has become, if anything, eminently mappable through its ritualistic repetitions" (Hills 223). The increased attention to space and mapping as further Discworld novels were released was not simply another layer of parody but a necessary step to avoid inconsistencies and maintain the overall homogeneity of a secondary world even as it remained constantly subject to meta-commentaries and ridicule.

Indeed, the maps and glossaries of the Discworld should be regarded not as mere addenda; they are integral to the extended narrative process of Pratchett's creation. While they too display much of the parody of earlier novels and remain humorous throughout, there certainly is the same serious attention to rules as in the general depth of the Discworld, and they fulfill their role to provide consistency and believability for the secondary world. Together with the frequent footnotes that adorn Discworld novels, these factors establish the Discworld as a space that is both dynamic (in the multi-layered stories we read) and fixed (in the maps and glossaries that provide additional information).[161] In particular, they emphasize the difference between an impersonal, fixed map and a personal, dynamic journey. As with narrative, setting places down on maps somewhat strips them of their emergent and rediscoverable nature—in the same manner as regarding identities as definite (be they Lilith's enforced identities in *WA* or how an alcoholic guard like Vimes is defined by his alcoholism) limits personal development and may petrify individuality. While the wider implications of slowly fixing a secondary world with additional content—be it textual or otherwise— did not become apparent until the final Discworld novels, the link between space and identity had emerged already much earlier.

Individuality and Maps
Spatial orientation is important for fictional characters despite fiction's preference for the temporal dimensions of narrative: Readers must be

---

[161] What Gérard Genette describes as *paratexts* or "productions [that] surround and extend" a text (Ekman 20).

implicitly (in text) or explicitly (via maps) able to locate characters in a given framework, which in turn is set in a specific fictional time *and* space. Breaking this rule, postmodern literature often depicts conflicting spaces and times that deliberately disturb expectancies. Given the conservative nature of much of genre fantasy and its "interconnectedness of character, plot, and setting" (Ekman 2), it is more important to *see* where the characters are going in a consistent secondary world since fantasy, despite its low-mimetic nature, places the same emphasis on the realistic depiction of space as high-mimetic fiction—for instance realist fiction of the 19th century. Within fantasy, this effect of believability and internal realism is often achieved via the aforementioned use of maps. To resume the game board metaphor, the Discworld maps provide readers not just with a frame of reference to visualize the characters' trajectory but underline another implication of mapping a secondary world: as with the Discworld deities' game board in *CoM*, a map of Pratchett's fictional realm gives readers a god-like perspective.[162] Just as reading a fantasy novel and following the journey of its characters with a finger across the frontispiece map, later Discworld novels allow us to see the trajectory of the journeys of Samuel Vimes or Granny Weatherwax from a broader perspective.

Yet crucially for Pratchett's fiction and its idea of narrative, what cannot be grasped from this perspective are the stories and individual fates of characters. Once again, the sophistication of the Discworld novels is exemplified by Pratchett's more mature treatment of characters. Compared to the later protagonists, Rincewind provides nearly no internal monologue: Instead of experiencing the Discworld from his perspective, we are given a much more auctorial view. The story of *CoM* and *LF* approaches a written map insofar as it offers little reflection from the characters' side—such a technique strips plot down to the basics that make a narrative a narrative, turning it into a series of connected events rather than a homogenous whole. Since cartography, like all fiction, effectively means simplifying things in order to make them more accessible and understandable, it likewise results in an abstraction of the actual. As Chris Philo stresses, this emphasis on the ideal within the representation of geography by using

---

[162] Besides the example of "Thud" (fig. 3), various other Discworld board games feature figurines of characters to be moved across a map of either Lancre or Ankh-Morpork. All of them put players into the position of the Discworld deities in *CoM* or *LH*.

statistics and symbols, for example, again leaves out the materiality of life, the Baudrillardian real: "I am concerned that, in the rush to elevate such [...] spaces in our human geographical studies, we have ended up being less attentive to the more 'thingy', bump-into-able, stubbornly there-in-the-world kinds of 'matter' (the material) with which earlier geographers tended to be more familiar" (60). Pratchett's rather reluctant agreement to map the Discworld reflects this idea of a tangible secondary world, the same way his characters prefer "realness" when readers experience the world through their eyes.

As we are reminded by the texts accompanying the Discworld maps, any attempt to trace the territory of Pratchett's secondary world on an objective level is betrayed by the strong personality—indeed, the subjectivity—of his cartographers and chroniclers (Butler, *Companion* 125). We have seen that the pragmatic, unsentimental attitude of the Discworld's protagonists does not overly rely on idealistic make-believe to tell them who to be and what to do—following the stereotypical patterns of fantasy would mean falling to the perils of narrative imperative. Where in *LotR* we have the consistent and immersive secondary world of Middle-earth filled with Tolkien's "intense attention to detail" (James and Mendlesohn, *History* 49), the main narrative is nonetheless a journey that closely follows the tracks on a map (allowing of course for certain dramatic detours, e.g. via Moria). In the first Discworld novels, which still closely emulate classic fantasy for parodist purposes, the travels of Rincewind and Twoflower across the Discworld achieve the same ultimately linear nature as Frodo's quest to carry the One Ring to a specific destination.[163] Thus, the initial journey across the Discworld has a lot in common with the fantasyland sweeps of stereotypical fantasy, the main difference being that Pratchett's secondary world had seen very little elaboration at this early stage. Only in later books was the Discworld a material, tangible world that did not serve as a mere background to the stories anymore but was of equal importance as the narrative.

Following characters along a mapped-out narrative which can also be pursued with the tip of a finger reveals a deeper problem going back to Pratchett's critique of stereotypical storytelling and

---

[163] Naturally because of their fragmented narrative and Pratchett's penchant for using as many parodies of classic fantasy as possible in these early iterations of the Discworld, both the world and the story are not as coherent as that of *LotR*.

its implications. Although rarely as obvious as in the prescribed life-stories of the people of Genua in *WA*, a general "sense of predestination permeates Discworld" (Pratchett and Briggs, *Turtle Recall* 119), and its characters often follow a specific pattern and are not allowed to or choose not to stray from their destined path—their individual choice is secondary to the dictates of stereotypical fantasy stories and the quickest way to their next plot point on the (narratological and cartographical) map. Once more, this is the game-board-perspective of the Discworld deities, who play dice over characters and move them from space to space. Narrative imperative applies to space as much as it dictates stories; like story and map, so the visual and textual are closely intertwined, and narrative and space also act in union and influence each other.

In fantasy, Foucauldian power dynamics can extend to the entirety of a secondary world: Regardless of whether it is theatre fantasy in the vein of Tolkien or a critique thereof in the works of authors such as China Miéville, the larger context of a secondary world often takes on a dominant role (Clute and Grant 804–05). In Tolkien's *magnum opus* as in derivative or critical fantasy, the fate of the secondary world eventually becomes so important as to enforce itself upon the main characters. As stated before, the hobbits are reluctant heroes, thrown into an adventure: their journey begins as a personal account of an epic undertaking, yet Bilbo and Frodo both finally succumb to narrative imperative: The power of the One Ring acts as an objectified narrative imperative, a plot device that marks the hobbits as "chosen ones" who need to fulfill their Campbellian journey in order to save the world and provide closure for the story[164] and the reader.

---

[164] This is why both Bilbo and Frodo travel to the Undying Lands at the end of *LotR*, a mythical land for mythical heroes of their corresponding era. Effectively, they do not belong to the material world any longer: they will become transcendent beings outside the time and space of Middle-earth—their story has ended. It is a development going hand in hand with the extensive genealogies and chronicles in the addenda to Tolkien's work. Perhaps less for the hobbits but certainly affecting characters such as Aragorn and Boromir, their ancestral background is ultimately their destiny: Boromir wants to prove himself to his father and his country whereas Aragorn, as the rightful heir of Isildur, becomes king of Arnor and Gondor. In Pratchettian logic, they *would* have the choice to play another role like Aragorn's Discworld equivalent Carrot, but in Tolkien's quasi-mythical world, the narrative imperative is decidedly more linear and each character must play a role in tune with the fate of the entire secondary world.

The narrative imperative applies not just to the fate and personality of characters but to their relation to space as well—the environment in the focus of the story that is told becomes more important than any spatial expanse set outside this focus. What effectively happens hereby is a denial of the extended *reality* of space. Details of personal experience, as well as the historical background, are overshadowed by an idealized and overarching need to save the entire secondary world. In derivative fantasy, readers thus often encounter the "crucial moments" of the story, comparable to points of interest on an itinerary, and rarely read about the smaller, non-significant journeys or events in between. Likewise, the maps in these works can be very rudimentary and serve little purpose beyond the plot:

> This is the result of an author producing a map, lazily perhaps, with the minimum needed for the story; the author has only mapped the places visited by the characters, rather than creating a robust and detailed map of regions reaching far beyond what is seen in the story. This is one example of why world-building should go beyond the story's needs and suggest a world much broader and more detailed than what the story gives the audience, since areas appearing on a map that do not appear in the story encourage speculation and imagination. (Wolf 158)

Besides the linear journey of *LotR*, Tolkien was certainly aware of the problem of bad cartography: Middle-earth is an elaborate and detailed literary space that allows for countless non-central diversions from the immediate plot of *LotR*, an idea exemplified by the numerous songs, poems, genealogies, etc., that add to the secondary world. None of them is crucial to heroic journey, and they would certainly interrupt narrative flow if they all formed part of the main text, but they also add to the believability and consistency—indeed the very inner-literary reality—of the secondary world, turning it into a realm whose culture and history are worth saving from destruction.[165]

By comparison, early Discworld novels were little more than A-to-Z journeys, representing the theatre fantasy or extruded fantasy product that copied Tolkien's apparent features without taking into account its deeper complexities and any features non-central to the main plot. Pratchett went beyond this imitation and parody in his later

---

[165] Perhaps herein lies the reason why to this day, Tolkien's text has not found an equal in genre fantasy: While many authors have tried, none have succeeded in emulating Tolkien's seemingly effortless and yet extensive additions to the main plot of a secondary world.

novels. The linear, broken-up journeys across the Discworld turned into more homogenous narratives allowing characters to remain in one place or move back and forth through the same spaces while simultaneously undergoing an internal journey more than once. In addition, through the non-central nature of Pratchett's main characters and a focus on marginal, everyday activities the novels reinforce the reality of experienced space and life as compared to the lofty ideals and impersonal grand narratives of epic and derivative fantasy: "As Granny Weatherwax once said, if you wanted to walk around with your head in the air, you needed to have both feet on the ground. Scrubbing floors, cutting wood, washing clothes, making cheese—these things grounded you, taught you what was real" (*W* 342–43). As with narrative, this character-centered approach to normally plot-driven genre fantasy is highly incongruous: It defamiliarizes the expectations of readers by remaining focused on characters instead of the "fate-of-the-world" scenario so typical for classic fantasy narratives, even though the elements in focus (everyday activities) are naturally familiar.

Surpassing the cravings for food and comfort of Tolkien's halflings whilst they are on their arduous adventures, Pratchett's protagonists, in fact, *need* to deal with their daily lives throughout the novels and cannot leave for heroic deeds for extended periods of time. Their professions—healer and advisor for Granny Weatherwax or city guard for Samuel Vimes—do not allow them to stray too far from their duties, as the community depends on them. The protagonists of Discworld novels are thus constantly in touch with the reality of living in the spaces of a secondary world—which, even though fictional, filled with supernatural content, and seen from a humorous perspective, is nonetheless seen as an autonomous reality that follows certain rules and needs specific social mechanisms to function.

In focusing on such mechanics, Pratchett appears to limit the storytelling potential of his world only superficially. While their journeys might be meandering in nature, the heroes of classic fantasy do not often stray from the path or remain where they are to partake in mundane activities such as cutting wood or mending their clothing— or if they do, these aspects of a secondary world are rarely mentioned in the scheme of grander stories as stereotypical plot elements take dominance. Pratchett, even more so than Tolkien, does not abandon the little stories in favor of the bigger ones. Like Tolkien's protagonists, Discworld characters do not serve as mere plot elements to save their world but possess a believable and personal connection to it—as pointed out before, Frodo misses the Shire when embarking on the journey to Rivendell and later on to Mount Doom. Yet the small, personal spaces such as his home in Bag End become secondary to the vast distances he traverses on his journey across Middle-earth.

Juxtaposing Tolkien's various maps, Ekman notes how the cartographic representations of the Shire and of Middle-earth underline different purposes: "Whereas [the Middle-earth] map has some traits in common with the Shire map, it offers a world-view different from the controlled safety of the hobbit lands: according to the larger map, Middle-earth is a wilder, older place, and the map is much more explicitly made to serve the story" (Ekman 55). From a cartographical perspective, as not simply the Shire but the wider space of the whole continent is at stake, Frodo must abandon personal concerns about his personal spaces/map in order to save the entire, bigger (world)map.[166]

While also acting as an extension to specific stories, the Discworld maps show far more features and aspects that focus on the "worldliness" of the world, acting as reminders of the down-to-earth nature of its inhabitants.[167] Tolkien's heroes lose part of their connection to smaller spaces as their journey progresses. While similarly devoted to their household and garden, Frodo and Bilbo do not possess the stubborn locality of a Granny Weatherwax, for whom tending to one's personal good and that of others in the immediate surroundings is as important as trying to save the entire (secondary) world. Thus, *LotR*, for all its personal detail in the map of the Shire, largely remains in a mythical, comprehensive idea of space over the course of the book. Pratchett, on the other hand, puts strong emphasis on a more hands-on and sociological approach to space on his secondary world, although we should not forget that he too fell victim to narrative imperative at first. The earliest Discworld novels are indeed parodies

---

[166] While no touristic journey as that of Twoflower in *CoM* and *LF*, Frodo's travels likewise show the tendency of fantasy to offer a wider perspective, both representative of the broadening of the hero's horizon and their role in the greater context of a secondary world.

[167] For example in the numerous references to agriculture and commerce in *The Compleat Discworld Atlas*: "Flat plains lie either side of the River Ankh, extending hubwards to the Carrack Mountains. The succulent fecundity of this region is legendary, and gives rise to a burgeoning vegetable bounty that is the finest brassica crop anywhere in the world." This statement is followed by extensive details about individual regions and their produce (Pratchett, *Atlas* 9–17).

of quest fantasy and place large-scale saving-the-world scenarios above individual growth, yet the later books feature narratives set in increasingly more personal and intimate realms—without ever fully abandoning the roots of fantasy in a mythical image of space.

While personal (read: tangible) spaces abound in Pratchett's later fiction, he nevertheless keeps addressing the problematic implications of people identifying with larger, more impersonal spaces despite their individual needs. Naturally, one of the easiest techniques to emphasize ideal space above personal space in classic fantasy is to have the secondary world threatened by war, a topic which Pratchett covered in his own manner. The two Discworld novels central to the conflict between abstract and real space both feature warfare as their main topic, although the perspective is all but the glorious reimagination of it that we encounter in so many fantasy worlds. In the aptly-titled *Jingo*, an armed conflict threatens to engulf the Discworld as a small island in the middle of an ocean is claimed by two rival nations.[168] Pratchett's bitter commentary on expansionist and militant views of cartography is as poignant as it is political in his book; yet his critique of imposing idealistic means on personal fates as a means to an end (winning a war) reaches a metaphysical level in the later novel *Thud!*. This book covers the long-standing conflict between dwarfs and trolls—a typical trope from fantasy that could easily be ridiculed but is handled seriously here.

What Pratchett shows in both books is how geography can form part of one's identity. Particularly the Battle of Koom Valley, considered the peak of centuries of conflict between Discworld dwarfs and trolls, presents borders "with regard to [...] opposing views on a key historical moment" (Gibson 59) that can exist mentally even though their material and historical sources may be doubtful:

> Koom Valley, Koom Valley. Vimes shook out the paper and saw Koom Valley everywhere. Bloody, bloody Koom Valley. Gods damn the wretched place, although obviously they had already done so—damned it and then forsaken it. Up close it was just another rocky wasteland in the mountains. In theory it was a long way away, but lately it seemed to be getting a lot closer. Koom Valley wasn't really a place now, not anymore. It was a state of mind. (*T!* 35)

---

[168] It is easy to see parallels both to the Falklands War and particularly to the 1991 Gulf War, both of which happened prior to Pratchett's writing of *Jingo*.

The evil connected with Koom Valley—both sides see this space as the epitome of the wretchedness of the other race, each stating that they were ambushed[169]—is much more complex than the one-sided depiction of so-called "evil" locations in classic fantasy. While the evil of Mordor is visible on a map of Middle-earth—in Lotman's terms, *good* is outside (such as the kingdom of Gondor) and *evil* is bred inside[170]— what happened in Koom Valley has left behind its spatial as well as temporal boundaries and "brought millennia of enmity" (Butler, *Companion* 368) to generation after generation of trolls and dwarfs, effectively creating a mental border of hate between the two species.

Going even further and reflecting the dangers of simplifying reality, the book also centers on a Discworld variant of chess called "Thud"—a game that reenacts the Battle of Koom Valley with figurines of dwarfs and trolls. Inspired by the novel, British game designer Trevor Truran created a commercial version of "Thud" in 2002, followed by a rerelease as "Koom Valley Thud" in 2005. Just like Rincewind in *CoM*, figurines on a game board are supposed to move in certain ways, and dwarfs are to remain in their roles of being opposed to trolls and *vice versa* (see fig. 3). As it turns out, however, such a binary opposition does not truly hold, as every game consists of two rounds, and players need to switch sides after the first one. Especially in the novel, this rule "compels empathy: […] the hereditary enemies troll and dwarf must learn the ways of the Other" (Webb, "Watchman" 99), be it in a game or in a wider context.[171] The game Thud is a narrative, too, and can be utilized to challenge or even shatter so-called eternal truths.

---

[169] Although what truly happened in Koom Valley is a historical tragedy: Dwarfs and trolls had planned to come together to sign a peace treaty, but due to fog in the valley, bad sight and misunderstandings left both sides with the impression of being ambushed by the other (*T!* 418), ending in the eponymous battle that was still remembered bitterly centuries later.

[170] And correspondingly the Uruk-hai marching from Mordor carry the evil within them into the lands outside—while evil is largely binary in *LotR*, it therefore certainly is mobile. Likewise, dwarfs and trolls in *T!* carry the hatred of Koom Valley with them through stories told and retold. Pratchett, as so often, internalizes the evil instead of showing it overtly as in cruel or ugly characters/races in stereotypical fantasy.

[171] At the end of *T!*, the petrified remains of the two leaders of the original Koom Valley conflict are found in a cave underground. They are frozen in midst of a game of "Thud"—and troll and dwarf king are each playing the opposite side (424–25).

Fig. 3: "Starting positions" by Terraliptar. The setup for a game of Thud. Dwarf figures are at the edges of the board; trolls are standing in the middle. See "Thud." (Used with permission of Terraliptar.)

In *T!*, Pratchett—and his protagonist Vimes, for that matter—struggles to bring centuries-old xenophobia[172] to an end by reconciling the two races. The groups of racist dwarfs and trolls in Ankh-Morpork have been led to *believe* that the other party is their enemy simply by being told stories about their wretchedness; stories handed down across generations to fuel hatred and force the believers into roles that offer no alternative or ground for discussion. Since the mind is constantly looking for patterns, the bigoted portrayal of race relations in the Battle of Koom Valley provides an easy and relatable blueprint that has been known for many generations and appears to have amassed truth and believability with each retelling. As with all Discworld characters, these groups are constantly confronted with a choice: Do they want to believe (and adapt to a role) a story that has been told to them, or do they want to find their own story and their own role? Reflecting on

---

[172] Fantasy and empirical reality are *very* close together in moments like these—here, Pratchett's mirror of worlds is most acerbic and direct.

these stereotypes, a dwarf claims: "'I need no axe to be a dwarf,' [...] 'Nor do I need to hate trolls. What kind of creature defines itself by hatred?'" (*T!* 421). Once more, the evil encountered in the Discworld has a real *motivation*, it is personal and not created by supernatural means or restricted to specific parts of the secondary world. This makes it more sinister yet also drastically realistic.

The examination of conflict on the Discworld reveals that there is no clearly delineated border between concepts such as "us" or "them" and "good" or "evil." Rather, Pratchett "shows a remarkable insight into the processes that breed and beget discrimination and terror" (Rana 6), a constant reminder of how "us" and "them" are constructs in any narrative. Particularly in the mid-to-late-period Discworld novels, "the issue of race and how to engage with the Other [...] governs the text" (Webb, "Watchman" 95). Here, the danger lies in the simplification of what is seen as "other" and, as a possible result, a devaluation of varied and different individual narrative identities and a preference for a grander but also more opposed ("us" versus "them") perspective.

Yet merely favoring personal "real" space over impersonal "ideal" space would leave out the complexities and interplay of the two forces at work in each novel. Pratchett, staying true to the ambiguous and incongruous core that is the driving force of the Discworld, focuses on combining everyday space with bigger motifs and journeys, laying bare the possibilities but also the potential for conflict inherent in this power dynamic. Personal space is paramount throughout the novels, yet remaining within one's boundaries would largely mean retaining the same identity—a lack of development which is in conflict with the dynamic nature of both the Discworld and the narrative identity of its protagonists. Going beyond the hobbits' return from the epic spaces of Middle-earth to the personal space of the Shire (or their ultimate journey to the Undying Lands) at the end of *LotR*, Pratchett's protagonists repeatedly leave and return to their comfort zone. And while these spaces might be far smaller than the world-spanning adventures of various classic and contemporary fantasy novels, they are by no means less relevant.

CHAPTER 8

FAIRY TALES AND SPATIAL IDENTITY

BEGINNING WITH *WS*, PRATCHETT'S FOCUS MOVED from world-spanning adventures to a more local Discworld setting. This shift in perspective, however, did not merely decrease the spatial scale to show an increased attention to characterization as opposed to world-making. Pratchett's choice of a more relatable scale also reflects the importance of space for the formation of an identity. Particularly in the Tiffany Aching books, the closest Discworld equivalent to coming-of-age novels, the importance of knowing lived space and one's personal connection to it is constantly stressed:

> The witches come from the land and from among the people who live there; witches are deeply enmeshed in the lives of the villages under their care, knowing and caring for individuals from the cradle to the grave—much of their power is a direct result of their deep understanding of the people and the land. (Butler, *Companion* 419)

Moreover, Pratchett's critique of fairy tales and their essential elements is expanded by this more complex portrayal of witches, abandoning both the one-dimensional "bad witches" as well as the simplistic spatial descriptions in classic fairy stories. Such simplification was transferred to much of genre fantasy in spite of its emphasis on the making of secondary worlds. We have seen that because fantasy authors tend to create worlds that then need to be saved, these secondary worlds (although elaborate) are often reduced to stage sets that allow for little attention to everyday, mundane activities but must instead be extensively and quickly traversed in order to reach a culmination.

Pratchett reintroduces the familiar to this framework and breaks narrative expectations by depicting his witches as characters preoccupied with their private lives as much as with the larger stories surrounding them. Their identity—indeed, their very sense of self—is derived from the dynamics between personal space and other space, between individuality and community.

Too Much Geography

The setting for Pratchett's Witches series of books, the kingdom of Lancre, is an ironic version of Tolkien's Shire, a small space of compressed landscapes: "Tolkien's Shire is said to be the south Midlands countryside; Lancre may well be a few select corners of South Bucks"[173] (Pratchett and Kidby [84]). Vital to the miniature aspect is the fact that Lancre is bigger than it appears to be, a sort of folded-in country that "gives visitors the feeling that it contains far too much geography" (Pratchett and Briggs, *Turtle Recall* 217). Both Pratchett's parody of mapping and the unmapped spaces of fairy tales become apparent in Lancre: due to its saturation in magic, the land of Lancre is itself warped and bent into a fairy-tale-like trickery which "topographically reflects the mood of anyone travelling through it" (Sayer 142), where places that seem close can be far apart and one path may lead down several roads.

Given this supernatural depth, Lancre is full of lore and magic, including gateways to other worlds. As a consequence of the magical overlapping of worlds and "geography" (Pratchett and Briggs' broad use of the term underlines the country's fickle relation to space), the "greatest concentration of natural magical talent in the Discworld is found in the Ramtop Mountains, especially in the small kingdom of Lancre" (Pratchett and Simpson 199). The standing magical field of the Discworld is particularly strong in Lancre: Magical incidents happen very frequently and are thus part of everyday life; likewise, witches belong to the land and are normally not taken as something out of the ordinary. Pratchett makes use of postmodern collage since he takes the abundance of fairy tales and folklore and turns all the clichés on their head to such a comic effect that the unfamiliar once more becomes refamiliarized and is not intrusive but indeed part of the world.

The bricolage nature of Lancre extends to its depiction in maps. Whereas other maps of the Discworld are surprisingly accurate, having seen several new releases and updates over the years, the map of Lancre seems to remain a parody of cartography, as its zigzagging roads and exaggerated mountainscapes show (see fig. 4). Once more employing the uniqueness of Discworld logic, the inaccuracies of the map of Lancre are explained by space distortion due to the high concentration of magic and the ensuing special features of the land:

---

[173] South Bucks being South Buckinghamshire, the area around Beaconsfield where Pratchett was born and grew up in.

The actual acreage of the kingdom is hard to calculate because of its mountainous nature and, in any case, it backs on to the Ramtops themselves and areas that are claimed by no man, troll or dwarf. The fact that there are at least two gateways into other dimensions in the country could also be held to give it a possibly infinite area. (Pratchett and Briggs, *Turtle Recall* 214)

Fig. 4: Lancre Map by Paul Kidby. An inaccurate but by no means incomprehensive map of Lancre. See Pratchett and Briggs, *Lancre*. (Used with permission of Paul Kidby.)

As the roots of Lancre lie in fairy tales and folklore, genres that remain very unspecific about their place and time, Pratchett is likely to have adopted this idea to account for the lack of exact cartography in the kingdom. While foregoing the "depthlessness" and very rudimentary notion of space in fairy tales (Lüthi 11) by depicting Lancre as a landscape with definite features and named towns, he nonetheless alludes to the vagueness of localization in folktales. Therefore, while the major landmarks of Lancre such as villages and the castle are signified on maps, the exact spatial and temporal expanses of Lancre remain unknown,[174] and stories might happen anywhere and anytime thanks to magic and narrative imperative. The map of the kingdom seems to provide an overview—one, however, which is fictional and bears no relation to a personal experience of space.

Pratchett thereby breaks the simplistic, reductive nature of fairy stories and exposes the problem in this kind of fiction when copied to other genres: Like the space, so the inhabitants of classic fairy tales are also simplified and portrayed in an either/or manner, "figures without bodies, without an inner world, and without an environment of their own" (Messerli 276). Hence most characters are either good or evil, and grey moral zones do not exist (Lüthi 15–16), and space is used as a similarly binary backdrop for their allegorical journeys—and as pointed out in the preceding chapter, even in a sophisticated text such as *LotR*, evil is still largely geographically confined (to Mordor, occupied Moria or Thangorodrim).[175] The allure of the simplicity and recognizability of fairy tales for fantasy fiction is obvious: precisely because fairy tales have universal appeal, characters are predominantly generic to make them relatable as heroes or to mark them as villains. Nevertheless, they are not set in exact locales as the secondary worlds of fantasy but in an equally generalized landscape that reflects the universality of fairy stories also spatially.

Compared to this, despite its inability to be mapped with precision, Lancre can be located on the Discworld in a specific place, and it replaces the dreamlike or allegorical quality of space in classic fairy tales with the same pragmatic approach that is also part of life on the whole of the Discworld. The practicality that comes naturally to Discworld inhabitants is apparent in the comparatively inaccurate mapping of Lancre, for instance in the naming of cartographic points of interest: Examples include the villages of The Place Where

---

[174] More unknown than the other Discworld maps of Ankh-Morpork and the Discworld itself, both of which are more precise. Naturally, all Discworld maps are inaccurate to a certain degree, but the map of Lancre has the most "white spots," so to speak.

[175] Or to Dagorlad, a plain to the north of Mordor and the Black Gate: it is a ravaged land of "mediated evil, clearly visible in [its] poisonous slag heaps and waste pits" (Ekman 201)—a result of various battles that took place there in the Second and Third Age.

the Sun Does Not Shine or A Rock and A Hard Place (Pratchett and Briggs, *Lancre* [26]).[176] In this context, personal experience and storytelling are combined to provide inaccurate yet navigable maps. As the Discworld itself, Lancre is not just a parody of a fairy-tale country or even just a genuine fantasy land but is simultaneously a country that is "real" for its inhabitants—in the same manner that its map ridicules the constructedness of fantasy maps and yet shows the cartographic features of the country portrayed. Mirroring this threefold complexity, there is more than meets the eye to the characters and events in the tales of Lancre: Witches can be good and helpful, self-proclaimed "just" kings might turn out to be cruel, and princesses do not necessarily have to get married unless they want to. Likewise, the Discworld equivalent of elves are not ethereal guardians à la Tolkien but horrible beings that like to manipulate and cause pain, and the archetypical big bad wolf is, as we have seen in Chapter 4, a poor animal cursed into thinking it is human. Vision can be deceptive in Lancre, as are expectation and reality.

Moreover, storytelling, identity, and mapping are linked in Lancre; places are intrinsically connected to stories. Compared to Rincewind's early journeys, which spend rather little time grounding the spaces traversed in a fictional background and like fairy tale space seem to be "a narratively built accretion and strung along as if on a straight line" (Messerli 278), Lancre and its stories appear to have naturally grown over an extended period of time. Lancre is like Genua insofar as it is equally dependent on and drenched in fairy stories. However, contrary to Lilith's kingdom, these stories have not been artificially forced upon people as part of a master narrative but have always formed a natural part of the community.

The practicality of this natural connection to land and story is exemplified by the *knowledge* Lancre's inhabitants possess about fairy tales. Since their country is basically a space where any fairy tale might happen thanks to the Discworld's abundance of magic (and

---

[176] Another example is the forest of "Your Finger, You Fool!"—a parody of the falsely-attributed Guugu Yimithirr expression "kangaroo" standing for "I don't understand you". While this linguistic myth has been debunked, it definitely inspired Pratchett (Pratchett and Briggs, *Turtle Recall* 422). A true case of phrase-turned-name is the French term *vasistas* for transom windows, derived from the recurring question "Was ist das?" ("What's that?") asked by German visitors in 18th-century France upon seeing this form of window there for the first time.

thus narrativium), the Lancrastians have grown used to them and the powers of narrative imperative:

> The people of Lancre are, on the whole, remarkably free from irrational beliefs. Things which in another universe would be considered superstitions are plain common-sensical facts in Lancre. People there don't *believe* that a horseshoe over the door keeps you safe from elves, they *know* it, and if you ask them why it works they can explain just why (the magnetic effect of iron disrupts the sixth sense so vital to an elf's well-being). (Pratchett and Simpson 255)

Pratchett's world can again be considered Kafkaesque with such absurd use of common sense, but all instances of incongruity seem to be explained. At a first glance the knowledge about the world is similar to the naïvete of fairy-tale characters where the wondrous is accepted as a given and "[t]he hero shows neither astonishment or doubt" (Lüthi 6–7) when confronted with supernatural elements. On the Discworld, however, the acceptance of such phenomena betrays a more intricate depth, namely the knowledge about superstitions and beliefs that is, in fact, true. Therefore, while the inhabitants of Lancre believe in the powers of iron over elves, for example, their knowledge of it is based on tested fact and not on naïve acceptance. Absurd as this familiarity with stories and corresponding behavior may be, it still makes sense in the inner-fictional reality of Pratchett's secondary world.

What is more, the fact that such knowledge is almost[177] superstition-free again underlines Pratchett's penchant for approaching a secondary world of fantasy with pragmatism and logic—although a total lack of superstition would be unwise in a world that shuns absolutes. A character exemplifying the dangers of not taking precautions against narrative conventions or even blatantly ignoring them, Discworld explorer Eric Wheelbrace proudly defies the fairy tale nature of the land, taking up a very rational—ironically too common-sensical—stance during his travels:

> The caves are rumoured to run everywhere in the kingdom; it is widely believed that there is a secret entrance in the castle. But— as any Lancrastian is delighted to tell the unwary traveller—they

---

[177] As the people of Lancre have grown up with and believe in stories, it is easy to make them believe in particular stories—for instance, the story of the wicked old witch—more strongly than in other ones, thus removing them from the reality of Discworld witches as benefactors of their community. Only by reminding the people that these depictions of witches as wicked old women in fact *are* stories, the witches can bring them back to what is real.

> are also one of those features that are not bound by the laws of time and space. Travel far enough in the caves, they say, and you will find mythical kings, asleep with their warriors; you will hear the roar of the Minotaur and the sheep of the Cyclops. Walk far enough and you will meet yourself, coming the other way. This sort of nonsense cuts no ice with a down-to-earth, experienced traveller like me, I can tell you. (Pratchett and Briggs, *Lancre* [4])

Pratchett once more plays with reader expectations and the treatment of clichés by letting a character in his secondary world snigger at the very supernatural features of that world. It is a behavior, however, that leads to his ultimate demise (Butler, *Companion* 373)—in Discworld logic, not believing in something all the others believe in (their literary belief ensures its existence, hence it exists) and not taking heed against it is a highly dangerous attitude, especially in Lancre. Again, a less self-centered approach to life holds the key to success: Wheelbrace refuses to acknowledge other points of view that might hold different truths; in a way, his identity derives from himself only and not from an exchange with others and the nature of the land surrounding him— it is fixed.[178] Ignoring the shifting rules of a secondary world means petrifying one's self in a manner and believing that things could—or should—not be any different.

In sum, it is the character of the land and the personal experience of Discworld characters that makes the relationship between Lancre and stories different from the fairy-tale dictatorship of Genua or the rudimentary and universal nature of classic fairy-story space and time. As the connection between land and individuality is natural and not enforced, they are not just in a balance but interdependent. All of Lancre's inhabitants display this interdependence,[179] but it is expressed most strongly (and importantly) in the novels' main characters, the witches of Lancre.

Land, Power, and Identity

The unique geography of Lancre and its occupants' practical attitude toward superstition is pivotal to life, be it for survival or to establish one's identity—even more so for the protagonists of the Witches

---

[178] In this regard, he is remarkably close to the danger that Vimes and Granny are constantly aware of: While not an evil person, Wheelbrace nonetheless thinks in absolutes and believes himself to be in the right precisely *because* he thinks so.

[179] As they naturally form part of a community in the villages and towns of the kingdom of Lancre.

novels. Most of them dwell in marginal locations of the kingdom[180] as in classic fairy tales, deep within woods and yet very much rooted in their surrounding community. Space is a source of power for the witches in spite of their marginal role, derived from their everyday life as part of a community. Such a symbiotic role of *living* in a space, even if fictional, must not be underestimated. And while critics such as Foucault or Lefebvre both draw attention to the dynamics between society and space,"Lefebvre's category of *lived space* [...] opens up the question of the individual's relation to place, and this involves memory and emotions" (Chanady 67; my emphasis). Home soil is considered magic both in a supernatural and a personal way, and being away from it for too long can have negative effects, as the witches know — they lose touch with the land and, more importantly, with themselves, as Granny's sister Lilith exemplifies. If we look back at her role in *WA* once more, it is clear that she has become so absorbed with her mirror image and dreams of power that she (ultimately) forgets where she once came from — her *real* space has been replaced with illusions of the *ideal*. Likewise, the general mistrusting nature of Granny stems from a deep fear that she too might lose contact with who she is and her source. Lancre is strongly conservative in this manner, reflecting the clear-cut boundaries of fairy tales despite the cragginess and overlapping dimensions of the country. To remember your roots is thus not simply a matter of nostalgia; on the Discworld (and in Lancre in particular), it is crucial to your well-being and self-knowledge. On the other hand, identity is subject to change in each book and cannot be drawn like an exact map, even though for a traditionalist like Granny, this plays into "the fears she has about her power" (Sayer 141) — namely falling from her careful balance between self-confidence and doubt.

The intimate relationship between place and character in the Witches novels, therefore, explains why they tell more intricately personal stories than the first Discworld releases.[181] Indeed, the

---

[180] Nanny Ogg could be said to be the exception to the rule: Unlike other witches both in personality and location, she lives in a large cottage in the center of Lancre and genuinely enjoys company — a stark contrast to the stern and isolated manner in which Granny Weatherwax and fellow witches live.

[181] For example, we learn about Unseen University in the first novels, but never get to know Rincewind's private room. In later installments of the Discworld, extensive accounts are given of the cottages of the witches and the streets of Ankh-Morpork.

everyday activities of the witches fit into their roles as wise women with great power and an equally strong reluctance to use said power. As part of this focus on their daily lives, their cottages are representations of this constant exchange between the everyday and the extraordinary; they reflect not just their personality[182] but "[t]heir witchcraft itself is embedded within domesticity" (Sayer 134), that is to say within their homes. The importance of this observation cannot be stressed enough: Although magic is so abundant on the Discworld that its very existence and elemental structure (narrativium) stems from it, the magic used by witches is not achieved by the all-empowering exploitation of these sources.[183] As Butler notes, "[w]itch magic is to a great extent organic, and their practices rarely attempt to force nature to take a contrary course" (*Companion* 418). In tune with the pragmatic and realistic nature of the Discworld in general, true magic happens when you do not have to use any and instead rely on knowledge of the land and yourself.

As Karen Sayer underlines, the witches do not just belong to Lancre—they *form* Lancre: "Setting is important in any novel, it often says something about the characters and might reflect their state of mind, but in Pratchett's witches' sequence, the witches and the land, like the witches and their communities, are particularly intimately linked" (141–42). Their power derives equally from the magical properties of the country and in relation to its other inhabitants. Yet this double connection to the land goes deeper; as Lancre is a transboundary and liminal space, the witches are furthermore also guardians of the borders between worlds—and indeed of the stories that might unfold should their guardianship or these borders weaken.

Therefore, when Granny Weatherwax dies at the beginning of the final Discworld novel *The Shepherd's Crown*, her passing tears a gash in the delicate fabric of time and space in the Discworld,

---

[182] Which is why any witch with common sense disapproves of gingerbread houses, as they are much too sticky and impractical. In addition, and more dangerously, they form part of the stereotype of the wicked old witch from folk tales.

[183] Pratchett is not afraid to show the dangers inherent in tapping into such unlimited magic. *Sourcery*, one of the earliest Discworld novels, shows Rincewind facing a Sourcerer—a magician who channels the raw creative power at the core of the Discworld. As with my earlier conclusions regarding Pratchett's personal experience with nuclear power and the portrayal thereof on his secondary world, the comparison between the *deus ex machina* magic of derivative fantasy and the dangers of using it on the Discworld once more becomes apparent.

allowing the mischievous elves[184] to enter Lancre and begin to destabilize the community:

> But in a world shimmering just the other side of the Disc, a world where dreams could become real—where those who lived there liked to creep through to other worlds and hurt and destroy and steal and poison—an elf lord by the name of Peaseblossom felt a powerful quiver shoot through the air, as a spider might feel a prey land on his web.
>
> He rubbed his hands in glee. A barrier has gone, he whispered to himself. They will be weak... (SC 43)

What is needed to drive back these harbingers of chaos and pain is a person similarly welded to her land and, derived from this attachment, her sense of identity. Having proved herself against the elves several times already in previous novels, the young witch Tiffany Aching fills in the spot left by Granny Weatherwax. Indeed, Lancre's proximity to other dimensions is explored most thoroughly in the Tiffany Aching books, a series of Discworld novels aimed at younger readers.[185] Although often seen as such by others in her first appearances, Tiffany is anything but a helpless child. Her adolescence reflects her increasing knowledge of the land and society near Lancre,[186] and as she adapts to its intricacies, she eventually masters her life while accepting and refining her role as a powerful witch. Thereby Tiffany Aching's coming of age is inextricably linked to her relationship to space. Much more so than most of the Discworld witches, Tiffany derives her sense of self and individuality from her knowledge and symbiosis with her land. Like her fellow witches, Tiffany feels estranged in foreign or urban areas, going there because she has to, but the finales of her books are always set in her homeland again, presumably the only place where the threat to the Discworld can be defeated—again with knowledge from the lore of the lands.

---

[184] In yet another nod to classic fairy tales, Pratchett's elves are not the near-divine beings that derive from Tolkien's portrayal of them in *LotR* but deceptive and cruel beings who dazzle others with their beauty to take advantage of them. The Wee Free Men, nefarious but ultimately helpful fairies, act as a similarly chaotic but ultimately benevolent counterpart to the cruel elves.

[185] Another book aimed at younger readers worth at least mentioning is *The Amazing Maurice and His Educated Rodents*, a Discworld book presenting a revision of the Pied Piper folk tale. As in the Tiffany Aching books, Pratchett's critique of fairy stories and their powers thanks to tradition is the major topic in this novel.

[186] Tiffany lives and grew up in the Chalk, a land close to Lancre, and often travels back and forth between the two in her novels.

In her last appearance in *SC*, Tiffany can defeat the elves by becoming fully aware of her personality as derived and nourished by the surroundings she grew up in. With Granny Weatherwax gone and the burgeoning threat of elves invading the Discworld, the young witch needs to stand not just as the moral but also the very geophysical center of her country, "becoming one with the land and the women who lived on it before her" (Butler, *Companion* 93). With her accrued good deeds throughout several novels and the people's confidence in her, she has amassed enough belief to achieve great power—a force that she could use to her own advantage and empowerment[187] but which (like Granny Weatherwax) she firmly controls by focusing on the everyday work of a witch. What is more, her benevolent (and more importantly, necessary) deeds further connect her to her land:

> The work that the witches do—cutting toe-nails, giving baths, cleaning rooms, delivering food, and sitting up with the dead—is not only work that desperately needs doing; it is also work that is *grounding*. It reminds the doer of what and who they are working *for*. Just as the witches anchor morality for the people, the people anchor the humanity of the witches. (Fellows 223–24)

Again, it is this forming part of a community, of remaining in contact with the real and not feeling superior to others (as Lilith, for instance), which is crucial to Tiffany's success. Even though the witches are ever under threat of being likened to their crooked counterparts from fairy tales[188] (and thus falling victim to narrative imperative and being twisted into a dark counter-ideal), the people still need them to take care of things nobody else is prepared to. Both parties anchor their connection and each other.

Their witches' communion with the land they inhabit shows that on the Discworld, it is not those who claim to be in power but those who are in touch with the land and its people who are the most powerful. Yet they do not prove their position by using power, in direct comparison with Tolkien's One Ring, "as a tool with one function: mastery" (Attebery, *Strategies* 33), but by *refraining* from using it whenever necessary. This is what both Tiffany and Frodo

---

[187] Also, when looking at Tiffany, Lilith is a perfect example of such wrong empowerment—putting herself center-stage, all the people of her kingdom become secondary to her.

[188] It remains debatable whether the inhabitants of Lancre are all equally well aware of the stories, but the true knowledge of the powers of narrative remains limited to the witches.

must learn on their journeys: Though power is alluring, it is ultimately corrupting and detracts from the reality of life in favor of an abstract and dehumanizing ideal.[189]

As Butler observes, the "prevalence of coming-of-age stories in the Discworld canon is hardly surprising, as the theme of identity and knowing oneself in general is strongly present" (*Companion* 92). Tiffany's books are unique, however, as they cover the whole adolescence of a Discworld child. This stands in stark contrast to the "adult" personal journeys of Pratchett's other protagonists: Vimes undergoes a self-mastery from alcoholic guard to duke, and Granny Weatherwax cements her role as the most powerful witch on the Discworld, yet their earlier lives remain largely hidden. With Tiffany, however, we see her progress from a child of nine years to young adulthood—a crucial timespan that forms her identity and sends her far across the Chalk, Lancre, and to other locations on (and beyond)[190] the Discworld. Her five appearances in books are also very reminiscent of the Campbellian "mystical journey" trope that appears so often in classic fantasy: "Why do you go away? So that you can come back. So that you can see the place you came from with new eyes and extra colors. And the people there see you differently, too. Coming back to where you started is not the same as never leaving" (*ISWM* 349). Even more so than Vimes and Granny, Tiffany accepts life changes without abandoning her roots. Identity, for this trio of Pratchett's protagonists, remains in an uneasy but necessary balance between embracing personal change and new influences while attempting to remain who you already are.

While Tiffany continuously leaves her moorland hamlet and later returns with new experience, her identity remains linked to where she comes from. Again, this dynamic emphasizes Pratchett's idea that both accepting change and keeping the memory of your roots defines who you are. Personal growth does not result from giving in to entitlement and forgetting your origins but rather from keeping your feet firmly on the ground[191]—Tolkien's critique of *ofermod* heroes and his hobbit

---

[189] Even though Frodo learns about the dangers of power not just through his own slow corruption by the One Ring but also by being physically confronted with its logical end in the form of Gollum.

[190] The land of the fairies and the elves that threaten to invade the Discworld.

[191] Be it in the form of a protective layer of cynicism in the case of Vimes or as a general feeling of mistrust for Granny.

protagonists with their unheroic longing for home come to mind. They, too, derive their identity from their cosy homes. Even though they go on grand adventures, Bilbo and Frodo constantly reminisce about the Shire and long to return. Arguably, the identity of the hobbits is not linked to narrative imperative as evidently[192] as that of Pratchett's protagonists—on Middle-earth, there is no literary belief operating on an ontological level and turning metaphors into actualities.

This is why narrative, as laid out in the first part of this book, is much more important for Discworld characters than for the protagonists of other fantasy—and even more so for the witches of Lancre and the Chalk. Stories make up Lancre; they have the power to shift beliefs and shape life. The geography of Lancre—although the land is small—is twisted and upside down because this, in an extended metaphor, is what stories in fairy tales provide despite their depthlessness. Underneath the surface of a simple tale, various different meanings can be uncovered. In the end, the space of the Discworld is as dynamic as its characters, and can undergo similar changes. While the stage of the Discworld—the parody of stereotypical fantasy—remains mostly intact until the final novels, the pragmatism at its core underlines the fact that from a postmodern perspective, no secondary world can remain locked within the same time for all eternity, in a stasis broken only by cataclysmic events that herald new eras. It has become clear that this conscious shift from a macrocosmic view to everyday life reflects the challenge which Pratchett poses to the grand stories of "epic" fantasy, replacing their centrality with an outsider's perspective. However, in the same manner that his protagonists experience small but significant changes in their lives, so the stories of the Discworld—and the Discworld itself—began to undergo subtle but nevertheless impactful changes with the books released in the late 2000s.

THE MODERNIZATION OF FAIRY TALES

For all its resistance to cartography and the fact that "Lancrastians seldom *change* anything that works" (Pratchett and Briggs, *Turtle Recall* 216), the land of fairy tales is slowly facing the implications of a more modern age spreading across the Discworld in the last novels written by

---

[192] Certainly, both of them receive calls to adventure and are assigned roles as burglar or Ringbearer as if they were given specific parts in a story, but Tolkien never reflects on narrative causality to the extent that Pratchett does.

Pratchett. The death of Granny Weatherwax[193] in *SC* is strangely poetic, as "[t]hose who fight for the bright future are not always, by nature, well fitted to live in it" (Pratchett, *Blink* 199). Apart from her advanced age, the Lancre we encounter in this book is embracing new stories of industrialization, and although the confrontations between traditional witch and modern technology would have certainly been funny to read, it is rather doubtful to see Granny forming a part of this rapidly changing Discworld.[194] What still matters is her moral code, which was passed on to Tiffany, who by the final Discworld novel is firmly in contact with the past of her land whilst also aware of the tidings of the future.

The advent of this new age was announced in preceding Discworld novels by the introduction of carriageways and semaphore towers but is fully heralded by the sound of steam engines as they break into the countryside, ever-deeper into the rural and remoter areas of the Disc: "A screaming whistle which screeched around the hills, setting everyone's teeth on edge. Down in the valley, the air now seemed to be full of fire as a huge iron monster tore along the silvery trail towards the town, clouds of steam marking its path" (*SC* 127). Such implications of technology as a threat to the integrity of the secondary world are present in the work of Tolkien as well. The end of the Third Age sees Middle-earth potentially transforming into a "prehistorical" Earth long after the events of *LotR*.[195] The feeling of loss associated with this development is reflected in the ending, and particularly in the appendices of the book.

Tolkien's melancholic approach to change, exemplified by his use of eucatastrophe, is likewise bound to the treatment of space. Saruman

---

[193] Granny has realized that although she is a living legend and one of the cornerstones of Lancre, the Discworld has changed and, in a way, left her behind. While she helped to bring about a large part of this change, the only reason why Granny did so, lies in her awareness and evasion of narrative imperative and bending the stories so that people do not get treated like things. Ironically, however, Granny's indomitable spirit was what oftentimes kept her from accepting change herself.

[194] Entering the field of speculation here, I also believe that Pratchett's ailing health had an influence on the passing of Granny Weatherwax in his last Discworld novel. Looking at his plans for novels which remained unwritten (none of them a new Witches book, however), it is well possible that Pratchett decided to go down a different road with *SC* when his illness became too severe.

[195] The depth and extensive background of Middle-earth in sources from empirical reality placed it "at the cusp of a final dramatic THINNING into the secular history of our own world" (Clute and Grant 951).

and the industrialization of Isengard act as an omen for the exploits to follow if Middle-earth is represented as a prehistoric, mythical age of our world, this implies that the magic space of Middle-earth will give way to a literally mundane space. Pratchett, particularly in his last Discworld novel, echoes the demystification[196] that Tolkien regarded as a consequence of the Enlightenment in the 17th and 18th centuries. Unsurprisingly, he links increased geographical exploration and mapping of the world with the loss of specific stories[197] and folklore: "It seems to have become fashionable soon after the great voyages had begun to make the world seem too narrow to hold both men and elves; when the magic land of Hy Breasil in the West had become the mere Brazils, the land of red-dye-wood" (OFS 29).

His fellow author and Inkling C. S. Lewis expresses similar disdain for such desacralization of space by new means of transport and treatment of space:

> The truest and most horrible claim made for modern transport is that it "annihilates space." It does. It annihilates one of the most glorious gifts we have been given. It is a vile inflation which lowers the value of distance, so that a modern boy travels a hundred miles with less sense of liberation and pilgrimage and adventure than his grandfather got from traveling ten. (182)

For Lewis and for Tolkien, industrialization and the disappearance of white spots on the world map inevitably has a negative influence on empirical reality, through a loss of mystery and sense of wonder which can be rediscovered only in supernatural texts. This pessimistic outlook is certainly one of the reasons why contemporary fantasy inspired by their works is still often set in quasi-medieval spaces with few technological developments beyond that era. Similar to cartography, which can be seen as "an attempt to tame the world around us, to transform it into a product of our own making, and, in being able to write and read it, cut it down to our size" (Armitt 60), so new technology and methods of traveling change the perception and experience of space. On the Discworld, however, space is not so much annihilated or destroyed but given new perspectives through

---

[196] Which on the other hand also allowed myths and fairy stories to enter a secularized world in the form of supernatural texts such as Gothic fiction, and, later on, fantasy.

[197] It must be noted that Tolkien (throughout his essay "On Fairy-stories") wrote about fairies as if they really had existed in empirical reality prior to being driven away by exploration and cartography.

different means of transportation. Narrative enmeshment, mapping, and technological development go hand in hand, and specifically in the last Discworld novels, we see the consequences of this process — both positive and negative.

As rural Lancre begins to undergo technological changes that stem from the urban melting-pot of Ankh-Morpork, its citizens must adapt to the new power dynamics of space and society — in Lefebvre's words, a new production of space. Not coincidentally, the elf queen — antagonist of the first Tiffany Aching book — is exiled in the last novel and eventually starts to realize that she is losing her place in the (Disc) world as new beliefs (and thus stories) replace old ones:

> Nightshade had the face of someone who had already begun to think about a world that had changed, a world with iron that was less welcoming for the fairy folk, a world that liked them enough in *stories* but had no real *belief* in them, gave them no way in; now she was looking closer and she was finding a new world she had never though about before, and she was trying to reconcile it with everything else she knew. (SC 231)

Her melancholy is rather similar to the exile of elves in the *LotR*; yet while in Tolkien's book they were very much part of the secondary world, on the Discworld their intrusion must be thwarted and the interlopers driven back to where they came from (another world/ space). Both novels see the fair folk exiled to make way for a new age — yet voluntarily so in *LotR* because "Middle-earth is losing its magic" (Ekman 64), after the destruction of the One Ring,[198] while the Discworld elves must be actively forced out of the Discworld.

Only the elf queen begins to understand that the occupants of the Discworld have started believing in railways and progress, abandoning old superstitions as exactly what they have now turned into — superstitions. Lancre may still "stand for the old" while the city of "Ankh-Morpork stands for the new" (Sayer 13), but the industrial revolution stemming from the urban space is slowly extending to the whole of the Discworld, blurring the borders "between town and country, between centre and periphery, between suburbs and city centres" (Lefebvre 97). Pratchett makes it clear that the elves are *still*

---

[198] Because the elves' power was bound to the One Ring via their three rings (Attebery, *Strategies* 33). Therefore, Frodo realizes "that the Elves must now dwindle away, the Ring having been destroyed" (Armitt 69) and joins them in their exile at the end of *LotR*, effectively becoming a myth or a story himself.

believed in, but (as in empirical reality) confined to stories. They can thus no longer enter the secondary world of the Discworld because their era of harnessing belief for dominance is over. Ironically, here we see the ideal (stories) influence the real (elves), and ultimately the "real" Discworld elves are replaced with the stories told about them.

Tiffany summarizes the elven exile into literature poignantly, informing the queen that "[y]ou are just… folklore now. You've missed the train, in fact, and you have only mischief left, and silly tricks" (*SC* 226). What she underlines is the fact that the elves on the Discworld are unable to adapt to their new environment—instead of accepting change and a different perspective, they insist that their worldview and superiority remain untouched.[199] Both in Middle-earth and on the Discworld, a loss of the supernatural in favor of the technological or progress in general results in an exodus. Yet Discworld elves had been trying to *force their way* from one world to another and are shut out at the end of *SC*, whereas the elves of *LotR* were part of Middle-earth and are *leaving* this space for the comparatively ethereal space of the Undying Lands. What Discworld elves ultimately lack is the realization that "the experience of a *world* is different and distinct from that of merely a *narrative* [and that it] is crucial to seeing how worlds function apart from the narratives set within them" (Wolf 11). The elves consider themselves the center of a narrative which they control (in which they can play with whomever they encounter at their leisure) and will not accept that what they invade is a whole world filled with sentient beings who have their own lives and agendas. Like Lilith, they see only themselves and their reflection whilst failing to accept the autonomy, perspective, and indeed the idea of other persons as individuals.

At the end of the final Discworld novel, Lancre has lost some of its "arresting strangeness": As the trains progress deeper into the Discworld, some of its more remote areas may remain unmappable but have definitely become more reachable. The belief in stories is still very active—otherwise, the inhabitants of Lancre would not take precautions against nightly visitations by using motifs from fairy stories—but as the Discworld changes, so do the stories and degrees of belief. It becomes clear that space and story are linked, and as Lancre embraces new means of transportation, this means that some of its

---

[199] Like the doomed Discworld explorer Eric Wheelbrace, although in their case the arrogance and feeling of superiority is obviously much more malicious.

stories also give way to new ones. Despite Tolkien's and Lewis' claims regarding the negative impact of fast transport and industrialization on empirical reality and the portrayal of technology in their work,[200] Pratchett also shows the positive effects of technological innovation in a secondary world of fantasy.

What is more, foregoing postmodern alienation in the face of the conforming powers of technology, many of his characters manage to adapt to these new challenges whilst keeping their moral code and identity largely intact. And although exodus seems to be the only option available to the elves in *LotR* at the end of the Third Age, who have failed in "their attempts to arrest change" (Attebery, *Strategies* 60), and thus continue to live in stasis, Discworld dwarfs and other races *adapt* and embrace these changes—particularly because they are not happening on a singular, cataclysmic scale and instead occur as part of the dynamics of their everyday life. Pratchett underlines the way stories change as the readers and tellers change; the space of the Discworld as part of its inhabitants' lives cannot remain stagnant and unchangeable either. Therefore, the Discworld elves with their primarily self-centered approach to life, unable to account for the perspectives of others, become locked out of the Discworld instantly "as if a strand connecting [...] two worlds had suddenly snapped" (*SC* 315), yet the signs of their diminishing power had been evident much earlier. As the Discworld changes, one could say, so does the focus of its belief, and technological and social change take center-stage as they spread from urban Ankh-Morpork to the countryside. This is the core and the fall of the Discworld elves: They are in love with the ideal (specifically: themselves), and all the world and its inhabitants are but a mere playground to them—in this respect, they too treated the realm they invaded as a stage or a game board and refused to accept its deeper implications and subtle changes.

This observation reinforces Pratchett's postmodern treatment of genres and the unresolved issue of simultaneously staging fantasy and attempting to evade the implications of this stage. For all its dynamic and often chaotic nature, narrative and space, as well as personality and experienced place, are interlinked on the Discworld, and prone

---

[200] Tolkien's dislike for modern technology evokes a parallel in the mass-production of later genre fantasy: As pointed out before, he clearly saw authors as creators, not as *producers* of secondary worlds.

to constant reconsideration as well as innovation. The very locus and motor of all innovation in Pratchett's secondary world is its biggest city, Ankh-Morpork. In this context, the Foucauldian dynamics between space and power, individuality and community abandon the fairy tale background for a decidedly urban stage that shows Pratchett's criticism of stereotypical fantasy not just by juxtaposing clichés but also by extending across genres and media.

CHAPTER 9

THE URBAN FANTASY OF ANKH-MORPORK

F ANTASY CITIES ARE OFTEN a cliché themselves and filled with "noise and people [...] and horsedrawn traffic" (D. Jones 34). The earliest depictions of the city of Ankh-Morpork in Pratchett's work are no exception to that observation, starting out as a parody of the quasi-medieval metropolises encountered in stereotypical fantasy novels. However, it quickly escaped these boundaries, taking cues and inspiration from eras ranging from the Renaissance to the Victorian Age. Pratchett considered the difference of an urban space as compared to a rural area as he wrote more novels set in Ankh-Morpork. Knowledge about the world and about one's self in a fairy-tale land such as Lancre is vastly different from the challenges one faces in a more crowded environment, shared with the multitude of other perspectives by fellow citizens. Since the focus of the Ankh-Morpork novels is both smaller and denser than the epic vistas of earlier Discworld books, this also meant that more attention had to be paid both to depiction and consistency—which is why Pratchett's urban space was the first to be mapped:

> I've always been mildly against mapping the Discworld. It's a literary construction, not a place. I like to leave it vague. But a city...a city is a made thing. It takes shape. It needs to stay that shape. You can be vague about the road to the Mountains of Mystery, but you need to know the way to the post office. (Pratchett and Briggs, *Streets* [1])

Again, practical matters and everyday life on Pratchett's secondary world are emphasized: a short trip to post a letter is a decidedly smaller adventure than the larger story that surrounds the journey to some grand destination. Likewise, the increased attention to a smaller space also led to a more accurate description of the social dynamics of a secondary world and an investigation into the mutuality of technological and social change.

Finding their most poignant appearances in *J* and *T!*, Pratchett had begun to explore the relationship between fantasy races and their stereotypical depiction already in earlier books. As it turned out, however, as in his first parodies, Pratchett's last novels did not feature the same sharp satire and critical examination of the genre as the mid-period books from the 1990s to the mid-2000s. Instead, towards the end of Pratchett's career, the tone of his fiction became more redemptive and humanist rather than the darkly humorous but ultimately positive outlook of the mid-period novels.

Evading the Stage Set

Classic fantasy is primarily non-urban and more intent on portraying an entire realm—in the works of J. R. R. Tolkien, Robert Jordan, and fellow authors of high fantasy, we encounter cities first and foremost as part of a much larger world. Their metropolises act as stations on the hero's journey, spaces that provide help and information but rarely feature as the main setting. Seen from the perspective of fantasy standing in this tradition where "travel is often a central part of a story's events" (Wolf 156), the secondary world as a whole is what is central, not a specific space or individual part of it, and so are corresponding maps. In his urban novels of the City Watch series, traveling the streets is likewise important, yet Pratchett both expands and focuses his view on the cartography of secondary worlds at this level, as Hills argues:

> Pratchett's relationship to mapping is postmodern, but only in a restricted and specific sense of this term. Rather than entirely rejecting the distinction between 'real' and 'fictional' mapping, [...] Pratchett instead seeks to undercut the generic expectations of fantasy cities and fantasy maps. He achieves this by focusing on material and distinctly unheroic concerns such as waste disposal, making Ankh-Morpork a narrative space which reverses and muddies any separation of 'pure' or abstracted culture versus 'filthy' or embodied nature. (218)

In a similar manner to his portrayal of Lancre and its complex relationship with "geography," Pratchett also avoids making Ankh-Morpork or its maps a mere parody of existing fantasy cities or a set piece for references to commercial products akin to *BotR*. His metropolis, particularly once the first books set entirely within Ankh-Morpork were released (starting with *GG*), grows to become its own distinct place instead—and starts to include aspects of urbanity that fantasy often neglects. For Tolkien as for many of his successors, "the guiding principle for inclusion is [...] the story, not size or social or political relevance" (Ekman 59), and consequently their cities are often decorative material rather than spaces where power dynamics are explored. Pratchett, while equally focused on storytelling, has a very politicized, at times almost Brechtian perspective on fantasy, and nowhere is this as clear as in his portrayal of the urbanity of Ankh-Morpork: The biggest stage of the Discworld is dotted with constant reminders of its materiality and how characters and protagonists deal with their current situation and state of affairs.[201] The question of which forces must be at work in order to keep the secondary world running beyond the main story of fantasy applies to the map of Ankh-Morpork as much as to its inhabitants and the narratives that unfold and influence the city as a whole. Already the first map of the city contains quarters responsible for specific purposes (Pratchett and Briggs, *Streets* [13–18]), and newer versions include the changes that have occurred over further novels set in Ankh-Morpork.

The complexity of Ankh-Morpork was expanded over the course of several novels, and this reflects Pratchett's thoughts concerning the inner workings of a secondary world. Within an urban context (such as Ankh-Morpork), he does not neglect the mechanisms that usually stay hidden beneath the main plot. Specifically, his concern is how a major city—even though fictional—can be kept alive and functioning as a whole, a factor that other authors rarely addressed:

> I tended to distrust fantasy cities when I was a kid. They were too much like stage sets. They didn't seem to *operate*. A city of even half a million takes a hidden army of farmers, fishermen and carters just to see it through the day. [...] But a humdrum city requires a thousand unseen things to happen like clockwork, because it is only a couple of meals away from chaos. (Pratchett and Kidby [6])

Again, what Pratchett does in each of his novels is point out and reflect those parts of fantasy which normally remain unconsidered. It should not be denied that there is a lot of irony and humor involved in this process of addressing non-heroic issues such as the problem of waste disposal. Yet the true question he keeps on asking is how cities and other settlements would, in fact, work in a realistic secondary world.

---

[201] Apart from Samuel Vimes, one of the most intriguing characters in this regard is C. M. O. T. Dibbler, an opportunistic seller of street merchandise and meddler in lucrative but oftentimes illegal affairs. He is one of the crooked mirrors of Ankh-Morpork, a city filled with possibilities—often including the possibility of fooling others for personal gain.

At the latest with the publication of *The Streets of Ankh-Morpork* city map in 1993, it became Pratchett's aim "to create a city that would not stop even if the story did" and which would eventually comprise "factories, workshops, high streets, slaughterhouses and suburbs, all of which are necessary to the running of a large city" (Butler, *Companion* 36–37) and cast a different light on urbanity in fantasy fiction.

In Ankh-Morpork, the implied dark underbelly of many fantasy cities is ever-present, as is Pratchett's humorous reconsideration thereof. Hence the river Ankh, so dirty and thick that it turns into slow-moving silt upon entering the city,[202] is still regarded as "incredibly pure [since] any water that has passed through so many kidneys must be very pure indeed" (Pratchett and Briggs, *Turtle Recall* 19). By paying attention to the more basic mechanisms of cities and incongruously expanding on them in a fantasy context, Shklovsky's concept of defamiliarization and Scarinzi's idea of refamiliarization become intertwined yet again: All that is left out of the pure ideal portrayed so often in the rudimentary urban spaces of classic fantasy emerges in Ankh-Morpork. Moreover, such grounding in facts of empirical reality and a focus on "the drawbacks of urbanity: crime, violence, dirt and stench" (Kowalski 23) reveals that although the Discworld (as any other secondary world) is fictional, "characters must have some source of food, clothing, and shelter to survive, and come from some kind of culture. On a larger scale, communities will likely need some sort of governance, an economy, food production, a shared form of communication, defense against outsiders, and other such things" (Wolf 39). The irony lies in the fact that these topics are incongruous for stereotypical fantasy insofar as they are normally not central to the stories we read—yet they receive increased attention in the "grittier" fantasy of Pratchett.[203]

Of course, Pratchett does not devote complete narratives to the description of interlocking processes like supply and demand for

---

[202] The main reason for this being that in most of the novels, the river is treated like a garbage pit and any debris or refuse is simply thrown into the already rank waters. A strong contender among the possible historical inspirations for the Ankh is the Thames during the Great Stink of London in 1858.

[203] Certainly, Pratchett was not the only contemporary fantasy author to address these topics: China Miéville's New Crobuzon is a similarly dirty and lived-in literary space, as is Jeff VanderMeer's city of Ambergris in *Shriek: An Afterword* and *Finch*.

food[204] and waste disposal—such meticulous attention to detail would arguably yield little narrative entertainment—but they feature in his books and emerge in the Discworld novels as a constant reminder of what is at work beyond the main plot:

> Slaving away in the shadows are the one million inhabitants of Ankh-Morpork, tradesmen with their own streets... narrative space is thus both *extended out* from the fictional narratives composed by Pratchett, and at the same time *cut out* of these narratives: civic life happens apart from the fictional narratives of the series—significantly, it happens elsewhere. (Hills 220)

The working dynamics of Pratchett's secondary world have always played a recurring role in the books—the introductory paragraphs of Ankh-Morpork in *CoM* already mention "ships in the Morpork docks [...] laden with grain, cotton and timber" (17),[205] although these factors did not achieve narrative prominence until the technological marvels and social implications of the later novels.

Nevertheless, the metropolis is far away from being nothing but a stage. In fact, Pratchett goes so far as to ridicule the "background" nature of fantasyland cities in one of his books. When a new recruit of the watch learns about the city in *MAA*, there is a sudden break in the narrative; an "unrealistically idealized" (Tiffin 168), picture is given dominance for a brief moment, and a "disneyfied" image replaces the overt realism of Ankh-Morpork:

> You expected him any moment to break into the kind of song that has suspicious rhymes and phrases like 'my kind of town' and 'I wanna be part of it' in it; the kind of song where people dance in the street and give the singer apples and join in and a dozen lowly matchgirls suddenly show amazing choreographical ability and everyone acts like cheery lovable citizens instead of the murderous, evil-minded, self-centred individuals they suspect themselves to be. (*MAA* 163)

The artificial happiness of Disneyland or countries like Lilith's Genua (and the potential threat residing therein) are reflected in this image of Ankh-Morpork. What is more, since descriptions like these belong to fantasyland, their corresponding spaces would remain in stasis, a stage that can be changed only by singular catastrophic events as we oftentimes encounter them in classic fantasy. The motor of the "real"

---

[204] While there is no in-detail coverage of the Discworld economy, a device that replicates the circulation of money in Ankh-Morpork plays a specific role in *MM*.

[205] How these ships navigate the nigh-solid river remains a mystery, however.

Ankh-Morpork, however, is progressive, organic change under the work and personal achievements of its inhabitants. Pratchett's suspicion of fictional cities that have been crafted according to a plan[206] or to a specific purpose instead of coming from "people [who] designed their streets by the age-old method, which was to follow the path the cows made down to the river" (Pratchett and Briggs, *Streets* [1]), is apparent. The occasionally brutal reality of Ankh-Morpork constantly remains within view in the Discworld novels. Like the people on the streets who will "cheer as readily at a wedding as at a hanging" (Pratchett and Kidby [33]), life in Ankh-Morpork is neither a fairy-story nor a dystopia but, as always with Pratchett, situated somewhere in between the two extremes.

URBAN GEOGRAPHY AND PERSONAL EXPERIENCE

Characters like Vimes exemplify how knowledge of one's surroundings[207] and facing the facts of inner-fictional reality (such as having to work) are vital for living an individual life on the Discworld, even more so in Ankh-Morpork than in Lancre. The city in its complexity that can be experienced only in fragments represents a "space as directly *lived*, with all its intractability intact" (Soja 67), shown in the limited yet personal perspective of a watchman. Again, while the final Ankh-Morpork city map provides a god-like overview with many additional facts concerning population density and specific places in specific districts, an exclusively objective perspective would leave the inner-literary reality and personal experience of the metropolis unaddressed. As Pratchett states in the introduction to the first map of Ankh-Morpork produced in 1993, cities must be explored in person to be experienced — "[t]he only accurate map is the one inside my head, and yours" (Pratchett and Briggs, *Streets* [2]) — and the same credo applies to his characters. Vimes (like Granny Weatherwax and Tiffany Aching in Lancre and the Chalk) has learned about his environment and role by growing up in them. He studies the city

---

[206] Perhaps reminiscent of "real" planned cities of modernist architects such as Le Corbusier or Lúcio Costa — another area where empirical reality and fantasy are very much related.

[207] Not knowing what to expect is exemplified best in the numerous attempts to plunder or conquer Ankh-Morpork through the ages, all of which resulted in the invading forces being either robbed themselves or becoming overwhelmed with the chaotic humdrum of the city (Pratchett and Briggs, *Turtle Recall* 23).

primarily by its feel underfoot and through personal experience, not by brooding over maps and historical recounting, and this is key to his survival and success against the forces of narrative conventions — because he *truly* knows the city by heart.

Such a narrative map, like narrative identity, is constantly shifting, unceasingly changing, and adapting to new situations and events. A city like Ankh-Morpork, with its chaotic layout and uncontrollable populace, is consequently the opposite of any fictional metropolis that has been planned in an abstract manner before building it.[208] Indeed, Pratchett began with very rudimentary outlines that would be expanded and filled in as he wrote further novels:

> In *The Colour of Magic*, Rincewind could run where he liked, because the city was still only vaguely mapped in my head; by *Night Watch*, the movements of Sam Vimes were plotted and timed on the *Mapp*. Indeed, the rooftop chase across Unseen University at the start of that book was written with reference to the *Mapp and* the limited-edition model made by Bernhard Pearson. The route and the lines of sight had to be right, otherwise people *would* complain. (Pratchett and Kidby [7])

Pratchett never went so far as to follow these measurements and a fixation of space at the cost of narrative flow or for the sake of an overview in the midst of a story. Indeed, the headstrong nature of his main character Vimes provides a pragmatic, non-ideal counterpoint to any exact delineations. The complexity of the space that is Ankh-Morpork may be shown in increased detail in official maps or on abstract lists and graph paper, but as its inhabitants know, its true form needs to be experienced in person; all of its potential and actual changes to be taken into account in a constantly shifting array of information.

Only by walking Ankh-Morpork can the city thus be understood, if only in fragments and never in totality. Vimes is aware of this—and so is its ruler, Havelock Vetinari. Although the tyrant often sees the city as a mechanism, he also understands "that [Ankh-Morpork's] social and economic system is the unintended, spontaneous result of millions of individual interactions" (Guilfoy 118), and that his leadership is in a precarious balance. Both men, while holding diametrically opposed

---

[208] While not an urban space, Eco's preliminary mapping of the abbey in *The Name of the Rose* is another way to address the reality of space in fiction — in his case, the realism stems from the detail given to his Italian abbey, which naturally could not have been extended to the vastly larger expanses of Ankh-Morpork.

attitudes towards power,[209] instinctively know that the city is not a fixed entity with a few variables but a dynamic process made up of thousands of individual choices and changes that happen every day—each of them a small story that forms part of a larger network of narratives which, channeling De Certeau, "compose a manifold story that has neither author nor spectator, shaped out of fragments of trajectories and alterations of spaces: in relation to representations, it remains daily and indefinitely other" (93). However, as various characters would attest, it is unadvisable to walk the streets of Ankh-Morpork in a manner that is too philosophical. When wandering the city, the goal of Vimes or other characters is not to come home with a *dérive* from a psycho-geographical excursion but far more immediate and practical-minded. While Ankh-Morpork too "is like a tree, growing ring after ring of brick and privet" (Self 35), it is a process that cannot truly be observed from a bird's-eye perspective or with the help of a map. To experience a city not fully but at least personally means to be aware of it sensually and physically—further aspects of the "real" that is so much present in Pratchett's fiction.

Vimes' patrols of the city are not simply his duty as a night watch officer but, like the witches' everyday tasks that help them be part of their community, they are also a conscious effort to remain grounded in reality. If space, as Foucault claimed, is intrinsically related to power, then in Ankh-Morpork, one deals with these dynamics best by walking through the city and experiencing them first-hand rather than studying them in an abstract manner. By choosing a personal journey, one may even find temporary release from the negative aspects of urbanity, such as powerlessness in the face of larger developments and postmodern alienation: "Disalienation in the traditional city, then, involves the practical reconquest of a sense of place and the construction or reconstruction of an articulated ensemble which can be retained in memory and which the individual subject can map and remap along

---

[209] While both traditionalists at heart, Vetinari—as critics have pointed out, he is a thinly veiled variant of the de Medici family, since his name is practically a pun on the meaning of "Medici" (James, "City Watch" 209)—is rather Machiavellian in his politics whereas Vimes strongly supports the everyday person on the street. However, they equally resent cruelty and stupidity and remain strongly aware of the ambiguity of human nature. In accordance with Pratchett's view, power (like magic) is only valuable when you do not have to make use of it—a credo that both Vimes and Vetinari follow.

the moments of mobile, alternative trajectories" (Jameson 50). Only by walking the city can one grasp it, although never in its totality (as maps make us believe we can), but by deriving a personal image of it—an image that is, like identity, in constant flux. Alienation is not something that can be overcome in the same manner that identity cannot be achieved in a fixed manner: the reconstruction of self never ends—it is subject to change, doubt, and reconsideration for as long as a life continues. Vimes and Vetinari assume identities (city guard or tyrant, respectively), but like Ankh-Morpork, they do not become petrified within these roles, as it would lead to clichéd behavior in the same manner as that of the heroes who "accept" their role in classic fantasy.

While the dynamics of power and space are rarely explored in an explicit manner on the Discworld—*Night Watch* being the most Foucauldian of Pratchett's books in this regard—they nonetheless form an important part of Ankh-Morpork. Ironically, we almost never encounter characters looking at a map of the city in the novels themselves. In the end, a map means power, dividing and categorizing seemingly holistic but ultimately superficial and non-subjective abstracts, whereas an actual journey allows observation of the city from another perspective with more freedom and is thus much more in tune with the practical nature of Discworld characters.

What is more, it allows them to break established patterns: "Whereas the tour or itinerary is fluid, the map is static, and whereas the map is associated with hegemonic social organization, personal spatial practice [...] illustrates the individual's deviation from imposed models and thus a relative degree of freedom from highly organized disciplinary society" (Chanady 68). Vimes' continuing mistrust of authority and expansive knowledge of shortcuts in the city provide him with freedom and uninhibited perspective on life. Once again, Pratchett's down-to-earth style becomes apparent, echoing De Certeau and Bourdieu when Vimes reminiscences about the reality of how a city *feels* as compared to how it looks on a map:

> He stood still for a moment, shut his eyes, and swivelled both feet like a man trying to stub out two cigarettes at once. [...] It was good to *feel* the streets with dry feet again. And after a lifetime of walking them, he *did* feel the streets. There were the cobblestones: catheads, trollheads, loaves [...] He bounced a little, like a man testing the hardness of something. 'Elm Street,' he said. He bounced again. 'Junction with Twinkle. Yeah.' He was back. (*NW* 124)

This is the perspective of a person consciously walking and recognizing the streets of a city without having to resort to a map. As in Iain Sinclair's London Orbital, his monumental study of psychogeography, "road and heart [are] always interlinked" (202), and experience is an internal map for Vimes. His knowledge of the city is not simply practical but furthermore necessary for survival both in his occupation as a policeman and to remain in this marginal role.

Vimes, like Vetinari, refuses to accept the superiority that lies in adopting a heroic, idealist perspective.[210] Both are parts of the authority that keeps Ankh-Morpork in check, but they go their own ways, individually, outside of maps and thus off established patterns. Eschewing a purely rational and abstract approach to space, "feet [have] a memory of their own" (*NW* 277) and ground characters in the inner-fictional reality of the Discworld to counteract ambitions or flights of idealist fancy à la Lilith Weatherwax.

What we see in the personal journeys of Pratchett's protagonists is a constant acknowledgment and breaking of patterns; here, the patterns of cartography and mapping a secondary world to juxtapose the individual with the communal. From the constant struggle to remain individual and still be part of a community—Vimes hides and protects his moral code with a shell of cynicism and yet accepts his role in the greater picture of Ankh-Morpork—stems another layer of the Discworld's relation to mapping and spatiality. Indeed, this struggle between individuality and conformity naturally applies to not merely to main characters but to every inhabitant of Pratchett's secondary world and extends to groups across races and social strata. In postmodern fashion, the seemingly fixed boundaries of these groupings turn out to be as artificial and constructed as examples from empirical reality—which does not make them invalid. Even though the Discworld's population includes typical and less typical[211] groups of fantasy species, such as vampires, zombies, trolls, and dwarfs, they are subject to critical reconsideration nonetheless.

---

[210] As mentioned before, Vetinari too sees the city and its inhabitants as highly independent beings. His philosophy of ruling, ironically, is providing as little obstruction and as much freedom as necessary. The crux of this freedom, however, is that it includes "the freedom to take the consequences of being a bloody idiot" (Pratchett, *City Guide* 12).

[211] For example, the "Igors," a clan of servants and experts in surgery. A combination of the clichéd hunchback assistant from *Frankenstein* films and Frankenstein's Creature itself, they form one of the more exotic groups on the Discworld.

In tune with the pragmatic attitude of the Discworld in general, the densely-populated area of Ankh-Morpork is inevitably a breeding ground for social problems and racial conflicts, and Pratchett is not afraid to address the topics in an ironic yet also serious manner. But it needs to be mentioned that by the late 2000s, the critical acuity of the Discworld begins to lose some of its edge:

> For the last few years of his life, Terry Pratchett was ill, and the progression of his illness had an effect on his writing. [...] Though the later novels retain the typical Pratchett style—wit, wordplay, wickedness—they seem to lack focus: characters aren't as well defined as they used to be, plots not as intricately interwoven; and in fact, despite the novels' length, they are not as extensive as they used to be. (Rana 8)

While always addressing the topics chosen—inequality, segregation, discrimination—with humor and thoughtfulness, Pratchett's last books indeed feature less satirical or critical fervor. Other than his illness, to be fair, it was also becoming increasingly difficult to adequately portray the rise in complexity as progress started to take a stronger hold on the Discworld in the final novels. The portrayal of an industrial revolution *and* the social rise of the goblins in *Raising Steam* (a species that had been introduced as a major theme only in the previous novel), to give an example, created two almost entirely new narrative spaces for the Discworld, none of which had the decades of refinement of the mid-to-late period books.[212]

URBAN DYNAMICS ON A SECONDARY WORLD

Pratchett's unsentimental and practical approach to depicting a fictional city within a fictional world is a far cry from many of the cities we encounter in the work of classic and contemporary fantasy authors. In *LotR*, the city of Minas Tirith is described with Tolkien's usual attention to detail (*RK* V.1. 982–85), yet within the appendices and addenda, his main fascination lies in providing background information about the languages and genealogy of the peoples of Middle-earth, not about its urban spaces and any inherent potential for change.[213] Pratchett, as we

---

[212] This observation should not be misunderstood as an attack on the final Discworld novels. It cannot be denied that their stories are less poignant, but they are still worth reading and form a crucial part of the series as a whole.

[213] Demographically, Minas Tirith is also very unlike the melting pot of Ankh-Morpork with its abundance of races. Once again, Tolkien's portrayal is comparatively static and binary—humans, dwarves, and elves do not cohabitate but each live in their own separate spaces on Middle-earth, and exodus is the only option viable for the latter once the Third Age ends.

have seen, puts his focus on the socio-economic and productive levels of a secondary world. Fittingly, he imagines such scenarios in his own reflections on Tolkien in a retrospective article about *LotR*: "My adult mind says that the really interesting bit of *LotR* must have been what happened afterwards—the troubles of a war-ravaged continent, the Marshall Aid theme for Mordor, the shift in political power, the democratization of Minas Tirith" (*Slip* 99). Pratchett sees Tolkien as a writer preoccupied with the epic and heroic dimensions of his tale and speculates about the stories that could have followed in the aftermath of the War of the Ring, which were only mentioned in the appendices, if at all. Ironically, in this light, Tolkien focuses more on invention[214] than on mimesis: Concrete topics from empirical reality are not part of Middle-earth, and Tolkien stressed that the comparison of the Ring War to any real-world conflict would be wrong, thus keeping *LotR* as universal as a fairy tale.[215]

Naturally, it must be kept in mind that Tolkien and Pratchett were writing nearly fifty years apart and thus cannot be compared with the same theoretical measurements. Nevertheless, in contrast to Tolkien's approach to fantasy, Pratchett clearly uses the Discworld as a stage to act as a "mirror of worlds [...] reflecting ideas from outside Fantasyland" (Langford 8), such as the First Iraq War, women's suffrage, and free press. While he is not afraid to include such serious topics inspired by actual events within his humorous framework, Pratchett's true focus still lies on the personal conflicts of his main characters that are no less important in the power-space dynamic as armed conflict. Ankh-Morpork, therefore, acts as a smaller stage that stands for non-eucatastrophical, dynamic change even more so than other areas of the Discworld.

Precisely because Pratchett was critical of the fantasy cities that simply worked because they should work (all processes were left in the background and barely addressed by the narrative, if at all), he underlined the importance of infrastructure on his secondary world, and consequently in Ankh-Morpork which "has been constructed, burned down, silted up, and rebuilt so many times that its foundations

---

[214] A reinvention based on mimesis of classic motifs from fairy tales and mythology, of course.

[215] But despite Tolkien's objections, "part of the popularity of the books is almost certainly down to many contemporary readers' assumptions that *LotR* was an allegory of the Second World War" (James and Mendlesohn, *History* 48)— or any other armed conflict, for that matter.

are old cellars, buried roads and the fossil bones and middens of earlier cities" (*MAA* 221). Following this literal depth, providing a map added to the believability and verisimilitude of the city instead of merely fixing the streets and routes indefinitely:

> Instead of limiting my options, which I'd feared, [the Ankh-Morpork map] opened them up. I began to see the neighbourhoods, the villages that had been swallowed by the sprawl, the way the city had grown. We had to build in the evidence of past ages—street names that didn't mean anything now, odd lanes, streets that curved around city wall [sic] that were moved centuries ago. (Pratchett and Kidby [7])

The development of Ankh-Morpork is reflected in its portrayal in later novels. As the series progresses, the city's rise in complexity is a repeated reminder of the change and hybridization that the Discworld as a whole underwent, ranging from the various topics addressed in individual novels down to the general innovations in characterization and plotting. Again, the core of Pratchett's fiction—the Discworld's humor, his characters' integrity, the metafictional commentaries—are in constant exchange with new features and ideas introduced in consequent novels.

Still, Pratchett does not provide a complete contrast to the negative potential of technological progress and the merits of tradition and inheritance in Tolkien's fiction (Habermann and Kuhn 263) by embracing the consequences of change *uncritically*—his attitude regarding progress is more complex. Beneath all the puns, jokes, and irony of the Discworld is a message of moral behavior that neither embraces nor abandons the eucatastrophical stereotype in fantasy for an entirely pessimistic or optimistic view on fantasy. Rather, it takes into account a wider scope of behavior for the inhabitants of his secondary world. Pratchett depicts a morality which applies (or should apply) to all the races in the melting pot of Ankh-Morpork. Therefore, Pratchett's postmodernism breaks many of the racial binaries of *LotR* and *H*. By allowing friendship between dwarfs and trolls and showing the darker side of elves, Pratchett's world proves a valuable alternative and more cosmopolitan approach to fantasy. Yet like the unshakeably suspicious Granny Weatherwax who states that "[p]rogress just means that bad things happen faster" (*WA* 250) and knows that conflict will always be a factor of life, no matter how harmonious it may seem, Pratchett is not so naïve as to neglect the problems that arise from different cultures cohabitating and is well aware that tensions between races may and will persist for all their peaceful relations. Particularly in an urban space such as Ankh-Morpork, social uprisings and racial segregation are often more pressing than in less densely populated areas.[216] Therefore, while Ankh-Morpork remains a city where "crime is utilized and can be considered as subtle form of taxation" (Pratchett, *City Guide* 8), racism and social problems must likewise be addressed to portray a believable and dynamic metropolis that naturally incorporates various species from fantasy.

Going further than merely portraying the struggles of friendship between stereotypically opposed fantasy races, Pratchett actively aims to show marginalized groups with the same interdependent dynamics as his entire world. Yet what was part of the larger, more complex narrative of Ankh-Morpork in books such as *MAA* and *T!* became a naturalized and somewhat simplified process by later releases. Particularly in novels like *Snuff* and *RS*, the Discworld enters what may be called a redemptive arc, exemplified in the race of goblins that feature centrally in the two books.

In *SN*, the Discworld inhabitants are confronted with the seemingly primitive creatures, and the reaction of the "civilized" Ankh-Morpork populace is as negative as in stereotypical fantasy:

> The City Watch appeared to contain at least one member of every known bipedal sapient species [...]. It had become a tradition: if you could make it as a copper, then you could make it as a species. But nobody had ever once suggested that Vimes should employ a goblin, the simple reason being that they were universally known to be stinking, cannibalistic, vicious, untrustworthy bastards. (*SN* 117–18)

By the next novel, the goblins have become a valuable addition to society, being accepted primarily due to their prowess with technology that is becoming the foundation of a modernized Discworld. What we can observe here is a slight change in tone and a certain loss of Pratchett's satirical wit compared to the earlier books that deal with racism. Even though *SN* "directly and specifically addresses slavery and the act of 'othering'" (Gibson 64), the treatment of goblins on

---

[216] Segregation of elves and dwarfs is explored more drastically by other authors such as the aforementioned Andrzej Sapkowski, but an equally interesting alternative of discriminated humans occurs in Steven Brust's Vlad Taltos books. Here, the protagonist is a mere human among a society of a vastly taller and more long-living species, and must deal with oppression and casual racism every day.

the Discworld is likewise far more direct and less nuanced than the conflict between dwarfs and trolls in *T!* and related novels.[217] Their employment as technicians follows the narrative necessity of finding a place of acceptance for the goblins within Pratchett's secondary world and is representative of the increasingly large advancements that happen across the entire Discworld. It appears that the social change on the Discworld eventually placed the anarchic humor within more solidified boundaries.

Pratchett had poked fun at the effects of "correct" moral behavior and social acceptance on a secondary world earlier. As a counterpart to the unresolved racial problematics between dwarfs, trolls, and other species, certain behavior is no longer acceptable by later novels. When a character tells Rincewind that his false teeth made from diamonds "were offensive to trolls" (*Interesting Times* 70), the satire of political correctness is indeed very on point, but it also underlines the change that has been set in motion. The function of humor in this framework is less to act as comic relief but to provide a contrast to the harsh truths that Pratchett emphasizes. Like Hutcheon's definition of parody that need not necessarily be humorous, the most serious moments in a Discworld novel are those that stand out from the array of jokes and sarcastic footnotes. Therefore, in *J*, both the "[l]unacies of racial prejudice" as well as "strict racialism" (James, "City Watch" 214), are less ridiculed than given emphasis. In this book, the city of Ankh-Morpork, like Koom Valley in *T!*, acts as a spatial source of pride, an identifier for its inhabitants to claim superiority over other spaces and nations. Yet as pointed out before, these binaries hold perils that reinforce narrative imperative. Indeed, the traditions and history of Ankh-Morpork act as a narrative imperative themselves and appear to give sufficient reasoning to denigrate others. Identity, as derived from such an idealistic and nationalist view of Ankh-Morpork, is less about personality or personal morality and more about conformity, fear, and feelings of supremacy.

Even though we are presented with a vastly different Ankh-Morpork in the final Discworld novels, the problems faced by the social process are not dropped altogether. Perhaps most prominent among

---

[217] Of course, it should again be stressed that the goblins feature in only two Discworld novels whereas the relationship of dwarfs and trolls was explored in at least five books—Pratchett therefore simply had had more *time* to cover the conflict between the latter two parties.

them are the "grags"—a group of fundamentalist dwarfs who try to enforce strict traditionalism in a generally progressive dwarf society. They are the main antagonists in *RS*, resorting to terrorist attacks and using rhetorics such as "all our mines will be full of stinking goblins ... unless we stand up for ourselves now!" (*RS* 151). Their fears and methods are eerily close to real-life examples, and Pratchett's inspiration is unmistakable. Thanks to the newly-inaugurated railway, the dwarf king manages to intervene in time and foil their plans to replace him on the throne. In an unprecedented moment and a further major shift for the Discworld, the king then proceeds to reveal that he is, in truth, a queen. This shift marks the end of another long journey: Pratchett had previously[218] established that his Discworld dwarfs "have no female pronouns like 'she' or 'her' [...] and no male pronouns either" (Pratchett and Briggs, *Turtle* 129), but he had not made it a pivotal world-changing plot point before.[219] Compared to earlier books, this Discworld is therefore undoubtedly more tolerant and aware of social changes, but likewise increasingly under the macrocosmic spell of the technological innovations that are gaining prominence like never before. Technology is turned into new global stories and myths— reflecting the progress of modernity in empirical reality.

With all of this in mind, Pratchett does not neglect the importance of cities as "characters" in themselves. Beyond the stench and grittiness of a city inspired by the medieval period lies a profound search for the nature or perhaps even personality of cities. When mapping Ankh-Morpork, Pratchett and Briggs were already aware that the city created in a few brush-strokes in *CoM* had developed into an entity of its own, akin to Leiber's city of Lankhmar[220] or Miéville's moloch New Crobuzon. As they state, "[w]e had to discuss the philosophy of the city. It had, without us consciously meaning it, developed a sort of architectural history" (Pratchett and Briggs, *Streets* [7]). In her reflections about spatial theory and the fantastic, Chanady concludes that Foucault

---

[218] Already in the first City Watch series novel (published in 1989), we learn that "[g]ender is more or less optional" (*GG* 36) for Discworld dwarfs. See also the footnote right below.

[219] Although it should be mentioned that one of the subplots of *MAA* revolves around the new dwarf recruit Cheery Littlebottom and her eventual decision to be openly female—which is unheard of in Dwarf society.

[220] Which was one of the major inspirations for the Ankh-Morpork of the earliest novels (Butler, *Companion* 230).

is interested not in the minute descriptions of institutions and spatial structures as such, but in the general social, political, and economic conditions that give rise to particular institutions and the way in which these institutions reflect our changing society. In an analogous way, spatial theory, rather than making us aware of the intricacies of the craft of writing, will shed light on the social conditions necessary for the emergence of the fantastic and its connection with our comprehension of the world. (Chanady 61–62)

By offering speculative spaces as an alternative to empirical reality, contemporary genre fantasy constructs elaborate scenarios that both reflect their historical conditions (with roots in mythology and folklore but also in current real-world topics) and may indeed also mirror urban developments from actual reality.

Pratchett does not go into detail concerning the making and evolution of Ankh-Morpork, as in Manzoni's exhaustive digressions from the main plots of his novels or the long lists of genealogies and linguistic background from his fellow fantasy authors. He instead includes enough allusions to hint at deeper mechanisms at work beyond the main story—which never break the flow of narrative even while his main characters may actively derail stereotypical stories. Nonetheless, space, for Pratchett as for Foucault, acts as a breeding ground for social developments and both the troubles and the potential that may come from them. In the City Watch books, Pratchett focuses on the struggles of the individual with these institutions, providing a very personal perspective on, at times, very impersonal (and indeed, inhuman) instances. Yet as the Discworld moves from its medieval fantasy outset to a more modern image, the side effects of this gradual change also begin to affect his choice in protagonists.

While several of the later Discworld novels—many of which are set in Ankh-Morpork—could be identified as examples of specific fantasy, this would again limit their range of topics covered. The fact that the Discworld turned its initial success into a long-term bestselling series is undoubtedly due to its adaptability and openness to further, newer influences, and its premier city is no exception to this incorporation of new content. As new subgenres and variations of the fantasy genre appeared towards the end of the 20th century, Pratchett did not remain limited to including topics and developments of empirical reality in his own novels but drew further inspiration from these literary developments. The consequences of this openness, however, detracted from the once-dominant focus on smaller, often more personal changes on the Discworld, featuring a new main character and plots that were both harbingers of bigger effects and which slowly changed not merely parts but the whole of Pratchett's secondary world.

CHAPTER 10

THE INDUSTRIALIZATION AND MULTIMEDIALITY OF THE DISCWORLD

WITH ITS RECURRING CAST of fantasy races and genre tropes such as magic and wizardry, the Discworld has always remained close to the outset of its earliest parodies. Nevertheless, the final Discworld novels undoubtedly portray a world that has evolved beyond its medieval design in *CoM*. Unsurprisingly, the city of Ankh-Morpork is both a basis for and reference point for such evolution. Having started out as a typical medieval/Renaissance metropolis of classic fantasy, Pratchett's city quickly began picking up traits from other eras of history.[221]

Most evident among the amalgam of history, and a clear indicator of the changes that the entire secondary world has undergone by the last novels, is the influence of the Victorian Age:

> While the series as a whole is fantasy, the great city of Ankh-Morpork is strongly reminiscent of Victorian London, with its vast divides between rich and poor, its small factories and manufacturing districts, guilds and apprenticeship systems; [...] the plots and corruptions gleefully reported in many thriving, competing newspapers; [...] the influx of racially diverse immigrants and the tensions they cause, the rural hinterland supporting the city; its growing international connections and its rapidly evolving technology. (Croft 4–5)

The Victorian era saw an intertwined counter-influence between these sociological and technological developments. They are currently receiving new attention in genre literature, specifically in the subgenres of Neo-Victorian and Steampunk[222] fiction. Especially as we look at the

---

[221] According to *The Art of Discworld*, Ankh-Morpork bears resemblances to medieval Prague and Tallin, 18th-century London and 19th-century Seattle and 20th-century New York (Pratchett and Kidby [6]).

[222] I use the term "Steampunk" to cover the literary genre. Steampunk as a cultural movement is of course a much bigger development (and parts of its crafting and artisan nature apply to the Discworld), but my focus lies on its novelistic techniques. Likewise, I use the term "Neo-Victorian" in some instances. Even though this genre of literature is certainly not identical with Steampunk, the two subgenres both exerted an equally strong influence on the Discworld.

Ankh-Morpork of the later Discworld novels in even more detail, it is evident that numerous elements from both subgenres find expression in the books. Besides adding to the refinement and believability of Pratchett's secondary world, they also act as harbingers of change—not just for Ankh-Morpork and the Discworld as a literary space but furthermore for the franchise itself.

While there had been maps, companions, and other releases outside of new novels since the 1990s, by the mid-2000s the amount of Discworld content published in other media began to expand considerably. Covering the entire scope of these publications would need its own separate study, yet there is one medium that should be given more attention in this chapter: the Discworld video games. Not only do they combine mapping and storytelling, they also offer a fresh perspective on Pratchett's literary space as well as his concept of narrative imperative.

THE VICTORIANIZATION OF ANKH-MORPORK

While there are few direct references to Victorian topics or its literary revival in Pratchett's books, he certainly is aware of their sources. Most obviously, *Dodger*,[223] a non-Discworld book set in Victorian London, clearly indicates Pratchett's indebtedness to Charles Dickens and Henry Mayhew, even featuring fictionalized versions of the two authors. As chroniclers of urban experience, Dickens and Mayhew find more than an echo in the crowded and "increasingly nineteenth-century city of Ankh-Morpork" (James and Mendlesohn, *History* 183) of the later books. But everyday life in the Ankh-Morpork of any novel already displays very Dickensian qualities at times: "Ankh-Morpork lives on the street. [...] The street is where you live, eat and get your entertainment while waiting for your turn in bed. The whole of the city is, in fact, a proto-mob. [...] What it craves, what it lives on, is entertainment. It is, generally, friendly" (Pratchett and Kidby [33]). In tune with the unapologetic but ultimately positive portrayal of social behavior in Discworld novels in general, the mob likes violence as much as any other source of distraction in a similar manner to everyday life on the streets in Mayhew's description of 19th-century London (76–81, 93–99). Nevertheless, it is not from this ambiguous

---

[223] Whose eponymous main character is unquestionably inspired by The Artful Dodger of Dickens' novel *Oliver Twist*.

behavior that social change may derive. Pratchett's hope for the future lies in smaller, gradually increasing changes and not in sweeping revolutions. In *NW*, we encounter a social upheaval which ultimately fails, as revolutions "always come around again" because "they're called *revolutions*" (*NW* 277; my emphasis). Change, in Pratchett's world, nearly always begins with the decision of an individual but often ends badly in the hands of larger movements.

Perhaps the best example for less drastic social change in Ankh-Morpork is the rise of the new City Watch, a clear parallel to the personal development of Samuel Vimes. When we first encounter the police force in *GG*, the Watch building is hardly more than a ruin, run by the alcoholic commander and his equally unfit officers Colon and Nobby. Yet by the end of this Discworld novel, the Watch has gained new enthusiasm and capability, much of it owing to the idealism of the new recruit Carrot and Vimes' determination to defend "his" city from a dragon. With the recurring routes of the City Watch across Ankh-Morpork, we can also mark the rising importance of a map for the later Discworld novels: As pointed out before, Pratchett found himself ensnared by the readers' imagination. A map became necessary because his audience was able to see and visualize the Discworld for itself—and the author needed to follow his own rules to avoid inconsistencies.[224] Moreover, it provided a basis for the Discworld novels that were to follow: by mapping the city, Ankh-Morpork was marked to become "a narrative space which effects [sic] the types of narratives which can unfold within its environs" (Hills 223), but this was not yet so with the first maps released.

Indeed, there is a city map at the front of *NW* (8)—however, this layout of the metropolis, the novel makes clear, is not what one should focus on. Likewise, in the earlier Discworld novel *MAA*, Carrot explains the intricacies and secret passages of the streets of Ankh-Morpork to the new recruits of the City Watch:

> 'Interesting thing,' he said. 'I bet there's not many people know that you can get to Zephire Street from Broad Way. You ask anyone. They'll say you can't get out of the other end of Shirt Alley. But

---

[224] One notable instance of inconsistency is the portrayal of the Patrician Vetinari. In the first Discworld novel, he is described as "cradl[ing] his chins in a beringed hand" (*CoM* 41). By his second appearance in *S*, his physical appearance is entirely different and has taken on its definitive form as "thin, tall and apparently as cold-blooded as a dead penguin" (*S* 76).

you can because, all you do, you go up Mormius Street, and then you can squeeze between these bollards *here* into Borborygmic Lane—good, aren't they, very good iron—and here we are in Whilom Alley. (*MAA* 30)

Mapping the streets mentally while walking is not simply useful but crucial when members of the City Watch are on duty: They need to know which shortcuts lead where, which back-alleys are dead ends in case of an emergency.[225] In other words, personal experience is necessary, and one cannot learn about shortcuts via maps. Moreover, if we compare *The Streets of Ankh-Morpork* of 1993 with *The Compleat Ankh-Morpork City Guide* of 2012, the first city map was anything but complete—and neither was exploring the city in the novels. With the novels released during those twenty years of Discworld, the completion and narrative density of Pratchett's secondary world had grown extensively, in the books as much as in the portrayal of Ankh-Morpork itself.

Consequently, the Ankh-Morpork of the 2000s and 2010s is a very different city from the Ankh-Morpork of the 1980s and 1990s. Pratchett gleefully took up technological revolutions such as the Internet and mobile phones and added them to his Discworld in slightly modified form. Innovations in empirical reality thus became innovations in the secondary world—and Pratchett eventually preferred to resort to an age known for its explosion of technological innovation, namely the Victorian era. In the final Discworld novel, there is a glimpse of an Ankh-Morpork that has begun to be reshaped and modernized on a large scale, a city with railway arches and trains passing overhead even though on the Discworld "railway was still in its infancy" (*SC* 175), but this is only the pinnacle of a long and dynamic process that began in earlier books. Pratchett again aims to provide the Discworld with a solid grounding in reality by not changing his secondary world

---

[225] Although the Discworld and Ankh-Morpork are fictional places, Pratchett treats them with the same earnestness as if they were real, thereby underlining the need for secondary belief of the readers despite his irony (which breaks belief again and again). Since London is a real place, Dickens had the opportunity to pace the streets himself and take notes to ensure an accurate fictional representation of reality when writing his novels; Pratchett, however, had to rely solely on the map of Ankh-Morpork. Nonetheless, his dedication to consistency within his secondary world rivals Dickens' approach to detail. The degree of consistency in the Discworld and Ankh-Morkpork is no small feat, especially when keeping in mind the constant jabs at the pitfalls of fantasy. Yet seeing that Pratchett's secondary world has evolved over such a long time as to reflect changes in the actual world (most prominently the rise of the Internet), it is not so much surprising.

fundamentally within one novel and one major social upheaval or eucatastrophic change; this gradual process, once again, is primarily achieved by his unsentimental approach to the genre.

Like the Discworld, the city of Ankh-Morpork is not regarded as a finished project stuck forever in the same time or anticipating a cataclysmic event as the end to an era, but—even more so than the Discworld—as an ongoing development with both positive and negative aspects. What is more, the subtle individual changes that the city undergoes with each new inhabitant and their interactions with others are not immediately apparent at all times:

> Against the dark screen of night, Vimes had a vision of Ankh-Morpork. It wasn't a city, it was a *process*, a weight on the world that distorted the land for hundreds of miles around. People who'd never seen it in their whole life nevertheless spent their life working for it. Thousands and thousands of green acres were part of it, forests were part of it. It drew in and consumed...
> ... and gave back the dung from its pens and the soot from its chimneys, and steel, and saucepans, and all the tools by which its food was made. [...] That's what civilization *meant*. It meant the city. (*NW* 390)

Although the image of this process is overwhelming,[226] surmounting the city walls of Ankh-Morpork and engulfing the surrounding countryside, there is nonetheless a positive side to the dynamics between space and power.

Compared to the regal ascension and restrictive social strata of classic fantasy, the Discworld offers various opportunities to achieve personal fulfillment without having to embark on an epic journey to save the entire world—an opportunity much more realistic than the stereotypical plots of derivative fantasy and also championing individual choice to a greater extent. Yet the disadvantages are not neglected (for example the sheer amount of waste[227] produced by an ever-more industrial city), thereby providing balance to the in-depth depiction of both the Discworld and, in more detail, of Ankh-Morpork.

Not just because of these traits, the last Discworld novels set

---

[226] Also strongly evocative of George Cruikshank's 1829 caricature *London Going Out of Town or the March of Bricks and Mortar* satirizing the expansion of London in the early 19th century.

[227] Exemplary for the organic social mobility in Ankh-Morpork is Harry King, who started out as a mere garbage collector but eventually becomes part of nobility due to his riches gained by his waste businesses (Pratchett and Briggs, *Turtle Recall* 207–08).

in Ankh-Morpork are seen as the most "Victorian"[228] of Pratchett's fantasy books. Here, "the effect[s] of a free press, the telegraph, and [...] technological advances" (Croft 4) alongside issues of immigration and urbanization have truly taken hold in the Discworld and particularly in Ankh-Morpork. They show the city as "the alchemist in reverse" (*Making Money* 146), turning not just gold[229] but everyone and everything that inhabits or enters its premises into something different. It is a process that stands on the threshold between past and future—a future that seems very different from the medieval outset of *CoM*. Ankh-Morpork, more so than ever before, becomes representative of the entirety of the Discworld. The power of this openness is immense:

> The city was no longer perceived as a place of privilege, as an exception in a territory of fields, forests, and roads. [...] Instead, the cities, with the problems that they raised, and the particular forms that they took, served as the models for the governmental rationality that was to apply to the whole of the territory. (Foucault, "Knowledge" 241)

Creating a living history, Pratchett constantly reminds readers both of Ankh-Morpork's age and its improvements that slowly spread out to the rest of the Discworld. Indeed, the future of the city grows out of this past, has been built on it like the newer quarters that have been erected on the remains of the old. Therefore, we see "the roofline [of Ankh-Morpork as] a forest of clacks towers, winking and twinkling in the sunlight" (*Going Postal* 88), a modern communication system rising out of a medieval cityscape. Pratchett's tone is humorous and places emphasis on the fact that the towers are "more effective than strapping a message to an owl or an albatross" (Butler, *Companion* 360); at the same time, the technological revolution implied by those means of communicating is constantly underlined.

The Discworld and Ankh-Morpork that we read about in the final novels have not yet fallen under the full spell of industrialization—the original secondary world, including its parodist core, remains visible. Nevertheless, the new narrative of technology as a modern myth finds representation in the main character of the final series of Discworld novels, Moist von Lipwig.

---

[228] Or, to be precise, "Neo-Victorian."
[229] *MM* addresses the abolition of the gold standard on the Discworld and the introduction of paper money—another technological and social revolution.

TECHNOLOGICAL CHANGE ON THE DISCWORLD

Vimes and Granny, with their knowledge of stories and the unpredictability of people, are both characters that remain steadfastly suspicious of change—for all their motivation to fight narrative conventions and rigid belief systems. The danger of change, according to Vimes, is that it is potentially "just waiting for some idiot to do the wrong thing, and Nature is bountiful where idiots are concerned" (*NW* 275). The main plot of *MAA* is a perfect example of such change going wrong, of technology mingling with social upheaval: Power in this manner finds its objectified expression in the "gonne"—the Discworld prototype of a rifle weapon—that is used by an assassin under a plan to bring a new order[230] to Ankh-Morpork by killing the Patrician. Vimes can foil the plot and restore the peace while the weapon does not appear in any further novels. The change and power inherent in this object would be too drastic a change for the Discworld. Yet looking at specific novels, technology has formed part of Pratchett's parody from the beginning. In *CoM*, the tourist Twoflower carries "a device for making pictures quickly" (52), an iconograph which, even though it is operated by a demon and thus to a certain extent magical, is nevertheless a machine. Consequent novels feature further equivalents of complex real-world technology: apart from the Discworld version of guns, they include spaceships, motorcycles, and personal organizers (Butler, *Companion* 359). Yet while these items are crucial for the plot or a character, none of them impacts the Discworld as a world—the inhabitants of the Discworld neither become a spacefaring folk nor do they mass-produce guns for warfare or security. Pratchett steered clear of making his mirror of worlds too exact a copy of empirical reality, in order to keep the integrity and role of its main characters intact.[231]

The stories of Rincewind, Granny, Tiffany, and Vimes hence involve little extended debate on technology or drastic social upheavals in a fantasy context except for dismissal or ignorance—and even then, the topic at hand is not an element that affects the Discworld on a

---

[230] Which is, ironically, an old order, namely the restoration of the royal bloodline to the throne of Ankh-Morpork. A counter-narrative, if you will.

[231] Too many dystopian elements would have not merely weakened but destroyed the Discworld's generally positively minded humor, bitter and satirical as it can be. Only rarely does Pratchett indulge in Orwellian satire (Smith 154) to point out the cruelties of war or the absurdities of politics.

macro-level. To adequately cover the decisive social and technological changes that the Discworld experienced in the last years prior to Pratchett's passing, I focus on the Discworld books whose overarching story is set around the implementation of innovation within a larger social context—the Moist von Lipwig novels.

Unlike the other main characters of the Discworld, whose relation to technology is suspicious at best, Moist von Lipwig is an accelerator of change for Pratchett's secondary world: Introduced to readers as "a natural born criminal, a fraudster by vocation, a habitual liar, a perverted genius and totally untrustworthy" (*GP* 24), he not only has a talent for setting ideas in motion, but as a con man knows how to embody different roles. Saved from the gallows by Lord Vetinari who also "only truly initiates change [...] when it is absolutely necessary" (Butler, *Companion* 398), and employs him for precisely this purpose, Moist turns the city's postal service "from a calamity into a smoothly running machine" (*MM* 26) and manages to revolutionize the Discworld's system of finances— ironically precisely due to his gifts for crime and fraud (Guilfoy 121). What is essential about Moist as a character is that he is practically forced into specific jobs which he at first resents but soon grows into.[232] In general, changing his identity is nothing new for him:

> Here was Moist von Lipwig walking through the city. He'd never done that before. The late Albert Spangler had, and so had Mundo Smith and Edwin Streep and half a dozen other personas that he'd donned and discarded. Oh, he'd been Moist inside (what a name, yes, he'd heard every possible joke), but *they* had been outside, between him and the world. (*GP* 70)

Granny and Vimes carefully hone their chosen roles as witch or watchman even as they adapt to new challenges. Moist, on the other hand, constantly had to create new personalities for lucrative opportunities and survival throughout his criminal life. His approach to theatrical performances is very encompassing and adaptable, making him the ideal—read: more impressionable—agent for change on a larger scale.

While Vetinari is no Lilith attempting to stage fairy-tale perfection,[233] he nonetheless arrests a talented con man at the beginning of *GP* and faces him with the choice to take on a specific occupation

---

[232] In order: Head of Ankh-Morpork's postal service (*GP*), bank manager (*MM*), and finally railway entrepreneur (*RS*).

[233] As pointed out before, he is very much aware of the perils of this false idealism.

that he does not want or to be executed for his crimes. Moist's role—and narrative—is enforced on him by the city's ruler from the start, much like that of Rincewind's role as tourist guide in *CoM* and *LF*.

Through this new main character who "knew about the zeitgeist [and] tasted it in the wind" (*RS* 91), Pratchett achieves the true introduction of technological innovation and thus bigger changes to the Discworld. Moist's revamping of the postal service enhances[234] the Discworld's equivalent of Morse code, effectively creating a telegraph line system (or even a rudimentary Internet, perhaps) for this secondary world: a vast system of semaphore towers that now act "as the principal method of communicating over long distances on Discworld" (Pratchett and Briggs, *Companion* 80). The common factor that all of these innovations emphasize is that although many inhabitants of the Discworld are reluctant about change, it is ultimately inevitable. However, this does not mean that it is accepted unanimously but, as always, deeply ambiguous since "people in Ankh-Morpork professed not to like change while at the same time fixating on every new entertainment and diversion that came their way" (*RS* 74). In empirical reality,[235] no less than on the Discworld, violent reactions sometimes occur against any new dynamics. As the fanaticism of the main antagonists in *RS*—the aforementioned "grags"—falls short of Pratchett's earlier, more complex reflections on evil, it is far more interesting to judge the reactions of the general Ankh-Morpork citizenry upon first seeing the railway. Besides marvel, there is a fear of the unknown and uncertainty, which would normally be reserved for the supernatural—incongruously, a piece of technology taken directly from empirical reality evokes such reactions on the otherwise down-to-earth Discworld.

Here, we come back to Pratchett's dichotomous attitude towards progress, which, for all its possible enrichment of life, does not automatically change the social conditions to the same extent. The results of this unbalanced development—alienation, mass consumption, fear

---

[234] The technology had existed before; however only through the entrepreneurial aptitude of Moist does it achieve acceptance and use on a wider scale. Incidentally, it also acts as another instrument of societal acceptance for goblins, who eventually take over the maintenance and operation of the semaphore towers.

[235] Perhaps the best historical example for open hate of new technology are the Luddites, although their fear was losing employment due to machines, not fear of innovation itself.

of loss of individuality—are all topics of postmodernist literature that are also addressed in Discworld novels through a fantasy lens. As in Pratchett's later fiction, "the themes of the Industrial Revolution [...] overlap nicely with those of steampunk" (Croft 4), and it is hence not surprising that this hybrid genre which is concerned with the same topics regarding the relationship between technology and human life found its expression on the Discworld as well:

> As an aesthetic, steampunk appeals to those who express discontent with the lack of tactile-focused beauty and the sense of disembodiment contained within today's technological design. It is not surprising, then, that in discussions about the purpose and meaning of technology in human lives, questions concerning steampunk subculture's political possibilities emerge. (Pho 185)

Similarly, the literary genre Steampunk is as little about simply escapism as fantasy—indeed, its major aim is also about portraying empirical reality in mimetic alternatives and variations of history. Like the Discworld (and the genres of fantasy and science fiction), its better examples were always a mirror of the real world.

What is more, both Steampunk and Discworld novels go beyond mere application of technology with supernatural or counterfactual extensions and feature the social backlash of such rapid development as well: "While [the Victorian] era featured great strides in aesthetics and technology, politically it was tainted by colonialism, imperialism, and racism" (VanderMeer and Chambers 39)—conflicts of equal importance to Steampunk as they are to Pratchett's fiction.

As Steampunk indeed tries to link past to future[236] and recreate both in our present, it is first and foremost a reconsideration of science fiction and fantasy as genres in themselves. Indeed, the triumph of new technologies had social consequences far from the speculative visions of many science fiction authors, processes which did not evade reflection by Pratchett's ambiguous change on his Discworld, nor in Steampunk literature:

> The popularity of steampunk in recent decades surely reflects changing experiences among the readers and writers of science fiction. [...] Today the science fiction future lies behind us. The works of Clarke, Asimov, and Heinlein have become, to modern readers, a kind of inadvertent steampunk with their giant, self-aware vacuum computers and nuclear powered dishwashers. (Haigh 30–31)

---

[236] In this regard, Steampunk acts as an example of retro-futuristic fiction.

The critical nostalgia of Steampunk sets the future in the past and is another method of evoking cognitive dissonance and producing incongruity: Contemporary authors of speculative fiction embrace the hybridity and merging of genres that were still differentiated rather clearly as "science fiction" or "fantasy" in the mid-20th century. Pratchett too expands his initial framework of fantasy with elements from established and emerging genres, Steampunk (and Neo-Victorian) elements being more prominent in the Moist von Lipwig novels. Herein lies another of the reasons why the final Discworld novels differ from the sharp satire of the mid-period books: While Pratchett still uses the same techniques to ridicule and criticize emerging topics in culture and empirical reality, his creation is becoming saturated (Wolf 49–51) — if not overfilled — with a plethora of existing and additional content.

We therefore encounter numerous counterparts to real-world technology on the Discworld that only appear ridiculous at first glance. More importantly, they underline the fact that while they are perhaps not all harbingers of change for the Discworld, any secondary world which remains forever within a progressless frozen time will eventually be considered stale and petrified both socially and historically. Since magic on the Discworld is not the *deus ex machina* device as in so many other fantasy novels but rather a tool, Pratchett considered it "inevitable that the combination of enthusiastic [wizardry] students and a disinterested faculty would lead to the creation of a machine to explore the unknown and to advance the search for knowledge" (Pratchett and Briggs, *Turtle Recall* 186–87), culminating in the construction of the Discworld computer Hex. Ironically, again and again, the wizards take on the role of scientists and focus their research on topics that have little to do with magic and more with rational knowledge. Like Steampunk, "simultaneously retro and forward-looking in nature" (VanderMeer and Chambers 9), Pratchett does not abandon the Discworld's past for a lightspeed science fiction future, but instead combines the two into an anachronistic mirror of historical advances[237] in technology — in his

---

[237] The Industrial Revolution of the Discworld does not happen out of the blue but is in fact implied to have originated long before the events of the final novels: In *Reaper Man* (the 11th Discworld novel, released in 1991), an inventor named Ned Simnel thinks about new forms of powering a rudimentary combination harvester when a whistling teapot distracts him (174–75). In *RS*, published in 2013, it is his son Dick Simnel who brings the idea of combining steam and mechanics to fruition, resulting in the Discworld's first steam engine.

case, they are not set in the Victorian Age but on a secondary world of fantasy that takes cues from that period.

Yet as Pratchett stated himself long before introducing game-changing innovations to his secondary world,

> once you invent the railways, you have seriously changed your civilization and there's no going back. Now you've got the bulk movement of people and materials over long distances, cheaply, and you're beginning a huge upheaval. You can't have a medieval society with railways *continuing to be a medieval society*, even if you've got dragons heating the boilers. (McCabe 269)

In tune with his unmitigated approach to fantasy, having the Discworld undergo the full consequences of an industrial revolution meant making these consequences a major subject of ensuing novels. This reveals one of the downsides of creating a secondary world that embraces dynamic change: as it incorporates additional content, the whole picture of the secondary world is modified with every new piece. The earliest Discworld novels already showed sparks of Pratchett's encompassing satire, yet they were little more than parodies of fantasy as a genre. The main strength of the Discworld—to be able to adapt a plethora of topics otherwise unused in fantasy—eventually detracted from it as a mirror of worlds, and the critical reflection slowly gave way to increased extension and densification of the secondary world.

Certain aspects of classic fantasy thus disappear as elements from other, more technologically or otherwise differently oriented genres find their way into the secondary world. This is expressed by a sense of nostalgia connected to the technological innovations on the Discworld, given prominence for example in the quiet lament of the final city guide regarding the revolutionary implications of a semaphore system across the Discworld: "Our Clacks system may not have the appeal of a traditional handwritten letter and by its very nature the message will be brief. But for guaranteed accuracy and speed of communication the Clacks system is second to none" (Pratchett, *City Guide* 32). Staying true to Pratchett's ironic and down-to-earth attitude, it is further classic characters from fantasy who begin to realize that their role in this emerging new world has become obsolete—not merely the heroes but also their former nemeses: "'Who really *appreciates* a good Dark Lord these days? The world's too complicated now. It don't [sic] belong to the likes of us anymore..." (*LH* 59). Like Granny Weatherwax, the brave new Discworld is not for them anymore, with novelties coming from Ankh-Morpork on a regular basis. Pratchett claims he "tried to capture the feeling of a city that would go on running *even if the story stopped*" (Pratchett and Kidby [7]), a quasi-autonomous mechanism fuelled by innovation as well as social and technological change.

It would be an overreach to imbue a fictional creation with anything but an implied narrative life beyond what has been written. What can be taken into account, however, is Pratchett's attention to detail and the crucial role of change on his secondary world, the perspective to see it as more than just background: "Discussing Ankh-Morpork in such terms is to treat it *as real*, to assert that civic life continues away from the spotlight and focus of the books' narratives" (Hills 220). Not the mockery and adaptation of technology within a fantasy world, but the dynamics of the Discworld reveal its closest resemblance to Steampunk and Neo-Victorian literature.

Middle-earth is a secondary world which is "densely interwoven" (Manlove, *Studies* 54), whereas many of the commercialized fantasy worlds can be considered specimens of fantasyland. Nonetheless, it has become clear that they share a general idea of stasis: In classic fantasy, the secondary world predominantly changes only during singular events. "Tolkien married the adventure fantasy with epic: suddenly, the journey on which the participants embarked had world-shattering consequences" (James and Mendlesohn, *History* 48), yet apart from such singular apocalyptic events, the world of Middle-earth and its descendants are locked in a pseudo-medieval age potentially lasting for centuries. It is here that we arrive at the true Steampunk features of the Discworld. Not only did Pratchett embrace the dynamic change that is found in Steampunk fiction and to an extent also in groundbreaking fantasy novels of the early 21st century,[238] he also reflected on the long-term changes this development might have, even though the subversive depiction of clichés became weaker in the late novels as the Discworld's focus shifted to the consequences of modernization. As Pratchett himself pointed out, there are "[p]lenty of good stories there, but before long, your world is going to be unrecognizable" (McCabe 269).

---

[238] Besides Jeff VanderMeer, Jasper Fforde, and China Miéville, further genre-defying fantasy authors of the late 20th and early 21st century include Scott Lynch, Erin Morgenstern, and Ben Aaronovich.

Therefore, Ankh-Morpork changed from its pseudo-medieval outset, and by extension so did the entire secondary world. The process of innovation also extended to culture, technology, and history—less an expansive back-story and mythology such as Tolkien's but rather a present-oriented and constantly evolving metanarrative of the Discworld as an ongoing process. This is clearly one of the reasons why for decades the Discworld novels have continued to be bestsellers: Pratchett was constantly aware of the changes in our world and incorporated them into his own, thereby keeping the Discworld up-to-date despite slowly moving away from its initial core topics. As part of this shift and openness, the Discworld has grown far beyond mere textual representation. Pratchett's fiction, at first visualized through maps and posters, soon found additional narrative opportunities in different media outlets. Today, there are "comics, a cookbook, diaries, merchandising, plays and television adaptations" (Butler, *Companion* 118), to name but a few publications outside of the novels—all of which provide new means of telling stories. Yet, one medium represents a more interactive version of staged narratives—namely the Discworld video games.[239] Due to their linear plots that players can explore in non-linear fashion, they are arguably one of the most pure forms of postmodern storytelling and offer yet another perspective on narrative imperative.

THE DISCWORLD FRANCHISE AND INTERMEDIAL NARRATIVES

Given the long-term success of Discworld, it is little wonder that the novels were adapted in other media. As laid out in the preceding chapters, maps were among the first intermedial releases that turned Pratchett's creation from a series of books into a franchise. The novels still remained central and continued to feature the most vital additions to the secondary world, but the inclusion of further media also added to its completion: "Thus, transmediality also suggests the potential for the continuance of a world, in multiple instances and registers; and the more we see and hear of a transmedial world, the greater is the illusion of ontological weight that it has, and experiencing the world becomes more like the mediated experience of the Primary World" (Wolf 247). The portrayal of a secondary world in different media can

---

[239] Covering the full scope of the Discworld's intermediality truly deserves a book of its own—one which I hope to see in the not-to-far future.

extend its believability and support the Tolkienian spell of suspension of disbelief.[240] Additional material is provided for the world to increase its verisimilitude outside of its main narratives, yet it remains based on the source text(s), a common-place event especially in genre literature such as *Harry Potter* and *LotR* but also the Discworld novels.

Looking at intermediality in literary theory, a definition of the term is as problematic[241] as it is for the other major concepts we have encountered throughout this book: Acting as an encompassing definition, intermediality has, like fantasy and postmodernism, a plethora of notoriously multitudinous meanings. Indeed, the critical assessment of the different medial expressions in narratology remains an open debate:

> While the concept of medium has become very prominent in narratology, there are so many candidates available to refer to the relations between narrative and media that terminology has become a true nightmare: what, if any, are the differences between transmediality, intermediality, plurimediality, and multi-mediality (not to mention multimodality)? (Grishakova and Ryan 3)

Judging from the Discworld releases after the first novels, Pratchett's oeuvre is hard to pinpoint within this vast array of possible definitions and subdefinitions: there are narratives spanning several media that are still considered part of the main Discworld stories[242] or part of the extended franchise that may reference or follow the plot of certain novels (the truly multi-medial Discworld video games). However, for the ease of analysis, I still mainly use the term "intermediality" in the following section.

---

[240] Or alternatively break it. Most controversial in this regard is the tendency to produce additional commercial value from existing material, exemplified by Peter Jackson's decision to turn Tolkien's thin volume *H* into three feature-length *Hobbit* films as with *LotR*. Jackson was heavily criticized and the films were panned—particularly because the main story was expanded with source material from Tolkien's notes in order to fill in material that would not have sufficed for three films otherwise.

[241] Linked to the problem of intermediality is the debate surrounding the term "medium" itself (Rippl 6). As a thorough examination of the different attempts at defining the term (and the implications thereof for a subsequent definition of intermediality) would need another full theory chapter, I leave these problems largely uncovered, opting for "a broad understanding of the term [...] of how meaning is generated" (9) instead.

[242] A good example being the employment of images and text in the illustrated novel *LH*.

CROSSING MEDIA AND NARRATIVE

After Terry Pratchett's passing in March 2015, his daughter and fellow writer Rhianna Pratchett announced that she would not continue her father's legacy by writing further Discworld novels, but might be involved in projects such as television adaptations. As she has been part of Pratchett's own media production company Narrativia (with the goal to create faithful Discworld screen adaptations) since its launch in 2012, her decision opens up a vast realm of speculation. Two animated features and three live-action Discworld films (released before the creation of Narrativia) exist so far, as well as a 2019 short film based on Pratchett's story "Troll Bridge." An animated movie adaptation of his Discworld book, *The Amazing Maurice and His Educated Rodents*, was released 2022. With Narrativia and its abundant source material, further films and series based on Pratchett's work have a good chance to emerge in the future.[243]

Yet looking at the crucial role of space and cartography on the Discworld, the most important first addition to the novels themselves were the maps and companions. Indeed, it is in these cross-media publications that the different nature of later Discworld releases becomes most evident, since even the style of writing changes to accommodate changes that the world itself is undergoing. *The Compleat Ankh-Morpork City Guide*, an illustrated book released in 2012, thus greets readers with the following message:

> We lay before you this most comprehensive gazetteer encompassing all the streets of Ankh-Morpork, as well as information on its principal businesses, hotels, taverns, inns, and places of entertainment and refreshment, enhanced by the all-new and compleat [sic] map of our great city state. For the first time ever, this work of cartographic excellence delineates in the most exquisite detail not just the main highways of the city but all roads, lanes, alleys and even ginnells [sic] and yards. (Pratchett, *City Guide* 4)

While Pratchett has always taken great care to keep the style of his novels consistent—that is to say, ironic, self-reflective, and succinct—in these companion works we encounter another, more ornate and precocious manner of writing.[244] It is reproduced again in the lengthily

---

[243] So far, the most successful endeavor of Narrativia is the BBC TV series *Good Omens*, based on the novel co-written by Terry Pratchett and Neil Gaiman.

[244] One could speculate whether Pratchett still wrote these guides himself, as his Alzheimer's disease had progressed by this time to impair his cognitive abilities to a larger extent. Certainly, they are collaborations with artists; yet how far Pratchett himself orchestrated this change in style remains debatable.

titled *Mrs Bradshaw's Handbook to Travelling upon the Ankh-Morpork & Sto Plains Hygienic Railway*, a 2014 companion to the penultimate Discworld novel and clearly a direct mirroring of George Bradshaw's guides from the 19th century.[245] The style and illustrations of this book indicate definite influences from Victorian and Neo-Victorian writing, imitating the language and culture of the era that also influenced the final novels to an extent. While less prevalent in the novels themselves, the two first Moist von Lipwig books feature chapter titles (which exist in nearly none of the other Discworld novels), and every chapter gives an overview of the content to follow in a mock-Victorian style à la Charles Dickens. This is a far step from the pseudo-medieval fantasy worlds parodied in *CoM*—the Ankh-Morpork of the 2010s features troll buses, dwarfen cuisine in railway wagons, and numerous other combinations of fantasy tropes with Neo-Victorian themes.

What all of these guides achieve is an intermedial densification of narrative enmeshment as stated by Wolf. They extend the narrative potential of the Discworld beyond mere text, thereby crossing borders between media as much as between genres. The process of these crossovers is one of intense communication: "Intermediality applies in its broadest sense to any transgression of boundaries between conventionally and culturally distinct media and thus is concerned with 'heteromedial' relations between different semiotic complexes and how they communicate cultural content" (Rippl 12). The combination of visual, textual, and also acoustic[246] elements adds a further dimension to the hybridization of Pratchett's oeuvre from the mid-1990s onwards. As with genres, so the extension of the Discworld to different media resulted in an additional authenticity of the secondary world. Once more, the ironic but nonetheless mimetic interpretation of examples from empirical reality gave the Discworld equivalents of technologies, maps, guides, and portfolios an aura of recognizability without ever fully destroying the suspension of disbelief. Indeed, the embracing of new technologies in a mock-Victorian style underlines

---

[245] Although Bradshaw was primarily known for his railway timetables (which were so popular that they became known as "Bradshaws" during the Victorian era), there were also numerous travellers' guides to various countries published under his name long after his death in 1853.

[246] Not limited to the video games set on the Discworld but also more prominently in "a soundtrack CD for *Soul Music From Terry Pratchett's Discworld*" and a (albeit non-Discworld) Pratchett musical (Butler, *Companion* 256–57).

the Discworld's proximity to Steampunk, also well-known for its portrayal in media other than writing (VanderMeer and Chambers 69–89). Nevertheless, for all their variety in style and content, what all of these expansions of the Discworld have in common is their lack of interactivity. The interplay between consumer and product is unilateral, meaning that we can read, view, or listen to the narratives, but we cannot actively influence their stories. Therefore, to give an example of storytelling in "which user input affects the behaviour of a text" (Herman et al., *Encyclopedia* 250) as well as image and sound, the interactivity of the Discworld video games is a perfect showcase of new possibilities for narrative—and simultaneously links back to the relation of mapping and storytelling on Pratchett's secondary world.

Indeed, perhaps the most crucial point of establishing the Discworld and Ankh-Morpork in several media was one of its first multifold transmedial adaptations: In 1995, video game developer Psygnosis published a *Discworld* adventure game[247] for PC, Mac, and later for PlayStation. As part of a genre typically associated with "elaborate video game worlds" (Wolf 141), the classic point-and-click nature of the first *Discworld* game offers maps to the player across which to navigate Rincewind—it is no wonder that he, the Discworld's quest-fantasy equivalent, should be the one to be sent on another journey in another medium. With *The Discworld Mapp* being released later that same year and the first city map having been published two years prior, the depiction of an accurate Ankh-Morpork map in the game was certainly no coincidence—indeed, the plot of the *Discworld* game is similar to that of *GG* (Butler, *Companion* 95), only with Rincewind as the main character instead of Vimes.

More importantly, in this and other narratives set outside the books, the audience could suddenly influence the way stories would develop to a certain extent, giving the concept of *immersion* a new meaning:

> In one sense, the experience of imaginary worlds has always required the active participation of the audience, whose imaginations are called upon to fill gaps and complete the world gestalten needed to

---

[247] It should be noted that this was not the first Discworld video game: In 1986, a text adventure game named *The Colour of Magic* was released for ZX Spectrum and Commodore 64. While important in its own right, I am not going to include it in my analysis as being entirely textual, the game misses what is central for this part of the book—namely visual elements and a virtual map by which the player may navigate the world.

bring a world to life. However, such participation does not actively change the events occurring in the worlds imagined; stories have predetermined outcomes, and their worlds are experienced vicariously through the characters in those stories. Nevertheless, just as the role of stories' main characters changed from observer to participant, interactive worlds changed the audience member's role from observer to participant. (Wolf 138)

Especially in an interactive medium such as video games, this change provides the audience with a certain amount of power to control the story: While video games[248] are often no exception from the classic patterns of storytelling and feature a beginning, a middle, and an end, the player is given a specific amount of freedom in regards to the sequence of events. Thus, in *Discworld* or its two sequels, for example, a choice of three related events may be experienced in any order—unlike in a fixed textual story,[249] where the sequence follows a given structure. This means that even as the main narrative cannot be changed, the player may approach individual points of it at their own choice and leisure.

The three Discworld adventure games also allow a non-linear exploration of the Discworld from a cartographical perspective: Story progression happens only if certain spaces are revisited at a later time to solve riddles and open new paths. In the same manner as readers are reintroduced to specific locations of the Discworld in several novels (prime examples being Lancre and Ankh-Morpork), the Discworld video games change spatially as well as temporally as the game progresses. What is more, the trademark irony of the Discworld is translated into the medium—hence Rincewind[250] and the

---

[248] To avoid confusion, I refer to Discworld games as video games instead of computer games even though they almost exclusively saw releases for personal computers. The term "video game" delineates the whole array of electronic games ranging from computers to consoles and handhelds—another encompassing term like fantasy and postmodernism.

[249] Keeping in mind the aforementioned Discworld text adventure game, there is a compromise between text and game worth mentioning, however: In Choose-your-own-adventure books, the main narrative is made up of a non-linear story, providing the reader with choices at given points. After every paragraph, the reader is expected to continue reading on another page—the entire text is a set of hyperlinks between individual sections of the book. An analog text adventure, one could say.

[250] Former Monty Python cast member Eric Idle is the voice of Rincewind in the CD-ROM version of the game, adding yet another excellent layer of sarcasm and nuanced humor.

narrator, while not as metafictional as later and more experimental video games (Thon 446–47), occasionally comment the actions of the player directly. Yet perhaps most interestingly for these interactive audio-visual representations of the Discworld in our context, players are given the same perspective as the Discworld's gods with their game board in *CoM* (see fig. 5 below):

Fig. 5: Psygnosis/Sony. A screenshot showing the city map of the 1995 Discworld video game, released two years after the publication of the first official Ankh-Morpork map. See *Discworld* 1995. (Used with permission of Psygnosis/Sony.)

Rincewind follows every click of the mouse and will pick up or interact with any object indicated. His path is both not determined (as he can go back to previous places and solve riddles in non-linear order) and at the same time very much preset (as he is under constant player-control). The Discworld video games therefore obviously allow for interaction and non-linearity unlike their purely textual counterparts in the novels, yet they are nonetheless set on "'hard rails' (which set limits on player choice in order to render a pre-structured experience)" (Herman et al., *Encyclopedia* 81). Indeed, for all their interactivity and the choices given to the audience, they ultimately offer *less* freedom to break story patterns: Player interaction cannot derail an overarching narrative to the same extent as achieved by the main characters in the books—or at least the player-choices remain within a given narrative corset.

With the release of the *Ankh-Morpork Map* for iPad in 2013,[251] the Discworld embraced another even more recent innovation, seamlessly integrating its city guide and map into the new medium of apps. Taking cues from Victorian culture, the maps and lists in the appendices to Mayhew's classic *London Labour and the London Poor* find their Discworld equivalent in the glossary and register of shops and street names in the tablet application (see fig. 6). These lists with corresponding locations, as well as a helpful commentator and tour guide to an already extensive compendium, intensified the Victorian style that Pratchett's companions had come to be known for. And even beyond an emulation in style, when we look at the hustle and bustle of Ankh-Morpork through the bird's-eye perspective of the iPad app, it is strongly reminiscent of Mayhew's 19th-century observations when seeing London from atop St. Paul's:

> A landscape of fact repeatedly knocks up against one of fairy-tale transformations: long lines of omnibuses are 'no bigger than tin toys, and crowded with pigmies on the roof'; brewers' drays are distinguished by the round backs of their horses, 'looking like plump mice'; the pavements are darkened 'with dense streams of busy little men, that looked almost like ants, hurrying along in opposite directions'. (qtd. in Douglas-Fairhurst xiii)

Mayhew effectively puts a layer of fiction onto the résumé of his real observations; in a similar manner, Pratchett creates the illusion that his fictional characters follow lives outside the narratives we read in the novels. The simulation of everyday life in a secondary world has achieved yet another layer of immersion; with the soundscape of a busy city and the countless characters freely walking the streets, "everything the user sees and hears is part of the controlled experience" (Wolf 48), and the illusion of a truly lively Ankh-Morpork.

The iPad app thus invests the Discworld with greater dynamics compared to the three Discworld adventure games. Reading a Discworld novel and then retracing the characters' itineraries with your finger on a paper map is enhanced; they speak or provide information as we tap on them on the iPad screen. Ironically, the app seemingly imbues characters with more freedom, while the players'

---

[251] Sadly, the app is no longer available on Apple Store by now. With the release of the iPad iOS 11 in 2015, all 32-bit apps—including the *Ankh-Morpork Map*—became incompatible and were deleted from the store. While I can attest that it *still* runs on my old iPad at the time of writing, this part of my analysis is therefore troubled by technical difficulties.

interactions and role in the narrative are reduced. Precisely because the app is less interactive than the other games—there is no overarching narrative as in *Discworld*, characters go about their business in Ankh-Morpork randomly and cannot be directly controlled—the impression of an independent life on the Discworld outside of the grand stories is again underlined. This is no stage with characters waiting for their cues; what we see in the Discworld app is the immersive simulation of a bustling city.

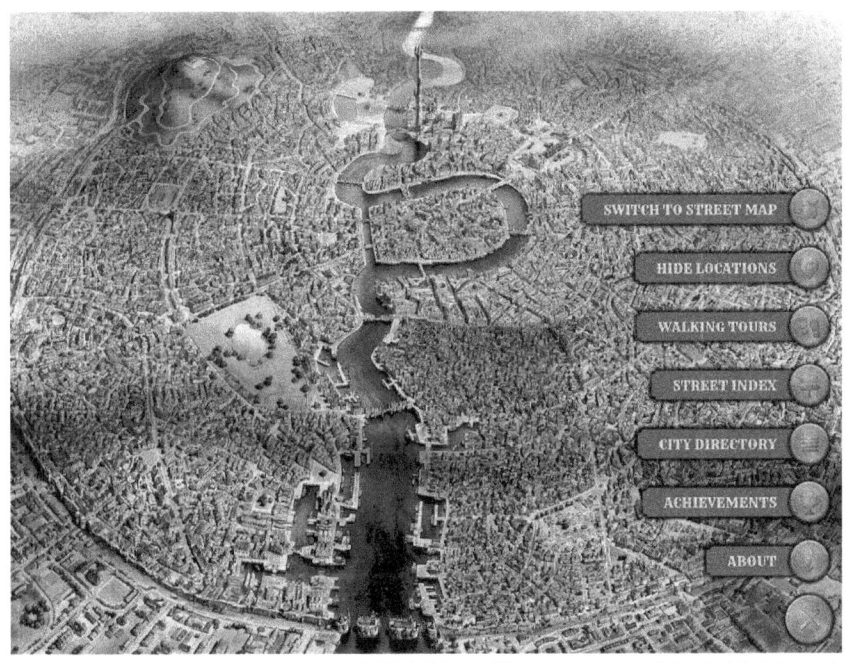

Fig. 6: Discworld Emporium/Transworld Publishers. The main screen of the Ankh-Morpork app. Upon zooming in, Discworld characters can be seen moving around in the streets and interacted with. See Pratchett, *Discworld: The Ankh-Morpork Map*. (Used with permission of Discworld Emporium/Transworld Publishers.)

It is still a stage, insofar as it *remains* an illusion and make-believe projection of a city that does not exist in empirical reality. However, it also abandons Pratchett's penchant to pit his characters against overarching narratives. There is hence far less intertextuality in the app, and novels are but alluded to. What we see and partake in are instead countless smaller narratives, personal character itineraries that provide us with glimpses into their lives as we tap on them. The Discworld app, perhaps, is the pinnacle of Pratchett's idea of a city that will go on even after the stories end.[252] By avoiding a parody of specific narratives, be they from genre fantasy or other literary or cultural contexts, the app achieves an interactive yet independent representation of a secondary world, a depiction of a fictional city that appears to be as unreal and yet realistic as a bird's eye view onto an existing metropolis.

Ankh-Morpork is the Discworld's most dynamic space to escape theatre-stage fantasy and Pratchett's largest[253] and most densely populated stage. By constantly shifting and changing, it underlines the equally altering aspects of personality and individuality in the face of narrative identity. It is a city that spins "cheerfully like a gyroscope on the lip of a catastrophe curve" (*GG* 111) and thus offers unprecedented opportunities to find a niche or a role. The threatening stasis of personality under the narrative imperative à la Genua is replaced with a postmodern, fragmented sense of self veiled with the mask of acting in a certain way—giving rise to the question of what *makes* a Discworld personality. The answer to this, as with anything on the Discworld, is belief. The active choice of a role within the framework of narrative imperative is led by necessity but also by then following this choice.

In this secondary world, where stories have power and metaphors can become real, taking on a specific role is powered by *believing* in this role. Whether a witch, a cynical guard, or a (to a lesser degree) scoundrel-turned-entrepreneur—believing in a role effectively means believing in oneself. Often, this belief precedes inner-fictional reality: As Death states, "YOU NEED TO BELIEVE IN THINGS THAT AREN'T TRUE. HOW ELSE CAN THEY BECOME?" (*HG* 423). For Tiffany Aching, believing that she is a witch might be untrue to begin with in her first novel, but by believing in her chosen role and her personal image of a witch (a powerful, independent woman) she acts *as if* she were a witch and thus eventually *becomes* a witch of her own making in later books. What is more, acting on one's beliefs can spread them to other people, leading them to accept the role of another person by believing the

---

[252] Indeed, starting up the app on an iPad always rearranges the characters' journeys through Ankh-Morpork: We never encounter the same characters in the same spots, some disappear and reappear completely, giving further impressions of itineraries that are not the same. Granted, it is all randomized and not truly personal as in the novels, but with suspension of disbelief, this version of Ankh-Morpork comes close to what Pratchett most likely envisioned as a fictional city running independent from stories.

[253] Judging by the number of inhabitants in one place.

illusion, "theater spilling into ordinary life" (Rayment 49), which eventually becomes accepted as part of reality. Nevertheless, characters like Granny Weatherwax emphasize that this choice is never easy or permanent and must be repeated every day. She herself has carefully established her role as *the* best witch of Lancre but also constantly has to keep this role firmly in check; otherwise, she might begin to believe in her chosen role too strongly and become arrogant. Likewise, Samuel Vimes struggles to remain the suspicious and cynical city guard underneath his wealth and noble title, just as Carrot wisely continues to keep his destined role of king secret by repeating his preferred role of watchman. Again, here we see the dynamics of the Discworld at work: Belief is never an absolute achievement but has to remain subject to change and doubt, as nearly everything else in Pratchett's secondary world.

The characters' choices are reflected by their surroundings and their knowledge thereof. Vimes knows Ankh-Morpork and how the city works, whereas Granny Weatherwax and Tiffany Aching have intrinsic knowledge of their land. This is why Rincewind, protagonist of the first novels, does not exhibit the same power to steer the plot: While based in Ankh-Morpork and at Unseen University, he does not know how to use these surroundings to his advantage. His role as failed wizard was not chosen but thrust upon him, exemplified by the spell that sprang into his mind and set the plot of *CoM* and *LF* in motion. Like Moist von Lipwig, he is driven by the plot, and characterization comes only second. Looking at Rincewind in later novels or in *The Science of Discworld* books, even though he has become professor at Unseen University, it is yet another role that he did not actively choose. At liberty to run away from all dangers but nonetheless bound to narrative imperative, he cannot escape his role as cowardly adventurer—a fact that he has become semi-aware of by *LH* (39). The full emancipation from theatre-stage fantasy did not happen until Pratchett wrote characters who actively chose their roles based on the environment they lived in.

Likewise, by mapping the Discworld, "Pratchett neither radically subverts the conventions of fantasy map, nor merely reproduces these conventions; his work both observes the co-ordinates of the fantasy genre and re-places these co-ordinates through a 'postmodern' emphasis on waste and marginality rather than upon heroic centrality" (Hills 236). In a Bakhtinian twist, Pratchett presents the

Discworld and especially the city of Ankh-Morpork in a down-to-earth, oftentimes grimy light, unlike the comparatively clean and superimposed secondary worlds of genre fantasy that appear much more like stages. Readers of Discworld novels are constantly reminded of the physical labor that keeps the society going and the effort that even main characters have to undergo in their daily toils. For all their role-playing, Pratchett's protagonists know that ideals in the end "[a]re mostly hot air, compared to the solid reality of a hard-boiled egg" (James, "City Watch" 208). Any real achievement or progress is earned not by entitlement but with continuous hard work.

The intertwining of story and world is a given on the Discworld: its protagonists become complex personalities through an intense exchange with the environment they live in and the preset stories they are faced with. While narrative is the driving force of Pratchett's secondary world, the larger stories are constantly juxtaposed with smaller stories at work that keep the world running—"extra information and events which fall outside of the main narrative threads" (Wolf 200), but which are no less important for the holistic image of a secondary world. Yet this image is never complete: like the characters that inhabit it, so the Discworld itself is only ever presented in fragments of stories and spaces. They form part of an ever-changing constellation, documented best by the final novels that solidified "the Discworld's gingerly dance towards industrial transformation" (Clute 25) and replaced folklore and classic fantasy with narratives of progress and a new understanding of space. The introduction of these new narratives was perhaps less fitting for a secondary world originally conceived as a postmodern parody and later a satire of stereotypical fantasy fiction, but it underlines the decisive factor for its success spanning more than three decades: Change.

A Reconsideration of Fantasy and Pratchett

Outlook

Mapping and Storytelling in a Postmodern Era

All fiction is about world-making, and fantasy perhaps more so than other genres or modes of literature. Pratchett's work defies categorization; it borders on fantasy and metafiction but belongs exclusively to neither. A Discworld novel is neither completely postmodern nor an example of classic storytelling—instead, it always uses elements of both. Contrary to the often fragmented and playful nature of postmodern narratives, Discworld stories have a clear beginning, middle, and end. Contrary to classic fantasy fiction, however, Discworld stories constantly break Tolkien's rule of secondary belief. Yet while this was the effect of mere parody in the first few novels, it evolved into an analysis of how fiction can affect lives: "While some postmodernist fictions provoke ontological reflection by projecting a plurality of worlds, others do so by troubling the very processes by which fictional worlds are constructed" (Herman et al., *Encyclopedia* 458). Channeling Hutcheon's ideas of postmodern irony and incongruity theory, Pratchett both affirms and challenges the human need for stories. Postmodernism uncovered what had been hidden but always present: The realization that in addition to fictional narratives set in other worlds, the cultural beliefs and systems of our actual world, whether historical or contemporary, display the same constructedness and narrativity.

Perhaps not as radical as Foucault's statement that truth "is undoubtedly the sort of error that cannot be refuted because it was hardened into an unalterable form in the long baking process of history" ("Nietzsche" 79), postmodernism nonetheless "works to show that all repairs are human constructs, but that, from that very fact, they derive their value as well as their limitation. All repairs are both comforting and illusory. Postmodernist interrogations of humanist certainties live within this kind of contradiction" (Hutcheon, *Poetics* 8). The Discworld and its inhabitants live this hybridity—the disillusionment of Pratchett's main characters is reflected by their conscious efforts to derail stereotypical narratives that claim to present an ultimate or unchangeable truth. As a mirror of empirical reality, Pratchett's secondary world does not shy away from exposing the challenges of a postmodern, fragmented quest for temporary meaning.

Yet for all its modern and critical approach to clichés and pre-patterned stories, the Discworld needs fictionality (and thus stories) to function—in the same manner as our empirical reality is a constantly shifting network of constructed meanings. Even so, Pratchett's creation cannot fully accept the free play of postmodernism:

> Here perhaps is one of the paradoxes of Pratchett's work. It is sometimes spoken of as postmodern but it cannot quite do without at least the idea of just the kind of transcendent signifier that postmodernism denies—whether that be the transcendent power of the gonne or of sourcery, or a trueborn king, or myth, or an ideal of art or opera. (Brown 299)

The Discworld rests in a delicate balance: Despite the elemental power of narrativium, Pratchett hardly ever allows the magic of storytelling to determine the entire cosmos of the Discworld with one unifying story like the save-the-world-scenarios[254] we know from countless typical fantasy narratives. For Discworld inhabitants, life continues after so-called happy endings (which rarely *are* happy endings for the characters through whose eyes we see the narratives unfold), yet in Pratchett's ultimately positive outlook, endings (even happy ones) are possible despite postmodern skepticism. They simply have to be accepted as temporary and subject to being changed into new beginnings.

The Discworld overcame its initial antithesis to classic fantasy (expressed most prominently in the Rincewind novels) and developed into a critical reflection of the genre's stereotypical elements and the powers of narrative. As Pratchett observed in 2004, the Discworld "was fantasy" and now "it uses fantasy" (Pratchett and Kidby [120]). Naturally, this was a process that could not be expressed in one book but took a longer process of sophistication—one which however did not remain fully exempt from petrification and serialization:

> Hence, while the Discworld series may have begun with a parodic approach to the genre of fantasy, over time it has 'solidified' into a form of fantasy which can no longer be so readily defined

---

[254] Except in the earliest books, where narrative was parodied and turned on its head but its patterns still remained unbroken.

> *negatively*—i.e. through its oppositionality to prior 'rules' of fantasy and world-construction—instead becoming *positively defined* through its own serialised identity. (Hills 234)

In other words, the Discworld is an experiment and dynamic process that began as a countermeasure to the blatant copies of Tolkien in the 1960s and 1970s, ridiculing their recurring elements and tropes in the Rincewind books. With the introduction of further main characters—mainly Samuel Vimes and Granny Weatherwax—Pratchett's treatment and sweeping criticism of genre fantasy refined itself into more acute analysis, and slowly the fast-paced ridicule gave way to more nuanced and subtle satire.

Ironically, by repeating the clichés of fantasy like Tolkien's imitators (naturally by turning them on their head), Pratchett's fiction eventually emancipated itself from imitation into something beyond mimicry and subversion. Pratchett's main topics—the power and prevalence of stories, the twin sides of morality, the complexities of progress—were always present but did not become truly apparent in the midst of all the jokes and puns of the earliest novels, emerging only in the finer ironies of later books. Indeed, each visit to the Discworld added layers to the flat world whose changes and challenges were linked to those of the characters. Again, in Pratchett's own words, "[t]he reason that Discworld has survived is that it's changed" (McCabe 272). It is ironic but ultimately unsurprising to see, then, that the predominant force that kept the Discworld running for so long—change—eventually detracted from the core issues of Pratchett's fiction and changed its focus from satire to saturation.

Likewise, the rising need to provide maps and a fixed continuity began as parody and overcame this definition as the series progressed further. At first, the serialization of the Discworld did not lead to mere repetitiveness but to an ever-increasing self-realization[255] and elaboration of its addenda. Only as an increasing number of Discworld maps—some of them in different versions—were published, Pratchett's secondary world began to become somewhat limited in its potential:

> Indeed, as Ricœur makes clear, the excessive predominance of narrative space can destroy narrative, leaving no stone unturned, no space unmapped, and no room for episodic 'reversibility' or

---

[255] In the case of the Discworld, the realization can be seen as literal—it became a space with its own intact account of an inner-fictional reality.

reinvention. Narrative becomes more and more configurational over time, tending towards its own exhaustion. (Hills 233)

While maps are a good method of orientation and credibility for fantasy fiction, they are often not as important as they seem—even though it "makes sense to read the map in the context of the entire text" (Ekman 43), it should primarily ensure that the world is represented in an overview but not show where evil lurks or even trace the narrative of the journey in advance. Such maps with predrawn routes are part of fantasyland, and can turn both represented world and story into an unimaginative stage with predictable events and locations.

The spatiality of the Discworld is inextricably linked to staging: Although petrification began to limit potential stories by the end, Pratchett never lost full sight of the dangers of narrative imperative.[256] The stage of the final Discworld novels may have become less satirical, but the power of stories is still prevalent and is still based on the same link to empirical reality: "In fact, what Pratchett defends in Discworld is that humans are so powerful they can make things happen just by thinking them. And story keeps everything hanging together, like a glue, providing meaning and structure to the universe" (McMurry 228). Like Hutcheon, Pratchett does not deny the constructedness of this or any other meaning; however, he also sees the necessity for such constructs: "TRICKERY WITH WORDS IS WHERE HUMANS LIVE. [...] HUMANS NEED FANTASY TO BE HUMAN" (*HG* 422), as Death points out. In this light, fantasy as a construct of a construct—a fictional world derived from constructs based in empirical reality—is not, as Plato feared, a shadow of a shadow but a mirror of a mirror, reflecting its topics around several corners if used cleverly.

Instead of dealing with the stereotypes of fantasy literature by either copying or actively avoiding them, Pratchett merges this conflict by seemingly re-enacting the clichés on his secondary world and then reflecting them in an open-ended manner: "Postmodernism [...] proceeds in three steps: undermine (deconstruct) all boundaries and

---

[256] Indeed, there is at least one instance when Pratchett himself is not entirely free of the forces of narrative causality, namely in *MP*: As Sawyer states, "[a] parody of Hollywood which includes an ape and a starlet among its *dramatis personae*, and has the possibility of a huge climbable building already built into the scenario can only end one way" (Sawyer, "Librarian" 129). The only major difference from the source film *King Kong* is the fact that in Pratchett's context, as pointed out in Chapter 6 of this study, it is a giant *woman* who abducts a normal-sized ape.

oppositions; create spaces of fusion, blends, collages; do not resolve contradictions but let all flowers, however incompatible, however disharmonious, bloom in one and the same garden bed" (Doležel, *Postmodern* 5). The stories of the Discworld are thus in a constant postmodern exchange between ideal and real, allowing space for both stereotypical fantasy plots as in *GG* or *WA* as well as the marginal main characters who aim to break these story patterns. Apart from revealing and ridiculing these patterns in his fiction, Pratchett also repeatedly stressed the crucial similarity of how stories are seen on Discworld and the power they hold in empirical reality.

Storytelling is vital for a plethora of fields and very much part of our minds. While possible-worlds theory in philosophy and in literature seem to be two linked but still different approaches to the topic of narratives in cognition, there is nonetheless a stronger relation between the two:

> The fact that fantasy literature continues to recycle stories that have been told for countless generations makes it seem repetitive and unoriginal as well as unrealistic—but it is the implication of "deep-rootedness" that gives fantasy its unique qualities and utilities, both culturally and psychologically. The fact that fantasy literature deals with the fictitious past of "once upon a time" makes it seem quaint and old-fashioned by comparison with stories that deal with the experienced world or the past of history—but our perceptions of who and what we are, and ought to be attempting to become, owe at least as much to our notions of that fictitious past as to our theories regarding the actual one. (Stableford, *Dictionary* xxxix–xl)

This relation has been emphasized by writers varying from authors of fantasy and the fantastic such as Neil Gaiman and Michael Ende to postmodern deconstruction[257] in the works of Paul Auster or Umberto Eco.

For Pratchett, the topic had been a principal feature of his books even prior to Discworld, yet it reached its full critical potential in the ever-more elaborate portrayal of a secondary world that literally runs on the power of stories. At the height of his talent, the relation between the role of storytelling in fantasy and in empirical reality was the core of Pratchett's creation:

---

[257] Of course, there are also various postmodern elements in the works of Gaiman and Ende—both, like Pratchett, address the power of stories or metafictional construction.

> Secondary worlds make us look differently at the Primary World, and are often used to comment on it. [...] At the same time, however, secondary worlds often differ greatly from the Primary World, making us more aware of its default assumptions. And as time went on, more and more of these defaults could be changed, as the imaginary-world tradition developed its own conventions and solutions to world-building problems. (Wolf 65–66)

Part of Pratchett's legacy is the constant reminder of both the power and the allure of stories, of their potential to turn lies into truth and question these truths in turn again. It is no small artistic feat to be open about the fictionality of one's creation and still achieve reader immersion. In light of these achievements, one question that remains at the end of this book is not just the literary evaluation of Pratchett's fiction, but in a wider sense that of contemporary and classic fantasy in general.

AFTERWORD
Fantasy Beyond Escapism

IN THE INTRODUCTION TO his famous *Literary Theory*, Terry Eagleton argues that any "belief that the study of literature is the study of a stable, well-defined entity, as entomology is the study of insects, can be abandoned as a chimera" (Eagleton 11). Even prior to the advent of postmodern reconsideration and the bridging between cultural boundaries, literature as a whole and its designated genres had always been subject to modifications that all reflected and were simultaneously results of changes that stemmed from empirical reality.

Therefore, Bloom's defense of the Western canon as something that "exists precisely to impose limits, to set a standard of measurement that is anything but political or moral" (Bloom 35) does not hold. With his position, we arrive at the question of whether art is more than simply a work of beauty and, more importantly, its value beyond entertainment:

> The romantic and modernist heritage of nonengagement insists that art is art and that ideological discourse has no place in the literary [...]. Added to this historical separation is a suspicion of the artistic, general in much of the Anglo-American world, a view that sees art as trivial, insignificant, imaginative and therefore cut off from the social and historical realities of life. (Hutcheon, *Poetics* 179)

The debate about the classifications and the worth of literature finally leads back to an argument that has always been part of Western cultural discourse: how is new literature compatible with the old? If a work of fiction employs hitherto unknown storytelling techniques, what role do they play within the canon? The literary canon, of course, is a construct itself, even though some critics still tend to regard it as a standard that is set in stone. But ironically, it is again the traditionalist Bloom who provides a solution to what makes a text canonical—one that betrays his own attitude: "The answer, more often than not, has turned out to be strangeness, a mode of originality that either cannot be assimilated, or that so assimilates us that we cease to see it strange" (3). Fantasy, with its innate "arresting strangeness," has been one of the major innovators in various strands of fiction, particularly since its breakthrough as a genre and later diversification in subgenres. Nevertheless, critics and scholars are often still reluctant to include it in canonic literature.

A large part of the unaltered skeptical attitude towards fantasy and low-mimetic reinvention stems directly from Enlightenment, from the repeated claims of having found one solid, fixed truth in rationalism. As a genre directly influenced by Gothic fiction, itself a reminder of the irrational aspects of life dismissed by Enlightenment philosophy, fantasy can, therefore, be regarded as a similar challenge to claims of superior or infallible knowledge. The phantoms conjured by fantasy are no less relevant for our time than the ones created by Ann Radcliffe or Horace Walpole were for their age. As Brown observes, one "of the most persistent 'myths' in the modern world is the myth that we've moved beyond myth: that we enlightened moderns have a purchase on truth that's fundamentally more secure" (269). This false sense of certainty points out one of the recurring fallacies in human cognition, namely the tendency to think in absolutes instead of allowing for flexibility once a new level of understanding has been reached.

Putting this certainty bias within the spectrum of literature, fantasy and "popular fiction" appear to be lower on the scale than high-brow or so-called canonic literature, even though their better examples may have similar impact and importance:

> Popular fiction is often dismissed as escapist and an easy accomplishment, but to achieve bestseller status a writer has to realise a heterogeneous appeal at least across class, gender and age perspectives. Bestsellers achieve their status by being culturally resonant. Popular fiction is therefore often considered to have a social function that extends beyond the passivity implied by escapism. (Moody 166)

What the Discworld has, more than anything else, is an ironic yet firm connection to empirical reality. Escapism is one of the recurring critical dismissals of fantasy, and the prime reason for this accusation lies in its supposedly simplified perspective. When any problem, small or large, could be solved by magic, when the dead can miraculously be returned to life or an army may be vanquished by sheer willpower, then we are in the territory of make-believe and wish fulfillment, a realm where the ideal triumphs over the real. In Pratchett's fiction, however, there rarely is an easy way out: bar a few exceptions, there are no *deus ex machina* characters or developments. In their stead, we have a secondary world peopled with an abundance of supernatural content, which nonetheless stays firmly grounded in a harsh and unadorned inner-fictional reality.

In a nutshell, on the Discworld, there is a price for everything,[258] and what may seem simple is rarely revealed as such. Magic, that wondrous element in so many other texts of fantasy, plays both a crucial, world-making role in Pratchett's fiction and yet remains largely unused by characters. In his secondary world, the perspective is up close and personal—save for a few books, it is never the world itself that is at stake but rather a few of the people who inhabit it. More specifically, they need to protect their moral code and personal integrity to continue doing good deeds for their community. Also, in union with Pratchett's skepticism towards artificial endings, everything on the Discworld is ongoing, an image of a dynamic exchange between real and ideal as opposed to absolute perfection: "Pratchett [...] differs from Aristotle in rejecting the attainment of an unchanging perfection. According to Pratchett, happiness is only found in continuing to work towards one's goals, and never in resting content with what one has accomplished" (Foster 181). Thus, morality is not achievement but always process; throughout their appearances in the novels, protagonists like Vimes and Granny find themselves in situations where they could take advantage of their own strength of morals and establish themselves as models as well as *ideals* of morality.

The imperfection of such assumed morality and superiority is based in humor, however with a serious undertone. Mendlesohn illustrates these two sides of the same coin by comparing comedy and tragedy:

> The crucial issue which underpins the moral schema of Pratchett's work is *choice* and thus the role of the individual. Pratchett demands that we view his fantasies through the eyes of a moral actor, and the humour of footnotes and incongruities which dominated the early work is by *Small Gods* [...] becoming subsumed into comedy, with all of comedy's power to illuminate human tragedy. The central figure of a Pratchett novel becomes the comedic hero, and a denial of the tragic spirit forms a principle current in the most powerful of his works. (Mendlesohn, "Faith" 239–40)

---

[258] Both philosophically and monetarily, as the profit-oriented nature of many Discworld characters—C. M. O. T. Dibbler being a perfect example—shows.

The main comedic value of Pratchett's protagonists derives from their seriousness in comparison to the general humorous portrayal and situations of the world they live in. But for Granny Weatherwax, Tiffany Aching, Samuel Vimes, Moist von Lipwig, and even for Rincewind, their world and life is no joke, but rather to be truly taken seriously: since they are not "heroes" in the stereotypical stories that unfold on the Discworld, their daily lives consist of hard work or simply survival. The fact that Vimes and Granny choose to be moral not for personal gain or entitlement but simply for the good of others[259] (Foster 186–90; James, "City Watch" 194–95) is what makes them stand out from standard narrative-driven heroics.

Choice, for Pratchett, also means having the *freedom* of choice, that is to say, the possibility of alternatives beyond one or perhaps two outcomes. Plenty of exemplary motifs show the problematics inherent to dealing in absolutes, be it a fairy tale dictator in *WA*, a conspiracy group hoping to re-establish monarchy in *GG* or countless other examples from the books. Even more, they reflect the critical reassessment of empirical reality—as all fiction, fantasy achieves its goal best when it does more than merely portraying an otherworldly realm of ideal escapism and wish-fulfillment:

> If [a fantasy writer] indeed achieves a quality that can fairly be described by the dictionary definition: 'inner consistency of reality', it is difficult to conceive how this can be, if the work does not in some way partake of reality. The peculiar quality of the 'joy' in successful fantasy can thus be explained as a sudden glimpse of the underlying reality or truth. (OFS 77)

At the core of this imperfection, of the unusually non-perfect endings of Pratchett's fiction and characterizations, is the postmodern questioning of all established truths and the revelation that binary oppositions are but reductions and simplifications in the end. The complexity of the Discworld, underneath a constant flow of jokes and references, lies in such breaking of dichotomies and narrative patterns and investigating—as well as questioning—the meaning behind them:

> Fantasy literature suspends established truth and reality. Yet fantasy theory relies on unquestioned norms of convention, and

---

[259] And to help people as directly as they can. There is no devotion to any "greater good" in them, as such vague descriptions are again too close to abstract narratives, which in the worst case do not value individual life other than as means to an end.

never asks what it means to suspend them. Theoretical definitions of fantasy rely on formal distinctions—the real vs. the unreal, the known vs. the impossible—without examining the premises upon which these antithetical notions are based. (Hull 35)

Naturally, Pratchett is first and foremost an author of fiction, and his work does not feature lengthy discourses on theoretical matters, yet he poignantly summarizes the problem and challenges of writing fantasy in a postmodern world. In one of his essays, he claims that "[t]oo much alleged 'fantasy' is just empty sugar, life with the crusts cut off" (*Slip* 105), and even though he does not address any particular authors or give examples, he most certainly means not just fantasy but also the world we live in. Contemporary contexts ranging from culture to politics may not be necessary to write good speculative fiction, but leaving the realities of life out of fantasy or life itself results in naïve make-believe. The Discworld's literary merit lies in the fragile balance between mimesis and invention, between humor and seriousness, and always between real and ideal.

With the passing of Terry Pratchett on the 12th of March 2015 and the publication of the final Discworld novel in September of the same year, a project spanning more than 30 years had reached its end—an end that did not close off the storyworld entirely:

> In creating his Discworld, Terry Pratchett has created a proper venue for the tournament of return; and with each new title it is Spring. The Discworld [...] has the aspect of a garden made by God [...] to play games in. The players (as we have said) disappear, at dusk, into air, into thin air; and with the dawn return. They are creatures of Comedy. Their ties to the world we know—the incipits which engender them from the books of this world—are never *closed*.
> [...]
> And that may be the secret of Terry Pratchett's success. We love the jokes—we ride the rollercoasters of slapstick with joy—and each time we hope Cinderella will find her slipper. But the true secret of Discworld is that it has remained free. Free of the dangerous pieties of transformative Healing. Free, in the end, of fantasy. (Clute 30)

The Discworld is and remains an ambiguous affair, and I could repeat many of the seeming contradictions and incongruities that have been discussed in this book. But seeing the self-ironic nature of Pratchett's fiction in a greater picture draws another comparison to Bakhtin's idea of the carnival: Like "a fire that simultaneously destroys and renews the world" (Bakhtin, "Characteristics" 127), so "[e]very

Discworld novel methodically destroys clichéd expectations of what other people should be like and how they should behave" (Butler, *Companion* 287)—and every time we reopen one of the books, we see a constellation of stereotypical content that will be torn down and shown in a new light. Yet while there has been no absolute finale in any of the books, this openness is ultimately what makes the novels so appealing; change kept the Discworld running for more than three decades, and the question of whether there is a true ending[260] to Pratchett's creation should best be left unanswered.

The experiment has turned into speculation. Perhaps we will be lucky enough to see further Discworld publications in different media, as films or in TV series, comic books and graphic novels, stage adaptations, or extended virtual explorations. Taking cues from Sam Gamgee's melancholic but also hopeful exclamation "Well, I'm back" at the conclusion of *LotR*, the Discworld remains open, postmodern in all its irony and self-referentiality but nonetheless with a satisfying sense of closure—even as it keeps reminding us that endings are only ever momentary. Because Pratchett knew that stories want to happen.

---

[260] Even the death of Granny Weatherwax as an end of her life is debatable since there are strong indicators throughout the last Discworld novel *SC* that she managed to transfer her consciousness to her cat.

WORKS CITED

Alber, Jan. "Unnatural Narratology: The Systematic Study of Anti-Mimeticism." *Literature Compass*, vol. 10, no. 5, 2013, pp. 449–60.
Alber, Jan, et al. "What Really Is Unnatural Narratology?" *StoryWorlds: A Journal of Narrative Studies*, vol. 5, 2013, pp. 101–18.
———. "What Is Unnatural about Unnatural Narratology?: A Response to Monika Fludernik." *Narrative*, vol. 20, no. 3, Oct. 2012, pp. 371–82.
Alber, Jan, and Rüdiger Heinze. "Introduction." *Unnatural Narratives—Unnatural Narratology*, edited by Jan Alber and Rüdiger Heinze, Walter de Gruyter GmbH, 2011, pp. 1–22.
Altman, Rick. *A Theory of Narrative*. Columbia UP, 2008.
Alton, Anne Hiebert, and William C. Spruiell. "Introduction." *Discworld and the Disciplines: Critical Approaches to the Terry Pratchett Works*, edited by Anne Hiebert Alton and William C. Spruiell, McFarland, 2014, pp. 1–14.
Armitt, Lucie. *Fantasy Fiction: An Introduction*. Continuum Books, 2005.
Armstrong, Helen. "Aragorn." *J. R. R. Tolkien Encyclopedia. Scholarship and Critical Assessment*, edited by Michael C. Drout, Routledge, 2007, pp. 22–24.
Attardo, Salvatore. *Encyclopedia of Humor Studies*. SAGE Publications, 2014.
Attebery, Brian. *Stories about Stories: Fantasy and the Remaking of Myth*. Oxford UP, 2014.
———. *Strategies of Fantasy*. Indiana UP, 1992.
Bakhtin, Mikhail. "Characteristics of Genre and Plot Composition in Dostoevsky's Works." *Fantastic Literature: A Critical Reader*, edited by David Sandner, translated by Caryl Emerson, Praeger Publishers, 2004, pp. 116–33.
———. *The Dialogic Imagination*. Edited by Michael Holquist, translated by Caryl Emerson and Michael Holquist, U of Texas P, 1981.

Bardon, Adrian. "The Philosophy of Humour." *Comedy: A Geographic and Historical Guide*, Vol 2, edited by Maurice Charney, Praeger Publishers, 2005, pp. 462–76.

Baudrillard, Jean. *Simulacra and Simulation*. Translated by Sheila Faria Glaser, U of Michigan P, 1994.

Beard, Henry N. and Douglas C. Kennedy. *Bored of the Rings. A Parody of J. R. R. Tolkien's* The Lord of the Rings. Gollancz, 2001.

Best, Steven, and Douglas Kellner. *The Postmodern Turn*. Guilford Press, 1997.

Bloom, Harold. *The Western Canon: The Books and School of the Ages*. Harcourt Brace, 1994.

Bolongaro, Eugenio. "Thomas Pynchon and the Contemporary Forms of the Fantastic." *Critical Insights: The Fantastic*, edited by Claire Whitehead, Salem Press, 2013, pp. 212–35.

Brown, James. "Believing is Seeing. Silas Tomkyn Comberbache and Terry Pratchett." *Terry Pratchett. Guilty of Literature*, edited by Andrew M. Butler et al., Old Earth Books, 2004, pp. 261–301.

Burns, Marjorie. "J. R. R. Tolkien: The British and the Norse in Tension." *Pacific Coast Philology*, vol. 25, 1990, pp. 49–59.

Butler, Andrew M. "Theories of Humour." *Terry Pratchett. Guilty of Literature*, edited by Andrew M. Butler et al., Old Earth Books, 2004, pp. 67–89.

———. *An Unofficial Companion to the Novels of Terry Pratchett*, Greenwood World Publishing, 2007.

Butler, Andrew M., et al. "Preface." *Terry Pratchett. Guilty of Literature*, edited by Andrew M. Butler et al., Old Earth Books, 2004, pp. vii–xiii.

Carroll, Noël. *Beyond Aesthetics: Philosophical Essays*. Cambridge UP, 2001.

———. *Humour: A Very Short Introduction*, Oxford UP, 2014.

Casey, Jim. "Modernism and postmodernism." *The Cambridge Companion to Fantasy Literature*, edited by Edward James and Farah Mendlesohn, Cambridge UP, 2012, pp. 113–25.

Chanady, Amaryll. "Rethinking the Fantastic and Related Modes: New Perspectives from Spatial Theory." *Critical Insights: The Fantastic*, edited by Claire Whitehead, Salem Press, 2012, pp. 61–77.

Chance, Jane. The Lord of the Rings: *The Mythology of Power*. Kentucky UP, 2001.

Clute, John. "Coming of Age." *Terry Pratchett. Guilty of Literature*, edited by Andrew M. Butler et al., Old Earth Books, 2004, pp. 15–31.
Clute, John and John Grant. *The Encyclopedia of Fantasy*. Orbit, 1999.
Critchley, Simon. *On Humour*. Routledge, 2002.
Croft, Janet Brennan. "The Golempunk Manifesto: Ownership of the Means of Production in Pratchett's Discworld." *Presentations of the 2010 Upstate Steampunk Extravaganza and Meetup*, edited by Gypsey Elaine Teague, Cambridge Scholars Publishing, 2011, pp. 3–16.
Curry, Patrick. *Defending Middle-earth: Tolkien, Myth and Modernity*. Houghton Mifflin Books, 2004.
De Certeau, Michel. *The Practice of Everyday Life*. Translated by Steven Randall, California UP, 1984.
De Fina, Anna and Alexandra Georgakopoulou. *Analyzing Narrative: Discourse and Sociolinguistic Perspectives*, Cambridge UP, 2012.
Dennerlein, Katrin. *Narratologie des Raumes*. Walter de Gruyter GmbH, 2009.
Dentith, Simon. *Parody*. Routledge, 2000.
Discworld. Windows PC Version, Psygnosis, 1995.
Doležel, Lubomír. *Heterocosmica: Fiction and Possible Worlds*. John Hopkins UP, 1998.
———. *Possible Worlds of Fiction and History. The Postmodern Stage*. John Hopkins UP, 2010.
Donald, Merlin. "Mimesis Theory Re-Examined, Twenty Years after the Fact." *Evolution of Mind, Brain, and Culture*, edited by Gary Hatfield and Holly Pitman, U of Pennsylvania P, 2013, pp. 169–92.
Döring, Jörg, and Tristan Thielmann. "Einleitung: Was lesen wir im Raume? Der *Spatial Turn* and das geheime Wissen der Geographen." *Spatial Turn. Das Raumparadigma in den Kultur- und Sozialwissenschaften*, edited by Jörg Döring und Tristan Thielmann, transcript Verlag, 2008, pp. 7–48.
Douglas-Fairhurst, Robert. "Introduction." *London Labour and the London Poor: A Selected Edition*, by Henry Mayhew, Oxford UP, 2010, pp. xiii–xliv.
Downes, Jeremy M. "Romancing the Quest: Quest Narratives in Changing Contexts." *The Hero's Quest*, edited by Bernard Schweizer and Robert A. Segal, Salem Press, 2013, pp. 56–79.
Eagleton, Terry. *Literary Theory: An Introduction*. Basil Blackwell Publisher, 1985.

Eco, Umberto. *On Literature.* Translated by Martin McLaughlin, Harcourt Books, 2005.

———. *Six Walks in the Fictional Woods.* Harvard UP, 1994.

Ekman, Stefan. *Here Be Dragons: Exploring Fantasy Maps and Settings.* Wesleyan UP, 2013.

Ellis, Markman. *The History of Gothic Fiction.* Edinburgh UP, 2007.

Fellows, Jennifer Jill. "Categorically not Cackling: The Will, Moral Fictions, and Witchcraft." *Philosophy and Terry Pratchett,* edited by Jacob M. Held and James B. South, Palgrave McMillan, 2014, pp. 204–27.

Fforde, Jasper. *The Well of Lost Plots.* Hodder and Stoughton, 2004.

Fimi, Dimitra. "Tolkien and the Fantasy Tradition." *Critical Insights: The Fantastic,* edited by Claire Whitehead, Salem Press, 2013, pp. 40–60.

Foster, Susanne E. "Millennium Hand and Shrimp: On the Importance of Being in the Right Trouser of Time." *Philosophy & Terry Pratchett,* edited by Jacob M. Held and James B. South, Palgrave MacMillan, 2014, pp. 179–203.

Foucault, Michel. "Nietzsche, Genealogy, History." *The Foucault Reader,* edited by Paul Rabinow, translated by Donald F. Bouchard and Sherry Simon, Pantheon Books, 1984, pp. 76–100.

———. "Space, Knowledge, and Power." *The Foucault Reader,* edited by Paul Rabinow, translated by Christian Hubert, Pantheon Books, 1984, pp. 239–56.

———. "Of Other Spaces." Translated by Jay Miskowiec, *Diacritics,* vol. 16, no. 1, spring 1986, pp. 22–27.

Genette, Gérard. *Narrative Discourse. An Essay in Method.* Translated by Jane E. Lewin, Cornell UP, 1980.

———. "Boundaries of Narrative." Translated by Ann Levonas, *New Literary History,* vol. 8, *Readers and Spectators: Some Views and Reviews,* autumn 1976, pp. 1–13.

Gibson, Mel. "'There Is No Race So Wretched That There Is Not Something Out There That Cares for Them': Multiculturalism, Understanding, Empathy and Prejudice in Discworld." *Terry Pratchett's Narrative Worlds: From Giant Turtles to Small Gods,* edited by Marion Rana, Palgrave McMillan, 2018, pp. 57–71.

Gilhus, Ingvild Sælid. *Laughing Gods, Weeping Virgins: Laughter in the History of Religion.* Taylor and Francis e-Library, 2004 [1997].

Glover, David and Scott McCracken, editors. "Introduction." *The Cambridge Companion to Popular Fiction*, Cambridge UP, 2012, pp. 1–14.

Gottschall, Jonathan. *The Storytelling Animal. How Stories Make us Human*. Houghton Mifflin Harcourt, 2012.

Grishakova, Marina and Marie-Laure Ryan, editors. *Intermediality and Storytelling*. Walter de Gruyter GmbH, 2010.

Guilfoy, Kevin. "Capitalism, Socialism and Democracy on the Discworld." *Philosophy & Terry Pratchett*, edited by Jacob M. Held and James B. South, Palgrave MacMillan, 2014, pp. 105–31.

Haberkorn, Gideon. "Debugging the Mind: The Rhetoric of Humour and the Poetics of Fantasy." *Discworld and the Disciplines: Critical Approaches to the Terry Pratchett Works*, edited by Anne Hiebert Alton and William C. Spruiell, McFarland, 2014, pp. 160–88.

———. "Seriously Relevant: Parody, Pastiche and Satire in Terry Pratchett's Discworld Novels." *Terry Pratchett's Narrative Worlds: From Giant Turtles to Small Gods*, edited by Marion Rana, Palgrave McMillan, 2018, pp. 137–57.

Habermann, Ina and Nikolaus Kuhn. "Sustainable Fictions— Geographical, Literary and Cultural Intersections in J. R. R. Tolkien's *The Lord of the Rings*." *The Cartographic Journal*, vol. 48, no. 4, *Cartographies of Fictional Worlds* (Special Issue), November 2011, pp. 263–73.

Haigh, Thomas. "Technology's Other Storytellers: Science Fiction as History of Technology." *Science Fiction and Computing: Essays on Interlinked Domains*, edited by David L. Ferro and Eric G. Swedin, MacFarland, 2011, pp. 13–38.

Halliwell, Stephen. *The Aesthetics of Mimesis: Ancient Texts and Modern Problems*. Princeton UP, 2002.

———, Translated. *The Poetics of Aristotle*. U of North Carolina P, 1987.

Herman, David. *Narrative Theory and the Cognitive Sciences*. CSLI Publications, 2003.

———. *Story Logic. Problems and Possibilities of Narrative* U of Nebraska P, 2002.

Herman, David, et. al., editors. *Narrative Theory. Core Concepts and Critical Debates*. Ohio State U, 2012.

———. *Routledge Encyclopedia of Narrative Theory*. Routledge, 2005.

Hills, Matthew. "Mapping Narrative Spaces." *Terry Pratchett. Guilty of Literature*, edited by Andrew M. Butler et al., Old Earth Books, 2004, pp. 217–38.

Ho, Elizabeth. *Neo-Victorianism and the Memory of Empire*. Continuum International Publishing, 2012.

Howard, Robert E. "The Phoenix on the Sword." *The Complete Chronicles of Conan*, edited by Stephen Jones, Gollancz, 2006, pp. 23–43.

Hull, Richard. "Fantastic Phenomenology: Quixote Reconsidered." *Substance*, vol. 18, no. 2, issue 59, 1989, pp. 35–47.

Hume, Kathryn. *Fantasy and Mimesis. Responses to Reality in Western Literature*. Routledge, 2014.

Hutcheon, Linda. *A Poetics of Postmodernism. History, Theory, Fiction*. Routledge, 2004.

———. "The Politics of Postmodernism: Parody and History." *Cultural Critique*, no. 5, *Modernity and Modernism, Postmodernity and Postmodernism*, winter 1986, pp. 179–207.

———. *A Theory of Parody. The Teachings of Twentieth-Century Art Forms*. Methuen, 1985.

James, Edward. "The City Watch." *Terry Pratchett. Guilty of Literature*, edited by Andrew M. Butler et al., Old Earth Books, 2004, 193–217.

———. "Tolkien, Lewis and the Explosion of Genre Fantasy." *The Cambridge Companion to Fantasy Literature*, edited by Edward James and Farah Mendlesohn, Cambridge UP, 2012, pp. 62–78.

James, Edward, and Farah Mendlesohn. *A Short History of Fantasy*. Middlesex UP, 2009.

———. "Introduction." *The Cambridge Companion to Fantasy Literature*, edited by Edward James and Farah Mendlesohn, Cambridge UP, 2012, pp. 1–5.

Jameson, Fredric. *Postmodernism, or, The Cultural Logic of Late Capitalism*. Duke UP, 1991.

Jolley, Nicholas. *Leibniz*. Routledge, 2005.

Jones, Diana Wynne. *The Tough Guide to Fantasyland: The Essential Guide to Fantasy Travel*. Firebird, 2006.

Jones, Steven Swann. *The Fairy Tale. The Magic Mirror of the Imagination*, Routledge, 2002.

Korkut, Nil. *Kinds of Parody from the Medieval to the Postmodern*. Peter Lang GmbH, 2009.

Kowalski, Karolina. *Popular Author Suspected of Literature. Sir Terry Pratchett's Discworld Series: Criticism, Secondary Worlds and Postmodernism.* 2010, U of Nottingham, unpublished MA thesis.
Lakoff, George, and Mark Johnson. *Metaphors We Live By.* U of Chicago P, 1980.
Langford, David. "Introduction." *Terry Pratchett. Guilty of Literature,* edited by Andrew M. Butler et al., Old Earth Books, 2004, pp. 3–13.
Lefebvre, Henri. *The Production of Space.* Translated by Donald Nicholson-Smith, Blackwell Publishing, 1991.
Leverett, Emily Lavin. "'At Times Like This It's Traditional That a Hero Comes Forth': Romance And Identity in Terry Pratchett's *Guards! Guards!*" *Terry Pratchett's Narrative Worlds: From Giant Turtles to Small Gods,* edited by Marion Rana, Palgrave McMillan, 2018, pp. 159–75.
Lewis, C. S. *Surprised by Joy. The Shape of My Early Life.* HarperCollins Publishers, 1998.
Lotman, Yuri M. *Universe of the Mind. A Semiotic Theory of Culture.* Translated by Ann Shukman, I. B. Tauris, 2001.
Lüthi, Max. *The European Folktale: Form and Nature.* Translated by John D. Niles, Indiana UP, 1982.
Lyotard, Jean-François. *The Postmodern Condition: A Report on Knowledge.* Translated by Geoff Bennington and Brian Massumi, Manchester UP, 1984.
Manlove, Colin. *The Fantasy Literature of England.* MacMillan Press, 1999.
———. *Modern Fantasy: Five Studies.* Cambridge UP, 1978.
Martin, Thomas L. *Poiesis and Possible Worlds: A Study in Modality and Literary Theory.* U of Toronto P, 2004.
Mason, Timothy. "Happy Endings in Terry Pratchett's *Witches Abroad.*" *Literary Happy Endings. Closure for Sunny Imaginations,* edited by Armelle Parey and Isabelle Roblin, Shaker Verlag GmbH, 2012, pp. 53–66.
Mayhew, Henry. *London Labour and the London Poor: A Selected Edition.* Oxford UP, 2010.
McAdams, Dan, and Kate McLean. "Narrative Identity." *Current Directions in Psychological Science,* vol. 22, no. 3, June 2013, 233–38.
McCabe, Joseph. *Hanging Out With the Dream King: Conversations With Neil Gaiman and His Collaborators.* Fantagraphics Books, 2004.

McCracken, Scott. "Reading time: popular fiction and the everyday." *The Cambridge Companion to Popular Fiction*, edited by David Glover and Scott McCracken, Cambridge UP, 2012, pp. 103–21.

McGuigan, Jim. *Modernity and Postmodern Culture*. Open UP, 2006.

McMurry, Margarida. "Story Matters. Story and its Concept in Tolkien and Pratchett." *Collision of Realities: Establishing Research on the Fantastic in Europe*, edited by Lars Schmeink and Astrid Böger, Walter de Gruyter GmbH, 2012, pp. 219–32.

Mendlesohn, Farah. "Faith and Ethics." *Terry Pratchett. Guilty of Literature*, edited by Andrew M. Butler et al., Old Earth Books, 2004, pp. 239–61.

———. *Rhetorics of Fantasy*. Wesleyan UP, 2008.

Meretoja, Hanna. *The Narrative Turn in Fiction and History. The Crisis and Return of Storytelling from Robbe-Grillet to Tournier*. Palgrave McMillan, 2014.

Messerli, Alfred. "Spatial Representation in European Popular Fairy Tales." *Marvels & Tales*, vol. 19, no. 2, 2005, pp. 274–84.

Miéville, China. *Perdido Street Station*. Pan Books, 2011.

"mimesis, n." *OED Online*. Oxford UP, Dec. 2014, 5 Feb. 2015.

Moody, Nickianne. "Death and Work." *Terry Pratchett. Guilty of Literature*, edited by Andrew M. Butler et al., Old Earth Books, 2004, pp. 153–70.

Morreall, John. *Comic Relief: A Comprehensive Philosophy of Humour*. Wiley-Blackwell, 2009.

———. "Philosophy of Humour." *The Stanford Encyclopedia of Philosophy*, edited by Edward N. Zalta, spring 2013, 9 Mar. 2015.

Mortensen, Peter. "'Civilization's Fear of Nature': Postmodernity, Culture, and Environment in *The God of Small Things*." *Beyond Postmodernism. Reassessments in Literature, Theory, and Culture*, edited by Klaus Stierstorfer, Walter de Gruyter GmbH, 2003, pp. 179–97.

Nagy, Gergely. "Gollum." *J. R. R. Tolkien Encyclopedia. Scholarship and Critical Assessment*, edited by Michael C. Drout, Routledge, 2007, pp. 246–48.

Neely, Erica L. "The Care of the Reaper Man: Death, the Auditors, and the Importance of Individuality." *Philosophy and Terry Pratchett*, edited by Jacob M. Held and James B. South, Palgrave McMillan, 2014, pp. 228–48.

Nikolajeva, Maria. "Fairy Tale and Fantasy: From Archaic to Postmodern." *Marvels & Tales*, vol. 17, no. 1, 2003, pp. 138–56.
Olsen, Lance. "Prelude: Nameless Things and Thingless Names." *Fantastic Literature: A Critical Reader*, edited by David Sandner, Praeger Publishers, 2004, pp. 274–93.
Pease, Donald. "From Virgin Land to Ground Zero: Interrogating the Mythological Foundations of the Master Fiction of the Homeland Security State." *A Companion to American Literature and Culture*, edited by Paul Lauter, Blackwell Publishing, 2010, pp. 637–54.
Plato. *The Republic*. Translated by Chris Emlyn-Jones and William Preddy, Harvard UP, 2013, 5 Feb. 2015.
Philo, Chris. "More words, more worlds. Reflections on the 'cultural turn' and human geography." *Cultural Turns/Geographical Turns: Perspectives on Cultural Geography*, edited by Ian Cook et al., Prentice Hall, 2000, pp. 26–53.
Pho, Diane M. "Objectified and Politicised: The Dynamics of Ideology and Consumerism in Steampunk Subculture." *Steaming into a Victorian Future. A Steampunk Anthology*, edited by Julie Anne Taddeo and Cynthia J. Miller, Scarecrow Press, 2013, pp. 185–210.
Potolsky, Matthew. *Mimesis*. Routledge, 2006.
Potts, Stephen W. "One for All: The Fantasy Quest in *The Hobbit, The Wizard of Oz*, and *His Dark Materials*." *The Hero's Quest*, edited by Bernard Schweizer and Robert A. Segal, Salem Press, 2013, pp. 221–36.
Pratchett, Terry. *A Blink of the Screen: Collected Shorter Fiction*. Doubleday, 2012.
———. *Carpe Jugulum*. Doubleday, 1998.
———. *The Colour of Magic*. Corgi Books, 1985.
———. *The Compleat Ankh-Morpork City Guide*. Doubleday, 2012.
———. *The Compleat Discworld Atlas*. Doubleday, 2015.
———. "Discworld & Beyond." *Locus Magazine*, issue 43, no. 4, Dec. 1999, pp. 4, 73–76.
———. *Discworld: The Ankh-Morpork Map*. Version 1.3. Random House, 2013.
———. *Eric*. Victor Gollancz, 1990.
———. *Going Postal*. Corgi Books, 2005.
———. *Guards! Guards!* Corgi Books, 1990.
———. *Hogfather*. Corgi Books, 1997.

———. "Imaginary Worlds, Real Stories." *Folklore*, vol. 111, no. 2, Oct. 2000, pp. 159–68.
———. *Interesting Times*. Corgi Books, 1995.
———. *I Shall Wear Midnight*. Corgi Books, 2011.
———. *Jingo*. Corgi Books, 1997.
———. *The Last Continent*. Corgi Books, 1998.
———. *The Last Hero*. Gollancz, 2001.
———. *The Light Fantastic*. Corgi Books, 1986.
———. *Lords and Ladies*. Corgi Books, 1993.
———. *Making Money*. Corgi Books, 2008.
———. *Men At Arms*. Corgi Books, 1994.
———. *Moving Pictures*. Gollancz, 1990.
———. *Mort*. Corgi Books, 1988.
———. *Night Watch*. Corgi Books, 2003.
———. *Raising Steam*. HarperCollins Publishers, 2013.
———. *The Shepherd's Crown*. Doubleday, 2015.
———. *A Slip of the Keyboard. Collected Non-Fiction*. Doubleday, 2014.
———. *Soul Music*. Corgi Books, 1994.
———. *Sourcery*. Corgi Books, 1989.
———. *Snuff*. Corgi Books, 2013.
———. *Thud!* Corgi Books, 2006.
———. *Wintersmith*. Corgi Books, 2007.
———. *Witches Abroad*. Corgi Books, 1992.
———. *Wyrd Sisters*. Corgi Books, 1989.
Pratchett, Terry, and Stephen Briggs. *A Tourist Guide to Lancre*. Corgi Books, 1998.
———. *The Discworld Companion*. Victor Gollancz, 1994.
———. *The Discworld Mapp*. Corgi Books, 1995.
———. *The Streets of Ankh-Morpork*. Corgi Books, 1993.
———. *Turtle Recall: The Discworld Companion…so far*. Victor Gollancz, 2013.
Pratchett, Terry, and Paul Kidby. *The Art of Discworld*. Victor Gollancz, 2004.
Pratchett, Terry, and Jacqueline Simpson. *The Folklore of Discworld*. Victor Gollancz, 2008.
Pratchett, Terry, et al. *The Science of Discworld*. Ebury Press, 2002.
———. *The Science of Discworld II: The Globe*. Ebury Press, 2003.
———. *The Science of Discworld IV: Judgement Day*. Ebury Press, 2013.

Prucher, Jeff, editor. *Brave New Words: The Oxford Dictionary of Science Fiction*. Oxford UP, 2007.
Rana, Marion. "Shedding the Light Fantastic on Terry Pratchett's Narrative Worlds: An Introduction." *Terry Pratchett's Narrative Worlds: From Giant Turtles to Small Gods*, edited by Marion Rana, Palgrave McMillan, 2018, pp. 1–20.
Rayment, Andrew. "'Feigning to Feign': Pratchett and the Maskerade." *Philosophy and Terry Pratchett*, edited by Jacob M. Held and James B. South, Palgrave McMillan, 2014, pp. 45–75.
Rescher, Nicholas. *Imagining Irreality: A Study of Unreal Possibilities*. Open Court Publishing, 2003.
Ricœur, Paul. "History as Narrative and Practice: Peter Kemp talks to Paul Ricœur in Copenhagen." *Philosophy Today*, no. 29, 1985, pp. 213–22.
Richardson, Brian. "What Is Unnatural Narrative Theory?" *Unnatural Narratives—Unnatural Narratology*, edited by Jan Alber and Rüdiger Heinze, Walter de Gruyter GmbH, 2011, pp. 23–40.
Rippl, Gabriele. "Introduction." *Handbook of Intermediality. Literature—Image—Sound—Music*, edited by Gabriele Rippl, Walter de Gruyter GmbH, 2015, pp. 1–32.
Roberts, Adam. "Gothic and Horror Fiction." *The Cambridge Companion to Fantasy Literature*, edited by Edward James and Farah Mendlesohn, Cambridge UP, 2012, pp. 21–36.
Ronen, Ruth. *Possible Worlds in Literary Theory*. Cambridge UP, 1994.
Rose, Margaret A. *Parody: Ancient, Modern, and Post-modern*. Cambridge UP, 1993.
Ryan, Marie-Laure. "From Parallel Universes to Possible Worlds: Ontological Pluralism in Physics, Narratology, and Narrative." *Poetics Today*, vol. 27, no. 4, winter 2006, pp. 633–74.
———. "Narration in Various Media." *The Living Handbook of Narratology*, edited by Peter Hühn et al., Hamburg University, winter 2013, 7 Oct. 2014.
———. *Possible Worlds, Artificial Intelligence, and Narrative Theory*. Indiana UP, 1991.
Sandner, David. "Critical and Historical Contexts: The Emergence and Evolution of the Fantastic." *Critical Insights: The Fantastic*, edited by Claire Whitehead, Salem Press, 2013, pp. 21–40.
———. *Fantastic Literature: A Critical Reader*. Praeger Publishers, 2004.

Sawyer, Andy. "The Librarian and His Domain." *Terry Pratchett: Guilty of Literature*, edited by Andrew M. Butler et al., Old Earth Books, 2004, pp. 109–31.

———. "Narrativium and Lies-to-children: 'Palatable instruction' in 'The Science of Discworld'." *Hungarian Journal of English and American Studies (HJEAS)*, vol. 6, no.1, spring 2000, pp. 155–78.

Sayer, Karen. "The Witches." *Terry Pratchett: Guilty of Literature*, edited by Andrew M. Butler et al., Old Earth Books, 2004, pp. 131–53.

Scarinzi, Alfonsina. "Enactive Literariness and Aesthetic Experience: From Mental Schemata to Anti-representationalism." *Aesthetics and the Embodied Mind: Beyond Art Theory and the Cartesian Mind-Body Dichotomy*, edited by Alfonsina Scarinzi, Springer, 2015, pp. 261–78.

Schallegger, René. "The Nightmares of Politicians: On the Rise of Fantasy Literature from Subcultural to Mass-cultural Phenomenon." *Collision of Realities: Establishing Research on the Fantastic in Europe*, edited by Lars Schmeink and Astrid Böger, Walter de Gruyter GmbH, 2012, pp. 29–49.

Schmid, Wolf. *Narratology: An Introduction*. Walter de Gruyter GmbH, KG, 2010.

Schnitker, Jan, and Rudolf Freiburg. "Introduction to Terry Pratchett." *"Do You Consider Yourself a Postmodern Author?": Interviews with Contemporary English Writers*, edited by Rudolf Freiburg and Jan Schnitker, LIT Verlag, 1999, pp. 175–78.

Self, Will. *Psychogeography*. Bloomsbury, 2007.

Senior, W. A. "Quest fantasies." *The Cambridge Companion to Fantasy Literature*, edited by Edward James and Farah Mendlesohn, Cambridge UP, 2012, pp. 190–99.

Shakespeare, William. *As You Like It*. Arden Shakespeare, 2006.

Sinclair, Iain. *London Orbital: A Walk around the M25*. Penguin Books, 2003.

Smith, Kevin Paul. *The Postmodern Fairy Tale: Folkloric Intertexts in Contemporary Fiction*. Palgrave MacMillan, 2007.

Smuts, Aaron. "Humour." *Internet Encyclopedia of Philosophy*. 2015 ed., 9 Mar. 2015.

Soja, Edward W. *Thirdspace: Journeys to Los Angeles and Other Real-and-Imagined Places*. Blackwell Publishing, 1996.

South, James B. "'Nothing Like a Bit of Destiny to Get the Old Plot Rolling': A Philosophical Reading of *Wyrd Sisters*." *Philosophy & Terry Pratchett*, edited by Jacob M. Held and James B. South, Palgrave MacMillan, 2014, pp. 25–45.

———. "Preface." *Philosophy & Terry Pratchett*, edited by Jacob M. Held and James B. South, Palgrave MacMillan, 2014, pp. x–xi.

Stableford, Brian. *Historical Dictionary of Fantasy Literature*. Scarecrow Press, 2005.

———. *Jaunting on the Scoriac Tempests and other Essays on Fantastic Literature*. Wildside Press, 2009.

Taleb, Nassim Nicholas. *The Black Swan: The Impact of the Highly Improbable*. Penguin Books, 2007.

Thomas, Melissa. "Teaching Fantasy: Overcoming the Stigma of Fluff." *The English Journal*, vol. 92, no. 5, *The Power of Imagination*, May 2003, pp. 60–64.

Thon, Jan-Noël. "Narratives across Media and the Outlines of a Media-conscious Narratology." *Handbook of Intermediality. Literature—Image—Sound—Music*, edited by Gabriele Rippl, Walter de Gruyter GmbH, 2015, pp. 439–56.

"Thud." *Boardgamegeek*. Boardgamegeek, 2010, 10 Dec. 2017.

Tiffin, Jessica. *Marvellous Geometry: Narrative and Metafiction in Modern Fairy Tale*. Wayne State UP, 2009.

Tolkien, J. R. R. *The Hobbit or There and Back Again*. HarperCollins Publishers, 2006.

———. *The Fellowship of the Ring*. HarperCollins*Publishers*, 2007.

———. *The Return of the King*. HarperCollins*Publishers*, 2007.

———. "On Fairy-stories." *Tolkien On Fairy-stories. Expanded Edition, with Commentary and Notes*. Edited by Verlyn Flieger and Douglas A. Anderson, HarperCollins Publishers, 2008, pp. 27–84.

———. *The Shaping of Middle-earth*. HarperCollins Publishers, 2002.

Vacek, Martin. "On the Possibility of the Discworld." *Philosophy & Terry Pratchett*, edited by Jacob M. Held and James B. South, Palgrave MacMillan, 2014, pp. 269–86.

VanderMeer, Jeff, and S. J. Chambers. *The Steampunk Bible: An Illustrated Guide to the World of Imaginary Airships, Corsets and Goggles, Mad Scientists, and Strange Literature*. Abrams Image, 2011.

Webb, Caroline. *Fantasy and the Real World in British Children's Literature: The Power of Story*. Routledge, 2015.

———. "The Watchman and the Hippopotamus: Art, Play and Otherness in *Thud!*" *Discworld and the Disciplines: Critical Approaches to the Terry Pratchett Works*, edited by Anne Hiebert Alton and William C. Spruiell, McFarland, 2014, pp. 92–107.

Westfahl, Gary. *The Greenwood Encyclopedia of Science Fiction and Fantasy: Themes, Works, and Wonders*, Vol. 2. Greenwood Press, 2005.

Winkler, Kathrin, et al. "Literary Studies and the Spatial Turn." *JLT* 6/1, 2012, pp. 253–70.

Wolf, Mark J. P. *Building Imaginary Worlds: The Theory and History of Subcreation*. Routledge, 2012.

Woods, Tim. *Beginning Postmodernism*. Manchester UP, 1999.

Wünsch, Marianne. *Die Fantastische Literatur der Frühen Moderne (1890–1930). Definition, Denkgeschichtlicher Kontext, Strukturen*, Fink, 1991.

Zima, Peter V. "Why the Postmodern Age Will Last." *Beyond Postmodernism: Reassessments in Literature, Theory, and Culture*, edited by Klaus Stierstorfer, Walter de Gruyter GmbH, 2003, pp. 13–28.

Zoran, Gabriel. "Towards a Theory of Space in Narrative." *Poetics Today*, vol. 5, no. 2, *The Construction of Reality in Fiction*, 1984, pp. 309–35.

Index

1960s culture/counterculture and society 21, 25, 37, 40, 133n143; fantasy literature of the period 21, 26, 27n38, 35, 50–51, 76, 104, 108, 237
1970s culture and society 40–41; fantasy literature of the period 37, 50, 76, 104, 108, 237
1980s culture and society 40–41; fantasy literature of the period 37, 51, 114, 125n132
1990s culture and society 37; fantasy literature of the period iiin3, 71n72, 114

A

A'Tuin, the Great (Discworld character/location) 50, 56, 62, 68n69, 125–27, 130
Aaronovitch, Ben 220n238
Adams, Douglas. *The Hitchhiker's Guide to the Galaxy* 41, 41n50
Alber, Jan 19–20
alienation 188, 197–98, 216
The Amazing Maurice and His Educated Rodents 180n185, 223
Amis, Martin. *Time's Arrow* 12n20
Ankh-Morpork (Discworld city) 57, 88, 103–08, 113, 155, 161n162, 169, 174n174, 178n181, 186, 188–206, 208–21, 223–32; concept of city running independently of the novels 229–30; sources and influences 205, 208; River Ankh 166n167, 193
Ankh-Morpork City Watch 103, 107, 203, 210–11
Anthony, Piers 3, 67
anti-heroes 29, 69, 85, 123
Apuleius. *The Golden Ass* 33
Arendt, Hannah 113
Aristophanes. *The Clouds* 33; *Peace* 50n54; *The Birds* 50n54
Aristotle. *Poetics* 7–9, 11, 23, 31, 243
art iv–v, 7, 9, 13, 17, 20; purpose of art 241

Asimov, Isaac 126, 217
Attebery, Brian 12–15, 21, 27, 32–33, 35, 47, 61–62, 81, 85; *see also* Extruded Fantasy Product; fuzzy set
Auster, Paul 115n125, 239; *City of Glass* 97

B
Bakhtin, Mikhail 17–19, 29, 37, 53, 69–71, 77, 231–32, 245; *see also* carnivalesque; chronotope; grotesque
Balzac, Honoré de 19
Baudrillard, Jean 89–90, 116, 162; *see also* hyper-reality
Beard, Henry N. and Douglas C. Kennedy. *Bored of the Rings* [*BotR*] iii, 37–38, 40–43, 47, 49–56, 63, 65, 67, 69–71, 78, 86, 118, 191
belief, power of (on Discworld) 82, 87n92, 91–92, 100, 103, 105, 128, 130–41, 169, 176–77, 181, 183, 186–88, 230–31, 238
Beowulf 15
binary oppositions, dichotomies 22, 74–75, 85, 101, 102n113, 108, 111–13, 168, 200n213, 204, 244
Blind Io (Discworld character) 63
Bloom, Harold 241
Bohr, Niels 138
Bonhoeffer, Dietrich 113
Bourdieu, Pierre 198
Borges, Jorge Luis 3; "On Exactitude in Science" 21, 152n153
Bradshaw, George 224
Bravd (Discworld character) 52
Brecht, Bertolt 192
Brewer's Dictionary of Phrase and Fable 65
Briggs, Stephen 152, 157, 205
British comedy tradition 40
Brooks, Terry iin2
Brust, Steven. Vlad Taltos series 203n216

C
C. M. O. T. Dibbler 192n201, 243n258
call to adventure 57, 79n79, 85, 86n91, 92n99, 183n192
Calvino, Italo 3, 115n125
Campbell, Joseph. *The Hero with a Thousand Faces* 82n85, 163, 182; *see also* call to adventure; hero's journey
capitalism 21–22

caricature (type of humor) 38, 53, 57
carnivalesque (Bakhtinian theory) 29, 245
Carpe Jugulum 112
Carrot Ironfoundersson (Discworld character) 107–10, 163n164, 210–11, 231
Carry-On films 40
Carter, Angela 36–37, 77, 80; *The Bloody Chamber* 76
The Chalk (region of Discworld) 180n186, 182–83, 195
Chandler, Raymond 104
change as theme (in Discworld and other fantasy) v, 40, 55, 66, 150, 184, 188, 202, 217–20, 232, 237, 246
Cheery Littlebottom (Discworld character) 205n219
Chesterton, G. K. 77–78, 118
Christianity 61, 74–75
chronotope (Bakhtinian theory) 17, 116; journey chronotope 55
"Cinderella" (fairy tale) 80
City Watch subseries of Discworld novels 103–08, 191, 205n218, 206
clacks (semaphore system in Discworld) 184, 213, 216, 219
Clarke, Arthur C. 126, 217; Clarke's Law 126n135
Clute, John 14n22, 27, 35, 54, 60, 61n64, 65; *see also* "fantasyland"; taproot texts; thinning
Cohen the Barbarian (Discworld character) 53n57, 120
Cohen, Jack 137–38
Coleridge, Samuel Taylor 79
The Colour of Magic (videogame) 225n247
The Colour of Magic [CoM] 27, 41, 49, 51–60, 63–68, 71, 73, 77–80, 84, 100, 120, 128, 130, 139, 154–56, 159, 161, 166n166, 168, 194, 196, 205, 208, 210n224, 213–14, 216, 224, 227, 231
coming-of-age novels 171, 182
commercialization and consumerism 22, 26, 27n38, 40, 51, 216
community, importance of (on Discworld) 98, 111, 147–48, 165, 176–81, 189, 197–99, 243
The Compleat Ankh-Morpork City Guide 211, 219, 223; *see also The Streets of Ankh-Morpork*
The Compleat Discworld Atlas 166n167
computers 144, 218, 226n248; *see also* Hex
consensus reality concept 91, 131–32, 134
conservatism, conservative features of fantasy 12, 21, 36n46, 40, 42, 47, 79–80, 161, 178

Costa, Lúcio 195n206
Cruikshank, George. *London Going Out of Town* ... 212n226

D

Dadaism ivn5
Dark Lord trope 35, 76n77, 219
The Dark Side of the Sun 41n50
De Certeau, Michel 197–98
Death (Discworld character) 50, 57–59, 64n67, 66, 132, 143, 230, 238
death 75n75, 132n140, 143
deconstructionism 36, 238–39
defamiliarization 77–78, 117, 165, 193
demons (Discworld characters) 76, 113n124, 214
detective fiction genre v, 14, 25–26, 103–06; *see also* mystery genre
Dick Simnel 218n237
Dickens, Charles 77, 209, 211n225, 224; *Oliver Twist* 209n223
Discworld series: classification and timeline of books in this study vi–i; assessment of series as a whole 47–51, 64–67, 76–82, 100–04, 235–40, 241–46; as satire 49, 50n55, 53, 64–65, 76, 78, 102, 148, 151, 191, 200, 203–04, 214n231, 218–19, 232, 237–38; focus on everyday life and pragmatism 65, 118, 122–23, 127–30, 152, 162, 165, 174–83, 188, 190, 193–200, 209, 212, 228, 232, 244; footnotes 67, 103, 138, 160, 204, 243; objects of parodies iii, vi–vii, 42–43, 51–53, 58, 62–68, 78–79, 157, 162n163, 224; sources 36–37, 40–41, 51–52, 61–65, 76–77, 100, 117, 138, 157, 209; technological development in Discworld v, 144, 183–90, 194, 200, 202–05, 208, 211–21, 224–25, 232, 237; treatment of endings and closure 119–20. Discworld as a secondary world: cosmology and cosmogony of 62, 127; prehistory of 158n158. Discworld characters: character-driven writing 67, 73, 165–66, 183, 232; marginalized protagonists 47–48, 58, 84–85, 92, 97n107, 98, 102–11, 123–24, 133, 165, 178, 199, 239; morality and moral codes in Discworld 76, 98–99, 106, 109, 112–14, 117n127, 143, 181, 184, 202, 237, 243; recurring characters 53n57, 70, 73, 155, 236–37; trope-savvy and self-aware protagonists 137, 143

Discworld extended texts (paratexts, illustrations, movies, video games, comic books, fanfiction, adaptations, guides, maps, etc.) iii, 148–49, 159, 160, 208–09, 221–24, 246; apps 228–30; board, computer, and video games 148–49, 161n162, 169, 209, 221–22, 224n246, 225–29; comic books 107n116, 221, 246; glossaries of 143–44, 160, 228; illustrations 159n160, 223n244; maps and cartography of 143–44, 151–62, 166, 172–74, 191, 196, 202, 205, 209–11, 221, 223–31, 237; media adaptions 221, 223; *see also* Kidby, Paul; Kirby, Jack; titles of individual maps, media adaptations, and games

Discworld (video game series) 225–29

The Discworld Companion 67n68, 88, 156

The Discworld Mapp [*Mapp*] 152, 156, 158, 196, 225

Discworld: The Ankh-Morpork Map (electronic app) 228–30

Disney movies and Disneyland 76, 88–90, 93, 107n116, 194

Dodger 209

Doležel, Lubomír 5, 10, 16, 19–20, 132, 149, 239; *see also* possible-worlds theory

Donald, Merlin 7–8, 32, 61, 81n81

Donaldson, Stephen R. Chronicles of Thomas Covenant 75

dragons (Discworld beings) 50, 105–06, 113, 120, 128, 131, 138, 210, 219

Dungeon Dimensions (Discworld location) 66, 76, 113

dwarfs (Discworld race) 79, 104, 117n127, 167–70, 173, 188, 199, 202, 204–05, 224; gender of dwarfs 205; *see also* grags; in other fantasy 27, 29, 33n43, 199, 200n213, 203n216; *see also under* Tolkien

dystopias and dystopic elements 89, 195, 214n231

E

Eagleton, Terry. *Literary Theory* 241

Eco, Umberto 19, 239; *The Name of the Rose* 18, 38, 196n208

Eisenhower, Dwight D. 133n143

Ekman, Stefan 9n16, 101n112, 158, 166

elephants (Discworld beings) 50, 62, 125–26

elves (Discworld race) 29, 175–76, 180–81, 182n190, 186–88, 202; in other fantasy and in folklore 29n40, 41, 185, 203n216; *see under* Tolkien

Ende, Michael 239

The Enlightenment 26n36, 185, 242

Eric 62n65, 68n70, 158n158
Eric Wheelbrace (Discworld character) 176–77, 187n199
escapism i, 8, 22, 27, 34, 36n46, 37, 72, 100, 217, 242, 244
Esmerelda "Granny" Weatherwax (Discworld character) 47, 69, 74, 85–88, 93, 95–115, 122, 133, 136, 161, 165–66, 177–82, 184, 195, 202, 214–15, 219, 231, 237, 243–44, 246n260
eucatastrophe 40, 55, 73, 98, 120, 184, 201–02, 212
evil *see* good and evil
evolution 7–8, 10, 23, 32, 140n150
Expressionism ivn5
"Extruded Fantasy Product" 35, 81, 164

F
fairy godmother figures 89, 99, 135
fairy tales 12n19, 32, 33n43, 47, 60–61, 64, 69, 74, 76, 80, 83n86, 85–93, 95, 97, 99–103, 107n118, 135, 138, 141, 171–78, 180–81, 183, 185n196, 187, 189, 201, 228,
fan fiction 101n111
fantasy as a genre i–v, 20–29, 33–43, 47–51, 54–55, 57, 60–61, 65, 67–69, 74, 77–87, 107–08, 113–14, 116–123, 125–26, 130, 142–43, 147, 150, 157, 159, 160–65, 171, 174, 185, 188–91, 206, 208, 212, 217–20, 230–32, 235–39, 241–45; definition 3–4, 12–19; tropes, clichés, formulas, and stereotypes of fantasy i–ii, 13–14, 26–43, 47–65, 70–74, 76–90, 94–97, 99–100, 103–07, 111–14, 117–19, 121–23, 127–28, 131–32, 135–38, 142–44, 150–51, 154–58, 162–65, 167–68, 170–72, 177–79, 182–83, 189–93, 198–99, 202–03, 206, 208, 212, 220, 224, 232, 236–39, 244–46
fantasy as a mode 13–14, 31, 33, 50, 77–78, 241–42
fantasy subgenres: Chestertonian 77–78, 118; classic ii, 17, 36n45, 41, 47–48, 51, 53, 57, 59, 70–71, 73–74, 78, 81n83, 83–85, 105–14, 117, 119–20, 123, 138, 142, 144, 162, 165, 167–68, 170, 182, 191, 193–94, 198, 200, 208, 212, 219–20, 232, 235–36, 240; "grimdark" 117n126; high 14, 35, 40, 83, 191; humorous or comic 28, 33–39, 50n55, 67, 71; immersive 120–24, 136, 153; mass market 24–25, 29, 35, 37, 51, 103–04; portal 54, 58; quest 54–55, 58–60, 66, 69–70, 72–73, 75, 80, 113, 121, 123, 154, 167, 225; theatre (James and Mendlesohn theory) 48–60, 63, 65–66, 68–69, 72, 94–97, 115, 122, 142, 154, 163–64, 171, 183, 188, 191–94, 201, 229–32, 238; urban (subgenre) 81n82, 103

fantasy, urban settings 104, 189–93
"fantasyland" 27, 35, 39, 53–55, 74, 86, 154, 162, 194, 201, 220, 238
Fforde, Jasper 220n238; *Thursday Next* series 122
Fiedler, Leslie iii–iv
film noir 104, 106
films, film industry in Discworld 136; in primary world vi, 77–78, 136, 238n256
Flaubert, Gustave. *Madame Bovary* 30, 73
Flynn, Errol 137
folklore and folk tales ii, v, 25, 49, 60, 63–65, 71, 75–77, 99, 100–01, 172–73, 179–80, 185, 187, 206, 232
Foucault, Michel iv, 147–48, 163, 178, 189, 197–98, 205–06, 213, 235
Frankenstein (creature, movies, book) 199n211
Fred Colon (Discworld character) 210
free press 201, 213
free will, active choice 48, 86, 88, 92–93, 97–99, 101–02, 113–14, 143, 198–99, 212, 230–31, 243–44
Freud, Sigmund 8n15
Frye, Northrop. *Anatomy of Criticism* 11–12
"fuzzy set" 14, 21, 33, 43, 47, 51

G
Gaiman, Neil 223n243, 239
game board imagery/metaphor 63, 65, 68, 82, 161, 163, 168, 188, 227, 245
Gardner, John 36
Genette, Gérard 17–18, 38, 54, 70–71, 160n161; *see also* hypertexts, paratextual material
genre literature (other than fantasy) and genre theory i, v, 3, 10, 13–14, 24–25, 43, 81, 112, 117, 188, 218, 222, 224, 241; *see also* specific genres
Genua (Discworld location) 88–93, 95, 109, 115, 131, 135, 163, 175, 177, 194, 230; *see also* Lilith Weatherwax, *Witches Abroad*
Gerber, Michael. *Barry Trotter* 38, 70, 78
Gerber, Michael. *The Chronicles of Blarnia* 38, 70
glossaries in fantasy novels 18n27, 83, 143; *see also* Discworld extended texts
goblins (Discworld race) 200, 203–05, 216n234

gods (of Discworld) 62–65, 79, 118, 127, 133n142, 161, 163, 167, 227; in other fantasy and in primary world 31, 50n54, 61–62, 65
Goethe. *Faust* 62n65
Going Postal [GP] 213, 215–16
gonne (Discworld weapon) 214, 236
good and evil 74–77, 79, 81, 85, 89, 97–100, 102n113, 108, 111–14, 168, 170, 174, 216; *see also* right and wrong
Good Omens (TV show) 223n243
Goodkind, Terry. *Sword of Truth* novels 36
Gothic genre vn6, 26, 185n196, 242
grags (Fundamentalist dwarf sect on Discworld) 205, 216
Granny Weatherwax *see* Esmerelda Weatherwax
Grant, John 27, 35, 54, 60, 61n64, 65; *see also* "fantasyland"; taproot texts; thinning
Grimm's fairy tales 87n93
grotesque (Bakhtinian theory) 53, 70
Guards! Guards! 47, 80, 82, 87n92, 103–07, 113, 117, 128, 131, 191, 205n218, 210, 225, 230, 239, 244
guards, watchmen, police 85, 95n103, 103, 105–07, 109n121, 114, 165, 195, 198, 210
Gytha Ogg 96n104, 178n180

H
"happy endings" 48, 85, 89, 100–01, 105–07, 111, 114, 120, 142, 156, 236
Harrison, M. John 27n38
Harry King (Discworld character) 212n227
Havelock Vetinari, the Patrician (Discworld character) 57n61, 108, 110, 113–14, 196–99, 210n224, 214–16
Heinlein, Robert A. 126, 217
Heraclitus 96
Herman, David 16n25
hero's journey 163–64, 182, 191; *see also* Campbell, Joseph
heroes and heroism 40, 52–53, 55–57, 59–60, 67, 69, 76, 83–86, 97n105, 102–08, 111, 118, 123, 136, 143, 154, 156, 165–66, 174, 176, 182–83, 191, 198–99, 219, 231, 243–44
Hex (Discworld computer) 218
Hindu mythology 50, 62, 82

history iv, 16, 23, 48, 54, 80, 88, 94n102, 133, 184n195, 208, 217, 221, 235, 239
Hobb, Robin iin2
Hogfather 132, 134–36, 230, 238
Homer 42n51; *The Iliad* 31; *The Odyssey* 38, 73n73, 82n85
horror genre v, 14n21, 25–26, 74
Howard, Robert E. 3; Conan the Barbarian stories 51–53
Hrun the Barbarian (Discworld character) 52–53, 84
humanism 117, 191, 235
Hume, David 81n81
Hume, Kathryn 91n97
humor, theories of 30–31; *see also* incongruity theory
Hutcheon, Linda 21–24, 31, 37–39, 42, 49, 61, 69, 83, 96, 98, 106, 204, 235, 238
hyperreality 89–90
hypertexts 17n26, 38

I
I Shall Wear Midnight 94n102, 182
iconograph (Discworld camera) 214
Idle, Eric 226n250
Igors (Discworld race) 199n211
immersion 10–11, 20, 30, 34, 39, 68, 123–24, 133n142, 153, 225, 228–29, 240
incongruity theory (theory of humor and/or postmodernism) 31–32, 49, 61, 235
individual development and growth (cognitive, social, etc) 7–10
individuality 65, 90, 93, 100, 109, 116, 121, 132, 136, 148, 160, 171, 177, 180, 189, 199, 206, 217, 230
industrialization (on Discworld) 21, 184–88, 200, 208, 212–13, 217–19, 232; in other fantasy and primary world 24–25, 185, 188, 217
Interesting Times 204
intermediality / transmediality 221–25
Internet (on Discworld) 144, 211, 216
intertextuality 38, 53, 138, 229
irony ii, iv, 24, 29–30, 36–37, 39, 41–42, 49, 51, 57, 62, 67–68, 77, 106, 118, 120, 123–24, 127–29, 157–58, 172, 192–93, 200, 202, 211n225, 223–24, 226, 235, 246
Iversen, Stefan 19n29

J

Jackson, Peter. *Lord of the Rings* and *Hobbit* movie series 107n118, 222n240
James, Edward 13, 29, 53, 68, 95; *see also* fantasy, theatre
Jameson, Frederic v, 198
Jingo 167, 190, 204
Johnson, Mark 14
Jonathan Teatime (Discworld character) 103n114
Jones, Diana Wynne 27, 36, 54; *The Tough Guide to Fantasyland* 35–36, 39, 154; *Howl's Moving Castle* 36n45; *Dark Lord of Derkholm* 36n45
Jordan, Robert iin2, 191; *The Wheel of Time* novels 36, 76n77, 85
Joyce, James. *Ulysses* 30, 38, 73
justice 74, 112

K

Kafka, Franz 12n20, 79, 176
Kant, Immanuel 115
Kay, Guy Gavriel. *Fionavar* trilogy 75
Kidby, Paul 63, 140, 159n160, 173
King Kong (movie) 238n256
kingship; return of lost king motif 75, 86n91, 105, 107, 154, 163n164, 214n230, 231, 236
Kirby, Jack 159n160
Koom Valley (Discworld location and battle) 167–69, 204
Kripke, Saul 5

L

Lacan, Jacques 109
Lakoff, George 14
Lancre (Discworld location) 98n109, 161n162, 172–84, 186–87, 190–91, 195, 226, 231; villages in Lancre 174–75
language, power and use of in fiction, philosophy of language 61, 68, 132, 134–35
The Last Continent 155n156
The Last Hero [*LH*] 63, 68n70, 125, 161n162, 219, 222n242, 231
Le Corbusier 195n206
Le Guin, Ursula K. 27n38
Lefebvre, Henri 151, 178, 186

Leiber, Fritz. Fafhrd and the Gray Mouser series 52; city of Lankhmar 205
Leibniz, Gottfried Wilhelm 5
Lewis, C. S. 185, 188; Narnia series 38, 54
Lewis, David 5
Lewis, Matthew Gregory. *The Monk* 26
"lies-to-children" 138n148
The Light Fantastic [*LF*] 41–42, 49, 55, 58–60, 64–66, 73, 75–77, 78n78, 80, 85, 100, 113, 122–26, 154–56, 161, 166n166, 216, 231
Lilith Weatherwax (Discworld character) 88–93, 97n107, 99–100, 109–10, 113, 115, 135, 142, 160, 175, 178, 181, 187, 194, 199, 215, 244
liminal spaces, thresholds, boundaries, borders i, iv, 101, 158n159, 167, 179, 186, 224; *see also* marginality
literary canon, Western canon 241–42
"Little Red Riding Hood" 69, 91–93
London 193n202, 208–09, 211n225, 212n226, 228
Lords and Ladies [*LL*] 70, 97, 101
Lovecraft, H. P. 52; Cthulhu mythos 66, 76
Lucas, George 82n85; see also *Star Wars*
Luddites 216n235
Lynch, Scott 220n238
Lyotard, Jean-François 22

M
Mage Wars (Discworld event) 130
magic (on Discworld) 58–59, 77, 86, 88, 92, 116, 123–34, 138–40, 142, 157, 172–75, 178–79, 197n209, 214, 218, 236, 243; in other fantasy and in general 9, 13, 33n43, 34, 47, 72, 86, 123–34, 179n183, 185–86, 208, 242–43
Making Money [*MM*] 194n204, 213, 215
Manlove, Colin 56
Manzoni, Alessandro 206; *The Betrothed* 18, 25n34
maps and mapping 185–86; in fantasy novels 83, 143, 147–48, 150–54, 156–64, 172–75, 190–91, 196–99, 209–11, 238
marginalized characters, marginality (on Discworld) 47–48, 74, 83–85, 92, 98, 101–02, 104–07, 109, 111, 123–24, 133, 165, 178, 199, 203, 231, 239; in other fantasy and in general 58, 74, 83, 102, 109
Marshall Plan 22n33, 201

Martin, George R. R. *Song of Ice and Fire* series 117n126
masquerade 97
Mayhew, Henry 209; *London Labour and the London Poor* 228
McBain, Ed 104
McCaffrey, Anne. Dragonworld series 51
media theory 149; definitions of media 222n241
Medici family 197n209
Men At Arms [*MAA*] 108, 194, 201–03, 205n219, 210–11, 214
Mendlesohn, Farah 3, 13, 14n22, 23, 53, 68–69, 95, 114, 121, 123, 153, 243; *see also* fantasy, theatre
metafiction, metatextuality, metanarrative 3, 14, 22–23, 39–40, 62, 68, 70, 82, 87, 93, 97, 103, 115n125, 123, 136–37, 139, 202, 221, 227, 235, 239n257; breaking the fourth wall, addressing the reader directly 68, 81n83
Meyrink, Gustav 12n20
Miéville, China 36n46, 117, 163, 220n238; *Perdido Street Station* 81n82, 130n139; *Iron Council* 130n139; New Crobuzon 193n203, 205
mimesis 6–17, 23, 30–34, 37, 61, 73, 85, 92, 102n113, 120, 151, 201, 217, 224, 245; high vs. low 11–12, 30–31, 106, 161, 242
modernism, modern literature iv–v, 21, 25, 195n206
Moist von Lipwig (Discworld character and book series) 128n137, 213, 215–16, 218, 224, 231, 244
money (on Discworld) 194n204, 213; banking 215n232
Monty Python's Flying Circus 226n250
Moorcock, Michael. Eternal Champion series 29n39
"mooreeffoc" effect *see* fantasy, Chestertonian
morality and moral growth in literature 59, 64, 69, 72–74, 76, 81, 105–06, 110–14, 174, 204, 237, 241; *see also under* Discworld
Morgenstern, Erin 220n238
morphic determinism 86, 114
Mort [*M*] 65–66, 87
Moving Pictures [*MP*] vi, 78, 132n141, 136, 238n256
Mrs Bradshaw's Handbook to Travelling upon the Ankh-Morpork & Sto Plains Hygienic Railway 223–24
music hall comedy 40
mystery genre 14n21
mythology (primary world) ii, iv–v, 13–15, 22, 25, 49–50, 60–65, 71, 74–75, 77, 82, 100, 135, 138, 151–52, 154, 185n196, 201n214, 205–06, 213, 236, 242

N

Nac Mac Feegle *see* Wee Free Men
names and naming 37, 52, 93, 135; place names 174–75, 202
Nanny Ogg *see* Gytha Ogg
narrative theory and narratology 10, 12n19, 17, 19, 22–23, 32, 54, 76, 80–83, 88, 128, 131, 137–38, 141–42, 151, 153–54, 161, 187, 194, 222, 235, 237–39; narrative fallacy 81, 138, 141;narrative identity, personal narrative 93, 101, 141–42, 170, 196–97, 230; narrative maps and geography 160, 197, 210–11; narratives of science and technology 137–38, 213, 232
narrative imperative, causality, or determinism 48, 73, 80–99, 102–19, 121–22, 131–38, 140–43, 148, 155–59, 161–66, 174–76, 181, 183, 184n193, 204, 209, 214, 216, 221, 227, 229, 230–31, 236, 238, 244, 246
Narrativia (production company) 223
narrativium (Discworld element) 133–38, 140–41, 176, 179, 236
Ned Simnel 218n237
neutrality 113
Nielsen, Henrik Skov 19n29
Night Watch [*NW*] vii, 71n71, 196–99, 210, 212, 214
Nightshade [Elf queen] (Discworld character) 186–87
"Nobby" Nobbs (Discworld character) 210
nostalgia 21, 79, 155, 178, 218–19
nuclear power 129–30, 133, 139, 179n183; nuclear accidents, radiation, and radioactive waste 130, 133, 139; nuclear war 130, 133n143

O

Octavo (Discworld object) 58–59
ofermod 108, 110, 182
Only You Can Save Mankind 84n88
oral storytelling and traditions 60, 64, 151
Orion (constellation) 77
Orwell, George 214n231
The Other, "othering" 170, 203

P

Paolini, Christopher. *Eragon* 85
paratextual material (maps, guides, games, etc.) 101n111, 153, 159, 160n161; *see also* Discworld extended texts

parody ii–iii, vi–vii, 24, 29–30, 33, 37–43, 47–73, 75–79, 83–84, 86–88, 92–93, 95–97, 108, 114, 117–19, 122, 127, 142–43, 150–51, 153, 156–57, 160–62, 172, 175, 183, 190–91, 204, 213–14, 219, 230, 232, 236–38
pastiche iii, 38–39, 51, 57, 65, 67, 70, 86
The Patrician *see* Havelock Vetinari
Pavel, Thomas 5
Peake, Mervyn. *Gormenghast* 30
Pearson, Bernhard 196
Peaseblossom (Discworld character) 180
Perec, George. *La Vie mode d'emploi* 153n154
philosophy (in general) 5–10, 31
phlogiston 134, 137
"The Pied Piper" (fairy tale) 180n185
planned cities 195n206, 196
Plato, *The Republic* 7–9, 31, 42, 238
poetry 7, 15, 61; bucolic 22
Ponder Stibbons (Discworld character) 125
popular culture v, 37, 41, 49, 65, 67, 71, 76–77, 138
possessiveness 75
possible-worlds theory (philosophical concept) 5, 9–11, 15–16, 19–20, 32, 139n149, 149, 239; for literary constructs, *see* secondary worlds
postal service (on Discworld) 215–16
postmodernism (in general) i–v, 3–4, 20–24, 30–31, 36–40, 42, 49, 62, 69, 118, 135, 137, 142, 183, 197, 199, 222, 226n248, 230–31, 235–36, 238–39, 241, 244–45; postmodern art, literature, and storytelling i–v, 3–4, 11–12, 14, 20–21, 23–24, 37–39, 42–43, 62, 68, 74, 81n83, 82–83, 96–97, 112, 118, 122, 142, 161, 217, 221, 235, 239; *see also under* Pratchett
power, power dynamics, abuse of power 75, 88–91, 98–100, 106, 110–11, 115–16, 135, 148, 155, 163, 170, 177–79, 181–82, 186, 189, 192, 197–98, 201, 212, 214
Prague 208n221
Pratchett, Rhianna 223

Pratchett, Terry—Biography and career iii, 27–28, 65; reporter on nuclear power for British Electric Board 130, 133n143, 179n183; collaborations 223n243–44; Alzheimer's disease 148n152, 184n194, 200, 223n244; death 215, 223, 245. Views and opinions: on fantasy 77, 118, 245; on hero characters 104; on "human" nature 117; on progress 216–17; on hope 210; on Tolkien 29, 201; on the influence of Tolkien 117, 164–65. As a writer: evolution of style and subject matter 49, 60, 66–71, 79, 82–87, 102, 112, 121–23, 128n137, 147–49, 153–61, 164–67, 170–71, 178, 183–86, 190, 194, 200, 202–12, 217–23, 232, 235–39; postmodern aspects of writing iii–v, 37–43, 50, 62–65, 68–69, 74, 81n83, 82, 93, 95–98, 101–02, 106, 112, 118, 120, 123, 134, 136, 139, 141–43, 172, 188, 191, 202, 217, 232, 235–36, 238–39, 244, 246; science fiction influences on and characteristics of work 41n50, 125–28, 130, 218–19; development of theory of narrative causality/narrativium 48, 80–82, 135, 137, 140–41; *see also* narrative imperative, narrativium. *See also* Discworld series; names of individual books and characters.
predestination and determinism 92, 133, 136, 143, 163; *see also* narrative imperative
Propp, Vladimir 47
prototype theory 14
psychoanalysis 8n15, 31
Pynchon, Thomas 3
Pyramids vi

Q
quests 27, 55, 119; *see also* fantasy, quest

R
Rabelais, François 33
race and racism, racial conflict 52, 144, 169–70, 190–91, 200, 202–04, 208, 217; discrimination 170, 200; prejudice 111, 204; segregation 29n40, 200, 203; xenophobia 169
Radcliffe, Ann 242; *The Mysteries of Udolpho* 26
railways, steam engines, and trains in Discworld 184, 186–87, 205, 211, 215n232, 216, 218n237, 219, 224
Raising Steam 200, 203, 205, 215n232, 216, 218n237
Ramtop Mountains (Discworld location) 172–73
Rankin, Robert 67

rationalism 242
reader expectations 42, 69, 80, 82, 96, 130, 165, 177; reader participation with text (reader response theory) 6, 9, 16n25, 20, 34, 149
realism as a mode, realism as a genre 13–14, 22, 26, 73, 116–20, 193
reality, empirical (our primary world) in relation to fictional worlds i, iv–v, 4–16, 19, 22–24, 31–36, 74, 77–79, 151, 96, 101n111, 114, 116, 119, 141, 157, 184–88, 201, 205–06, 211, 214, 216–18, 224, 236, 238–42, 244–45
Reaper Man [*RM*] 218n237
redemption, redemptive themes 191, 203
refamiliarization 79, 82, 87, 112, 117, 129, 172, 193
religion vi, 54, 61, 64, 117, 144
Renaissance era 190, 208
revolutions 210
Rhys Rhysson, Low King of the Dwarfs (Discworld character) 205
Richardson, Brian 12n19–20, 19n29
Ricœur, Paul 97, 237
right and wrong 76, 99–100; *see also* good and evil
Rincewind (Discworld character), Rincewind subseries 52–60, 66–69, 72, 80, 84–85, 92, 95n103, 102, 114, 123, 154–57, 161–62, 168, 175, 178n181, 179n183, 196, 204, 214, 216, 225–27, 231, 236–37, 244
"Robin Hood" (folktale) 137
rock music vi, 78, 132n141
romance (medieval genre) v, 13, 22, 108
Roundworld Project 138–41
Rowling, J. K. *Harry Potter* novels iii, 54, 71n72, 110n122, 153, 222
Rushdie, Salman. *Midnight's Children, The Satanic Verses* 12n20
Ryan, Marie–Laure 5, 10–11, 16n25, 19

S
salvation as theme in literature 55, 120; *see also* eucatastrophe
Samuel "Sam" Vimes (Discworld character) 47, 69, 74, 85, 95n103, 102–15, 122, 133, 136, 160–61, 165, 167, 169, 177n178, 182, 192n201, 195–99, 203, 210, 212, 214–15, 225, 231, 237, 243–44; as aristocrat 109–10, 133, 182, 231; alcoholism 110, 160, 182, 210; moral code 199, 243–44
Sapkowski, Andrzej. Witcher series 29n40, 203n216
satire (in general) 33–34, 38, 67, 69
Scarinzi, Alfonsina 79, 193; *see also* refamiliarization

Schmid, Wolf 10–11
Schwarzenegger, Arnold 53
science 124–27, 131, 133–34, 137–42
science fiction genre vn6, 14, 25, 41, 65, 81n82, 125–28, 130, 217–18; space opera sub-genre v
The Science of Discworld (multiple books) 59n63, 68n69, 127n136, 131, 137–41, 231
Seattle 208n221
secondary belief 30, 70, 123, 128, 150, 211n225, 235
secondary worlds (theory of, construction of in general) i, iv–v, 7n12, 9–12, 15, 16n25, 20, 22, 25–27, 30, 33–35, 39–40, 43, 53–56, 60–61, 67–68, 73, 78, 83n86, 91, 98, 101n112, 115–16, 121–28, 139, 147, 150–55, 158–67, 171, 174, 183–84, 188n200, 191–93, 218–20, 232, 240; *see also* possible-worlds theory; world-making
Sellar and Yeatman 40
semantics 5–6
Serafini, Luigi. *Codex Seraphinianus* 11n18
Shakespeare, William iii, 40, 66, 77; *As You Like It* 96; *Hamlet* 66; *Macbeth* 66, 86–87, 131–32
The Shepherd's Crown [SC] 179–81, 184, 186–88, 211, 246n260
Sherlock Holmes 38
Shklovsky, Viktor 77, 193; *see also* defamiliarization
Shrek (movie) 88n95
signifier and signified v, 236
Sinclair, Iain. *London Orbital* 199
slapstick comedy 60, 245
slavery 17, 75, 203
"Sleeping Beauty" (fairy tale) 69, 93
Small Gods [SG] vi, 64, 158n158, 243
Snuff [SN] 113n124, 203
social issues, problems, dynamics, change, protest 21, 103, 116–17, 188, 190, 200, 203–06, 210–17, 220
social mobility, status 105, 200, 212
Socrates 70
Soja, Edward 16, 195
Soul Music [SM] vi, 78n78, 132n141
Soul Music from Terry Pratchett's Discworld (CD) 224n246
Sourcery [S] 120, 127, 157, 179n183, 210n224

space and spatiality iv–vi, 15–19, 22, 147–201, 204, 206, 209, 212, 223, 226, 232, 237
space travel in Discworld 214
speech acts 134–35
Stableford, Brian 35
Stalnaker, Robert 5
Star Wars 82n85
Steampunk literary genre, style, and social movement vn6, 208–09, 217–20, 225
Stewart, Ian 137–38
storytelling ii, vi–vii, 6–10, 17, 23, 25–26, 43, 60–61, 64n67, 73–74, 80–82, 86–87, 102–03, 111–12, 128, 131, 133–36, 142–43, 149, 151, 158, 162, 175, 209, 221, 225–26, 235–39; see also narrative imperative
Strata 125
Streets of Ankh-Morpork, The 158, 190, 192–93, 195, 202, 205, 211
sub-creation 9, 23, 30, 38, 43, 61
Summoning Dark (Discworld entity) 113n124
Superman/Clark Kent 66, 107n117
supernatural elements in literature (in general) iin1, 11–14, 22, 26n36, 30–31, 33–35, 50, 63, 72, 85, 103n115, 116, 165, 176–77, 185, 187
supernatural literature genre i, vn6, 27, 30, 71n71, 74, 185n196
surrealism 25
suspension of disbelief 24, 32, 34, 37, 39–40, 42, 56, 65, 68, 70, 124, 127, 133n142, 150, 222, 224, 230n252
Swift, Jonathan 33, 70
Sybil Ramkin, Lady (Discworld character) 108n120

T
Taleb, Nassim Nicholas. *The Black Swan* 141; see also narrative fallacy
Tallin 208n221
taproot texts 14n22, 60
technological development and change (in primary world) ivn5, 24–25, 61, 126, 144, 184–88, 205, 208, 211, 214, 216–18, 224; as modern mythology 213; see also under Pratchett, Tolkien
Thames River 193n202
thaum (Discworld unit of magic) 129, 131, 139
"thinning" (Clute and Grant theory) 27, 184n195
Thud! [*T!*] 109, 113n124, 143, 167–70, 190, 203–04

Thud, Koom Valley Thud (real-world and Discworld games) 161n162, 168–69
Tiffany Aching (Discworld character and book series) vi, 64n66, 71n72, 74, 171, 180–82, 184, 186–87, 195, 214, 230–31, 244
time and linearity iv–v, 12n20, 16–19, 22, 54, 83n86, 88, 116, 125, 139n149, 147, 159, 161, 173, 177
Tolkien, J. R. R. Legendarium. Texts: *The Hobbit* 35n44, 83, 85n90, 108, 202, 222n240. *The Lord of the Rings* [*LotR*] in general 8, 14, 21–22, 32, 34–35, 40, 53–54, 55, 59–60, 69–70, 73–75, 78, 83, 85–86, 92, 98, 107, 113, 125, 138, 162, 163n164, 164, 166, 170, 174, 201; *LotR*'s influence on fantasy genre and Discworld i, iin2, 24–27, 29, 32, 35–37, 39–40, 48–51, 53–54, 59–60, 67, 70, 72, 74–75, 78–79, 81n82, 83–84, 108, 117, 118, 120–21, 124, 152, 155, 156, 162–64, 188n200, 191–92, 220, 237; *LotR* parodies *see* Beard and Kennedy, *Bored of the Rings*. *The Silmarillion* and cosmology 62, 65. Paratexts related to Middle-earth 34, 65, 152, 159, 162–64, 200–01; maps 38, 152–54, 164, 166, 168, 170; notes 222n240. Topics within legendarium: Races and race relations 75n76, 200n213, 202; Elves 27, 75n76, 180n184, 186–88, 200n213; Hobbits 79n79, 84–86, 154–55, 163, 165, 170, 182–83; Orcs 27, 75n76, 86, 168n170. Characters: Aragorn 75, 86n91, 107–08, 163n164; Bilbo 37n48, 73, 79n79, 83, 85, 92n99, 108, 154–55, 163, 166, 183; Boromir 163n164; Frodo 37n48, 47, 53, 57n61, 58, 73, 75, 79n79, 83, 85, 86n91, 92n99, 108, 154–55, 162–63, 166, 181–83, 186n198; Gandalf 37n48, 57n61, 85n89–90; Gollum 75, 182n189; Gríma Wormtongue 86; Sam Gamgee 57n61, 83n87, 246; Saruman 85n89, 184–85; Sauron 62, 75–76, 113. One Ring 59, 75, 83n87, 92n99, 162–63, 181, 182n189, 186. Locations: Isengard 21, 185; Minis Tirith 200–01; Mordor 168, 174, 201; Shire 21, 166, 170, 172, 183; Undying Lands 163n164, 170, 187. Topics related to legendarium: Middle-earth as a secondary world 8, 19, 25–27, 33, 91, 126, 154, 162, 184–85, 220; narrative imperative in works 85n90, 108, 155, 163, 183; technology and industrialization 184–88, 202
Tolkien, J. R. R. "Ofermod" 108, 182; *see also* ofermod
Tolkien, J. R. R. "On Fairy-stories" 8–9, 11–12, 23, 30, 33–34, 39–40, 42–43, 60–61, 63–64, 75n75, 77–78, 100, 128, 185, 235, 244; *see also* eucatastrophe, secondary belief, Secondary World, sub-creation
A Tourist Guide to Lancre [*Lancre*] 173–77
tragedy genre 9, 70, 243
transportation, modern (in primary world) ivn5, 185

Triple Goddess 64
"Troll Bridge" 223
trolls (Discworld race) 50, 104, 117n127, 167–70, 173, 199, 202, 204, 224
Truran, Trevor 168
Trymon (Discworld character) 75
Turtle Recall see Discworld Companion
Twoflower (Discworld character) 54–58, 68n70, 80, 84, 100, 128, 154, 157n157, 162, 166n166, 214

U
Unseen University (Discworld location) 59, 125n131, 127n136, 139–40, 155, 178n181, 196, 231
utopia 50n54, 89

V
vampires (Discworld race) 199
Vance, Jack. *The Dying Earth* 30
VanderMeer, Jeff 220n238; city of Ambergris 193n203
Vetinari *see* Havelock Vetinari
Victorian and Neo-Victorian era and style 25, 190, 208–09, 211, 213, 217–20, 224, 228; *see also* Steampunk
video games (in general) 84n88, 226–27; *see also under* Discworld extended texts; names of specific games
villains 74, 76, 85–87, 102–03, 113, 132, 174
Virgil 42n51
Vorbis, Inquisitor (Discworld character) 103n114
Voynich manuscript 11n18

W
Walpole, Horace 242
war 35, 130, 144, 167, 201, 214n231; *see also* World War I, World War II
Weasel (Discworld character) 52
Wee Free Men (Discworld race) 180n184
Wicca 64
Wilde, Oscar 70
Williams, Tad iin2
Wintersmith [W] 99, 165

witches (of Discworld) 64, 86–87, 93–99, 101, 171, 175–77, 230; as midwives and healers 87n93, 98n108, 181, 197; "cackling" 99, 110; relation to lands and homes 171–72, 178–83; *see also* individual names; in fantasy and folklore in general 50, 53, 67, 85n89, 87, 93–94, 97–100, 106, 114, 118, 124, 132, 171, 176n177

Witches Abroad [WA] 47–48, 64n66, 69, 82, 86–101, 109–10, 115, 119, 121, 131–32, 135, 142, 156, 159–60, 163, 178, 202, 239, 244; *see also* Genua; Lilith Weatherwax

Witches subseries of Discworld novels 64n67, 87, 90, 95–98, 100n110, 171–79, 184n194; *see also* Tiffany Aching subseries

The Wizard of Oz 69

wizards (in fantasy in general) 35, 50, 57, 59, 85n89, 118; for wizards of Discworld, *see* individual names; Unseen University

Wodehouse, P. G. 40

wolf (unnamed Discworld character in *WA*) 91–93, 175

Wolf, Mark J. P. 17, 19, 125, 153, 156, 224

World War I iv, 24–25

World War II 21–25, 201n215

world-making 4, 15–20, 22, 26–27, 33, 42–43, 48, 54, 60, 116–34, 150, 153, 159, 164, 171, 235, 243; *see also* secondary worlds

world-turtle (primary world folklore) 50, 62

Wright, Joseph. *An Experiment on a Bird in the Air Pump* 140

Wünsch, Marianne 33n43

Wyrd Sisters [WS] vii, 66, 80, 87, 98n109, 127, 131–32, 171

Z

zombies (Discworld race) 199